WATTERS · LEYH · ALLEN · BOSY · BRYANT · LAIHO

LUMBERJANES™

END OF SUMMER

Published by

BOOM! BOX™

Ross Richie .... CEO & Founder
Joy Huffman .... CFO
Matt Gagnon .... Editor-in-Chief
Filip Sablik .... President, Publishing & Marketing
Stephen Christy .... President, Development
Lance Kreiter .... Vice President, Licensing & Merchandising
Bryce Carlson .... Vice President, Editorial & Creative Strategy
Kate Henning .... Director, Operations
Elyse Strandberg .... Manager, Finance
Sierra Hahn .... Executive Editor
Dafna Pleban .... Senior Editor
Shannon Watters .... Senior Editor
Eric Harburn .... Senior Editor
Elizabeth Brei .... Editor
Sophie Philips-Roberts .... Associate Editor
Jonathan Manning .... Associate Editor
Gavin Gronenthal .... Assistant Editor
Gwen Waller .... Assistant Editor
Allyson Gronowitz .... Assistant Editor
Ramiro Portnoy .... Assistant Editor
Kenzie Rzonca .... Assistant Editor
Rey Netschke .... Editorial Assistant

Michelle Ankley .... Design Lead
Marie Krupina .... Production Designer
Grace Park .... Production Designer
Chelsea Roberts .... Production Designer
Madison Goyette .... Production Designer
Crystal White .... Production Designer
Samantha Knapp .... Production Design Assistant
Esther Kim .... Marketing Lead
Breanna Sarpy .... Marketing Coordinator, Digital
Grecia Martinez .... Marketing Assistant
Amanda Lawson .... Marketing Assistant, Digital
José Meza .... Consumer Sales Lead
Ashley Troub .... Consumer Sales Coordinator
Morgan Perry .... Retail Sales Lead
Harley Salbacka .... Sales Coordinator
Megan Christopher .... Operations Coordinator
Rodrigo Hernandez .... Operations Coordinator
Zipporah Smith .... Operations Coordinator
Jason Lee .... Senior Accountant
Sabrina Lesin .... Accounting Assistant
Lauren Alexander .... Administrative Assistant

BOOM! BOX™

LUMBERJANES Volume Twenty, November 2021. Published by BOOM! Box, a division of Boom Entertainment, Inc. Lumberjanes is ™ & © 2021 Shannon Watters, Grace Ellis, Noelle Stevenson & Brooklyn Allen. Originally published in single magazine form as LUMBERJANES No. 75, LUMBERJANES: END OF SUMMER No. 1, LUMBERJANES: FAREWELL TO SUMMER FREE COMIC BOOK DAY SPECIAL 2020. ™ & © 2020 Shannon Watters, Grace Ellis, Noelle Stevenson & Brooklyn Allen. All rights reserved. BOOM! Box™ and the BOOM! Box logo are trademarks of Boom Entertainment, Inc., registered in various countries and categories. All characters, events, and institutions depicted herein are fictional. Any similarity between any of the names, characters, persons, events, and/or institutions in this publication to actual names, characters, and persons, whether living or dead, events, and/or institutions is unintended and purely coincidental. BOOM! Box does not read or accept unsolicited submissions of ideas, stories, or artwork.

BOOM! Studios, 5670 Wilshire Boulevard, Suite 400, Los Angeles, CA 90036-5679. Printed in China. First Printing.

ISBN: 978-1-68415-743-3, eISBN: 978-1-64668-321-5

THIS LUMBERJANES FIELD MANUAL BELONGS TO:

NAME:_____

TROOP:_____

DATE INVESTED:_____

FIELD MANUAL TABLE OF CONTENTS

LUMBERJANES
FIELD MANUAL

For the Advanced Program

Tenth Edition • August 1985

Prepared for the

**Miss Qiunzella Thiskwin
Penniquiqul Thistle Crumpet's**

CAMP FOR  HARDCORE LADY-TYPES

"Friendship to the Max!"

A MESSAGE FROM THE LUMBERJANES HIGH COUNCIL

miss Quinzella Thiskwin
Penniquiqul Thistle Crumpet's
Camp for
HARDCORE LADY TYPES
FRIENDSHIP to the MAX!

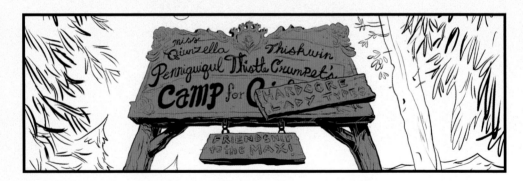

Seasons change and so, too, do we all. And while change can be daunting, and the unknown frightening, all things must end at one point or another. Whether it be the summer, or childhood, or the last box of popsicles in the freezer, nothing can last forever. But even when an end draws near, the era that's closing won't be gone for good. The times you shared, the things you learned, the friends you made, the smell of rust in a sprinkler, the tack of spilled lemonade, the itch of mosquito bites, the sound of cicadas…no matter where you go, no matter how grown up you become, you will carry those memories with you wherever you go. Everything you see and feel—good and bad, beloved and abhorred—becomes a part of the kaleidoscope that is you, just as you become one tile within the mosaics that make up your varied communities, from your school, to your family, to your town or city, to your world. From one angle, in one group, you might be just a small piece, but every masterpiece is made up of countless small parts—brushstrokes, molecules of clay, pieces of broken glass—all coming together to make a more beautiful whole.

We of the high council have cherished having you scouts as a part of the mosaic of our Lumberjanes organization. And while the end of summer each year is bittersweet, we know that you will all go back to your classes again rested, full of new knowledge and growth, and ready for teachers and books once more. You will become a part of your school community, and you will carry with you everything that you learned over the summer months. You and your school will be stronger for the adventures you had, the friends you made, and the things you discovered about yourself and your world. We hope that you will take these experiences with you, into your future, just as your classmates and teachers will, teaching and learning from each other, and always changing and growing, even when it's scary.

THE LUMBERJANES PLEDGE

I solemnly swear to do my best
Every day, and in all that I do,
To be brave and strong,
To be truthful and compassionate,
To be interesting and interested,
To pay attention and question
The world around me,
To think of others first,
To always help and protect my friends,
[redacted]
And to make the world a better place
For Lumberjane scouts
And for everyone else.

THEN THERE'S A LINE ABOUT GOD, OR WHATEVER

LUMBERJANES™
END OF SUMMER

Written by
Shannon Watters & Kat Leyh

Illustrated by
Brooklyn Allen, Alexa Bosy, & Kanesha C. Bryant

Colors by
Maarta Laiho

Letters by
Aubrey Aiese

Cover by
Kat Leyh

Series Designers
Grace Park & Marie Krupina

Collection Designer
Chelsea Roberts

Editor
Sophie Philips-Roberts

Executive Editor
Jeanine Schaefer

*Special thanks to **Kelsey Pate** for giving the Lumberjanes their name.*

Created by
Shannon Watters, Grace Ellis, Noelle Stevenson & Brooklyn Allen

LUMBERJANES FIELD MANUAL

CHAPTER
SEVENTY-FIVE

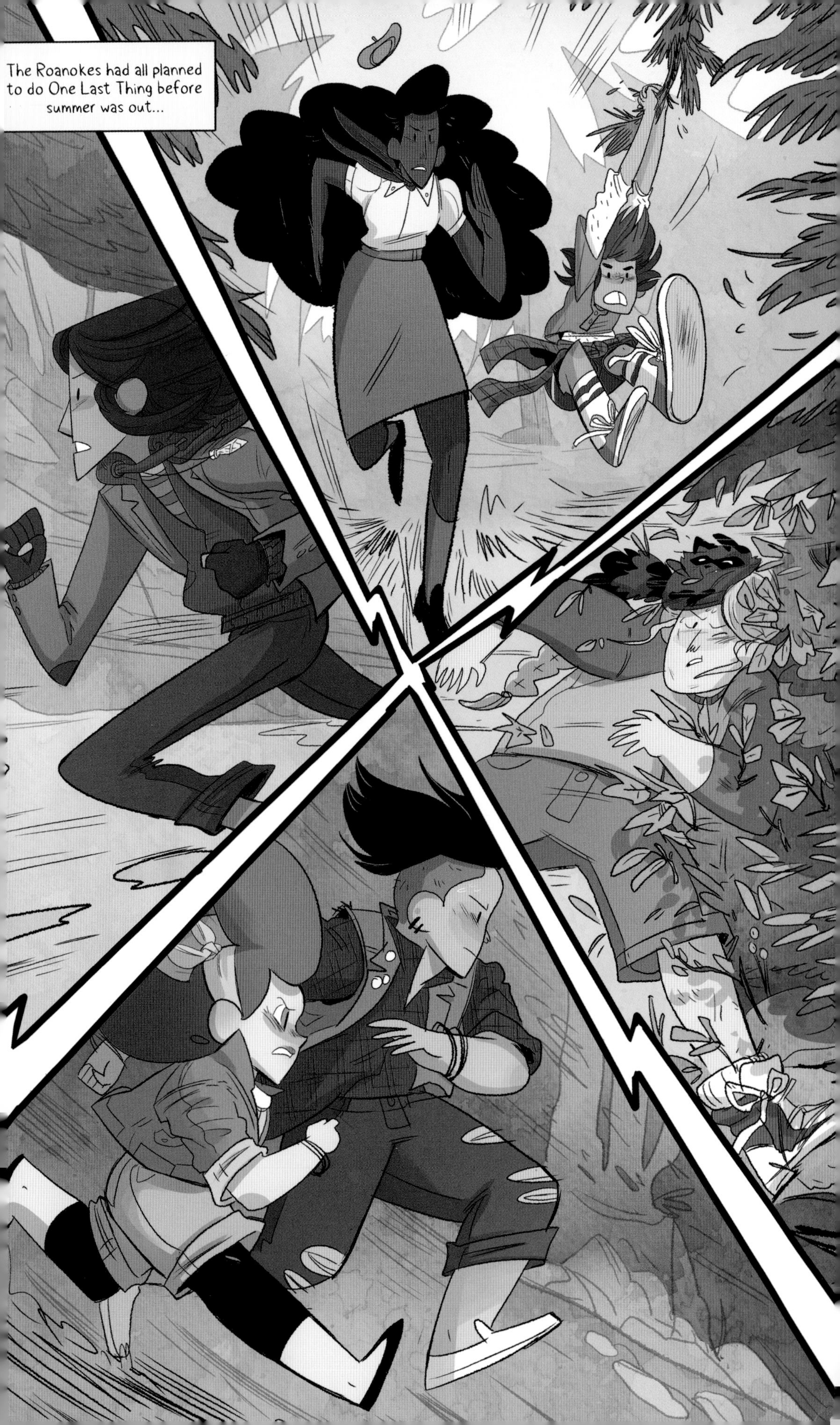
The Roanokes had all planned to do One Last Thing before summer was out...

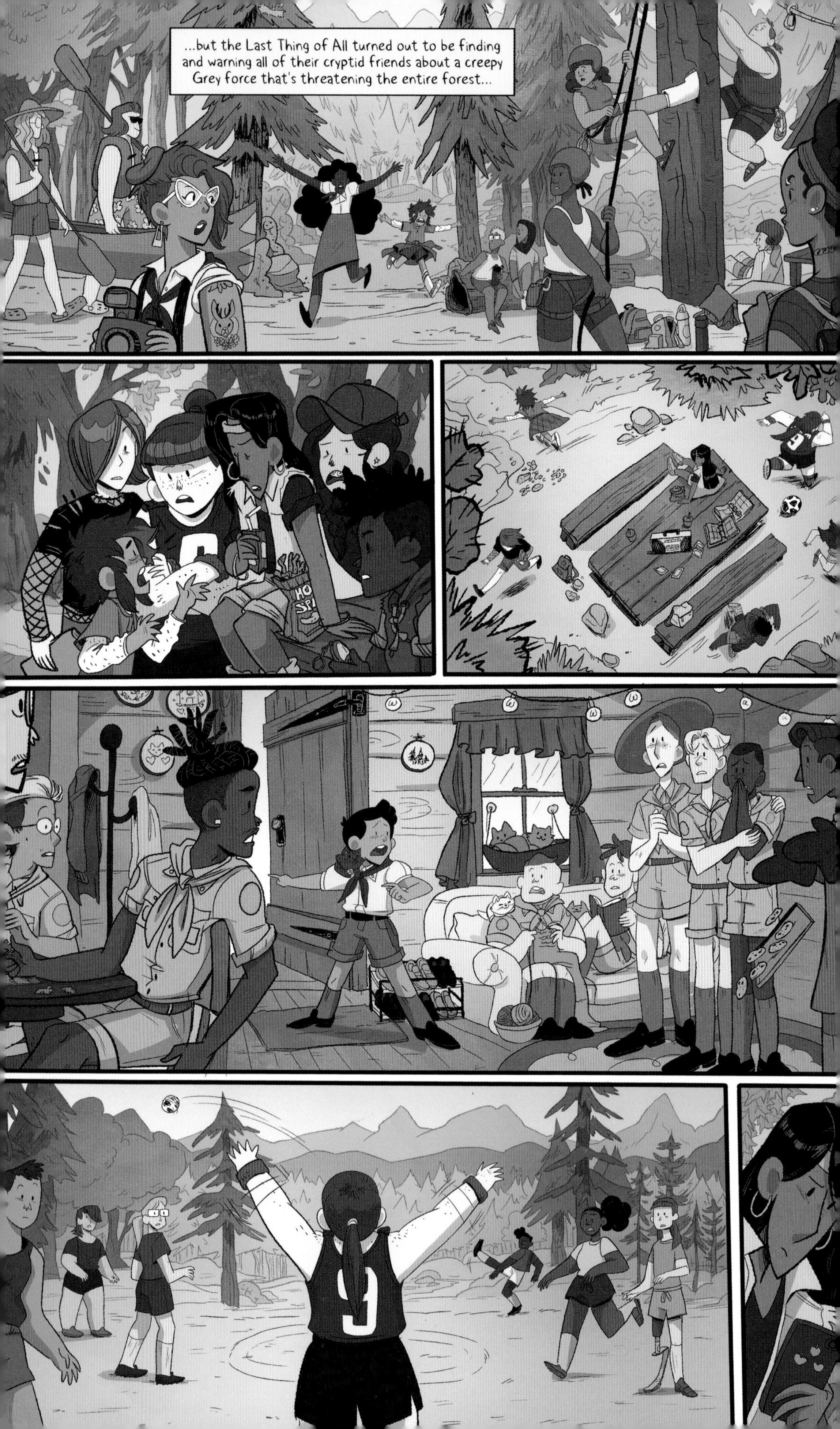
...but the Last Thing of All turned out to be finding and warning all of their cryptid friends about a creepy Grey force that's threatening the entire forest...
HO
SPI

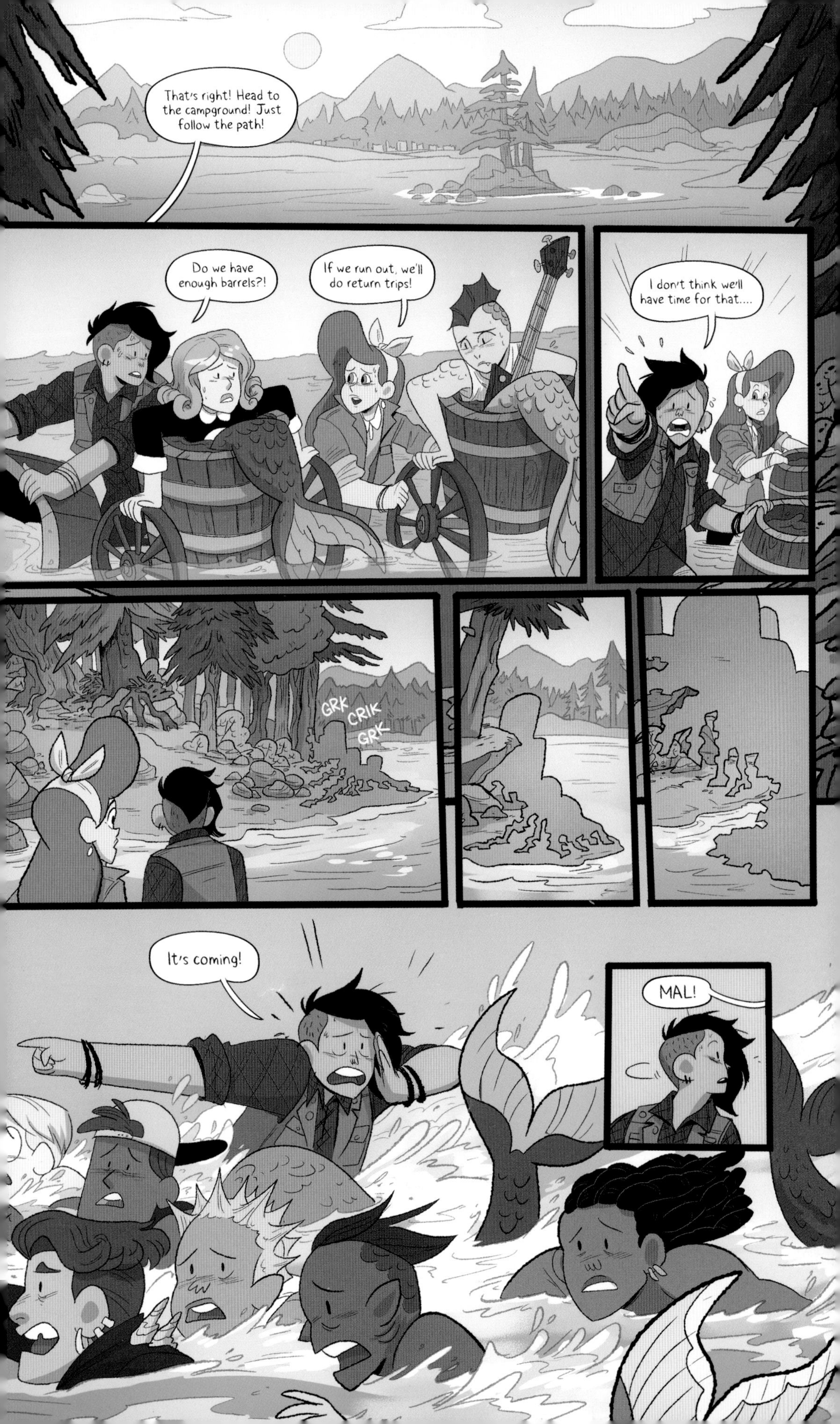
That's right! Head to the campground! Just follow the path!
Do we have enough barrels?!
If we run out, we'll do return trips!
I don't think we'll have time for that....
GRK
CRIK
GRK
It's coming!
MAL!

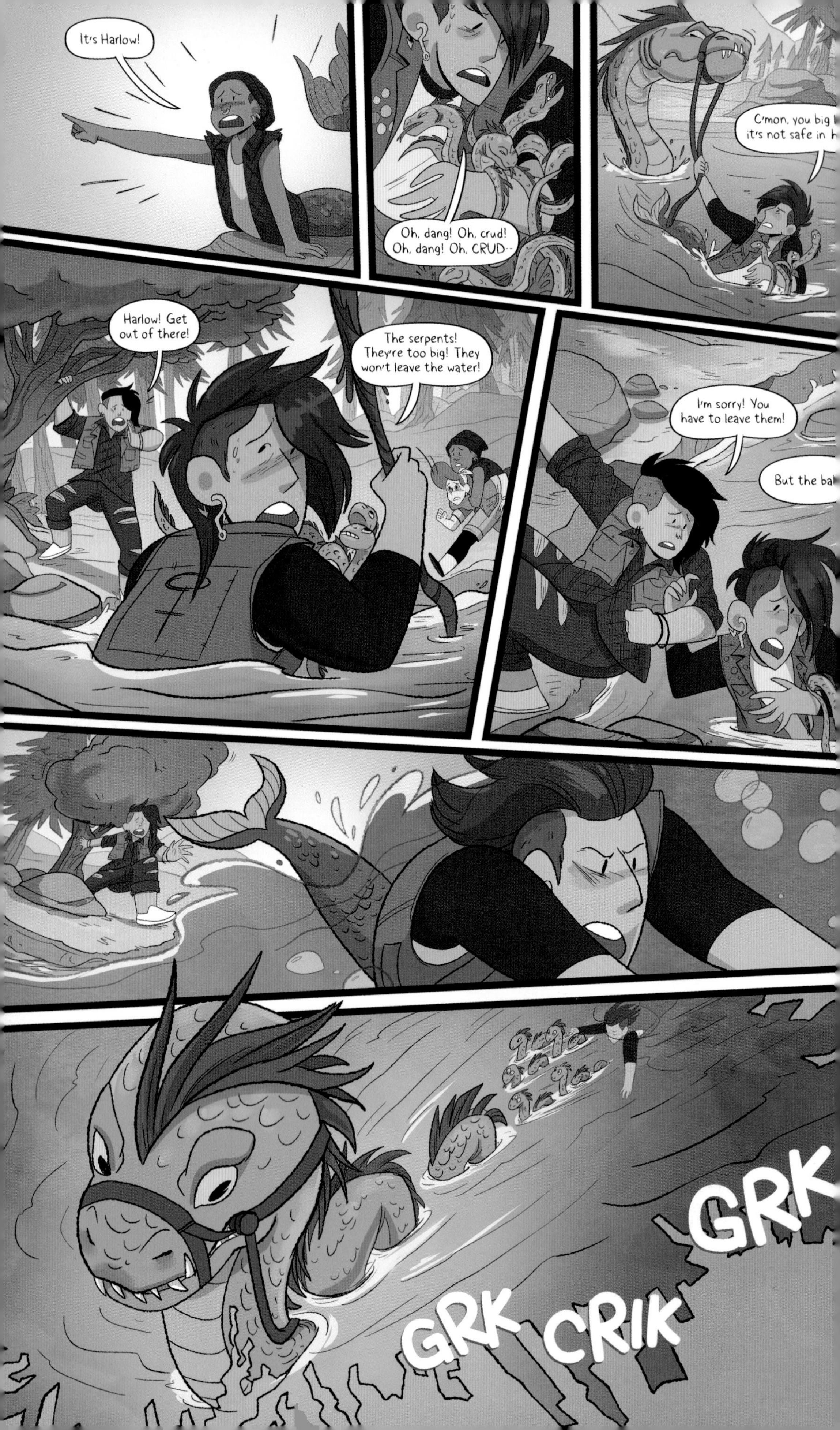
It's Harlow!
Oh, dang! Oh, crud! Oh, dang! Oh, CRUD--
C'mon, you big
it's not safe in
Harlow! Get out of there!
The serpents! They're too big! They won't leave the water!
I'm sorry! You have to leave them!
But the ba
GRK
GRK
CRIK

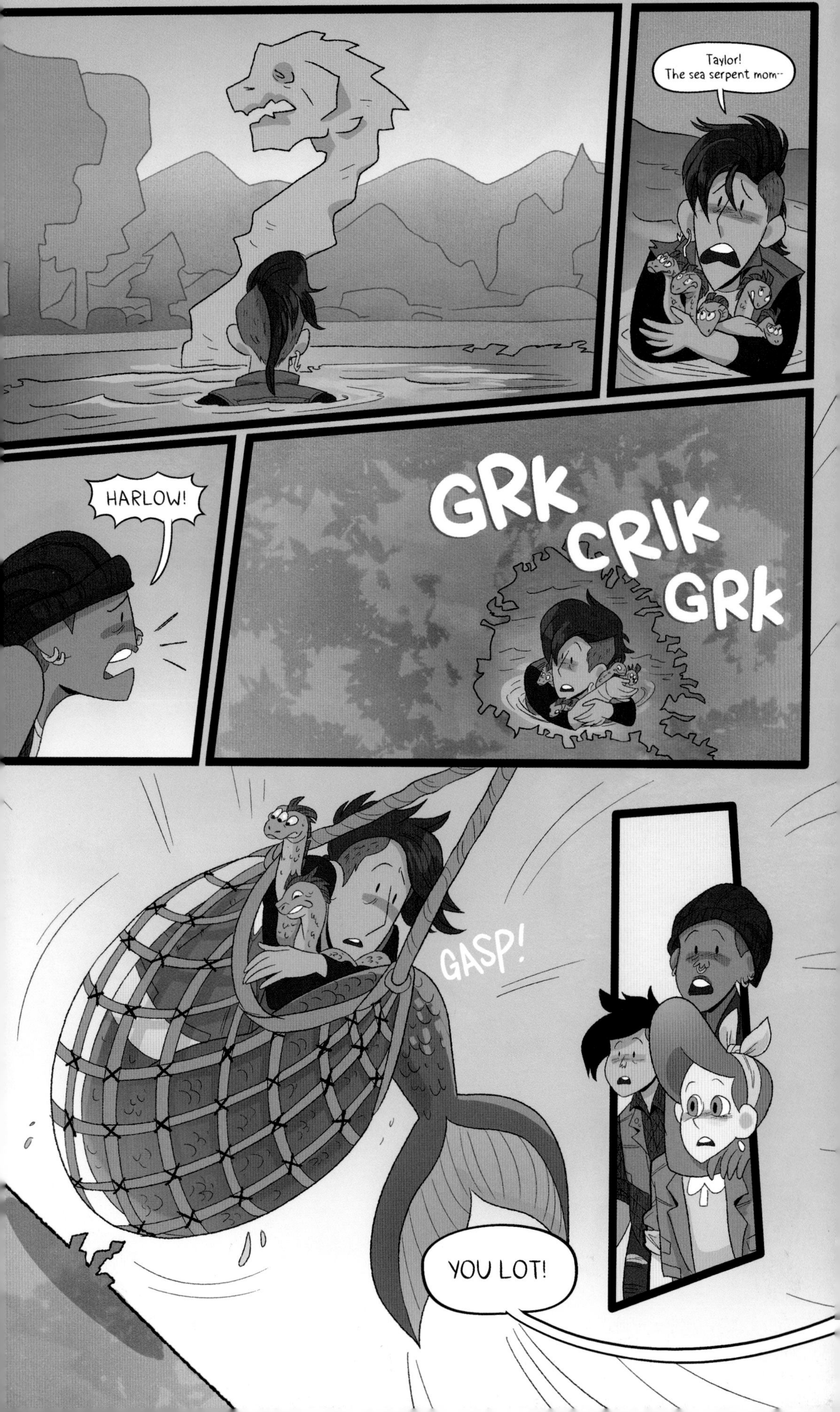
Taylor!
The sea serpent mom--
HARLOW!
GRK
CRIK
GRK
GASP!
YOU LOT!

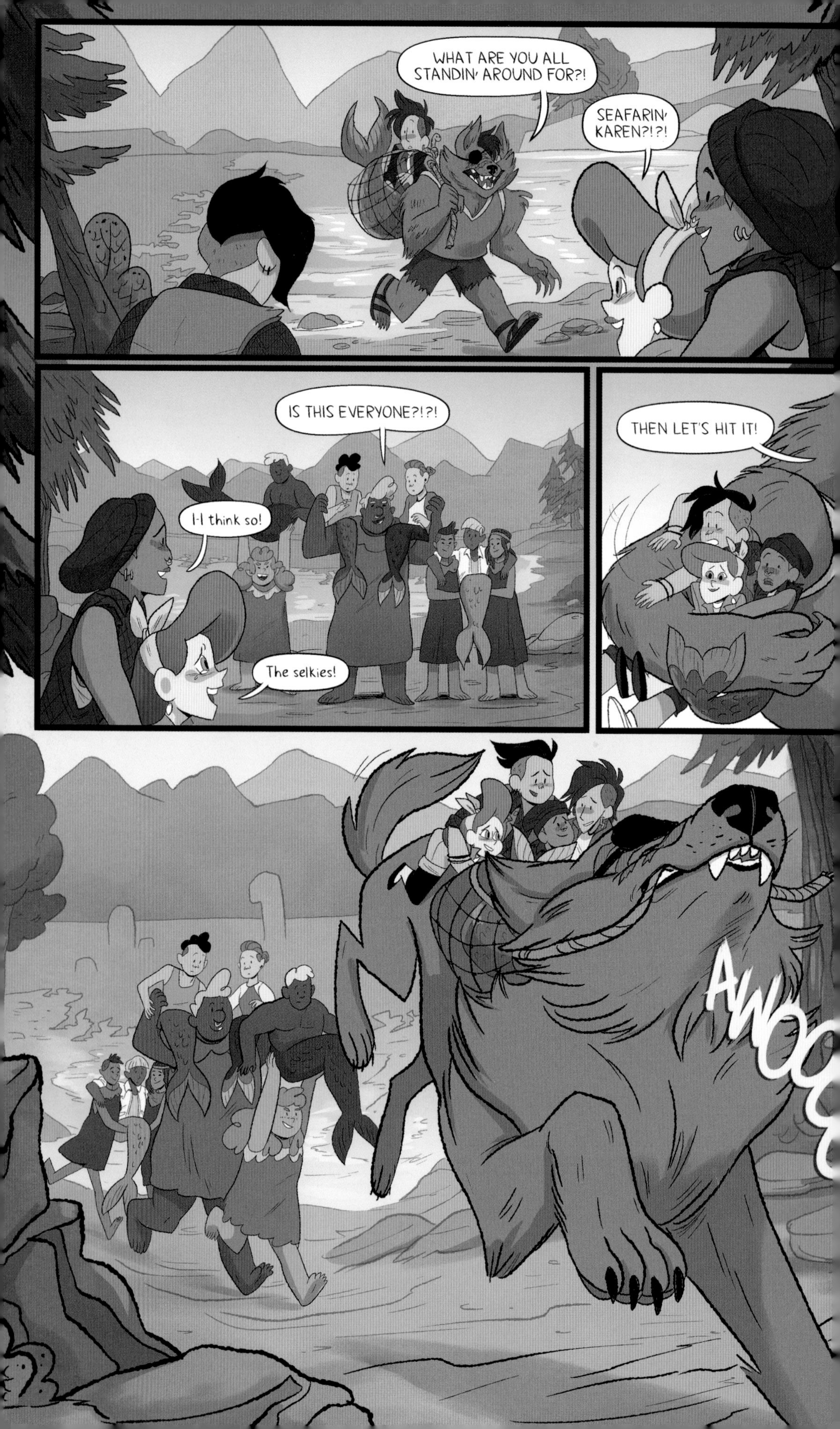
WHAT ARE YOU ALL STANDIN' AROUND FOR?!
SEAFARIN' KAREN?!?!
IS THIS EVERYONE?!?!
I-I think so!
The selkies!
THEN LET'S HIT IT!
AWOO

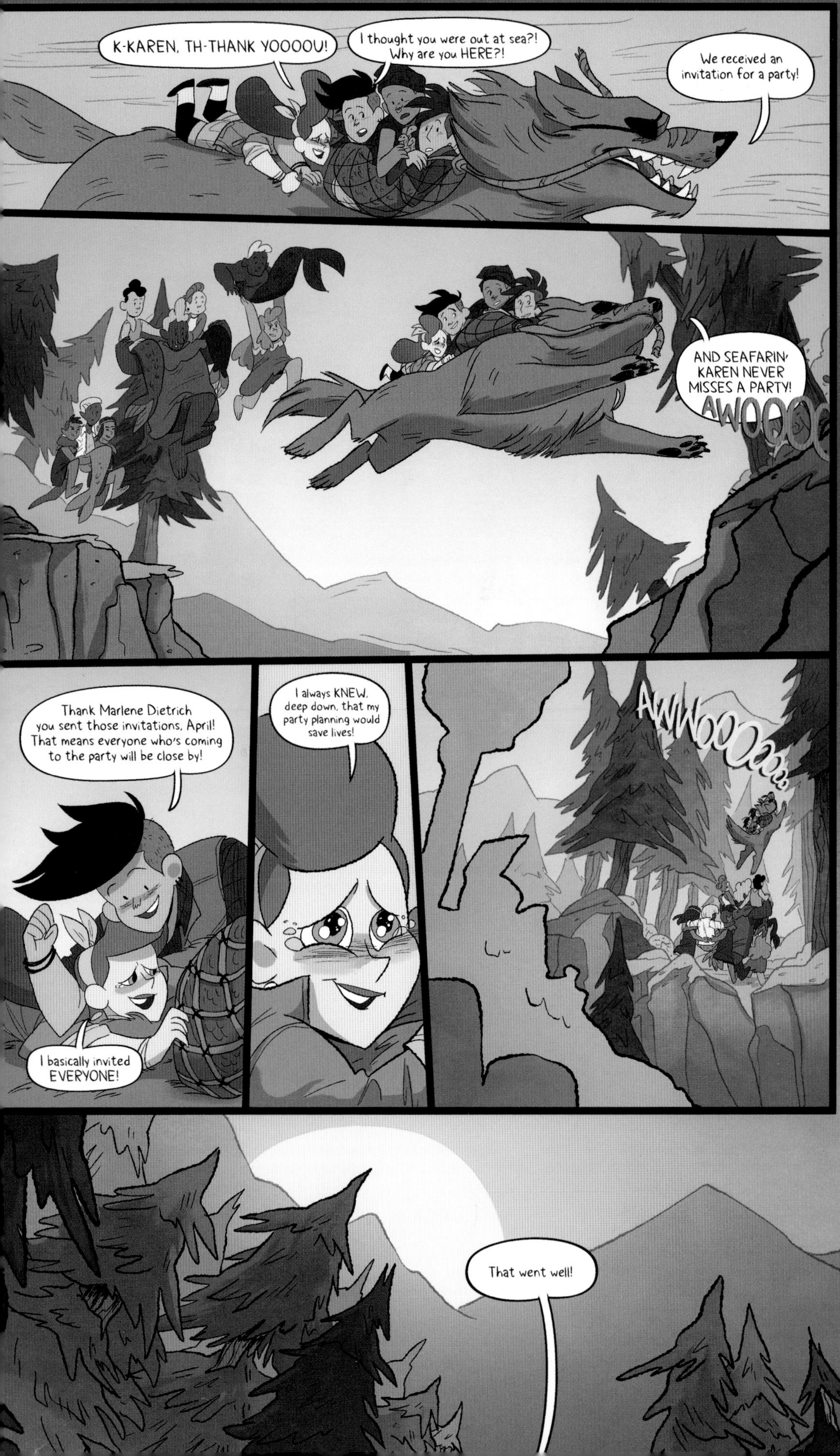
K-KAREN, TH-THANK YOOOOU!
I thought you were out at sea?! Why are you HERE?!
We received an invitation for a party!
AND SEAFARIN' KAREN NEVER MISSES A PARTY!
AWOOOO
Thank Marlene Dietrich you sent those invitations, April! That means everyone who's coming to the party will be close by!
I basically invited EVERYONE!
I always KNEW, deep down, that my party planning would save lives!
AWWOOOOooo
That went well!

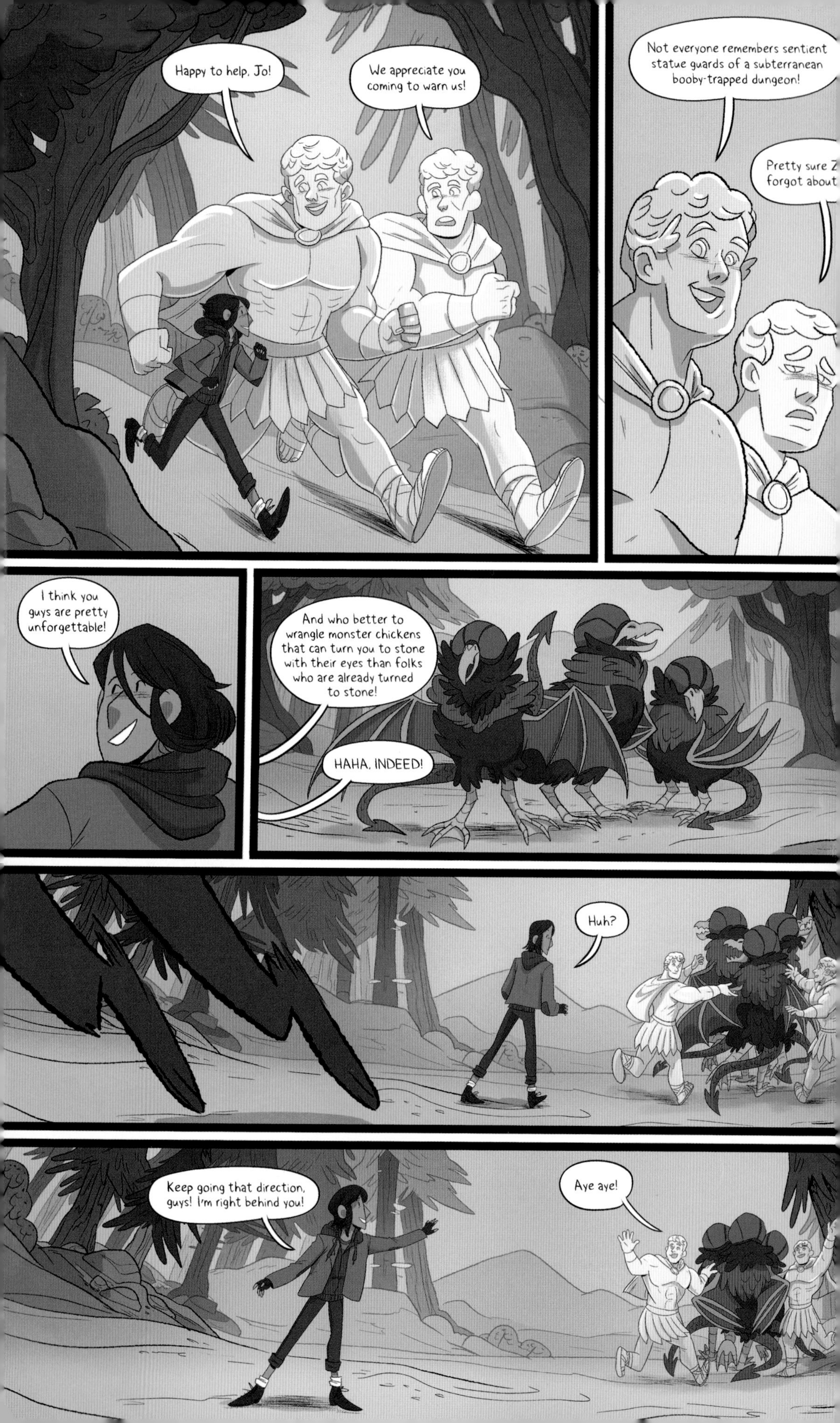

Happy to help, Jo!
We appreciate you coming to warn us!
Not everyone remembers sentient statue guards of a subterranean booby-trapped dungeon!
Pretty sure Z forgot about
I think you guys are pretty unforgettable!
And who better to wrangle monster chickens that can turn you to stone with their eyes than folks who are already turned to stone!
HAHA, INDEED!
Huh?
Keep going that direction, guys! I'm right behind you!
Aye aye!

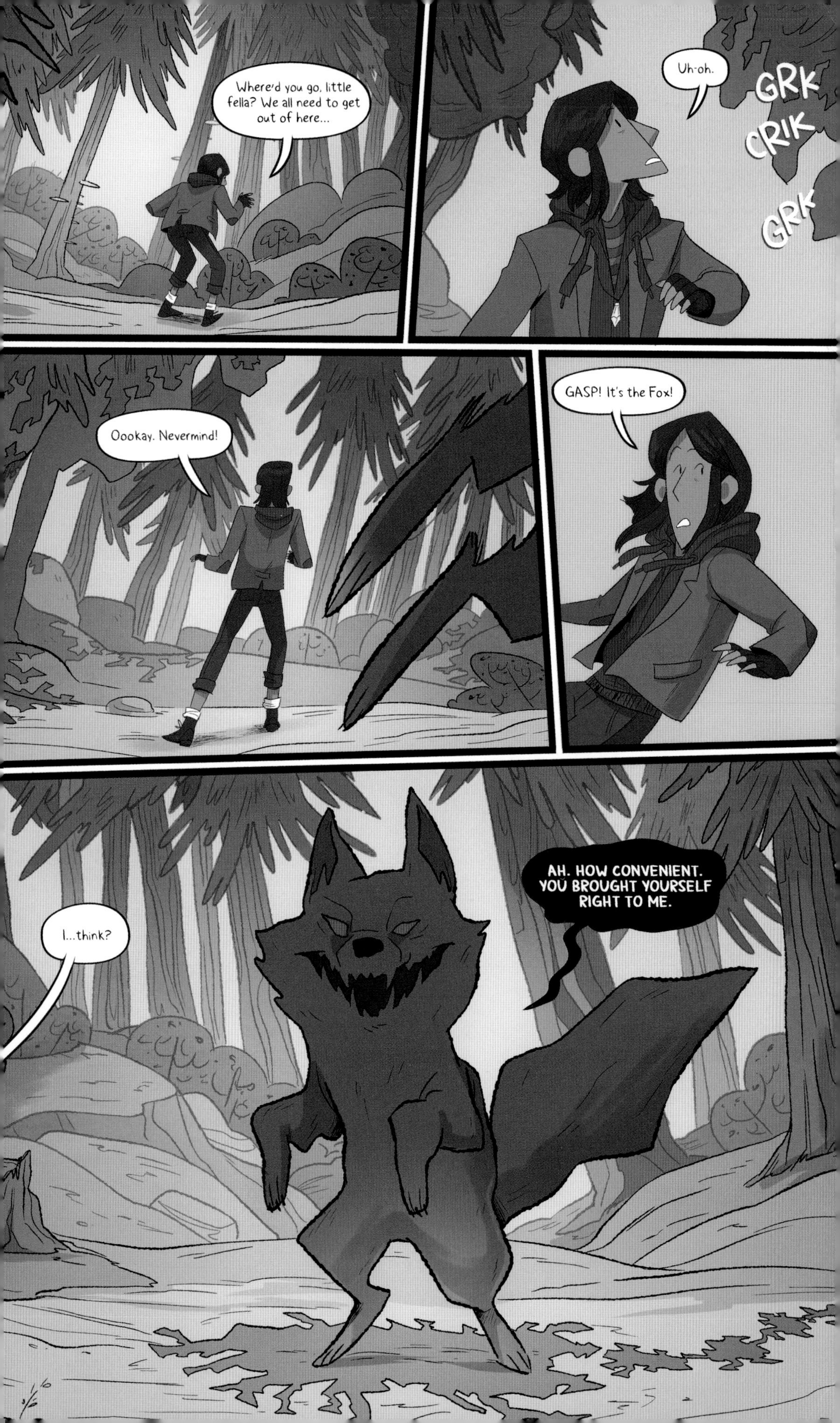
Where'd you go, little fella? We all need to get out of here...
Uh-oh.
GRK
CRIK
GRK
Oookay. Nevermind!
GASP! It's the Fox!
I...think?
AH. HOW CONVENIENT. YOU BROUGHT YOURSELF RIGHT TO ME.

IS THE CAMPGROUND THIS WAY? IT IS SO EASY TO GET...LOST HERE... SO CHAOTIC.
BUT I WILL SOON HAVE EVERYTHING... STRAIGHTENED UP.
BUT FIRST, I NEED TO GET YOU LUMBERJANES TAKEN CARE OF...
No no no...
No...
"...this can't be happening."
BREEEEEEATH

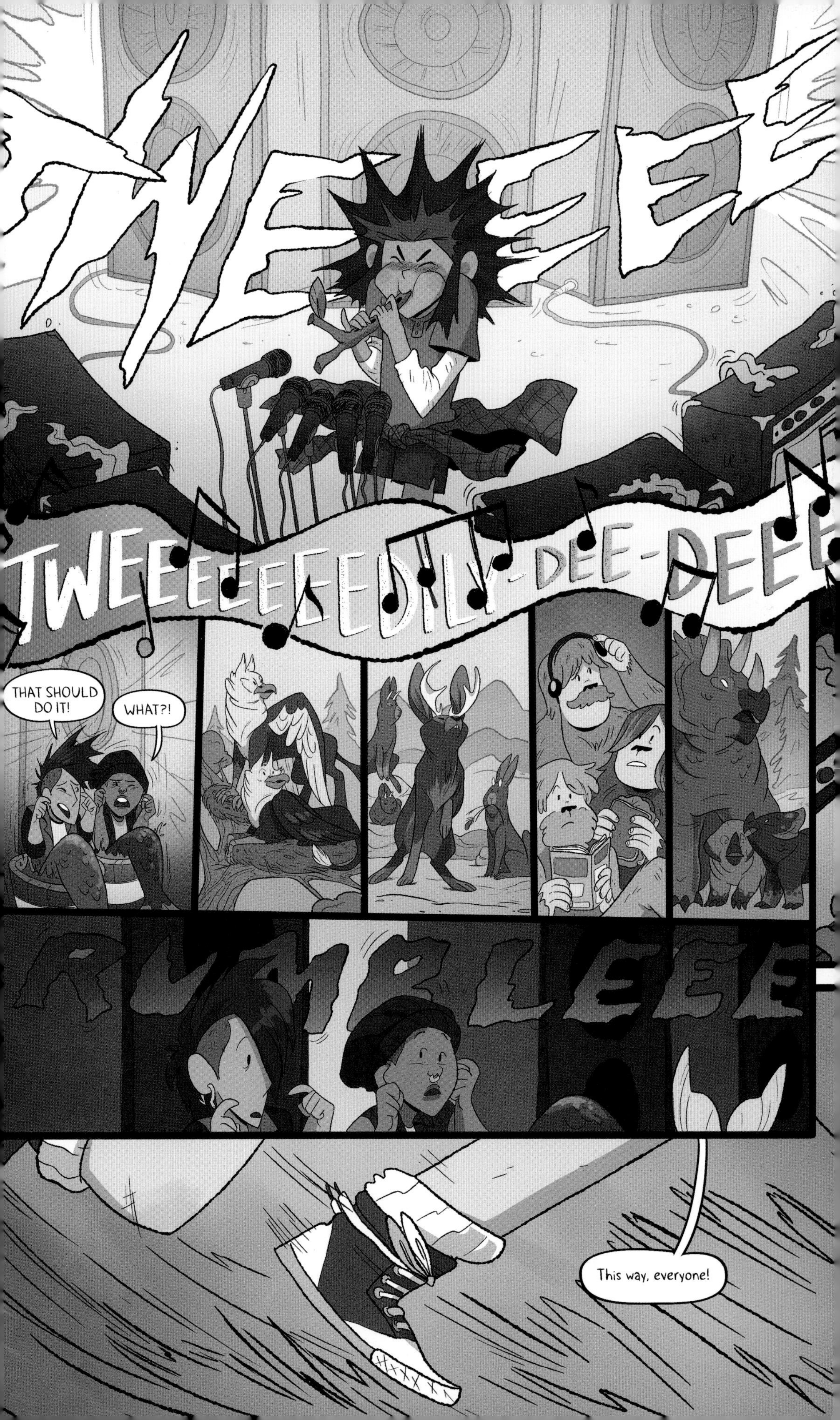
THEEEEE
TWEEEEEEDILY-DEE-DEEE
THAT SHOULD DO IT!
WHAT?!
RUMBLEEE
This way, everyone!

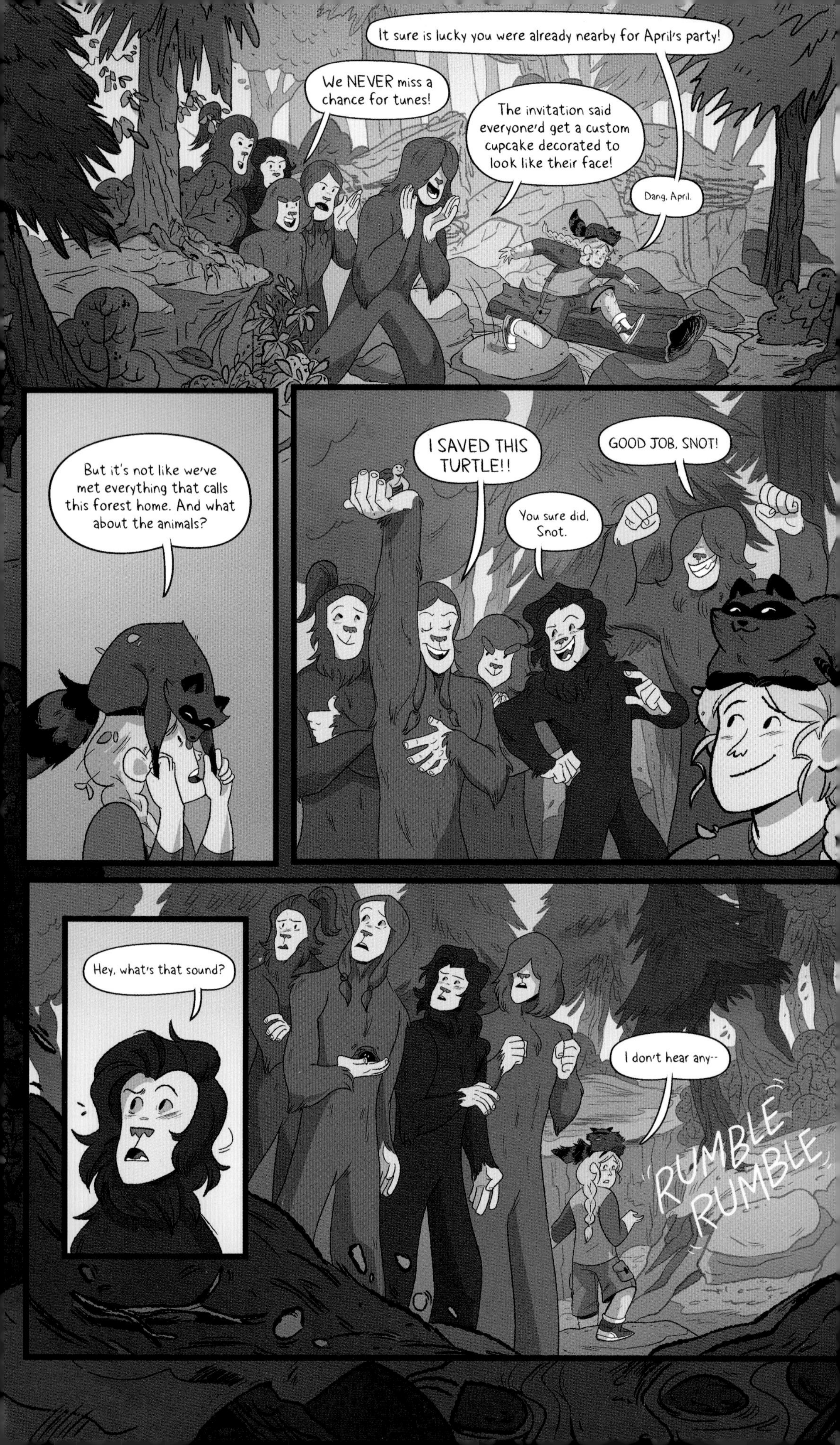
It sure is lucky you were already nearby for April's party!
We NEVER miss a chance for tunes!
The invitation said everyone'd get a custom cupcake decorated to look like their face!
Dang, April.
But it's not like we've met everything that calls this forest home. And what about the animals?
I SAVED THIS TURTLE!!
You sure did, Snot.
GOOD JOB, SNOT!
Hey, what's that sound?
I don't hear any--
RUMBLE
RUMBLE

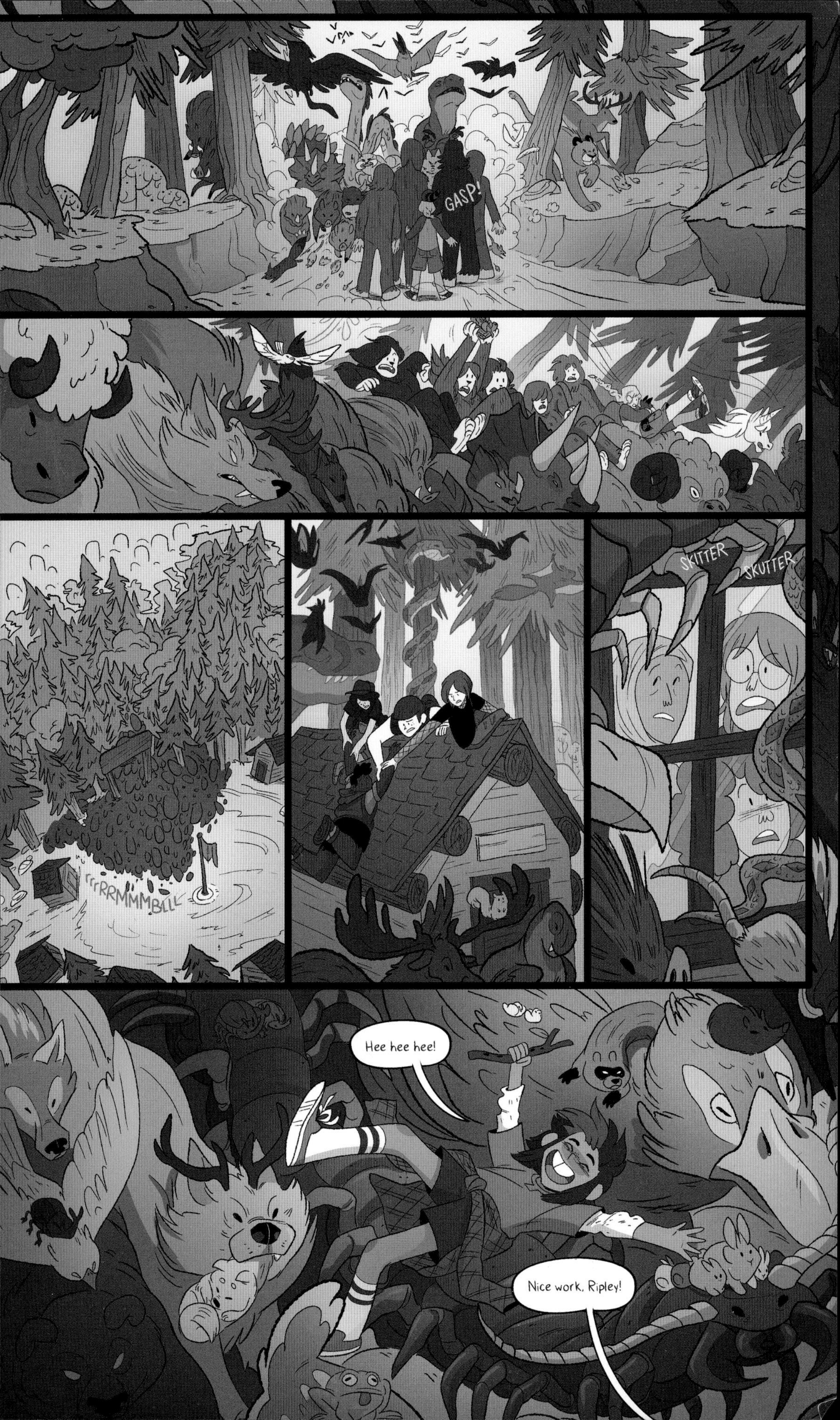
GASP!
SKITTER
SKUTTER
rrrRRMMMBLLL
Hee hee hee!
Nice work, Ripley!

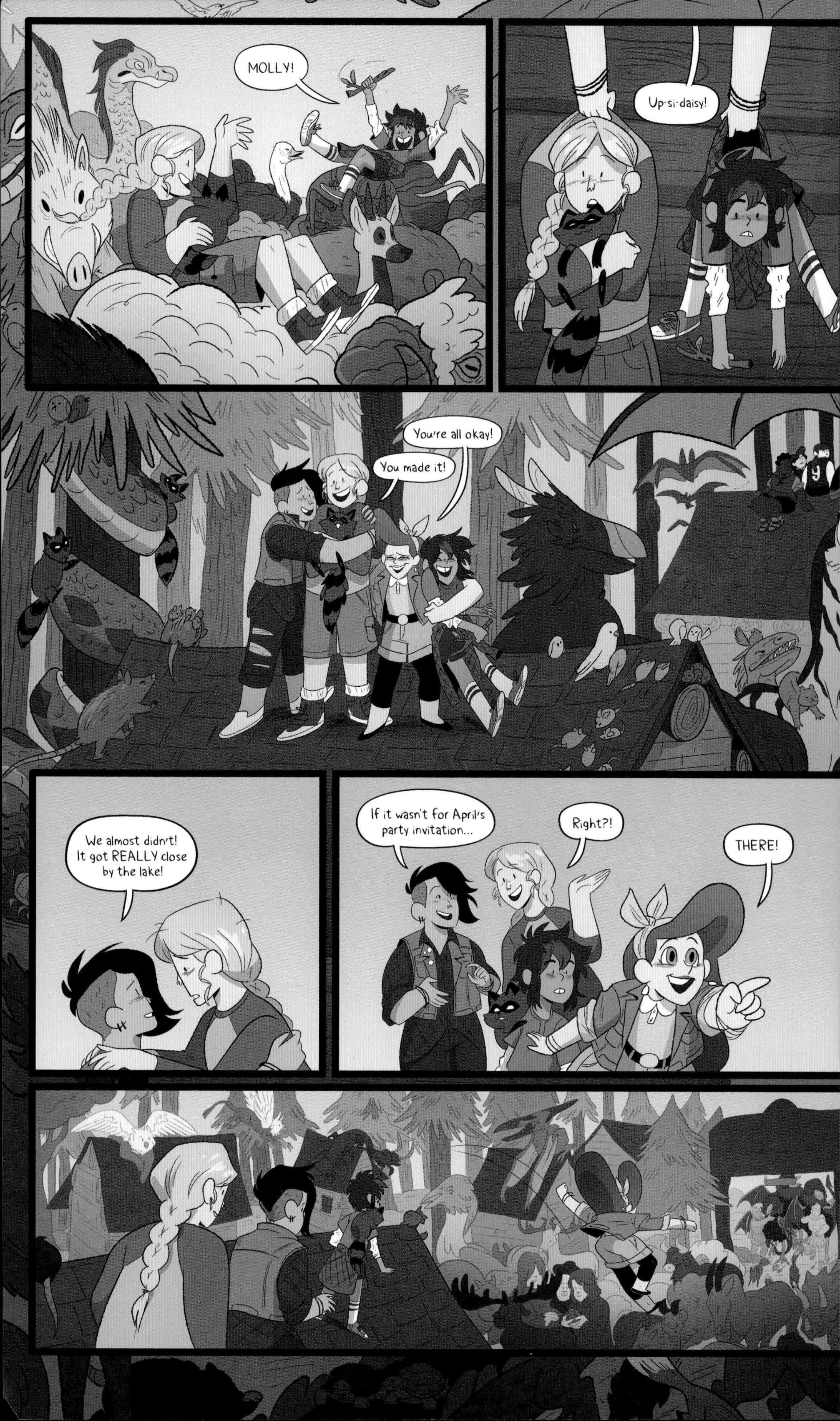
MOLLY!
Up-si-daisy!
You're all okay!
You made it!
We almost didn't! It got REALLY close by the lake!
If it wasn't for April's party invitation...
Right?!
THERE!

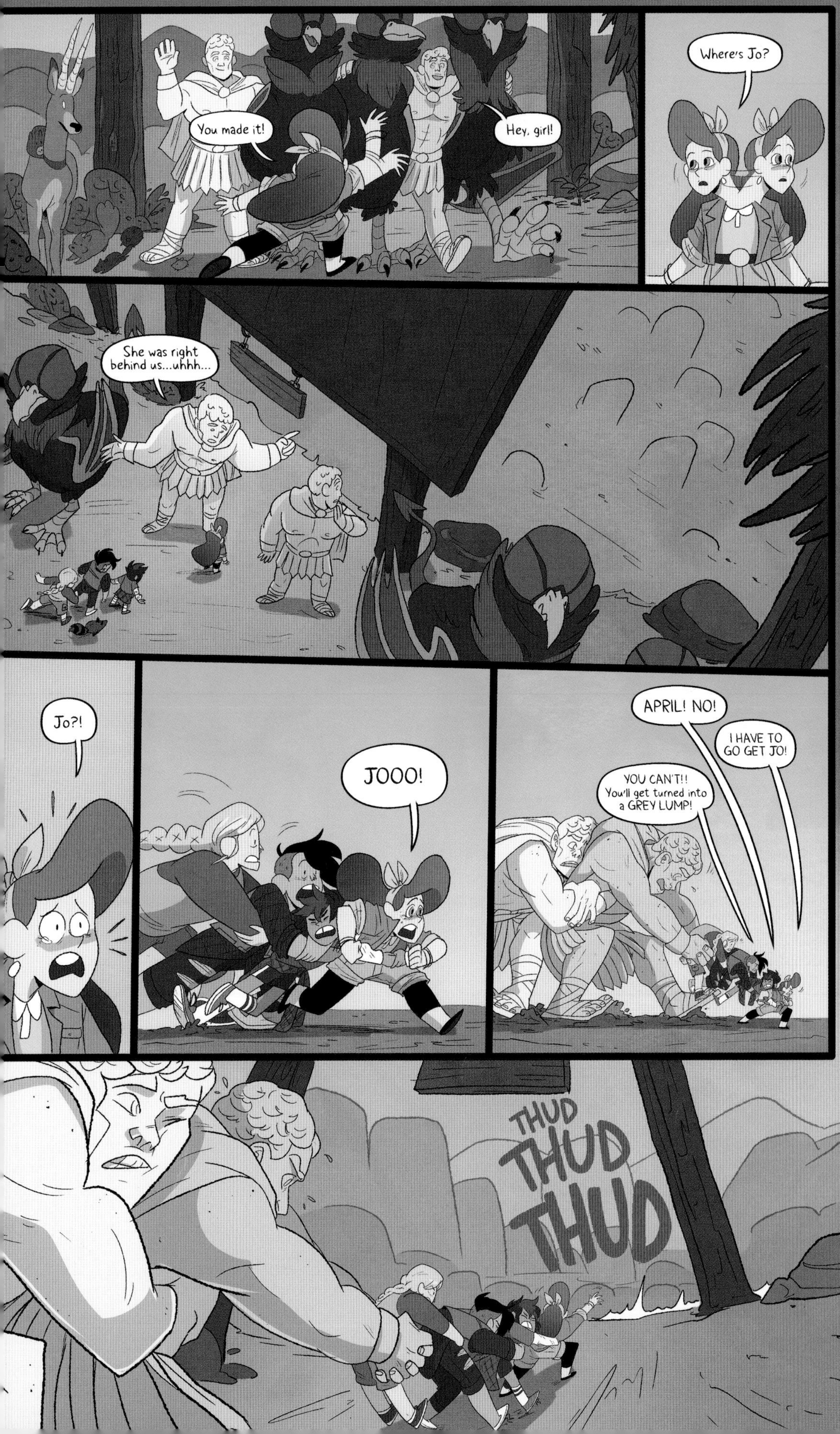
You made it!
Hey, girl!
Where's Jo?
She was right behind us...uhhh...
Jo?!
JOOO!
APRIL! NO!
I HAVE TO GO GET JO!
YOU CAN'T!! You'll get turned into a GREY LUMP!
THUD THUD THUD

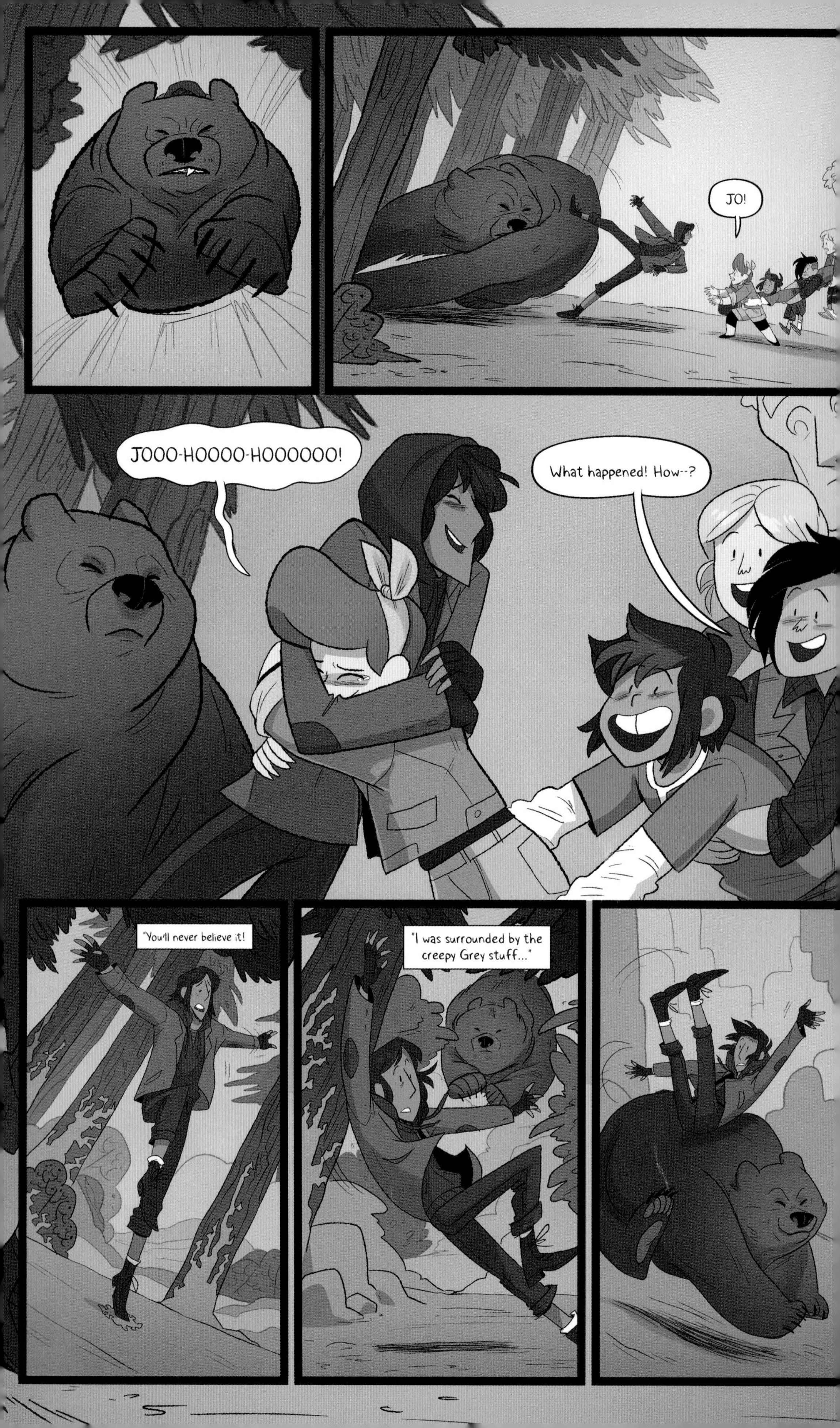
JO!
JOOO-HOOOO-HOOOOOO!
What happened! How--?
"You'll never believe it!
"I was surrounded by the creepy Grey stuff..."

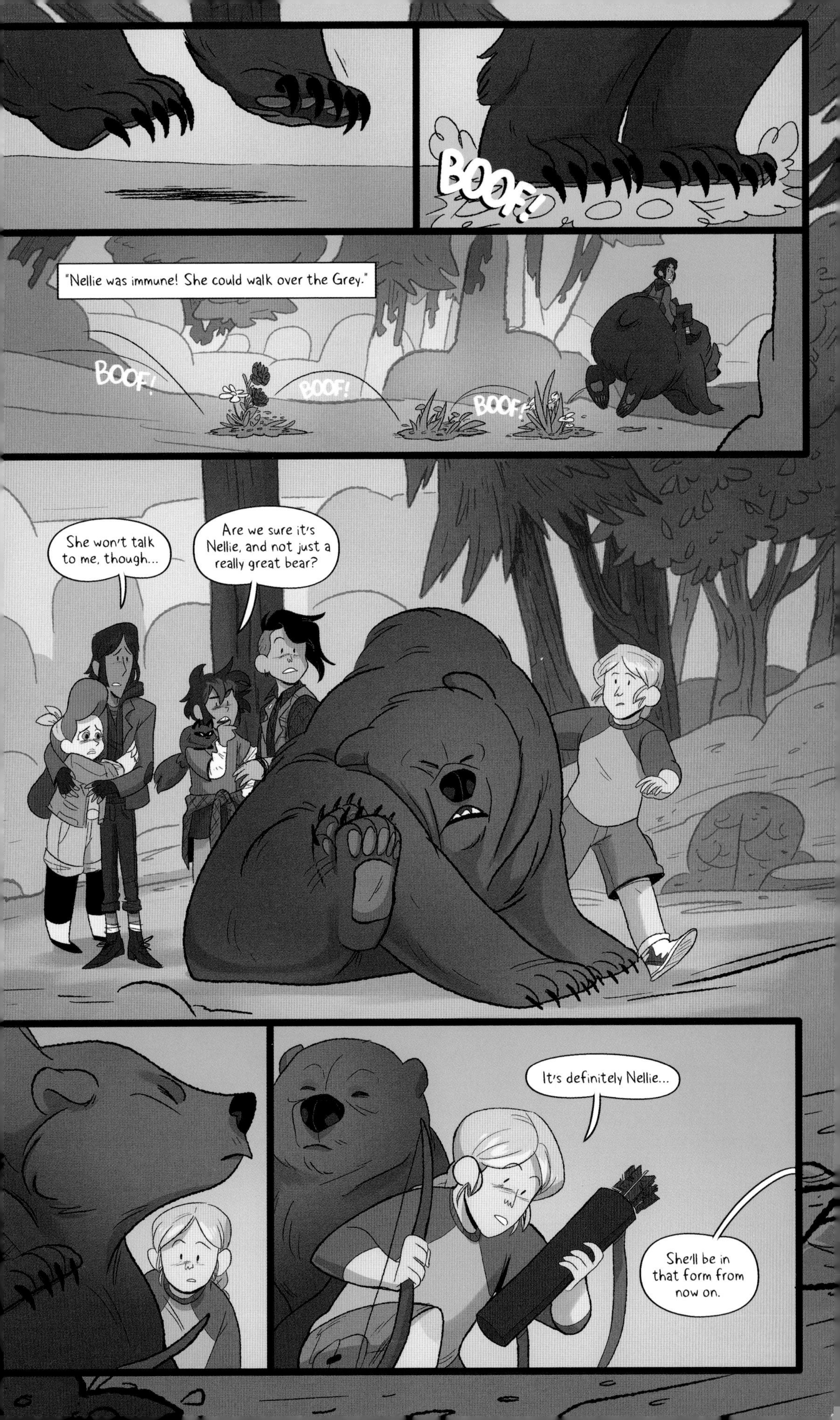
BOOF!
"Nellie was immune! She could walk over the Grey."
BOOF!
BOOF!
BOOF!
She won't talk to me, though...
Are we sure it's Nellie, and not just a really great bear?
It's definitely Nellie...
She'll be in that form from now on.

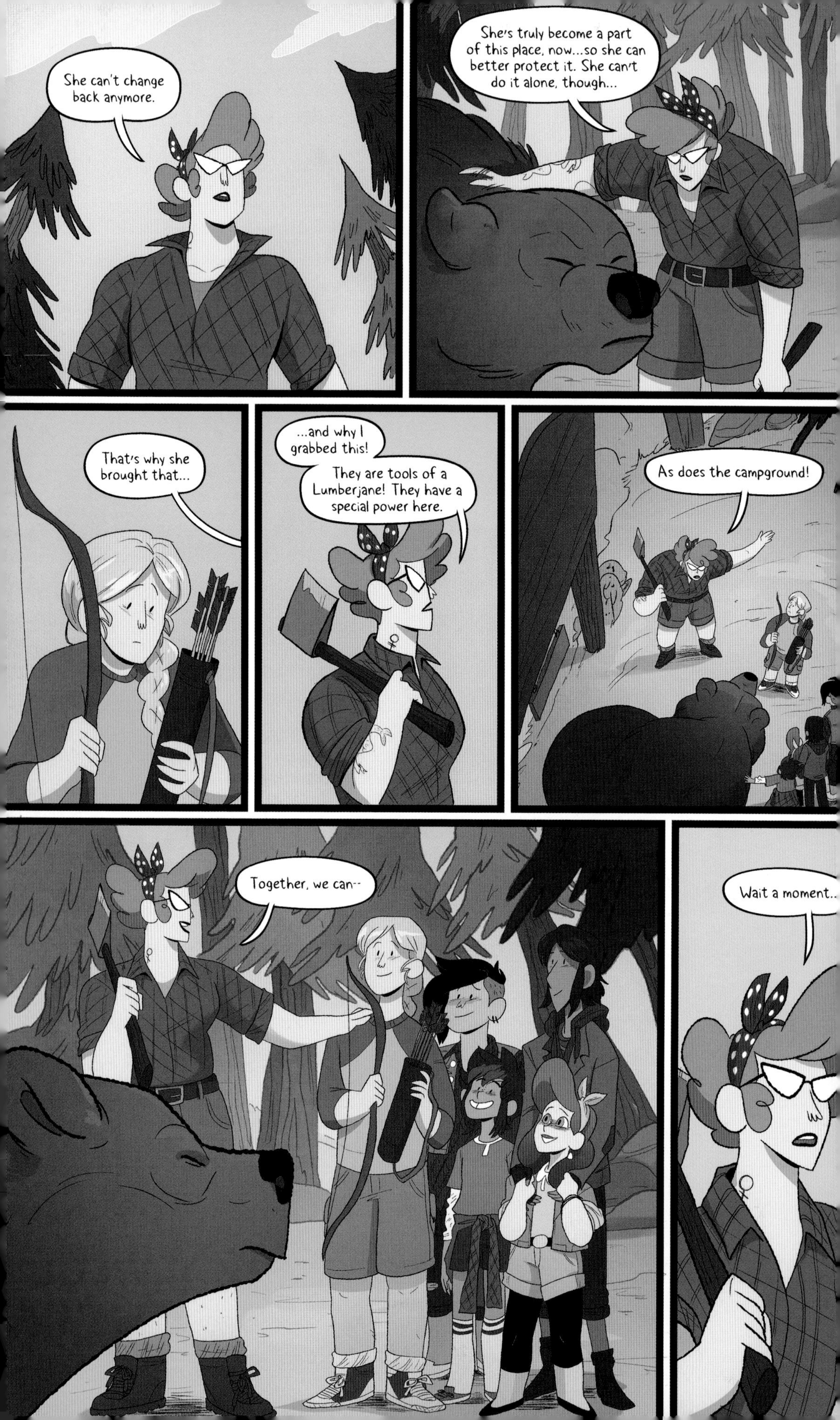
She can't change back anymore.
She's truly become a part of this place, now...so she can better protect it. She can't do it alone, though...
That's why she brought that...
...and why I grabbed this!
They are tools of a Lumberjane! They have a special power here.
As does the campground!
Together, we can--
Wait a moment...

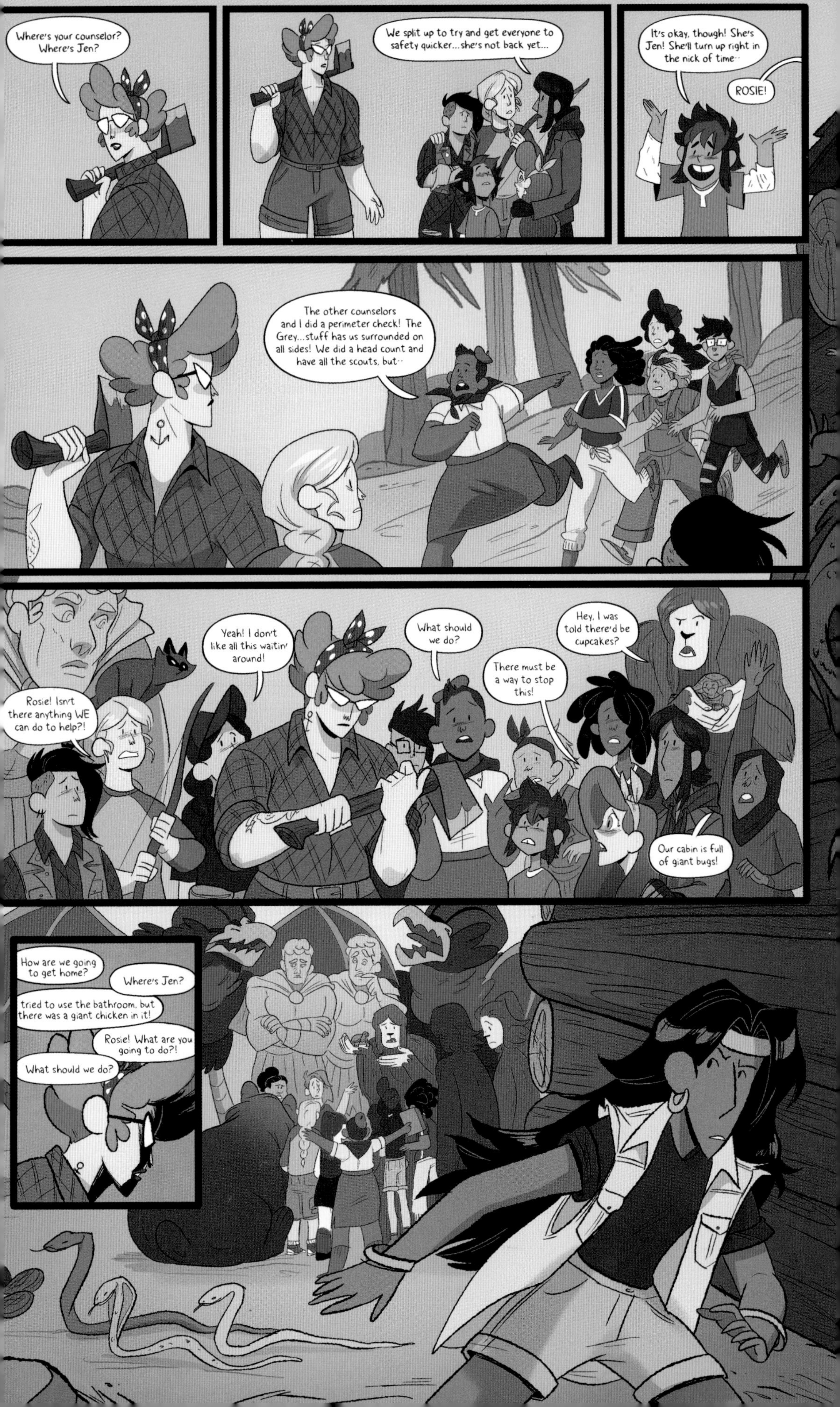
Where's your counselor? Where's Jen?
We split up to try and get everyone to safety quicker...she's not back yet...
It's okay, though! She's Jen! She'll turn up right in the nick of time--
ROSIE!
The other counselors and I did a perimeter check! The Grey...stuff has us surrounded on all sides! We did a head count and have all the scouts, but--
Rosie! Isn't there anything WE can do to help?!
Yeah! I don't like all this waitin' around!
What should we do?
There must be a way to stop this!
Hey, I was told there'd be cupcakes?
Our cabin is full of giant bugs!
How are we going to get home?
Where's Jen?
tried to use the bathroom, but there was a giant chicken in it!
Rosie! What are you going to do?!
What should we do?

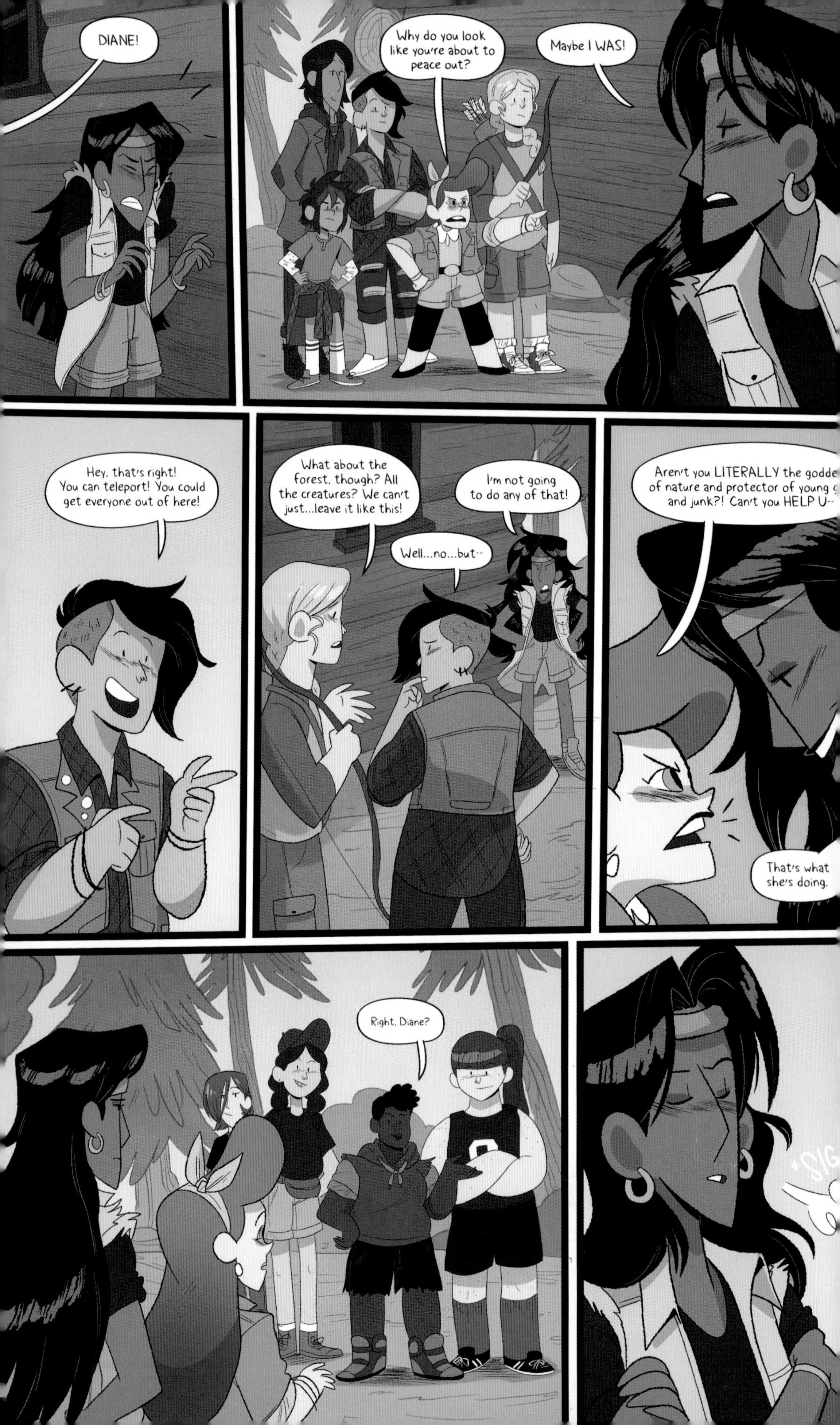
DIANE!
Why do you look like you're about to peace out?
Maybe I WAS!
Hey, that's right! You can teleport! You could get everyone out of here!
What about the forest, though? All the creatures? We can't just...leave it like this!
I'm not going to do any of that!
Well...no...but--
Aren't you LITERALLY the godde of nature and protector of young g and junk?! Can't you HELP U--
That's what she's doing.
Right, Diane?

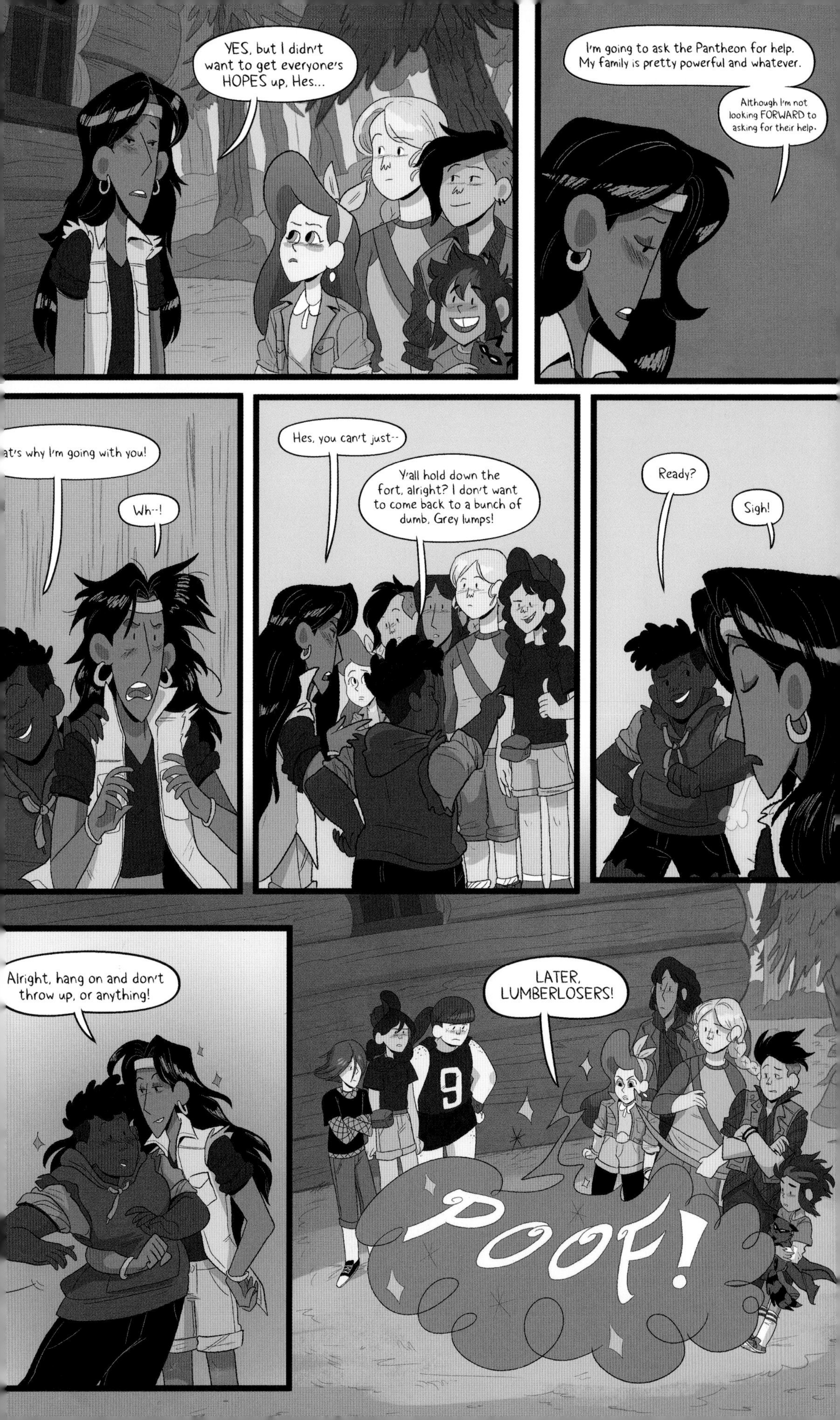
YES, but I didn't want to get everyone's HOPES up, Hes...
I'm going to ask the Pantheon for help. My family is pretty powerful and whatever.
Although I'm not looking FORWARD to asking for their help.
at's why I'm going with you!
Wh--!
Hes, you can't just--
Y'all hold down the fort, alright? I don't want to come back to a bunch of dumb, Grey lumps!
Ready?
Sigh!
Alright, hang on and don't throw up, or anything!
LATER, LUMBERLOSERS!
POOF!

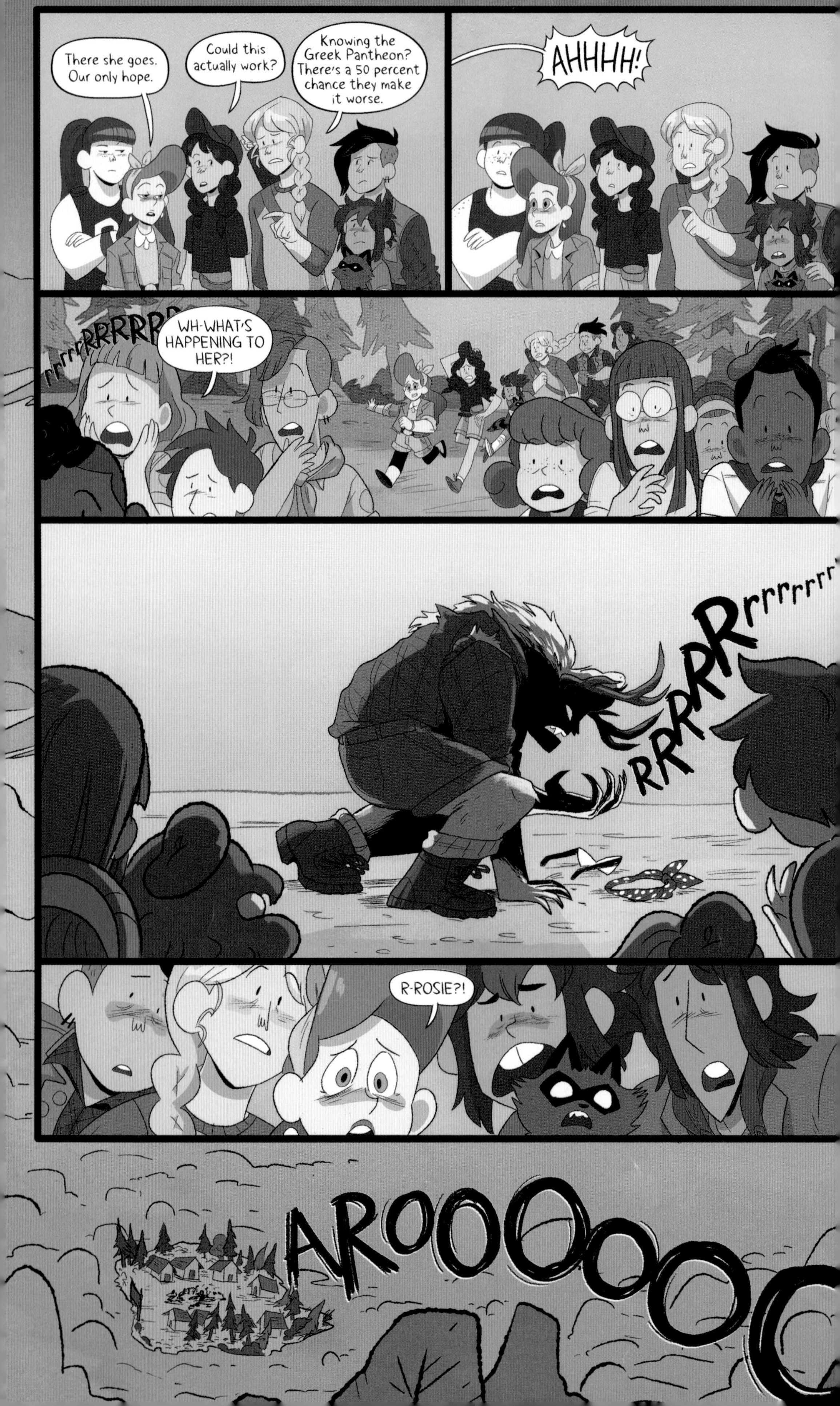
There she goes. Our only hope.
Could this actually work?
Knowing the Greek Pantheon? There's a 50 percent chance they make it worse.
AHHHH!
rrrrrRRRRRR
WH-WHAT'S HAPPENING TO HER?!
RRRRRRrrrrrrr
R-ROSIE?!
AROOOOOOO

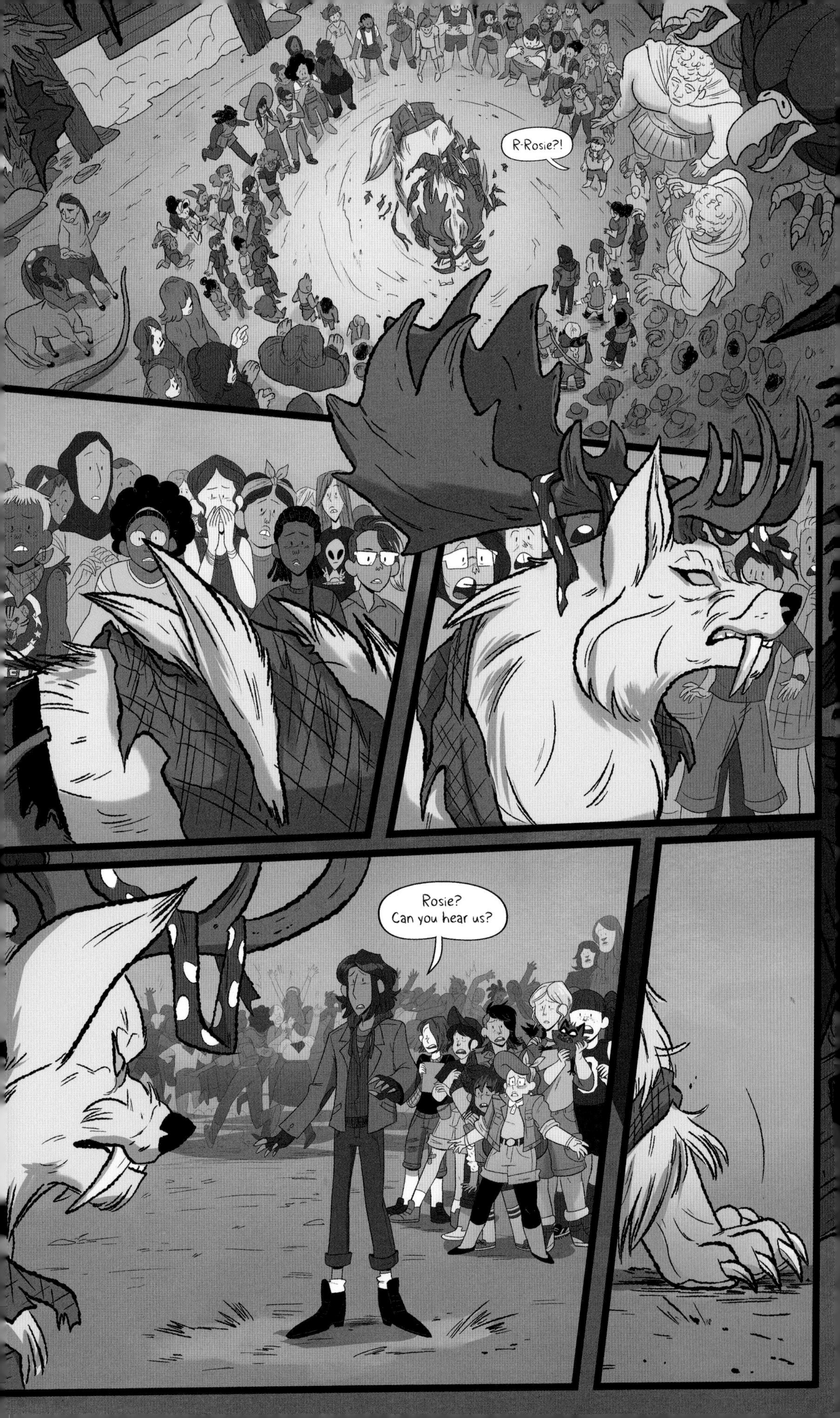
R-Rosie?!
Rosie?
Can you hear us?

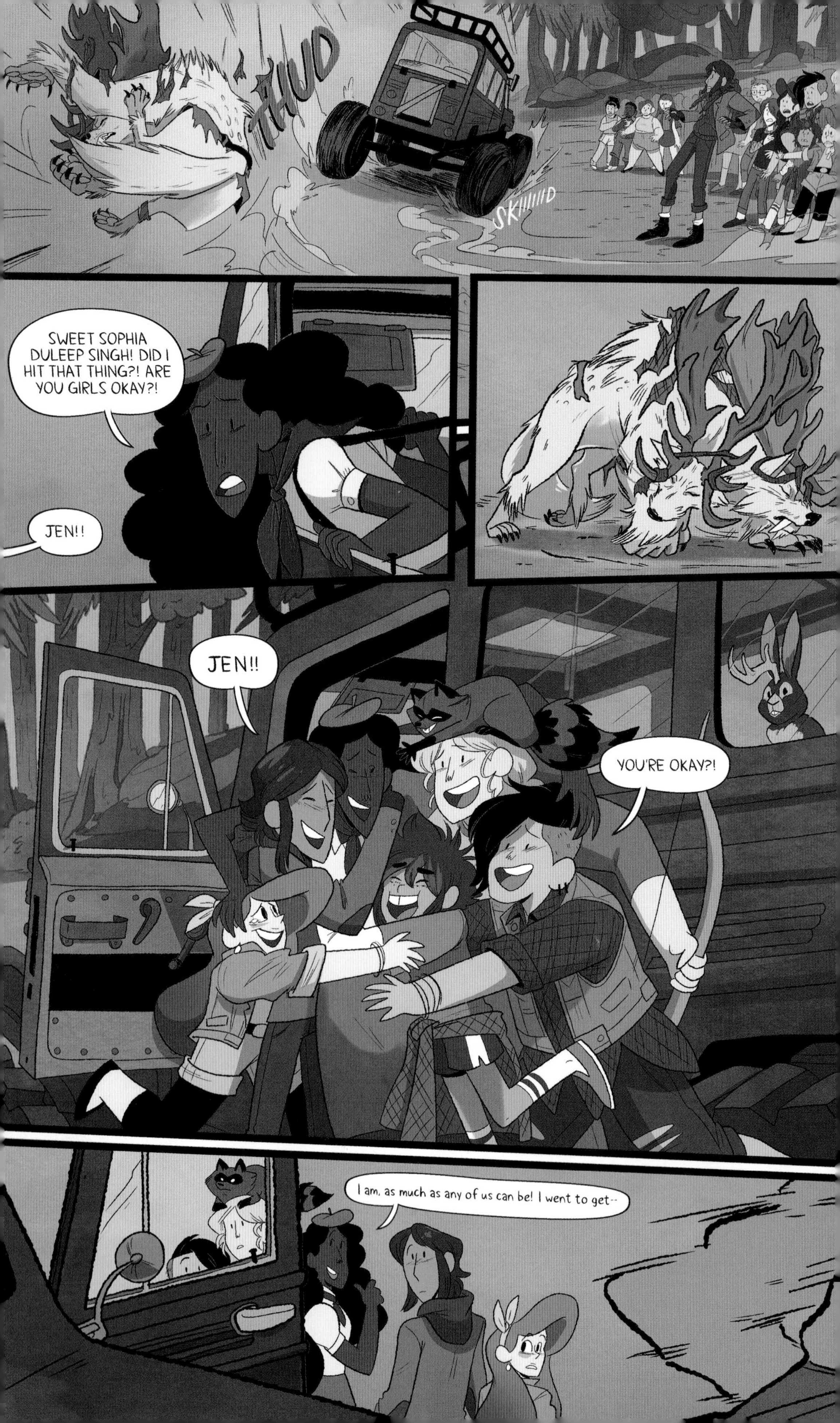
THUD
SKIIIIIID
SWEET SOPHIA DULEEP SINGH! DID I HIT THAT THING?! ARE YOU GIRLS OKAY?!
JEN!!
JEN!!
YOU'RE OKAY?!
I am, as much as any of us can be! I went to get--

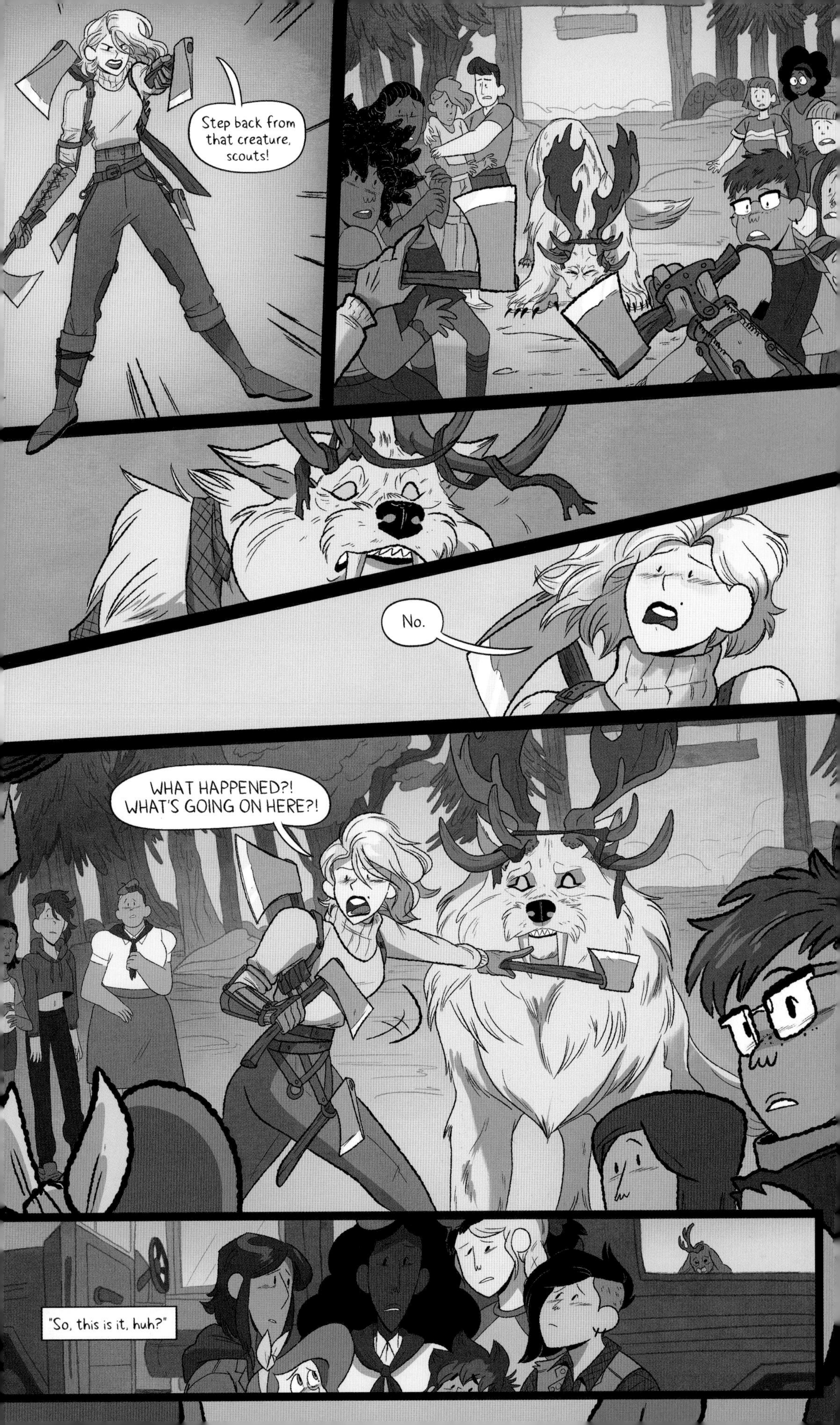
Step back from that creature, scouts!
No.
WHAT HAPPENED?! WHAT'S GOING ON HERE?!
"So, this is it, huh?"

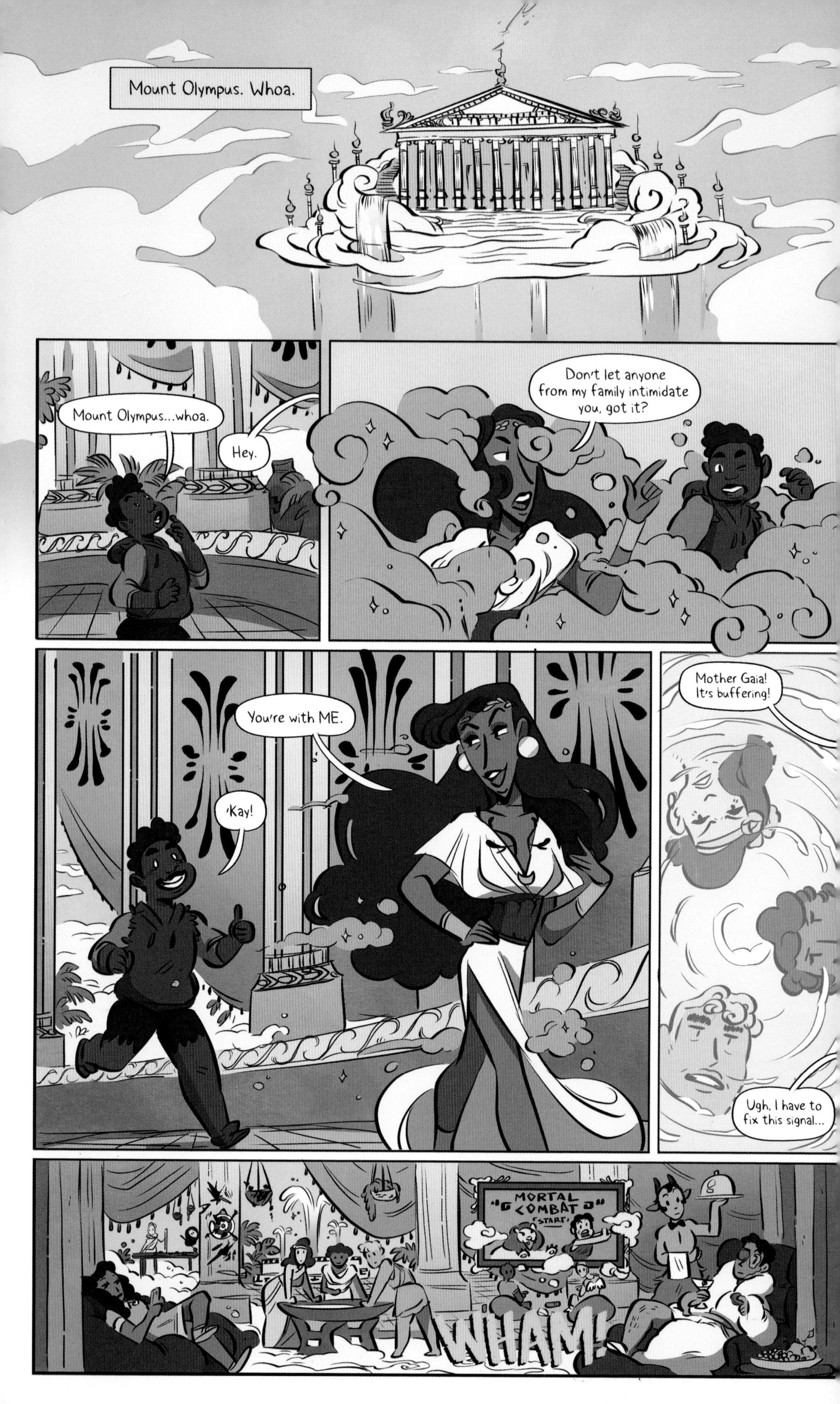

Mount Olympus. Whoa.
Mount Olympus...whoa.
Hey.
Don't let anyone from my family intimidate you, got it?
You're with ME.
'Kay!
Mother Gaia! It's buffering!
Ugh, I have to fix this signal...
MORTAL COMBAT
START
WHAM!

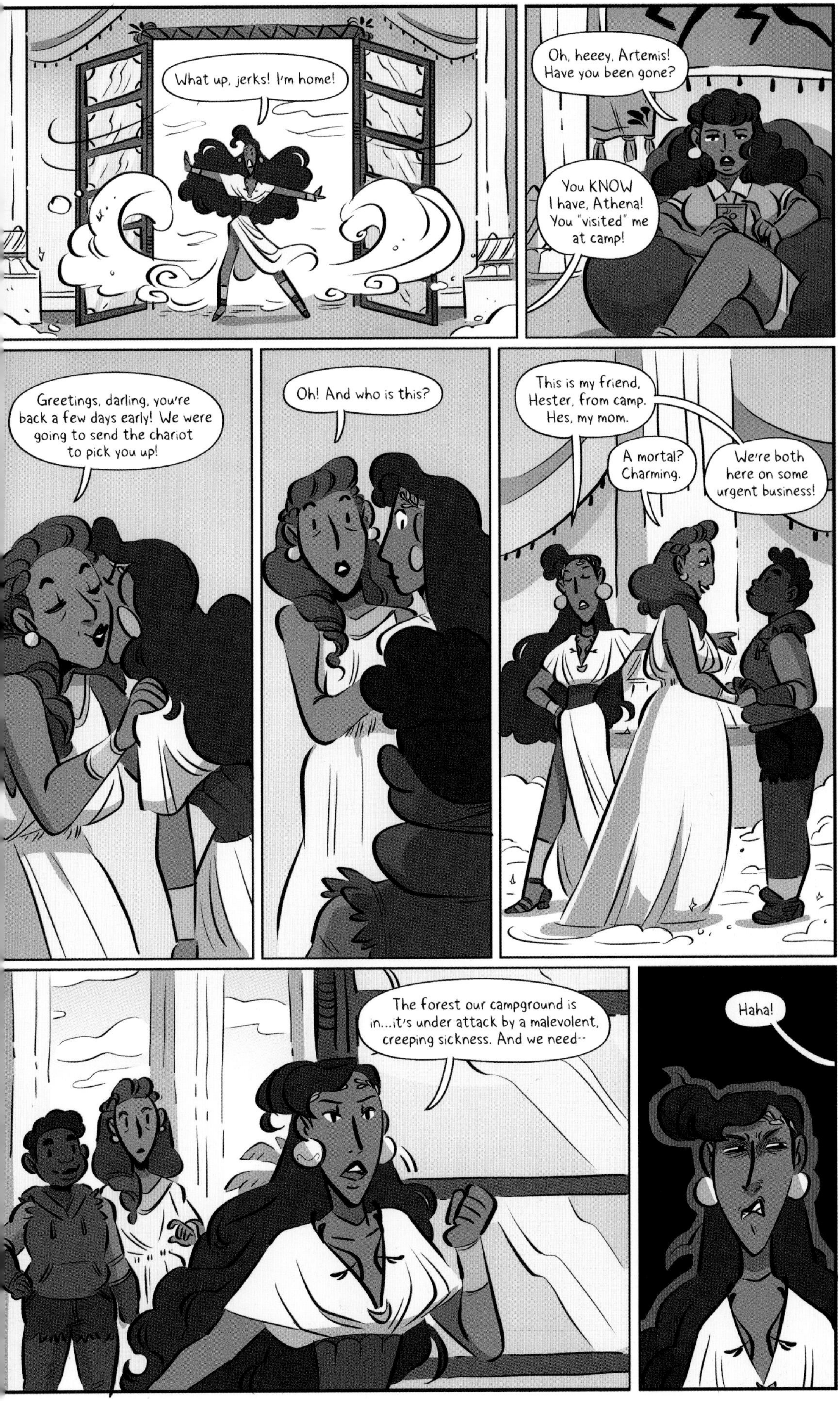
What up, jerks! I'm home!
Oh, heeey, Artemis! Have you been gone?
You KNOW I have, Athena! You "visited" me at camp!
Greetings, darling, you're back a few days early! We were going to send the chariot to pick you up!
Oh! And who is this?
This is my friend, Hester, from camp. Hes, my mom.
A mortal? Charming.
We're both here on some urgent business!
The forest our campground is in...it's under attack by a malevolent, creeping sickness. And we need--
Haha!

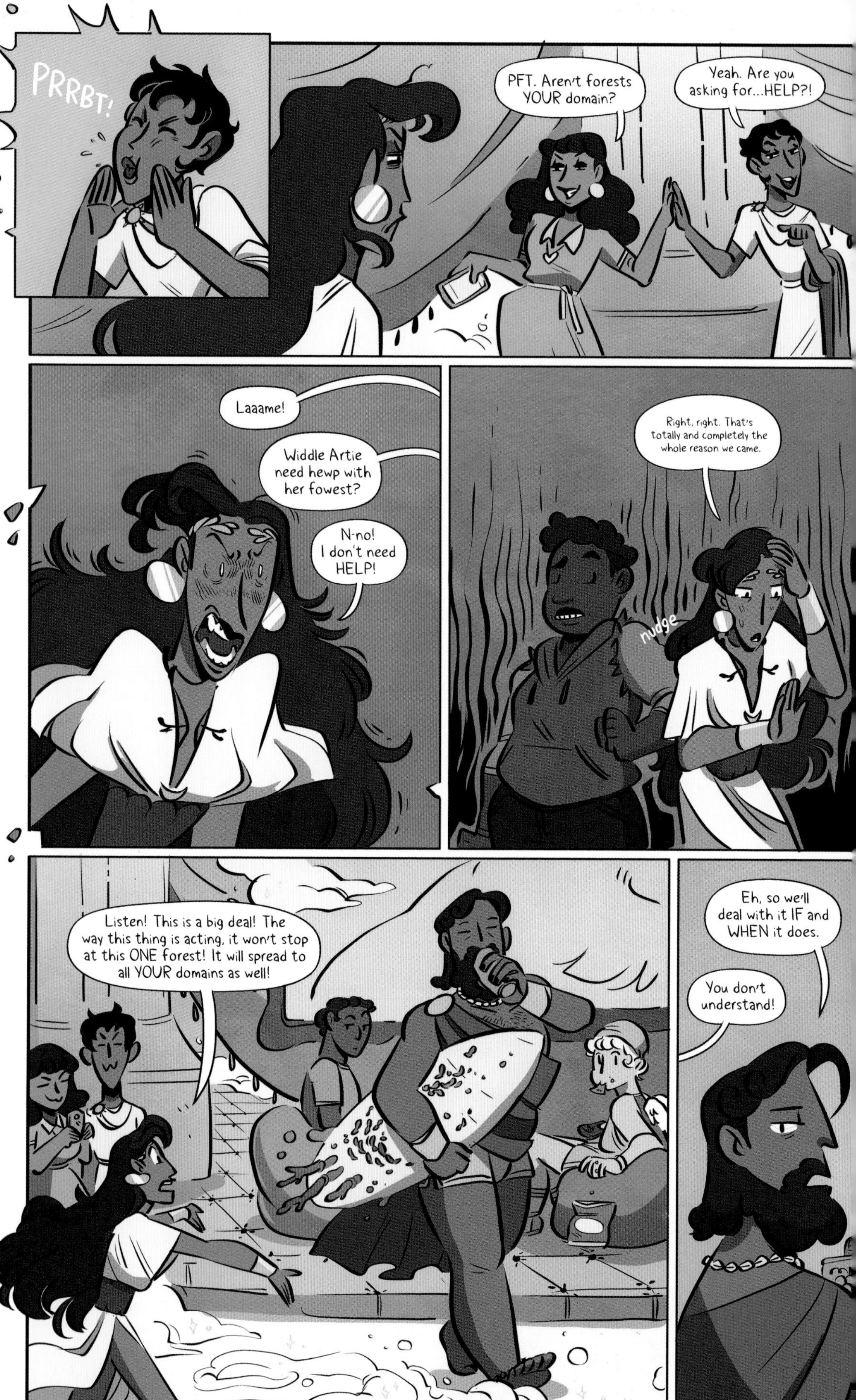
PRRBT!
PFT. Aren't forests YOUR domain?
Yeah. Are you asking for...HELP?!
Laaame!
Widdle Artie need hewp with her fowest?
N-no! I don't need HELP!
Right, right. That's totally and completely the whole reason we came.
nudge
Listen! This is a big deal! The way this thing is acting, it won't stop at this ONE forest! It will spread to all YOUR domains as well!
Eh, so we'll deal with it IF and WHEN it does.
You don't understand!

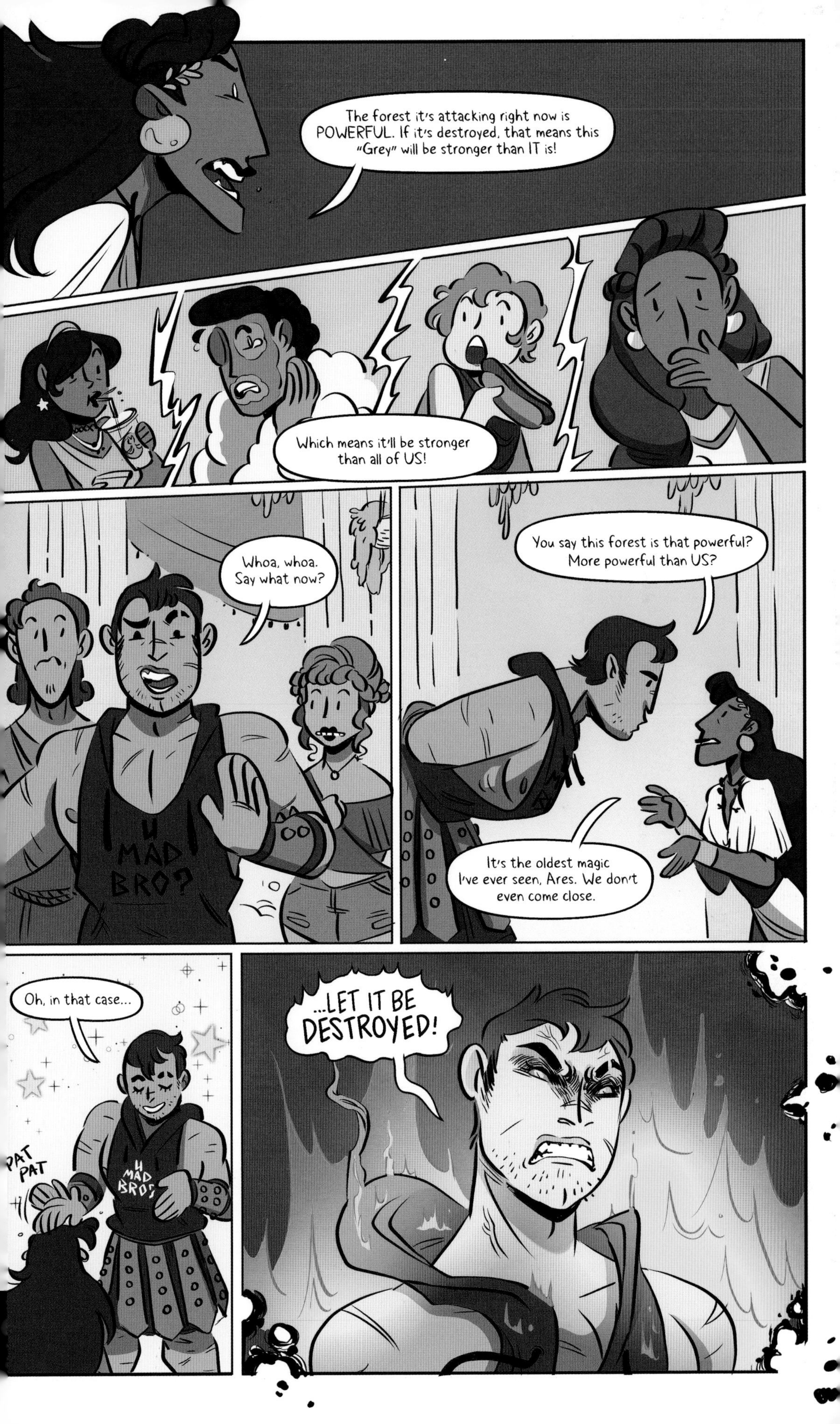
The forest it's attacking right now is POWERFUL. If it's destroyed, that means this "Grey" will be stronger than IT is!
Which means it'll be stronger than all of US!
Whoa, whoa. Say what now?
You say this forest is that powerful? More powerful than US?
It's the oldest magic I've ever seen, Ares. We don't even come close.
Oh, in that case...
PAT PAT
...LET IT BE DESTROYED!

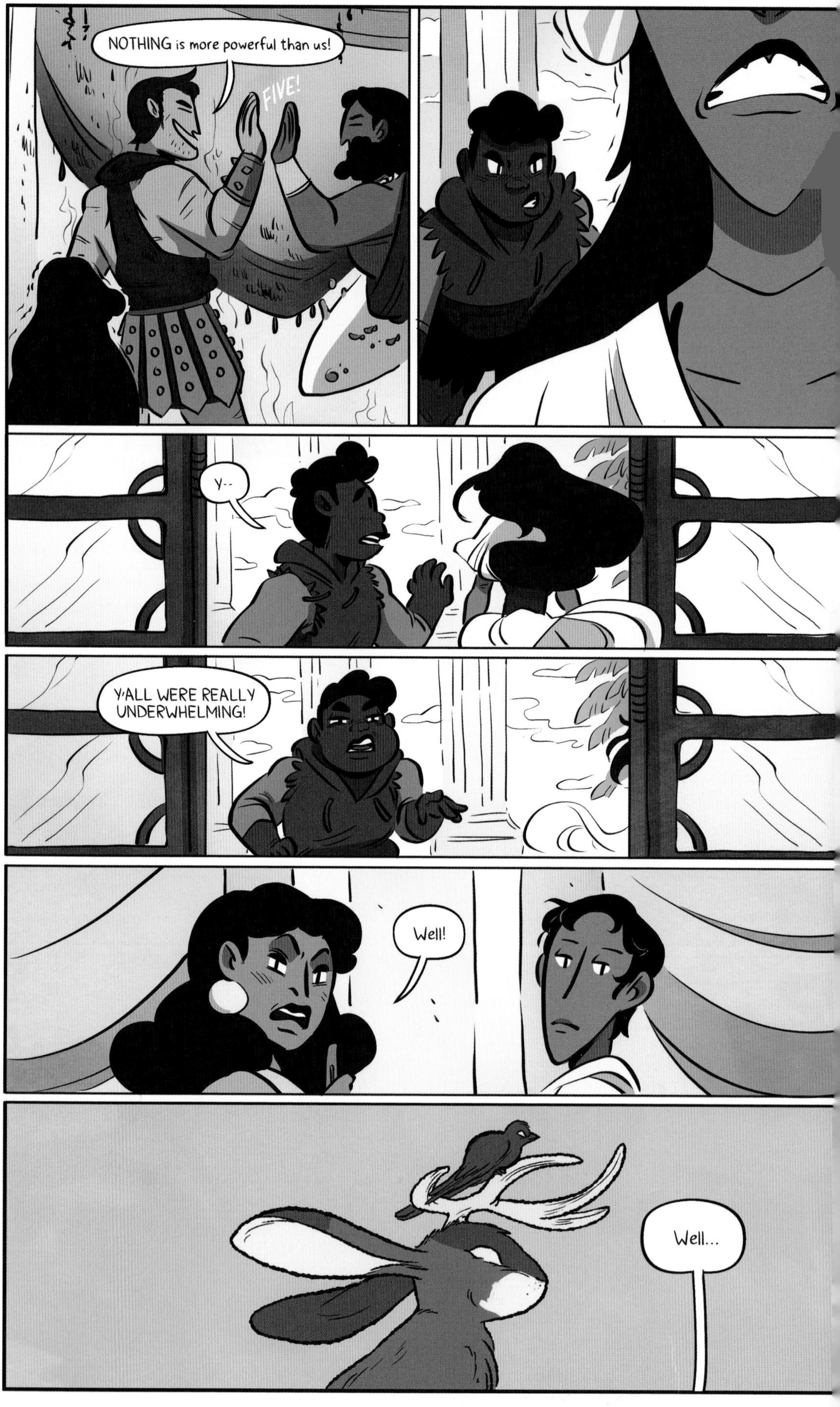
NOTHING is more powerful than us!
FIVE!
Y--
Y'ALL WERE REALLY UNDERWHELMING!
Well!
Well...

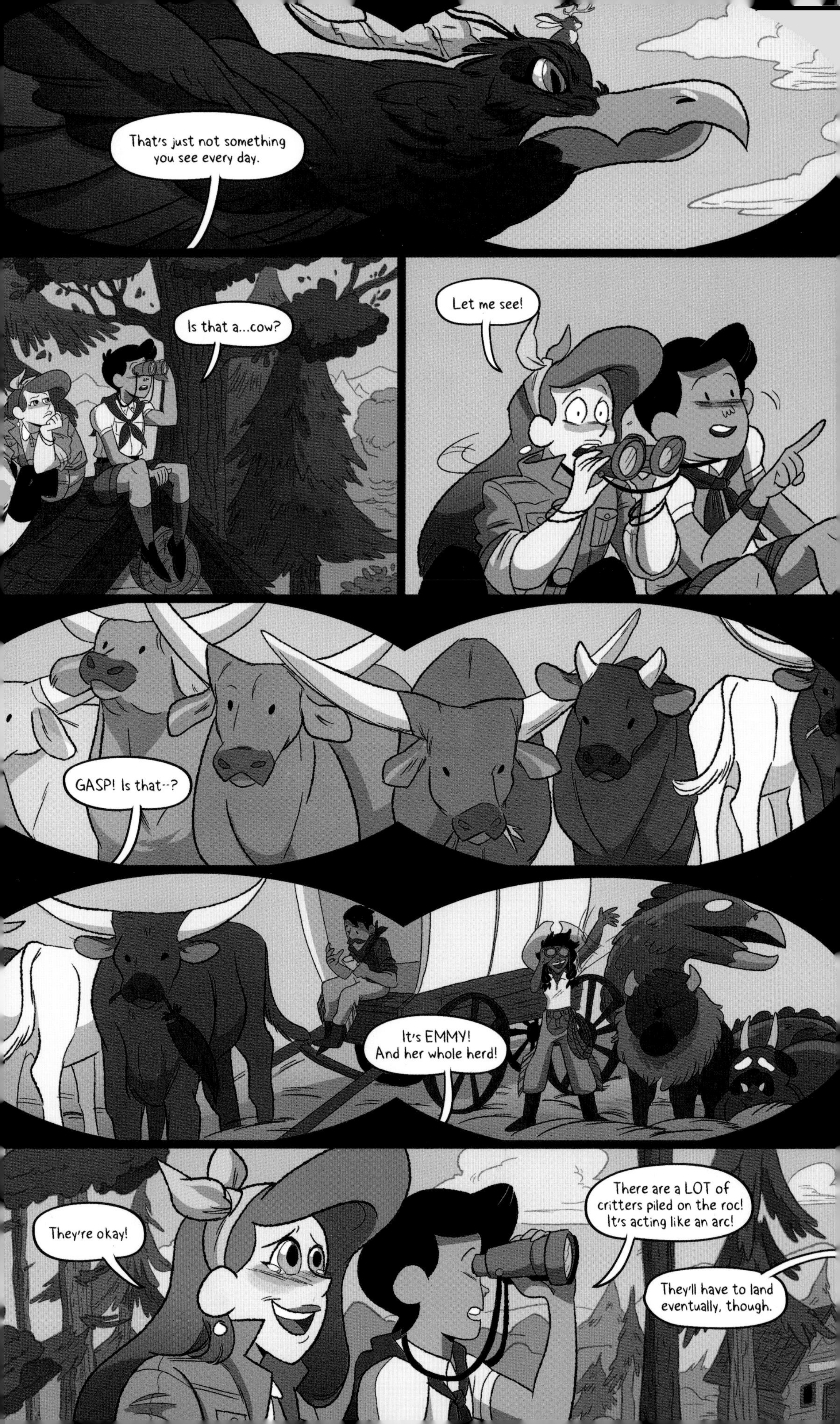

That's just not something you see every day.
Is that a...cow?
Let me see!
GASP! Is that--?
It's EMMY! And her whole herd!
They're okay!
There are a LOT of critters piled on the roc! It's acting like an arc!
They'll have to land eventually, though.

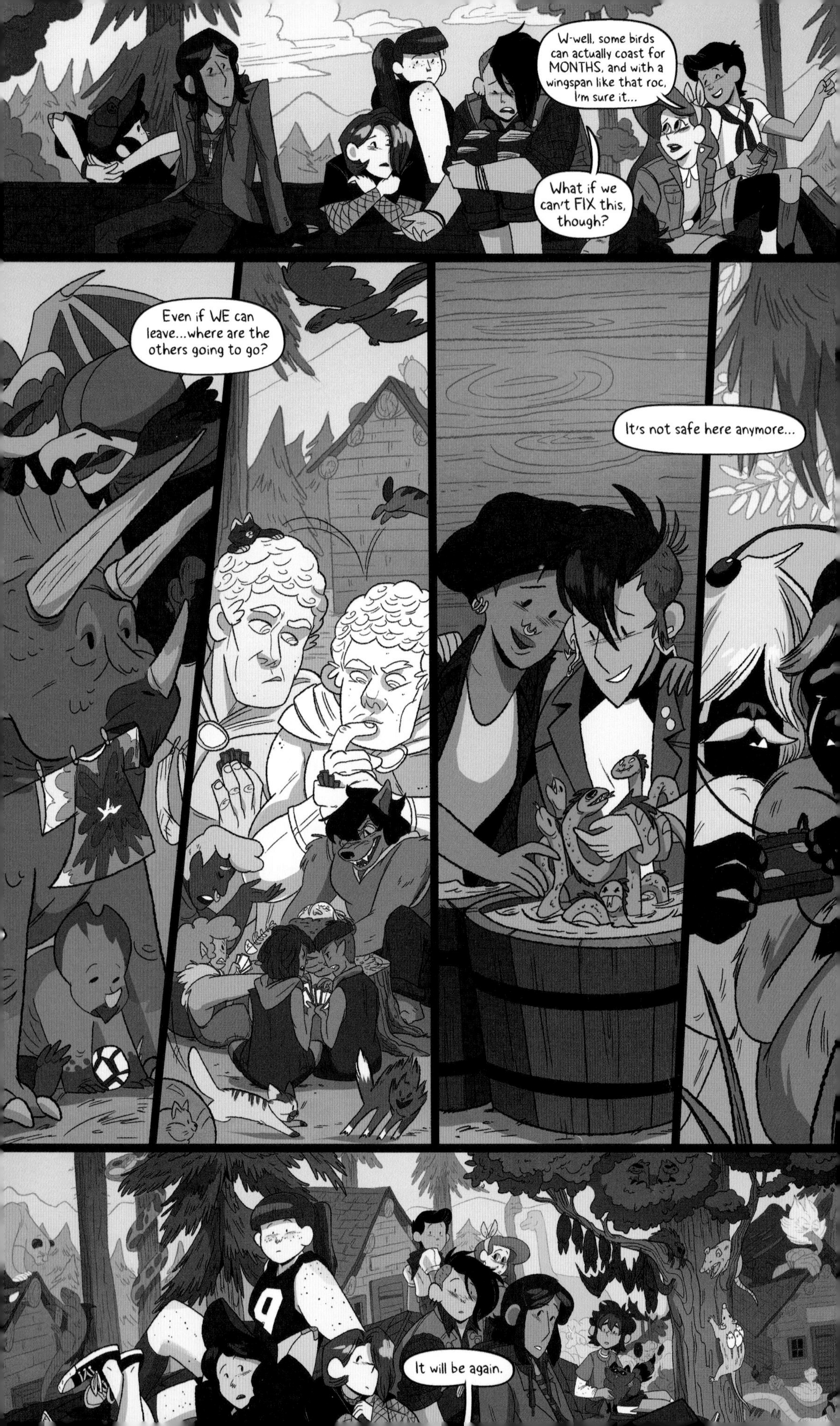
W-well, some birds can actually coast for MONTHS, and with a wingspan like that roc, I'm sure it...
What if we can't FIX this, though?
Even if WE can leave...where are the others going to go?
It's not safe here anymore...
It will be again.

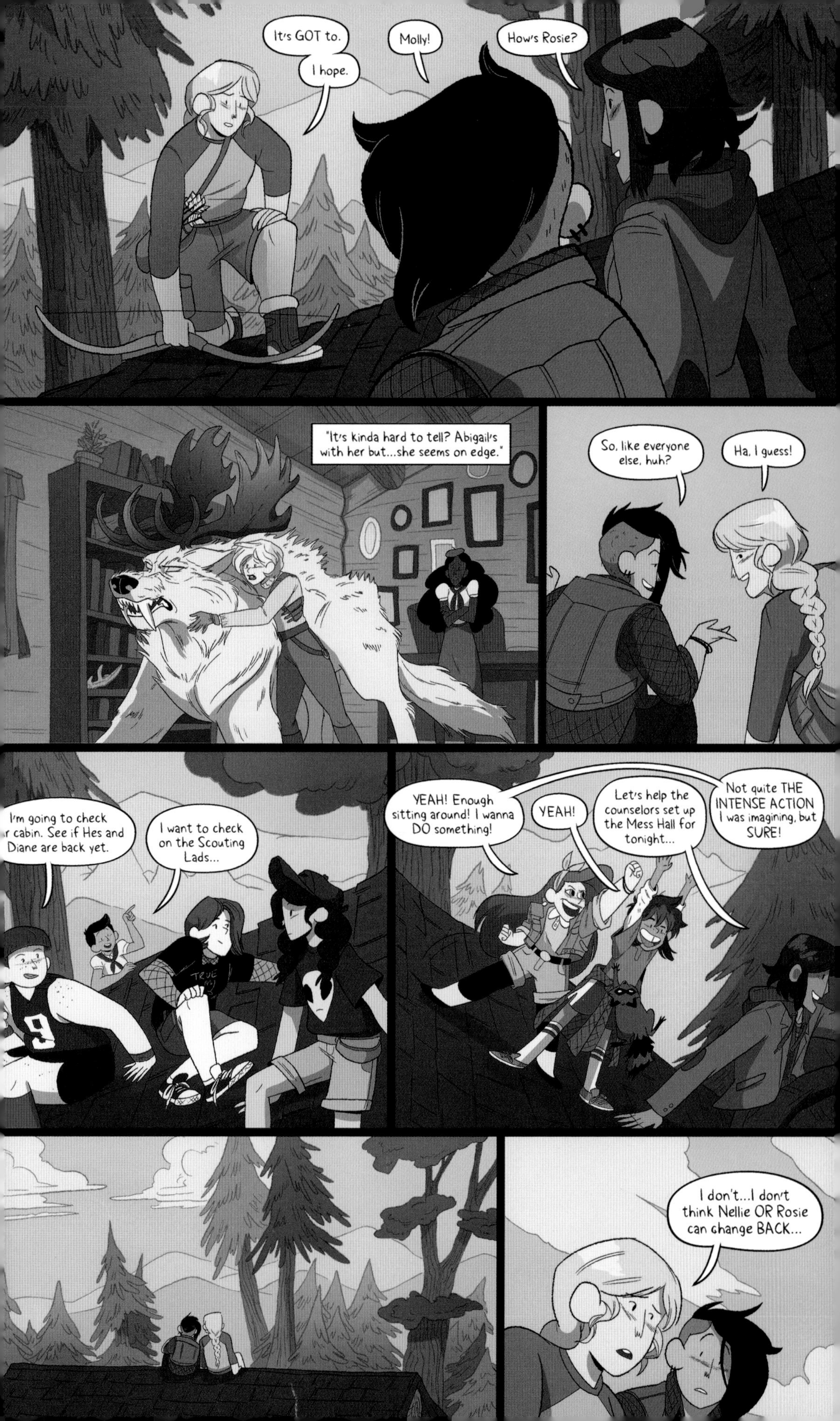
It's GOT to.
I hope.
Molly!
How's Rosie?
"It's kinda hard to tell? Abigail's with her but...she seems on edge."
So, like everyone else, huh?
Ha, I guess!
I'm going to check r cabin. See if Hes and Diane are back yet.
I want to check on the Scouting Lads...
YEAH! Enough sitting around! I wanna DO something!
YEAH!
Let's help the counselors set up the Mess Hall for tonight...
Not quite THE INTENSE ACTION I was imagining, but SURE!
I don't...I don't think Nellie OR Rosie can change BACK...

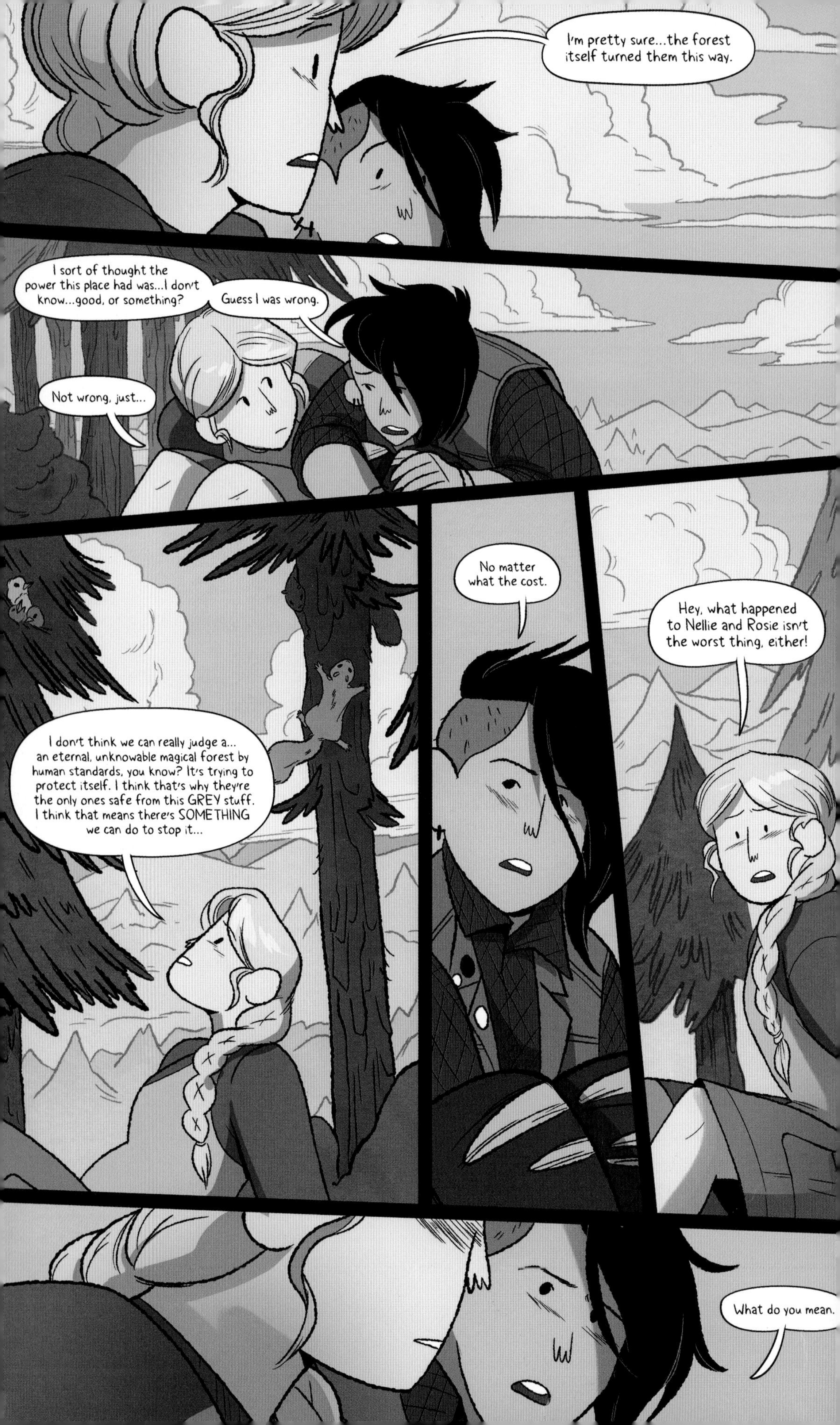
I'm pretty sure...the forest itself turned them this way.
I sort of thought the power this place had was...I don't know...good, or something?
Guess I was wrong.
Not wrong, just...
I don't think we can really judge a... an eternal, unknowable magical forest by human standards, you know? It's trying to protect itself. I think that's why they're the only ones safe from this GREY stuff. I think that means there's SOMETHING we can do to stop it...
No matter what the cost.
Hey, what happened to Nellie and Rosie isn't the worst thing, either!
What do you mean.

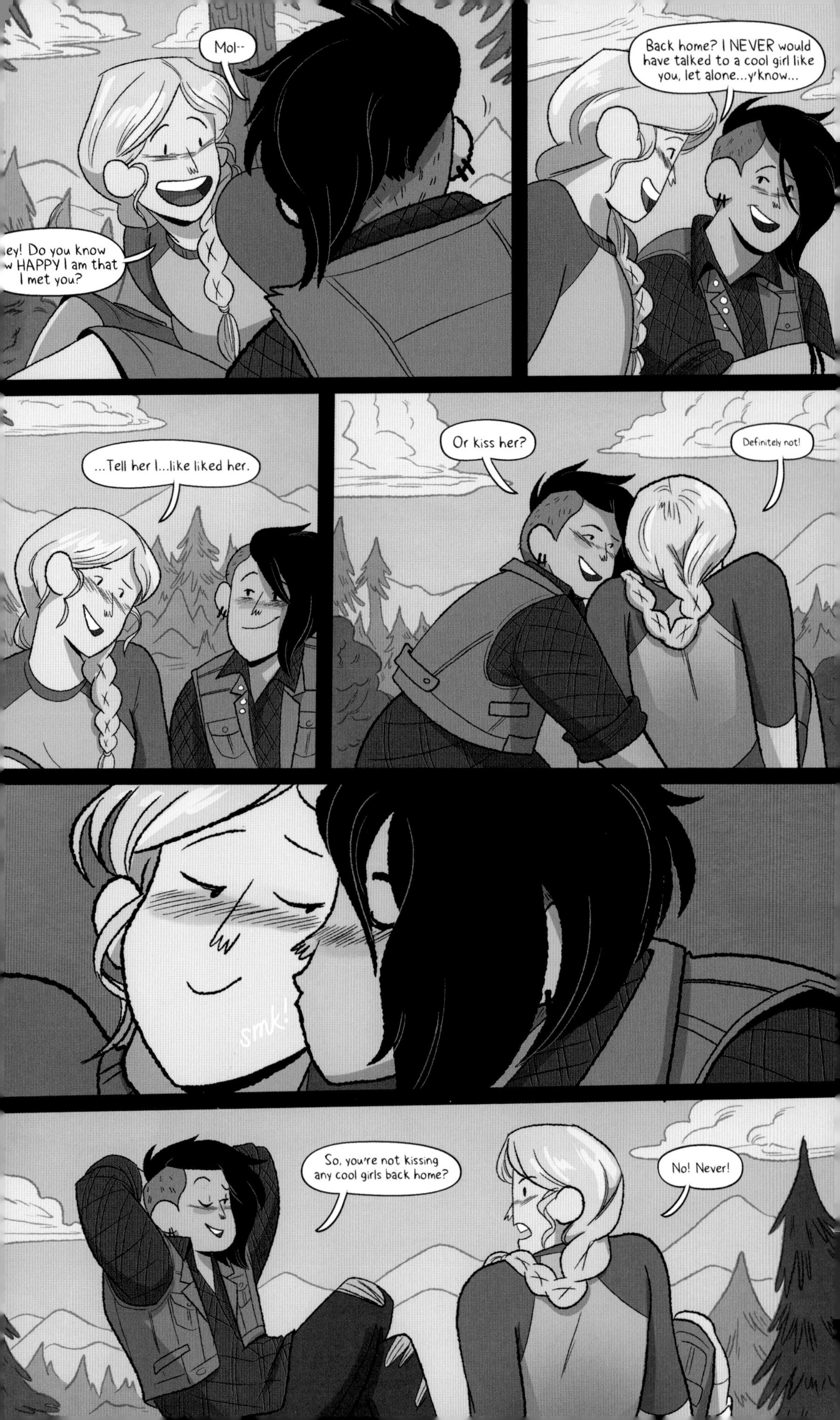
Mol--
ey! Do you know
w HAPPY I am that
I met you?
Back home? I NEVER would have talked to a cool girl like you, let alone...y'know...
...Tell her I...like liked her.
Or kiss her?
Definitely not!
smk!
So, you're not kissing any cool girls back home?
No! Never!

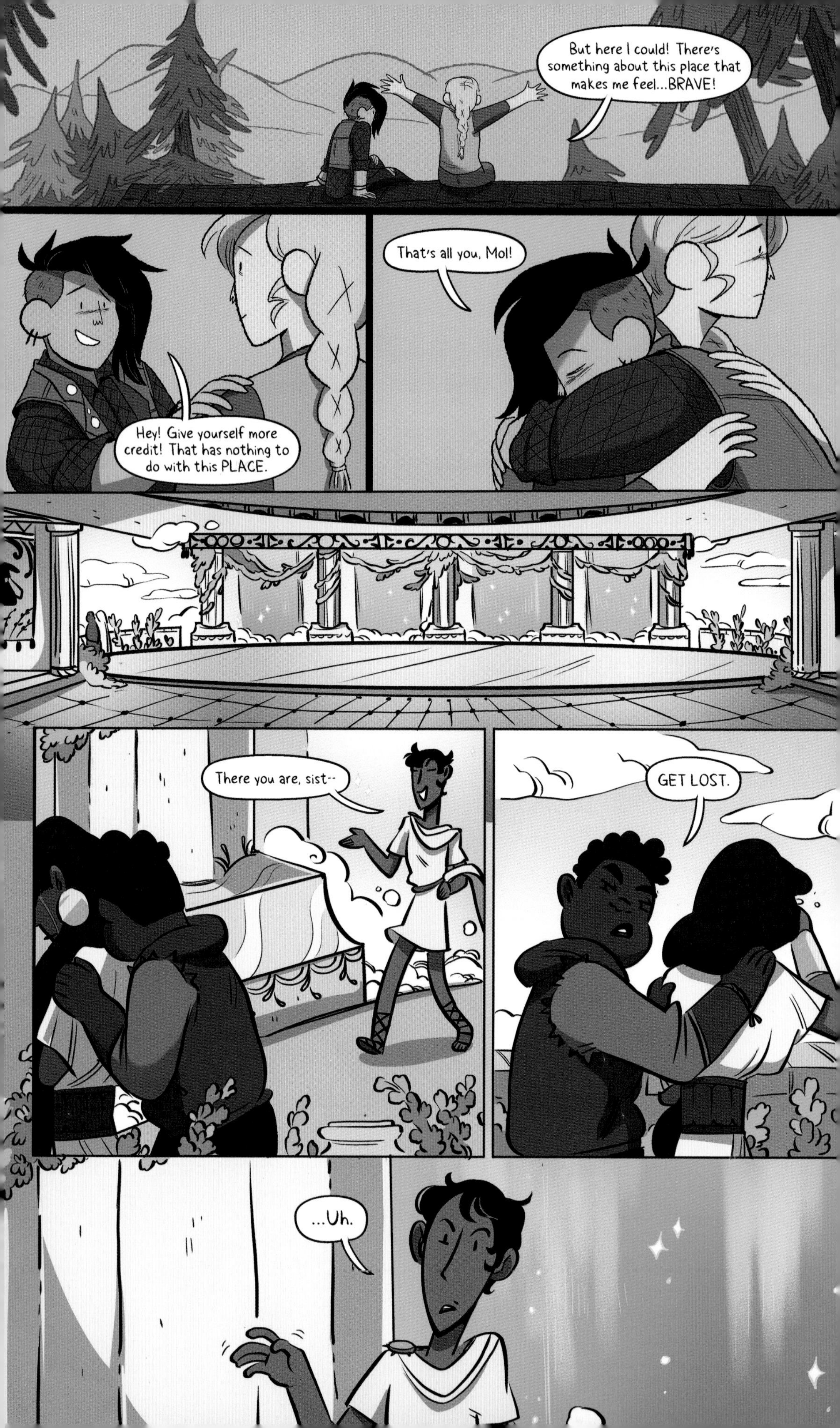

But here I could! There's something about this place that makes me feel...BRAVE!
Hey! Give yourself more credit! That has nothing to do with this PLACE.
That's all you, Mol!
There you are, sist--
GET LOST.
...Uh.

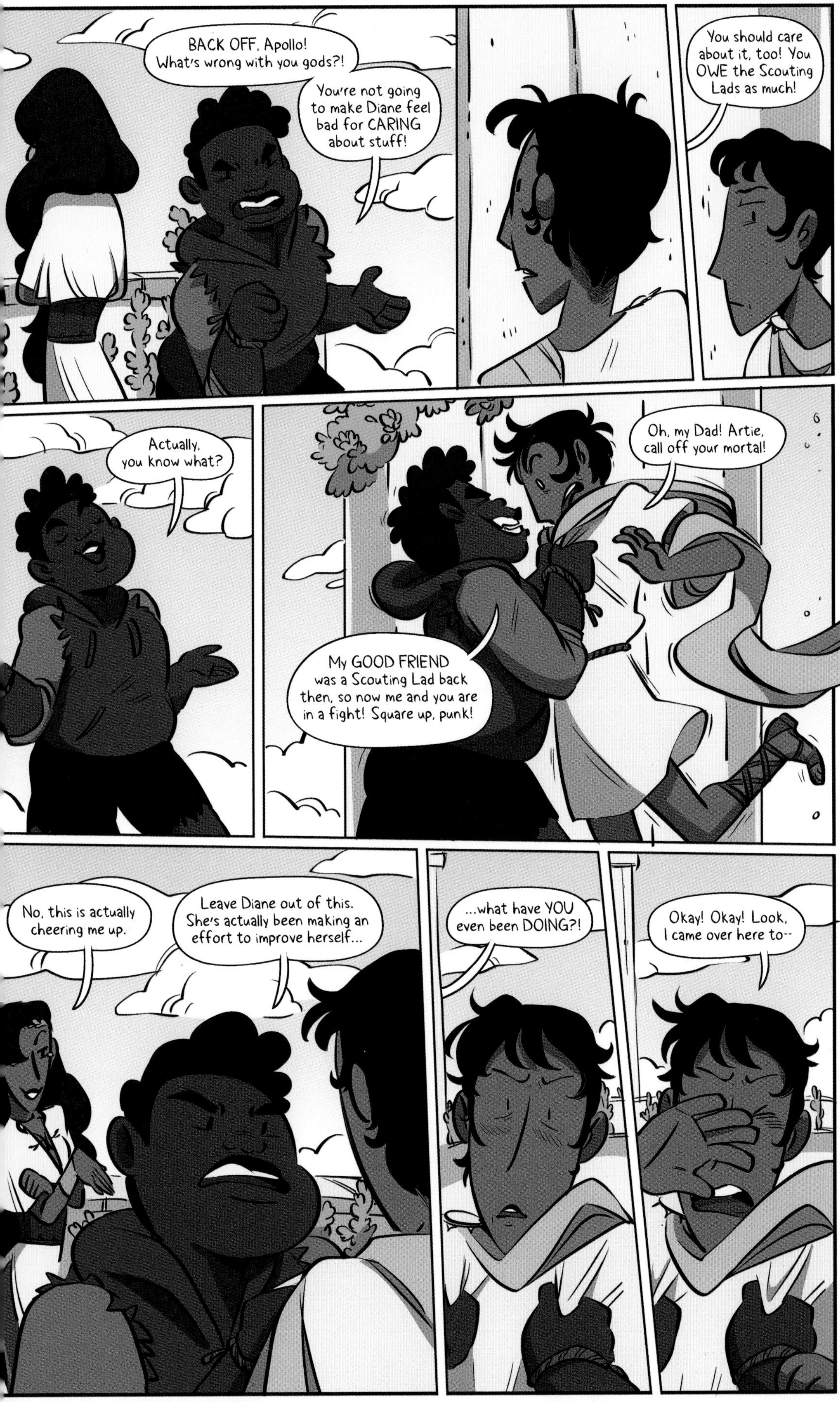
BACK OFF, Apollo! What's wrong with you gods?!
You're not going to make Diane feel bad for CARING about stuff!
You should care about it, too! You OWE the Scouting Lads as much!
Actually, you know what?
Oh, my Dad! Artie, call off your mortal!
My GOOD FRIEND was a Scouting Lad back then, so now me and you are in a fight! Square up, punk!
No, this is actually cheering me up.
Leave Diane out of this. She's actually been making an effort to improve herself...
...what have YOU even been DOING?!
Okay! Okay! Look, I came over here to--

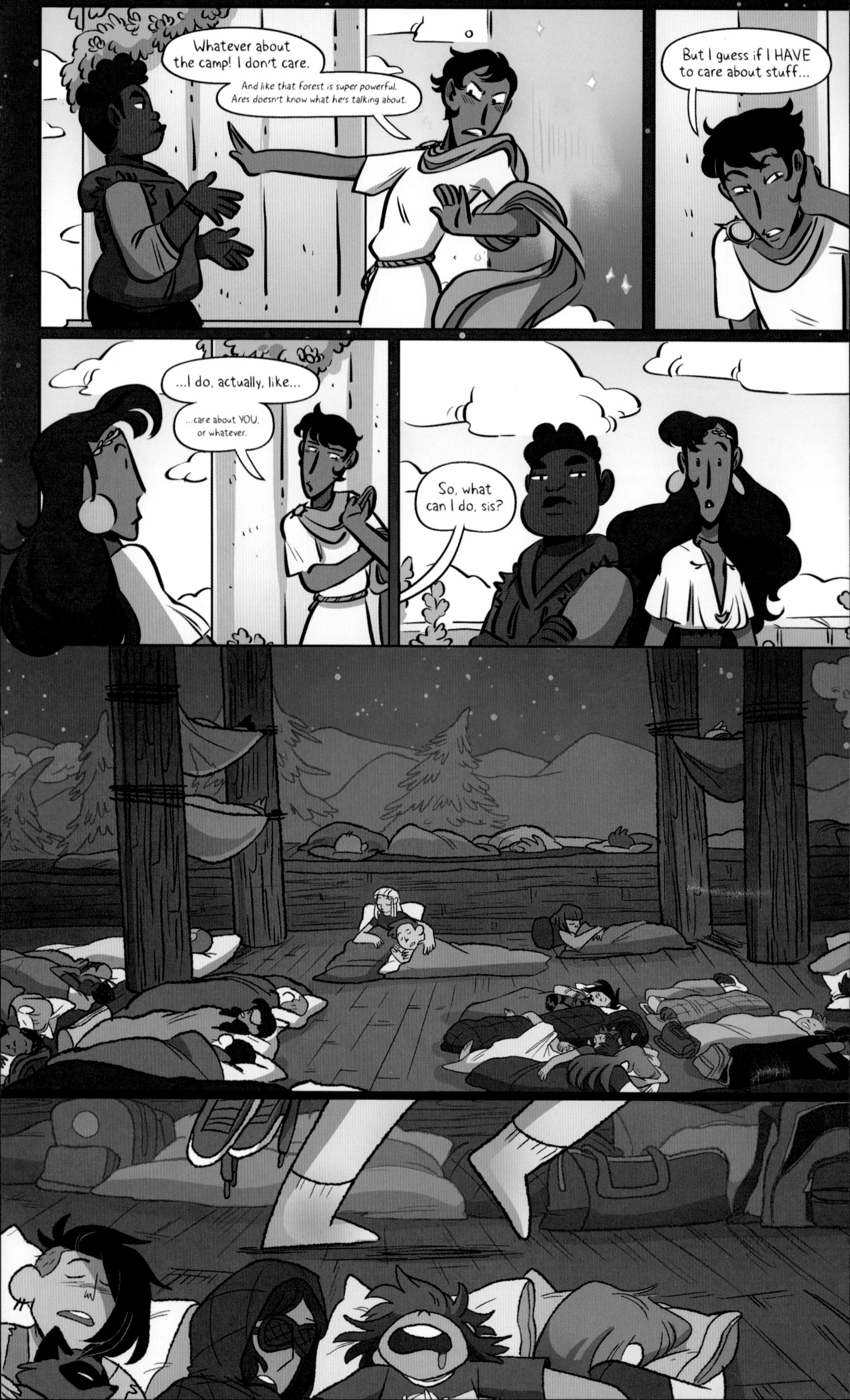
Whatever about the camp! I don't care.
And like that forest is super powerful. Ares doesn't know what he's talking about.
But I guess if I HAVE to care about stuff...
...I do, actually, like...
...care about YOU, or whatever.
So, what can I do, sis?

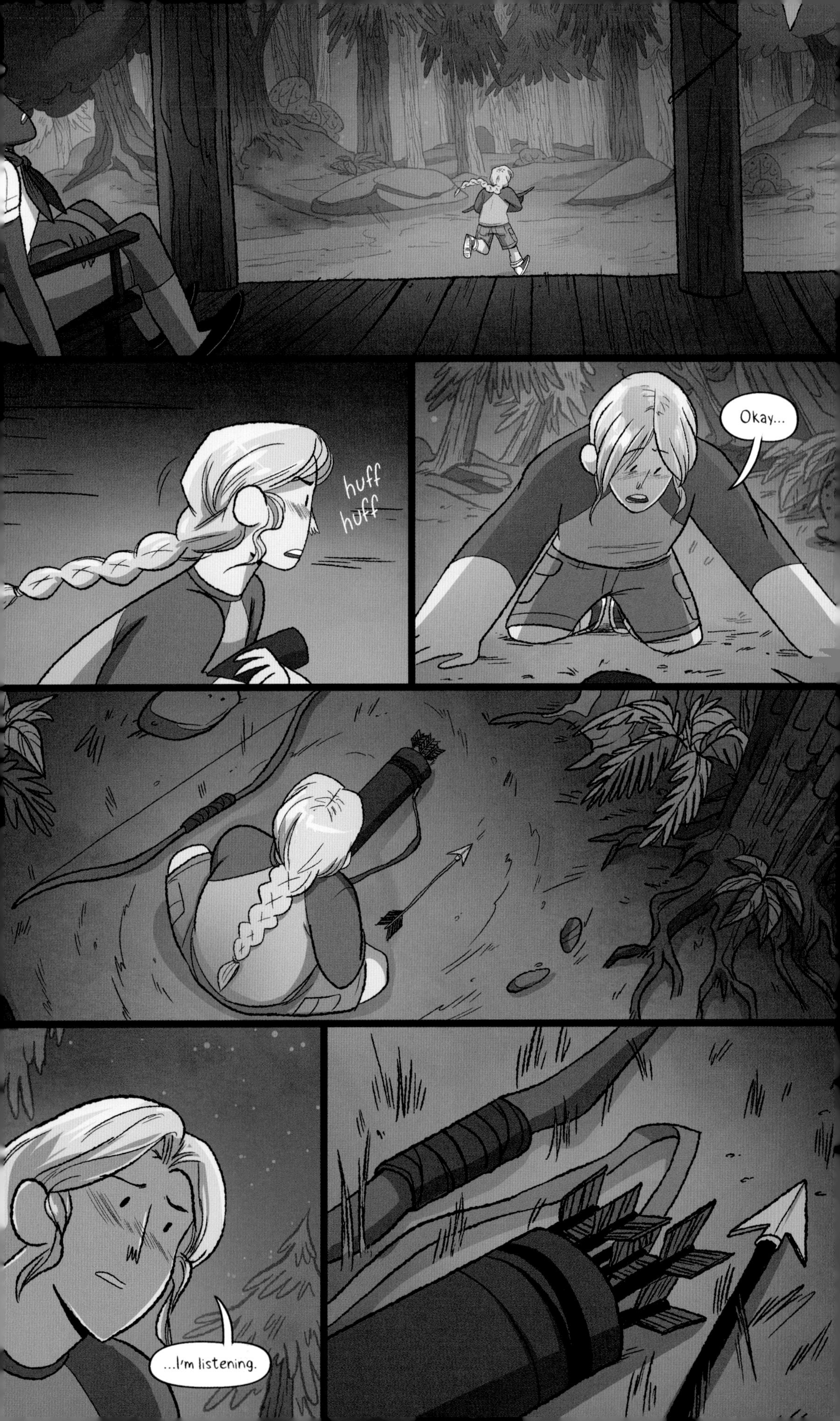
huff huff
Okay...
...I'm listening.

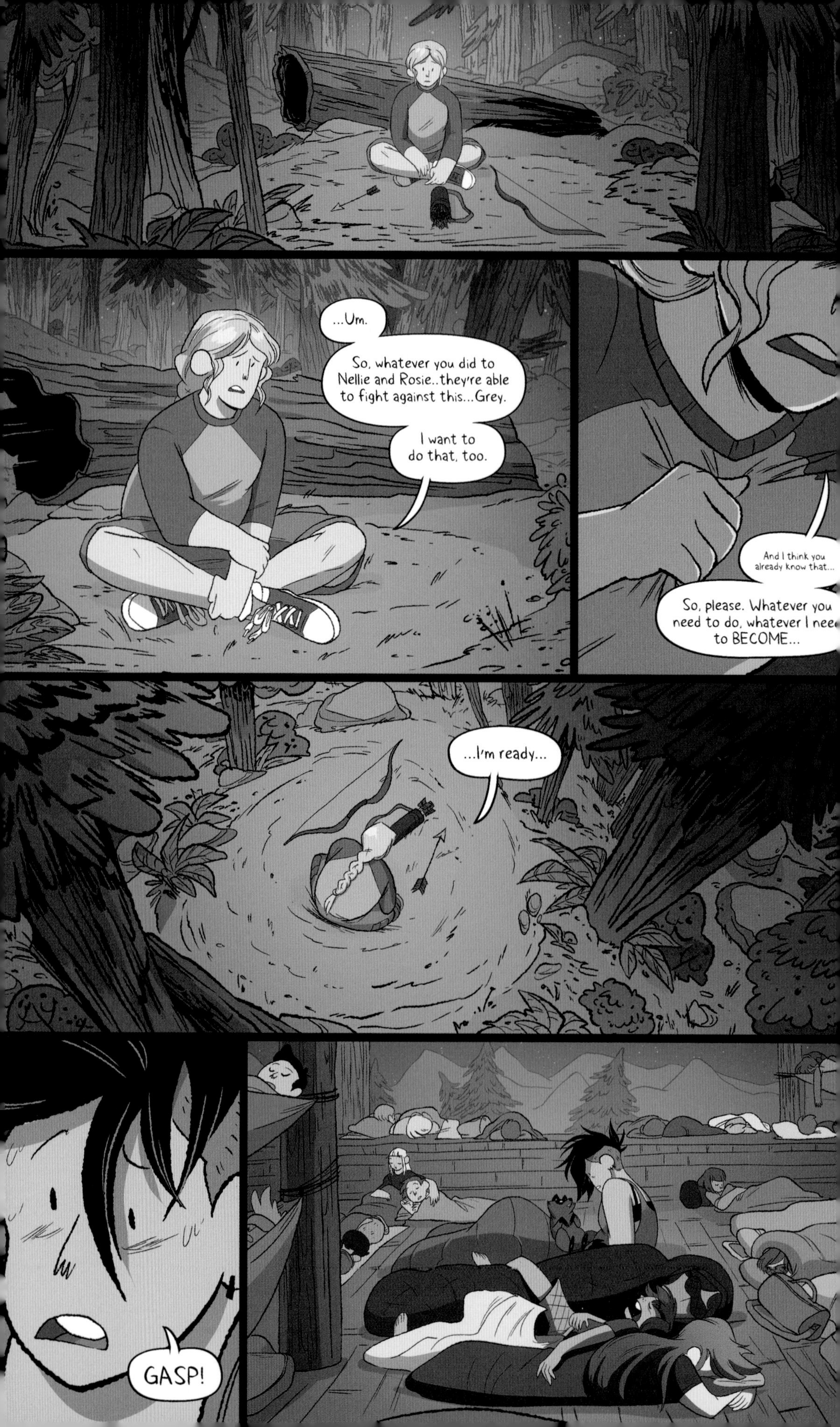
...Um.
So, whatever you did to Nellie and Rosie..they're able to fight against this...Grey.
I want to do that, too.
And I think you already know that...
So, please. Whatever you need to do, whatever I nee to BECOME...
...I'm ready...
GASP!

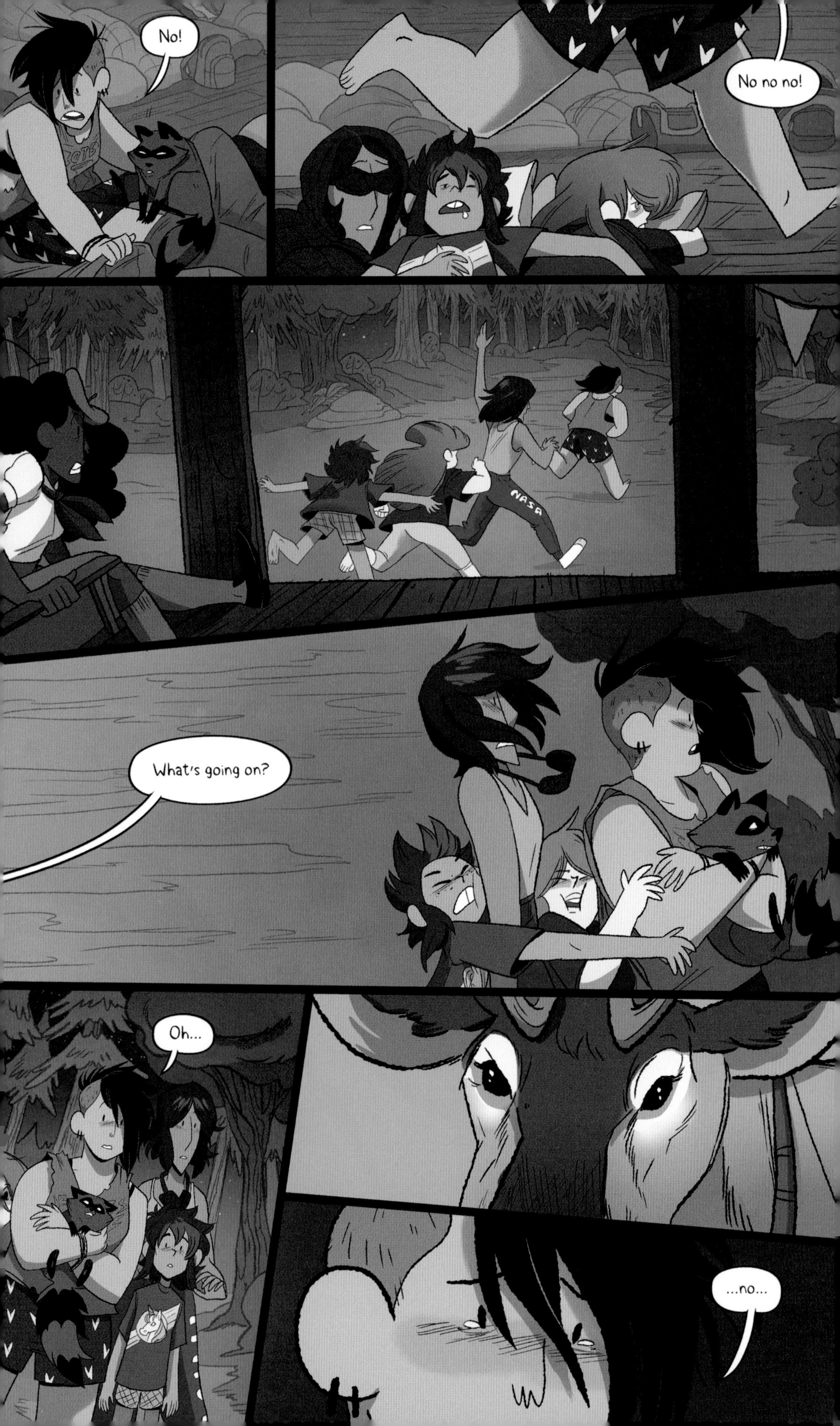
No!
No no no!
What's going on?
Oh...
...no...

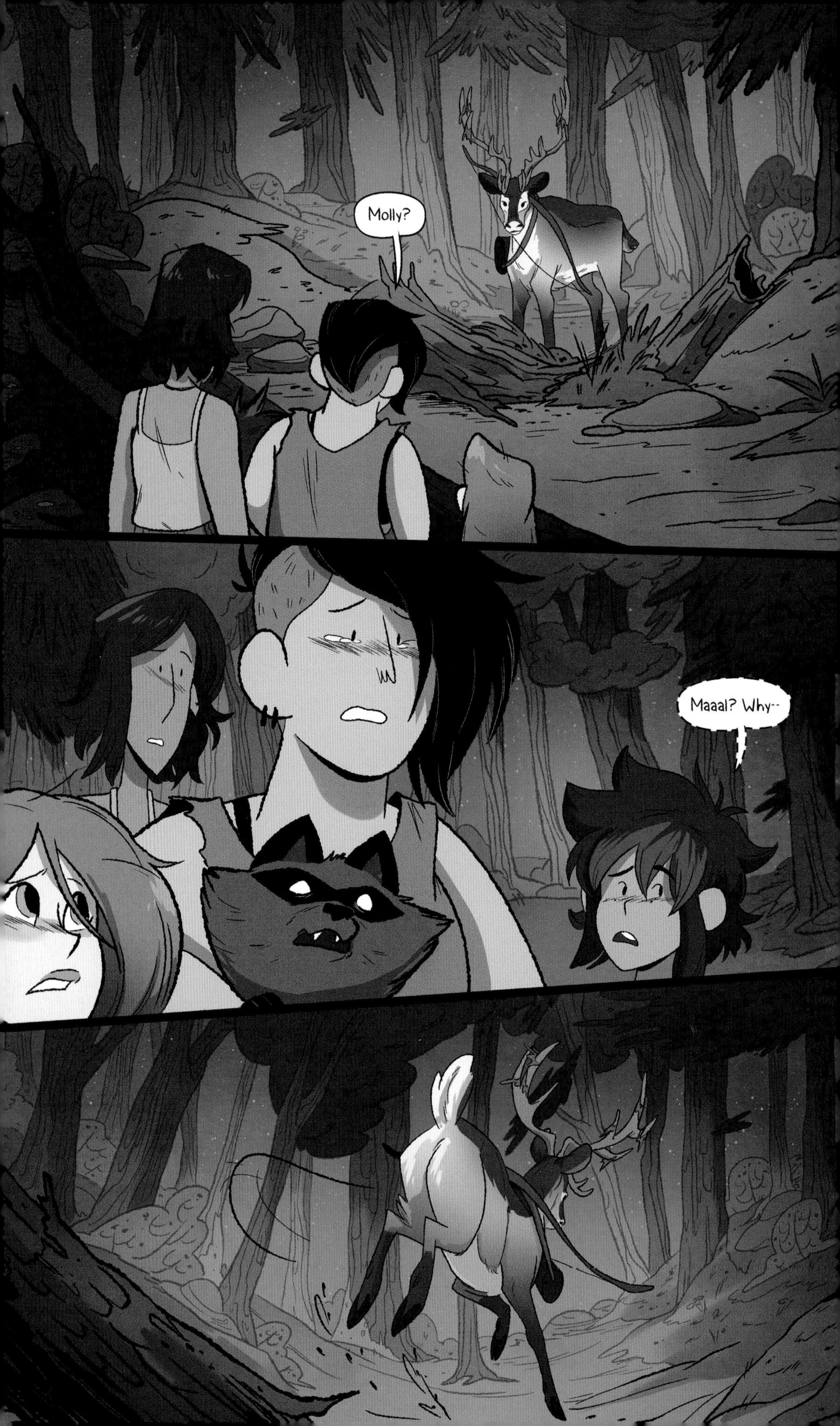
Molly?
Maaal? Why--

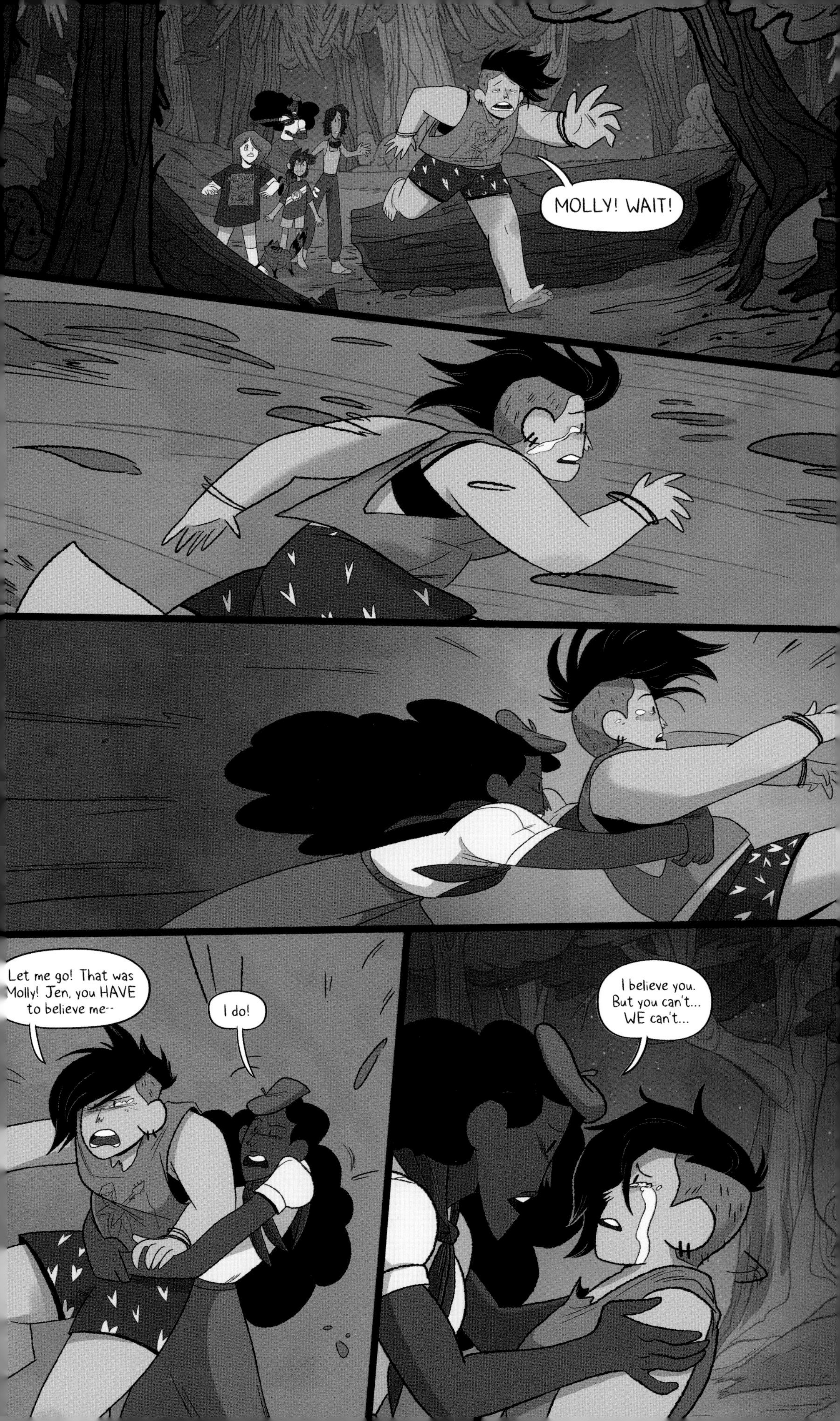
MOLLY! WAIT!
Let me go! That was Molly! Jen, you HAVE to believe me--
I do!
I believe you. But you can't... WE can't...

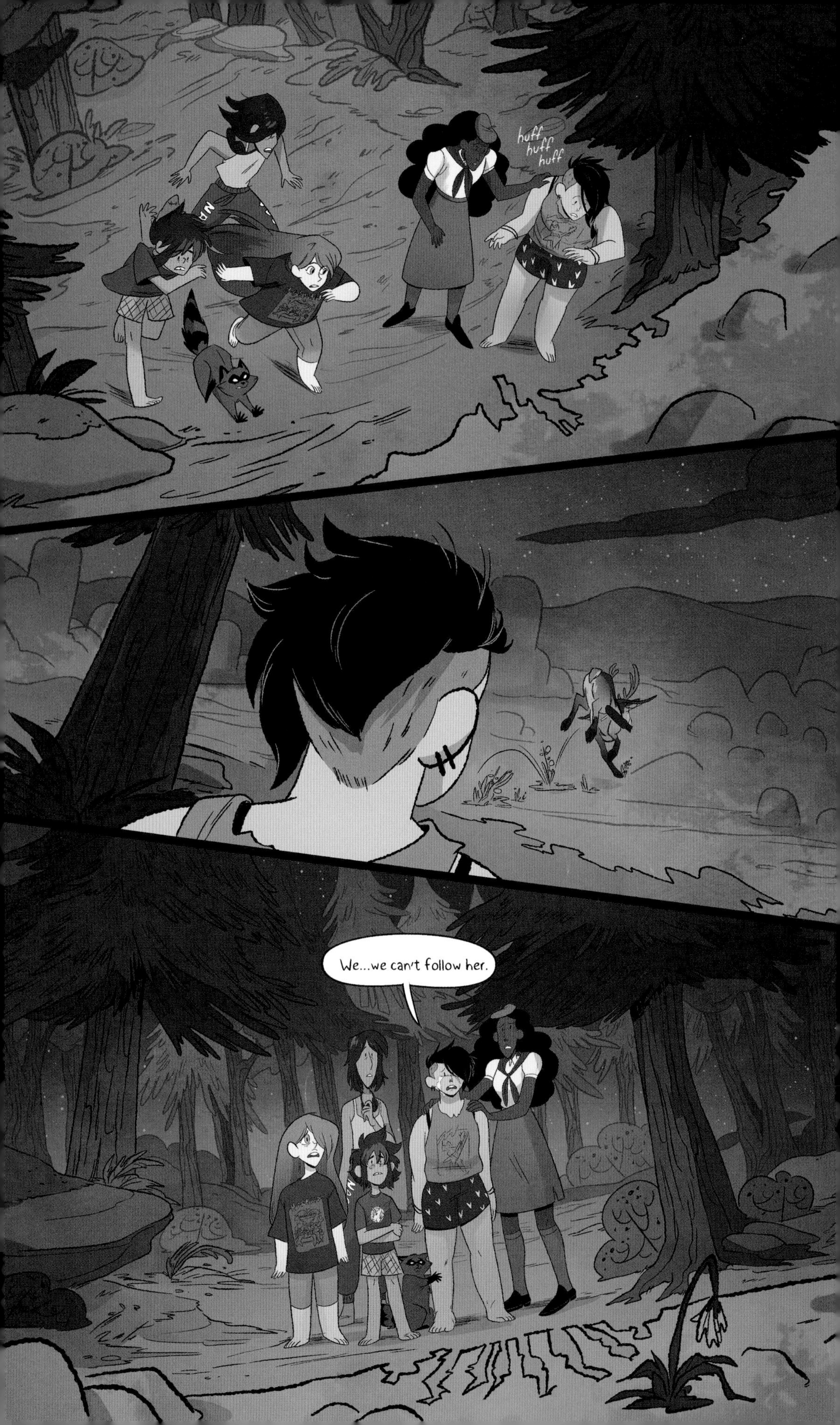
huff
huff
huff
We...we can't follow her.

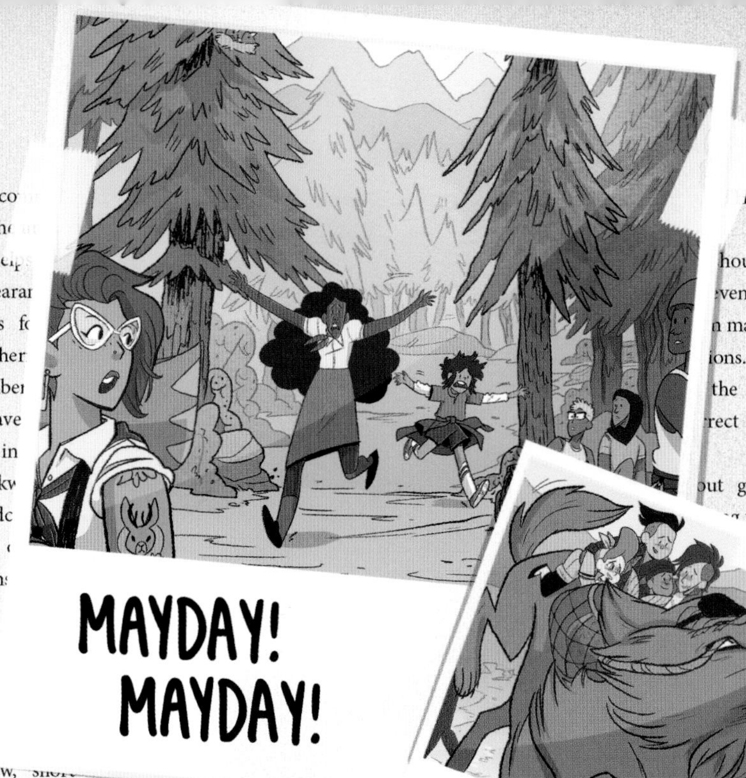
MAYDAY! MAYDAY!

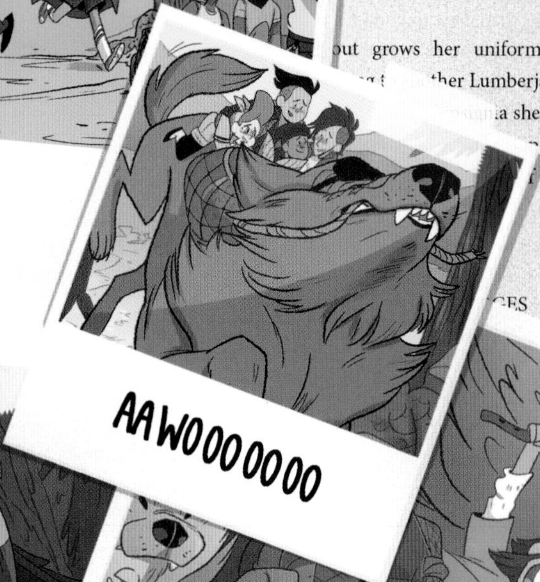
AAWOOOOOOO

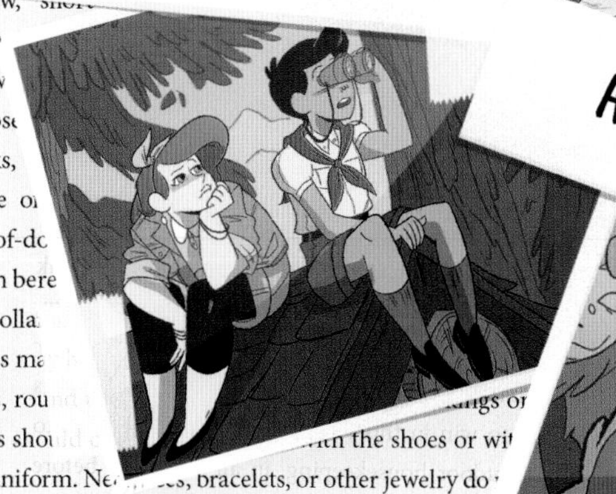

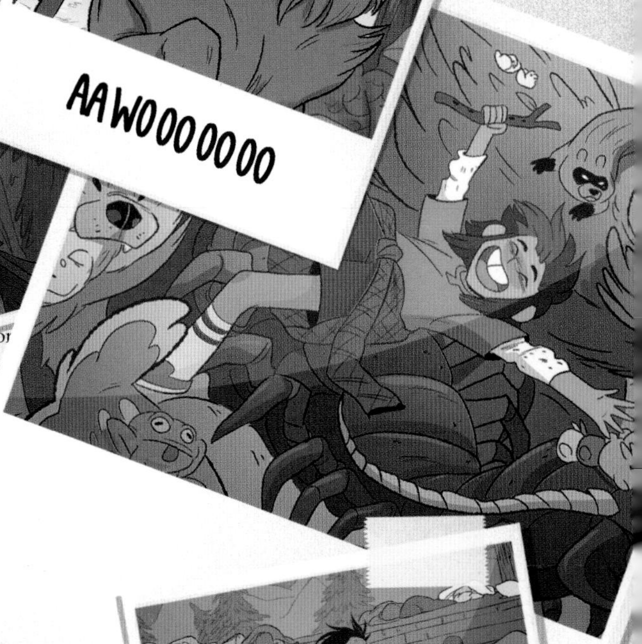

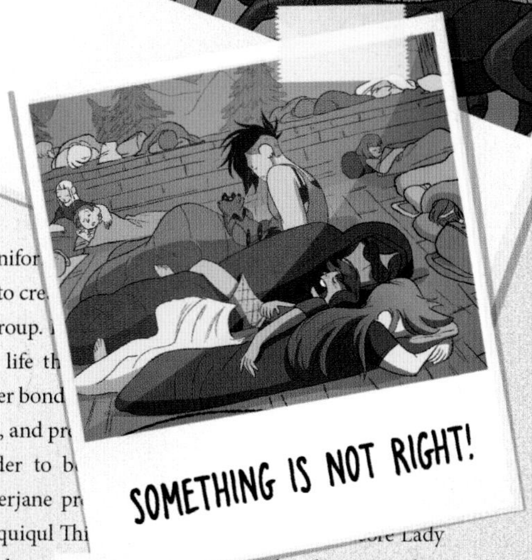
SOMETHING IS NOT RIGHT!

will co

The

It he

appeara

dress f

Further

Lumbe

to have

part in

Thiskw

Hardc

have

them

HE UNIFORM

hould be worn at camp
events when Lumberjanes
n may also be worn at other
ions. It should be worn as a
the uniform dress with
rrect shoes, and stocking or

out grows her uniform or
ther Lumberjane.
ia she has
her
her

The
yellow,
emb
the w
choose
slacks,
made o
out-of-do
green bere
the colla
Shoes ma
heels, rou
kings or
socks shou ith the shoes or wi
the uniform. Ne es, bracelets, or other jewelry do
belong with a Lumberjane uniform.

HOW TO WEAR THE UNIFORM

To look well in a uniform demands first of uniform be kept in good condition—clean pressed. See that the skirt is the right length for your own height and build, that the belt is adjusted to your waist, that your shoes and stockings are in keeping with the uniform, that you watch your posture and carry yourself with dignity and grace. If the beret is removed indoors, be sure that your hair is neat and kept in place with an inconspicuous clip or ribbon. When you wear a Lumberjane uniform you are identified as a member of this organization and you should be doubly careful to conduct yourself in a way that will show everyone that courtesy and thoughtfulness are part of being a Lumberjane. People are likely to judge a whole nation by the selfishness of a few individuals, to criticize a whole family because of the misconduct of one member, and to feel unkindly toward an organization because of the

The unifor
helps to cre
in a group.
active life th
another bond
future, and pr
in order to b
Lumberjane pr
Penniquiqul Thi ore Lady
Types, but m s will wish to have one. They
can either bu uniform, or make it themselves from
materials available at the trading post.

LUMBERJANES FIELD MANUAL

LUMBERJANES: END OF SUMMER

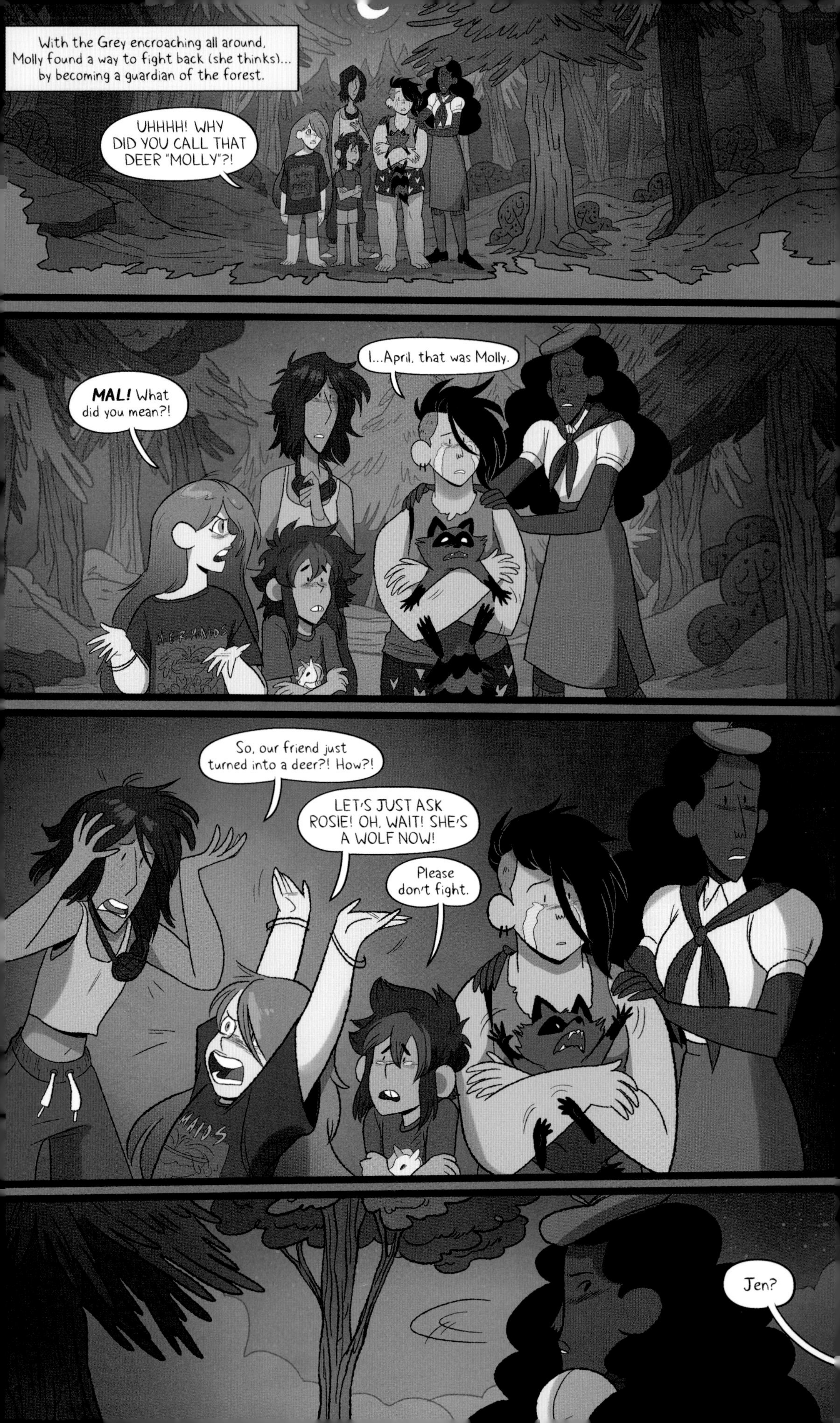
With the Grey encroaching all around, Molly found a way to fight back (she thinks)... by becoming a guardian of the forest.
UHHHH! WHY DID YOU CALL THAT DEER "MOLLY"?!
MAL! What did you mean?!
I...April, that was Molly.
So, our friend just turned into a deer?! How?!
LET'S JUST ASK ROSIE! OH, WAIT! SHE'S A WOLF NOW!
Please don't fight.
Jen?

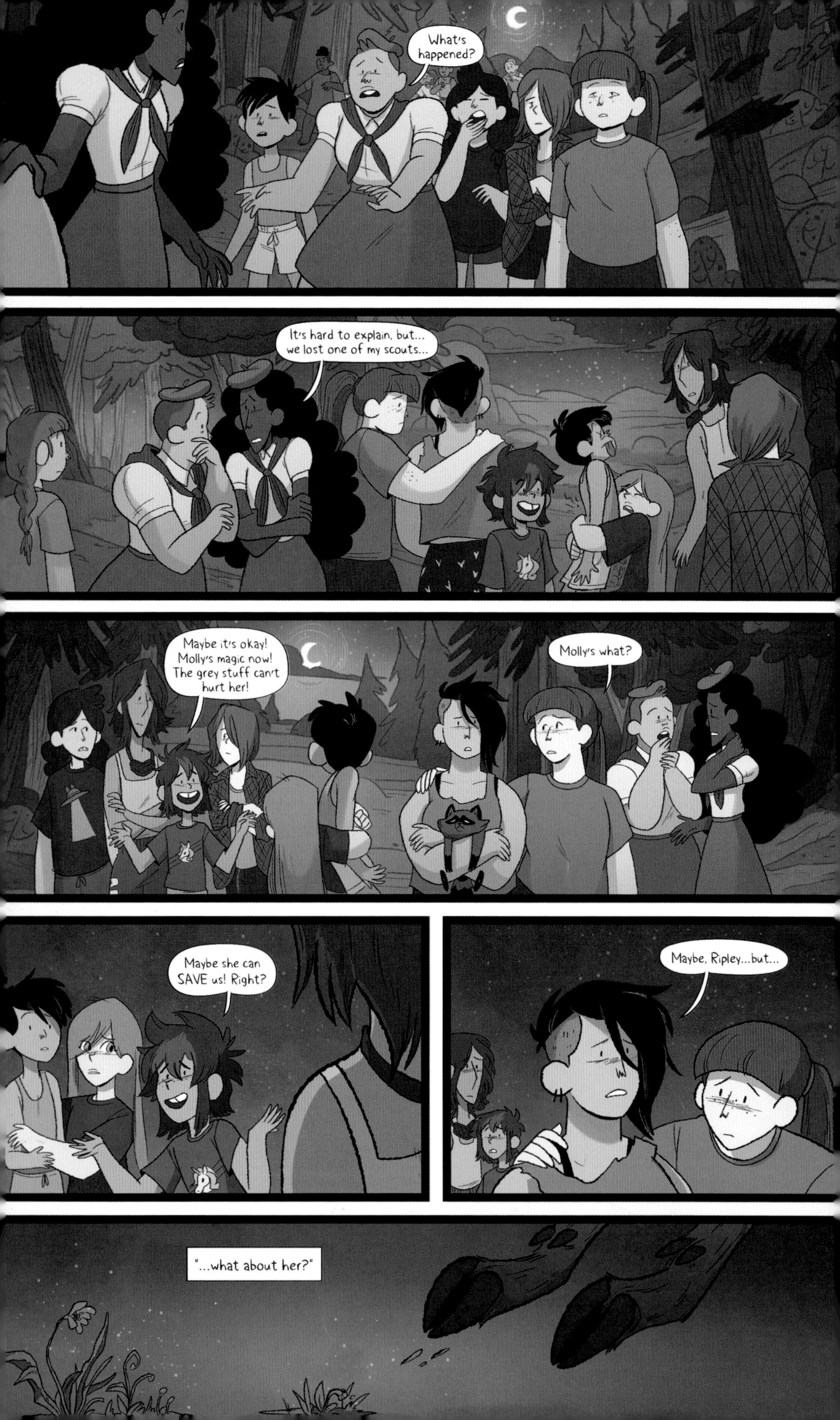
What's happened?
It's hard to explain, but... we lost one of my scouts...
Maybe it's okay! Molly's magic now! The grey stuff can't hurt her!
Molly's what?
Maybe she can SAVE us! Right?
Maybe, Ripley...but...
"...what about her?"

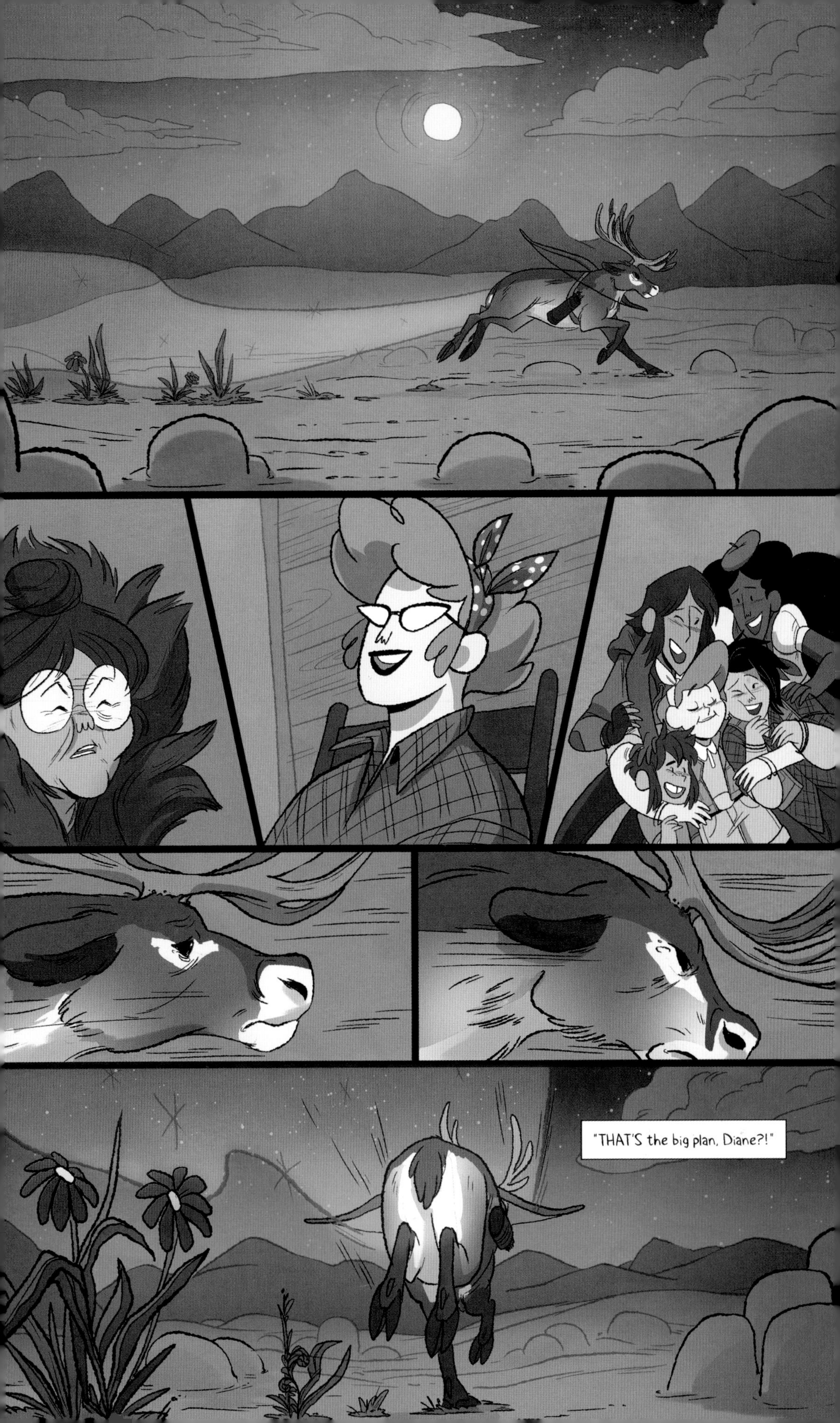
"THAT'S the big plan, Diane?!"

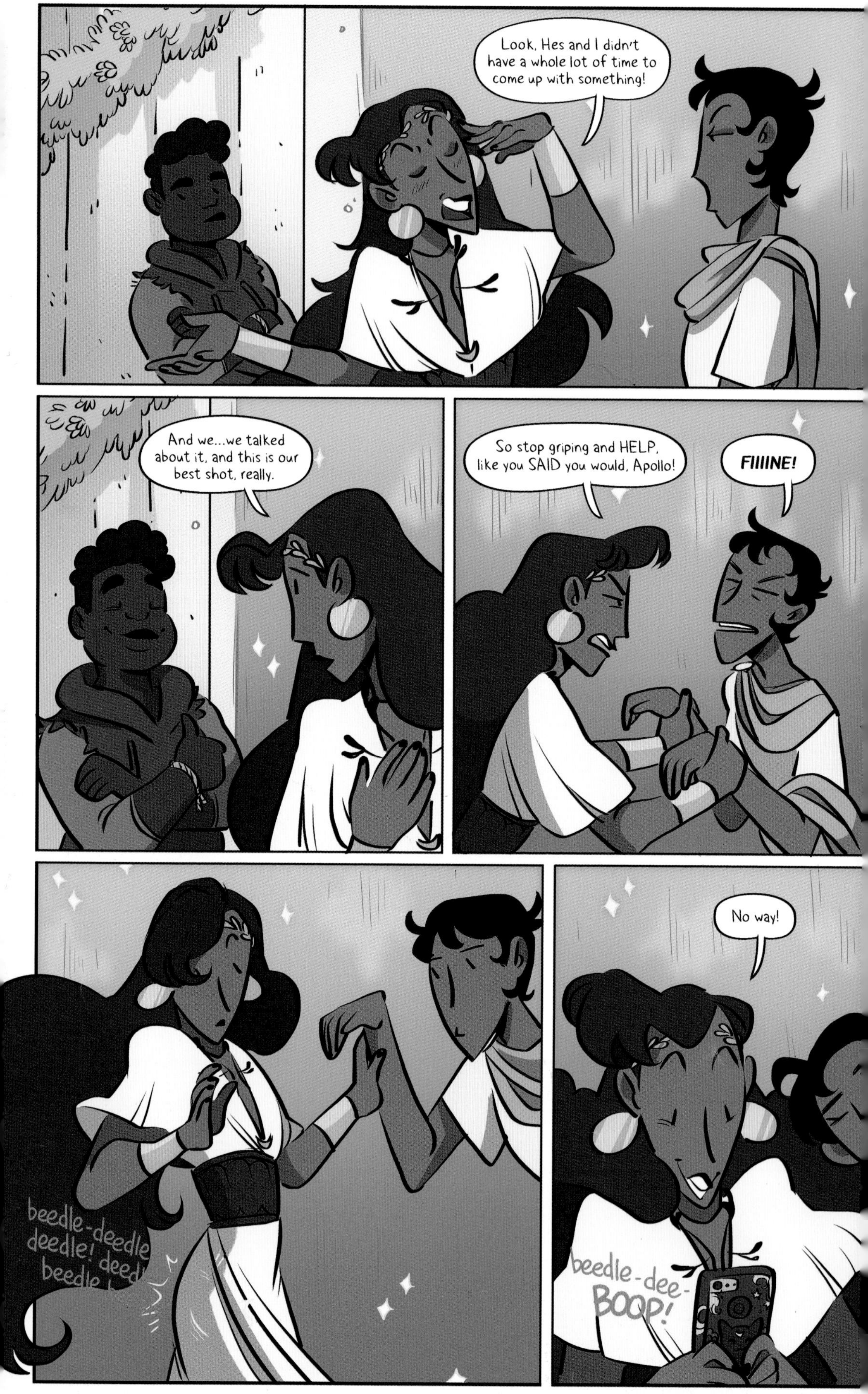
Look, Hes and I didn't have a whole lot of time to come up with something!
And we...we talked about it, and this is our best shot, really.
So stop griping and HELP, like you SAID you would, Apollo!
FIIIINE!
No way!
beedle-deedle deedle! deed! beedle
beedle-dee-BOOP!

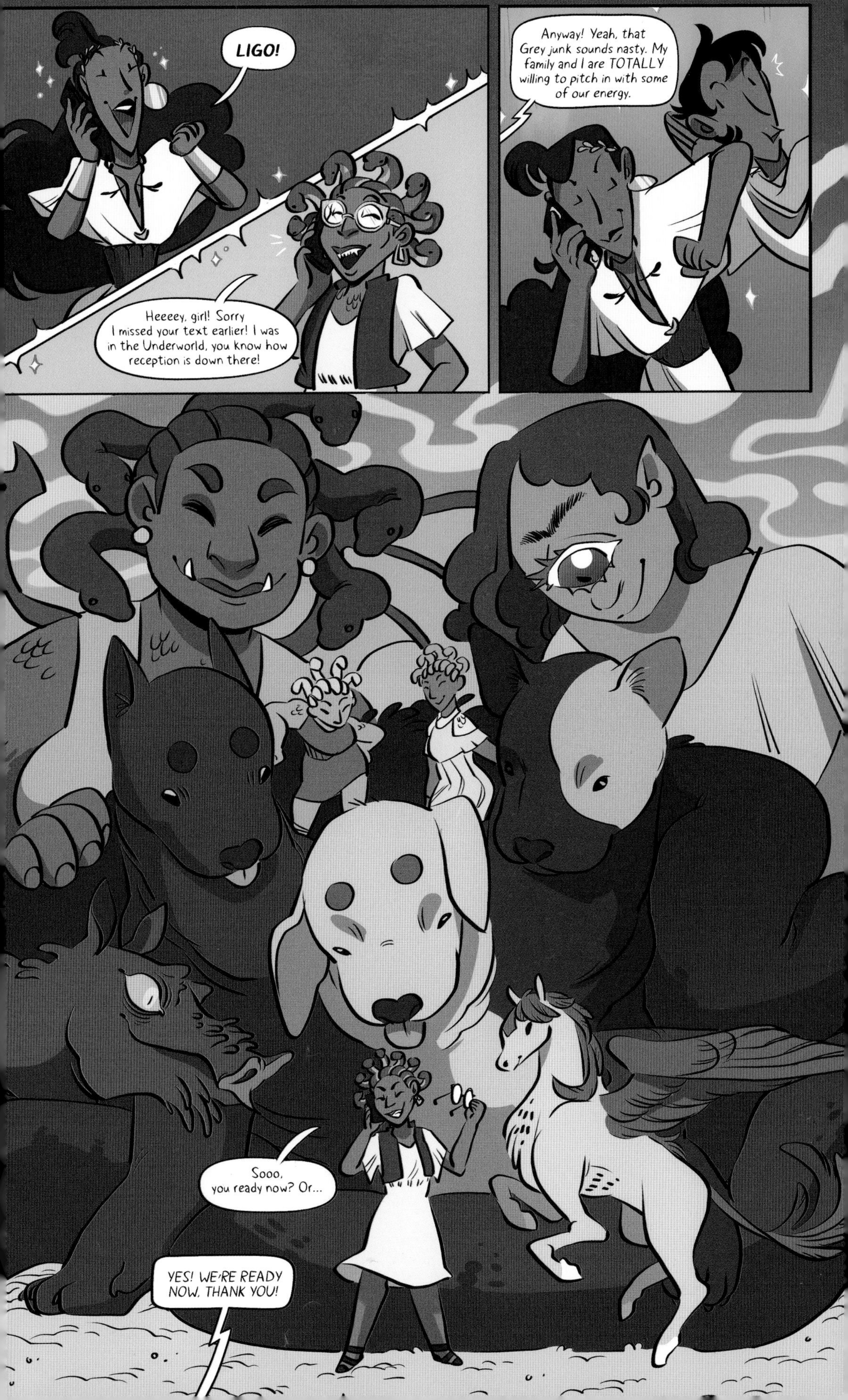
LIGO!
Heeeey, girl! Sorry I missed your text earlier! I was in the Underworld, you know how reception is down there!
Anyway! Yeah, that Grey junk sounds nasty. My family and I are TOTALLY willing to pitch in with some of our energy.
Sooo, you ready now? Or...
YES! WE'RE READY NOW, THANK YOU!

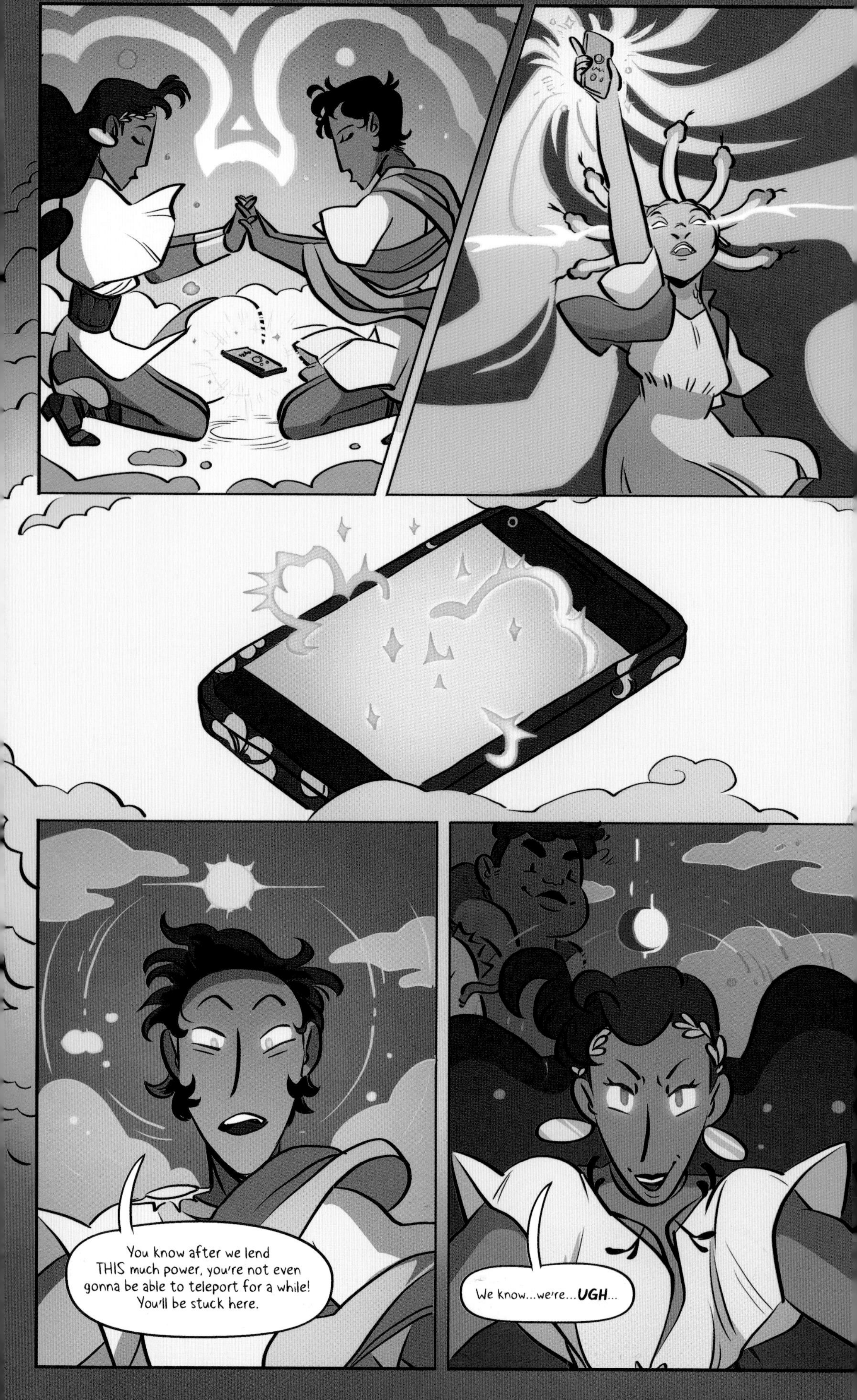
You know after we lend THIS much power, you're not even gonna be able to teleport for a while! You'll be stuck here.
We know...we're...**UGH**...

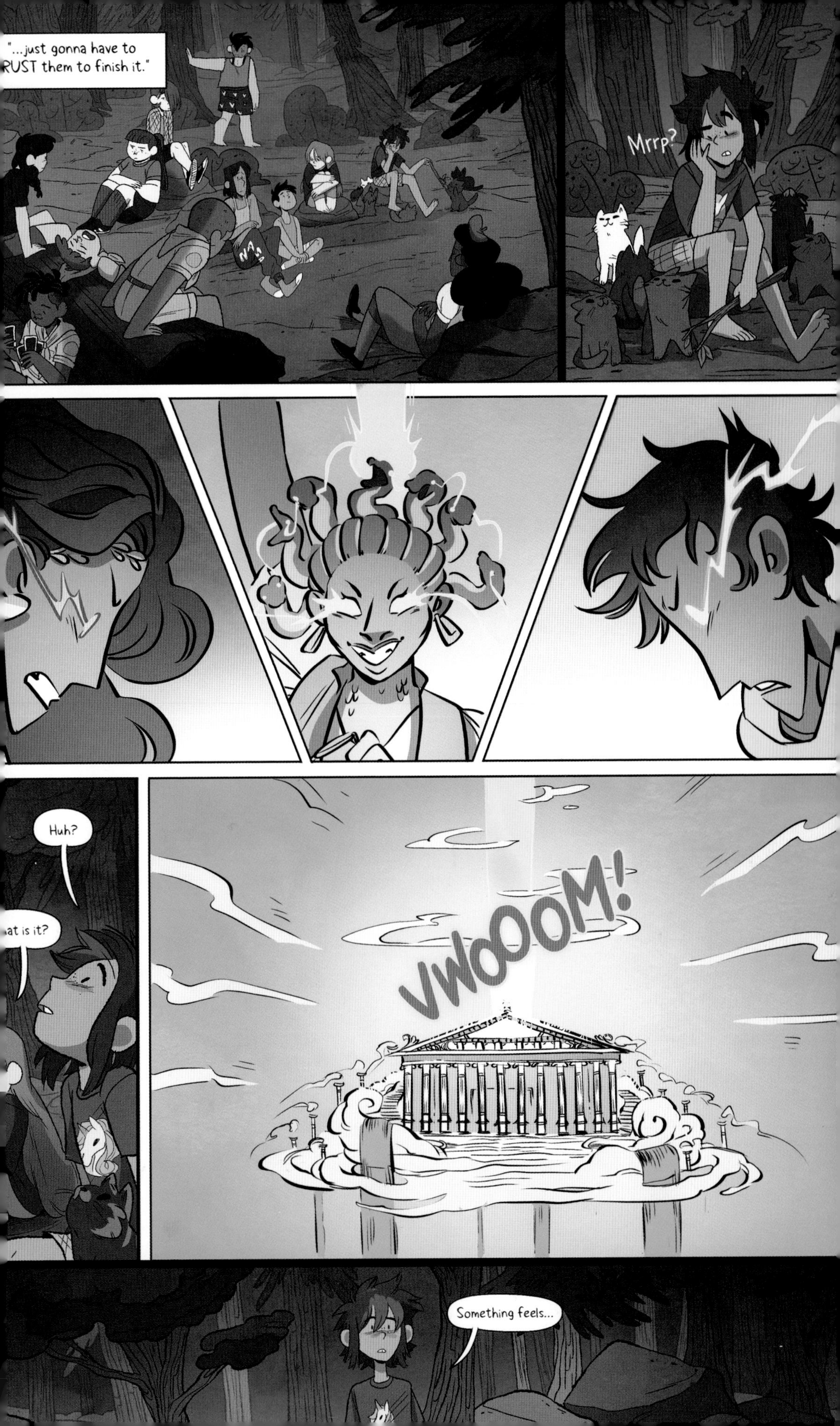
"...just gonna have to
RUST them to finish it."
Mrrp?
Huh?
at is it?
VWOOOM!
Something feels...

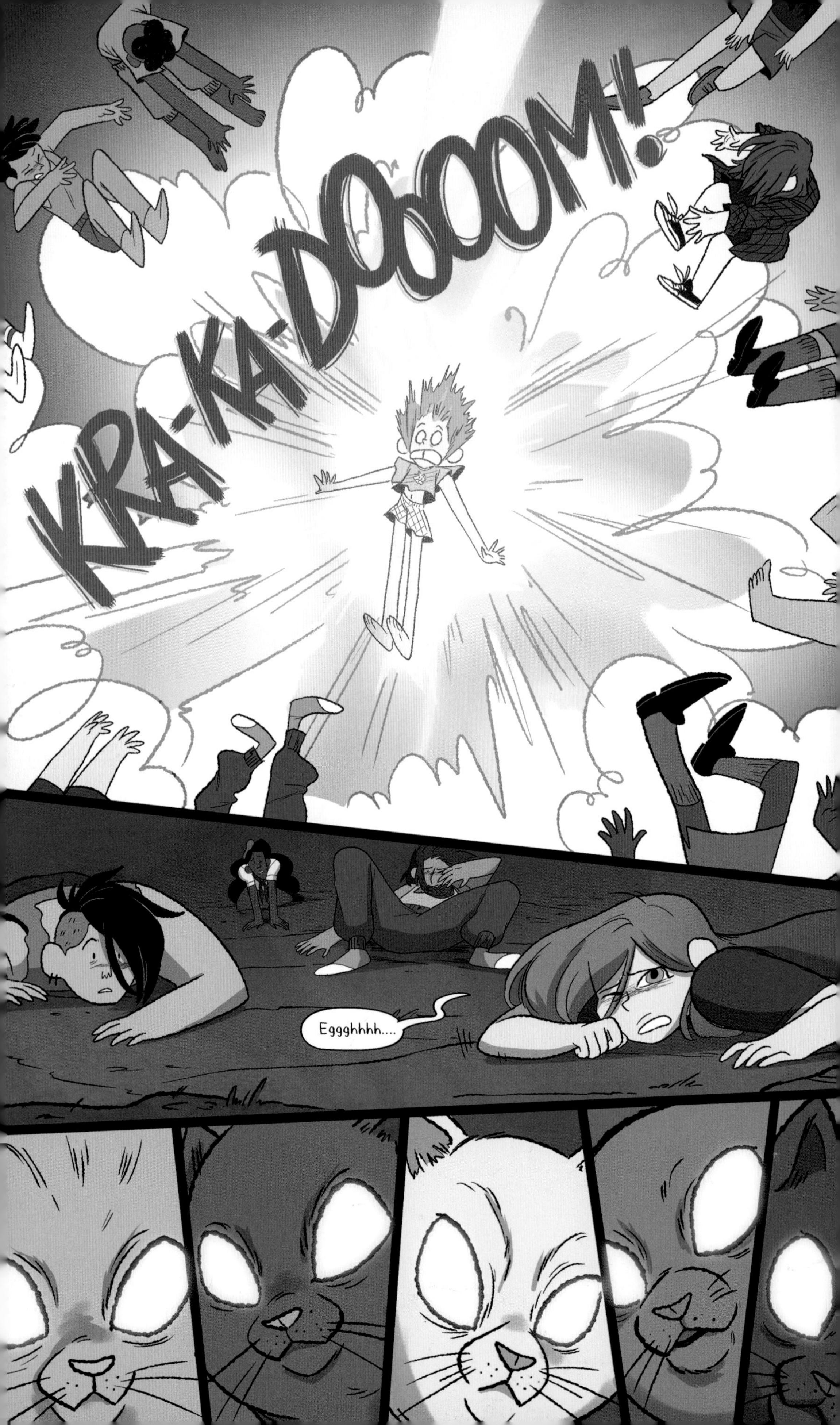
KRA-KA-DOOOOM!
Eggghhhh....

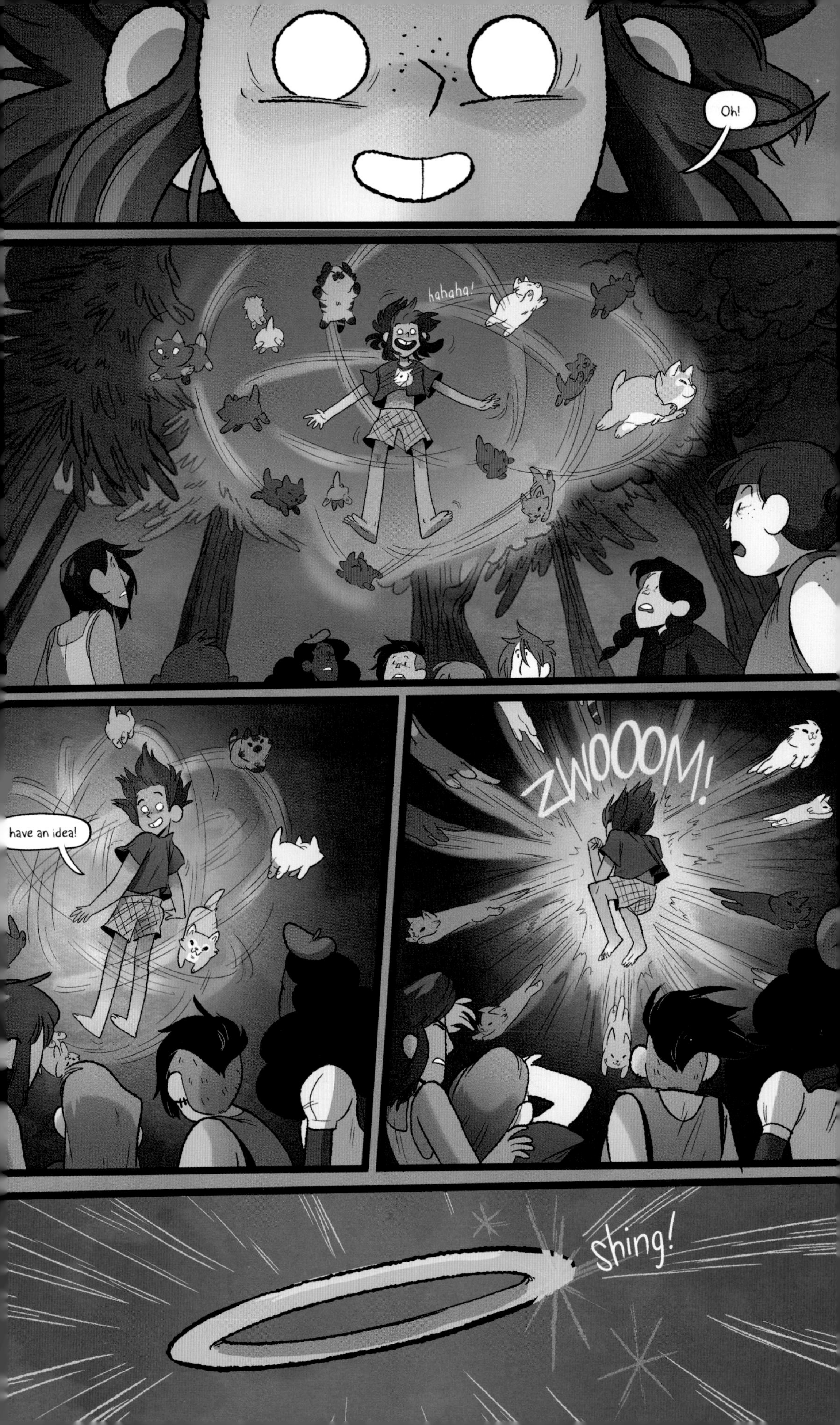
Oh!
hahaha!
have an idea!
ZWOOOM!
shing!

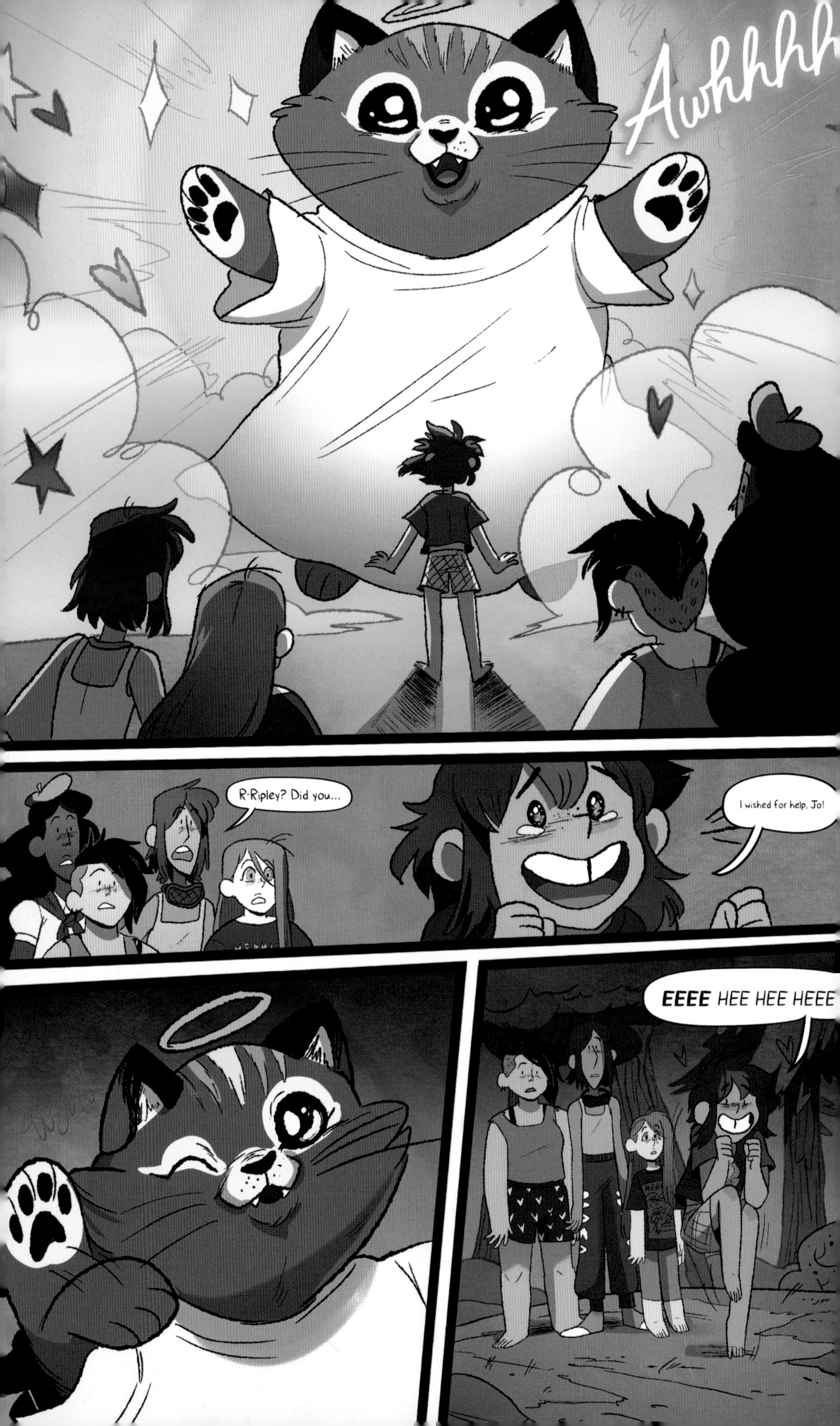
Awhhhh
R-Ripley? Did you...
I wished for help, Jo!
EEEE HEE HEE HEEE

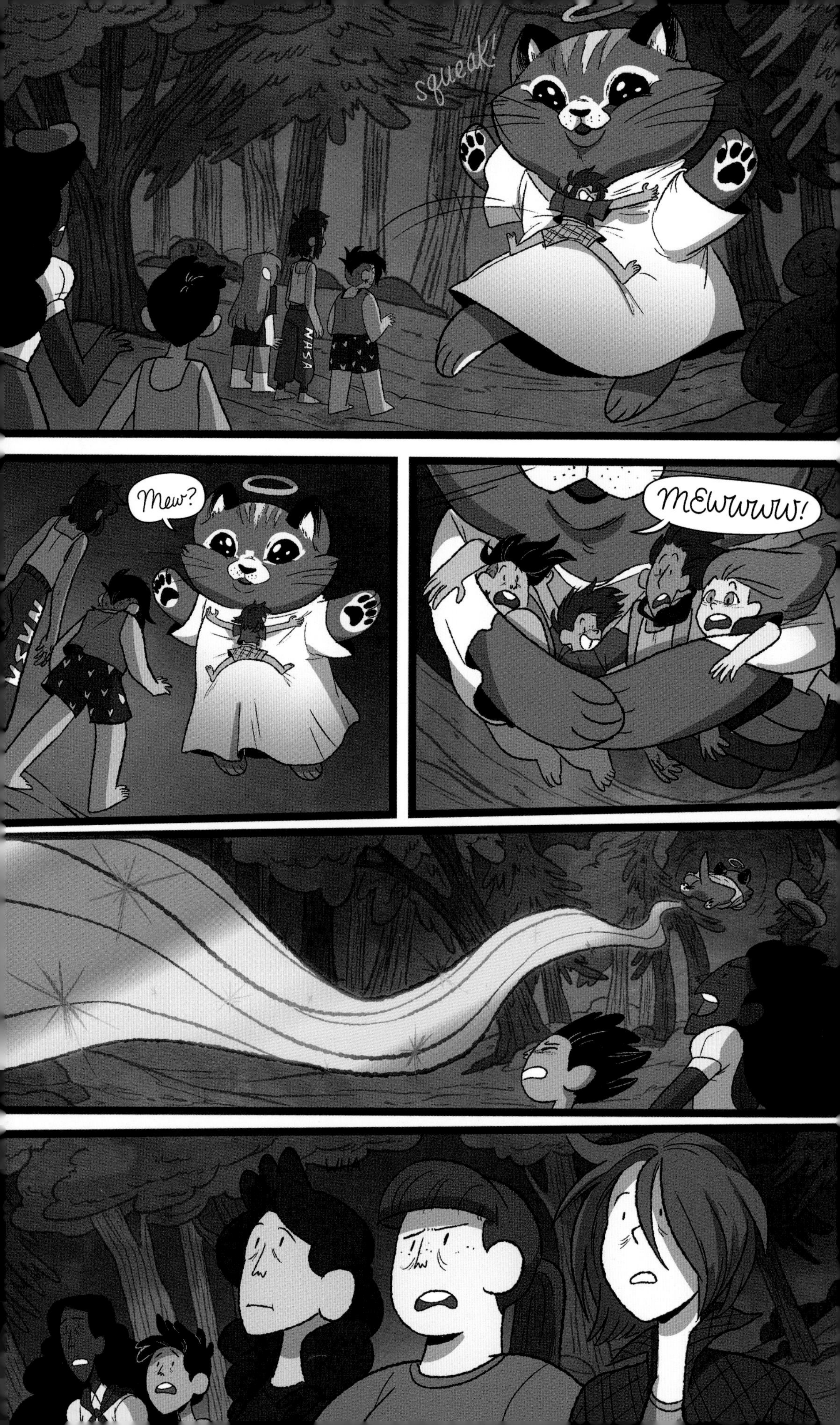
squeak!
NASA
Mew?
MEWRWRW!

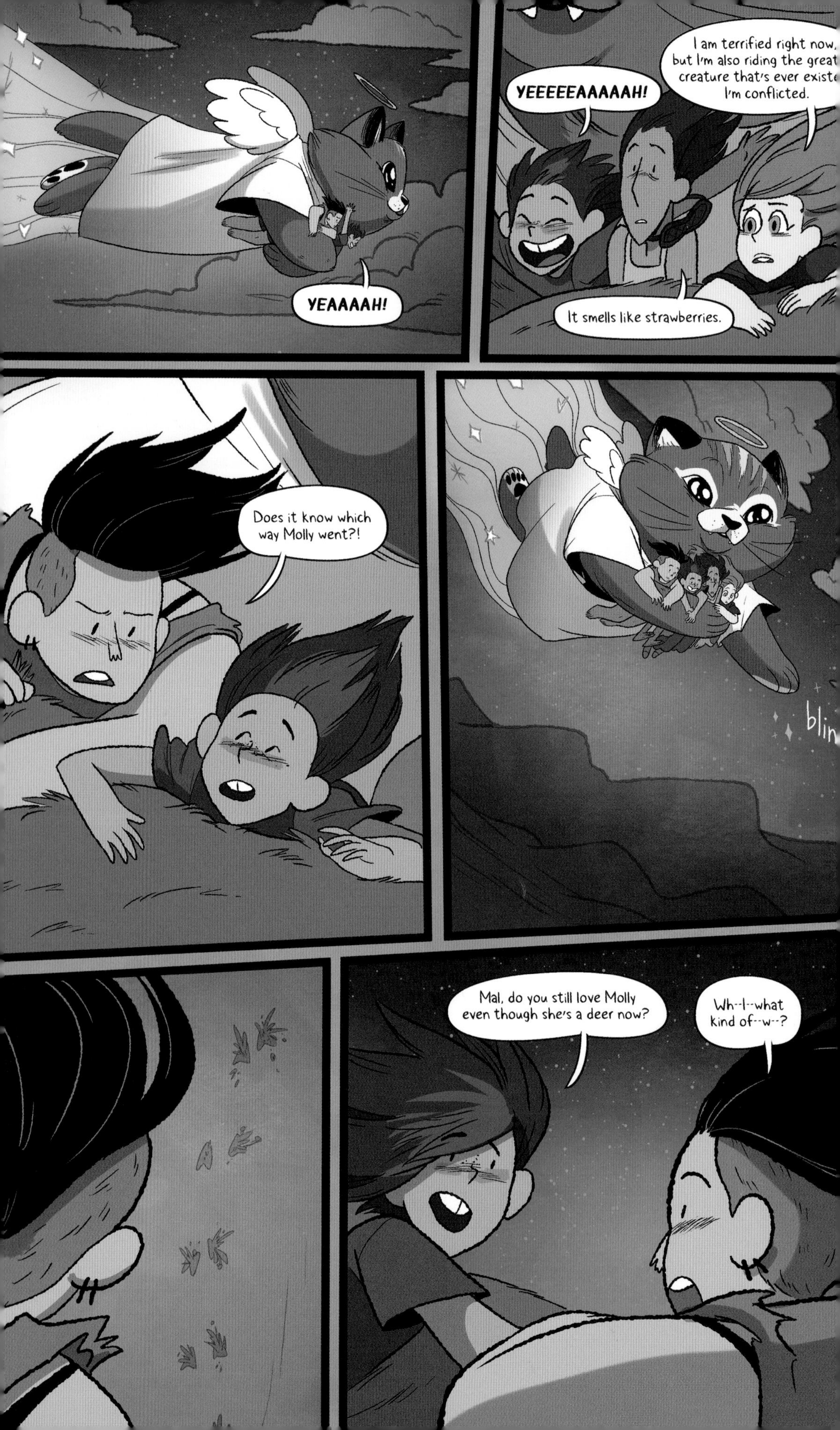
YEAAAAH!
YEEEEEAAAAAH!
I am terrified right now, but I'm also riding the great creature that's ever existe I'm conflicted.
It smells like strawberries.
Does it know which way Molly went?!
blin
Mal, do you still love Molly even though she's a deer now?
Wh--I--what kind of--w--?

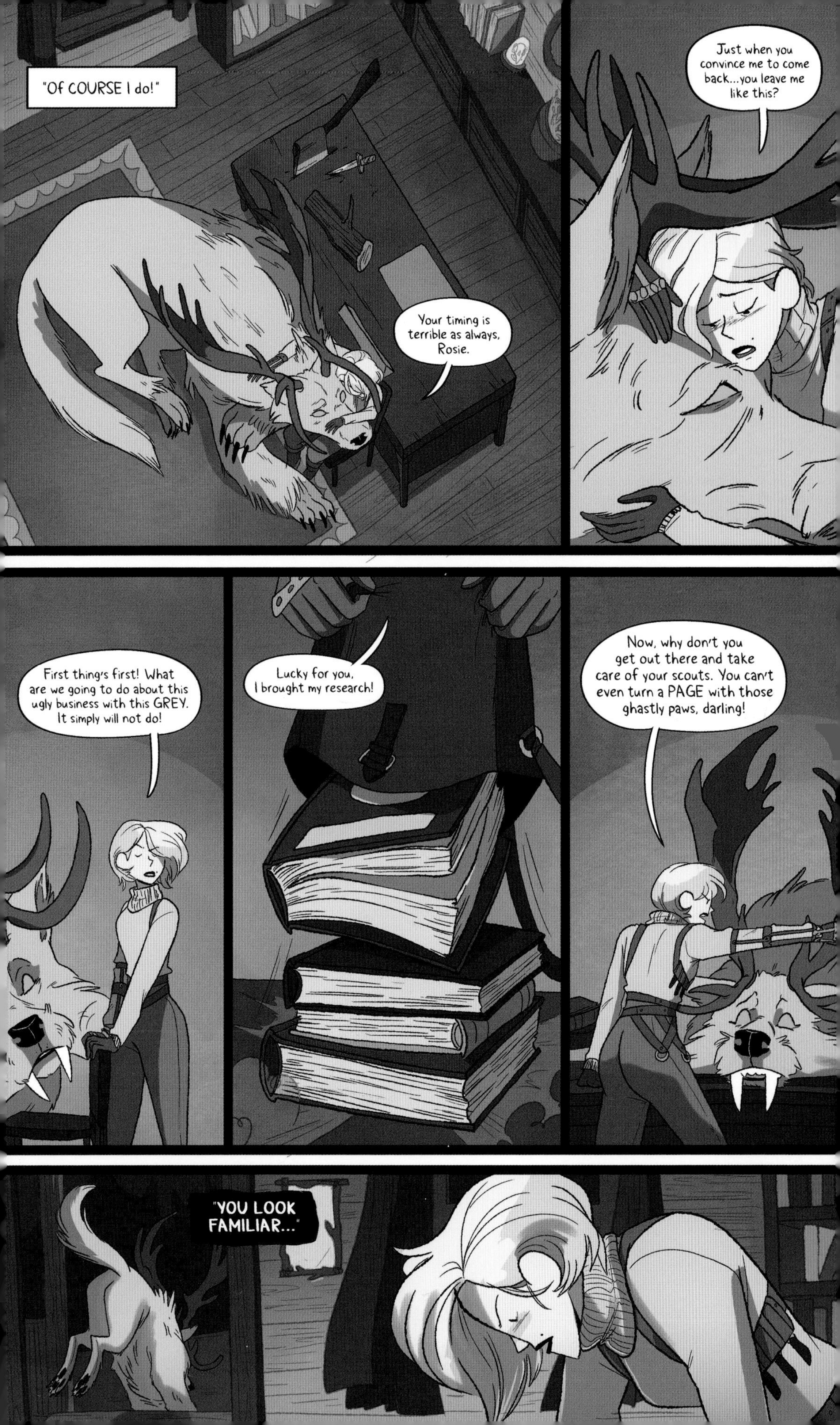
"Of COURSE I do!"
Your timing is terrible as always, Rosie.
Just when you convince me to come back...you leave me like this?
First thing's first! What are we going to do about this ugly business with this GREY. It simply will not do!
Lucky for you, I brought my research!
Now, why don't you get out there and take care of your scouts. You can't even turn a PAGE with those ghastly paws, darling!
"YOU LOOK FAMILIAR..."

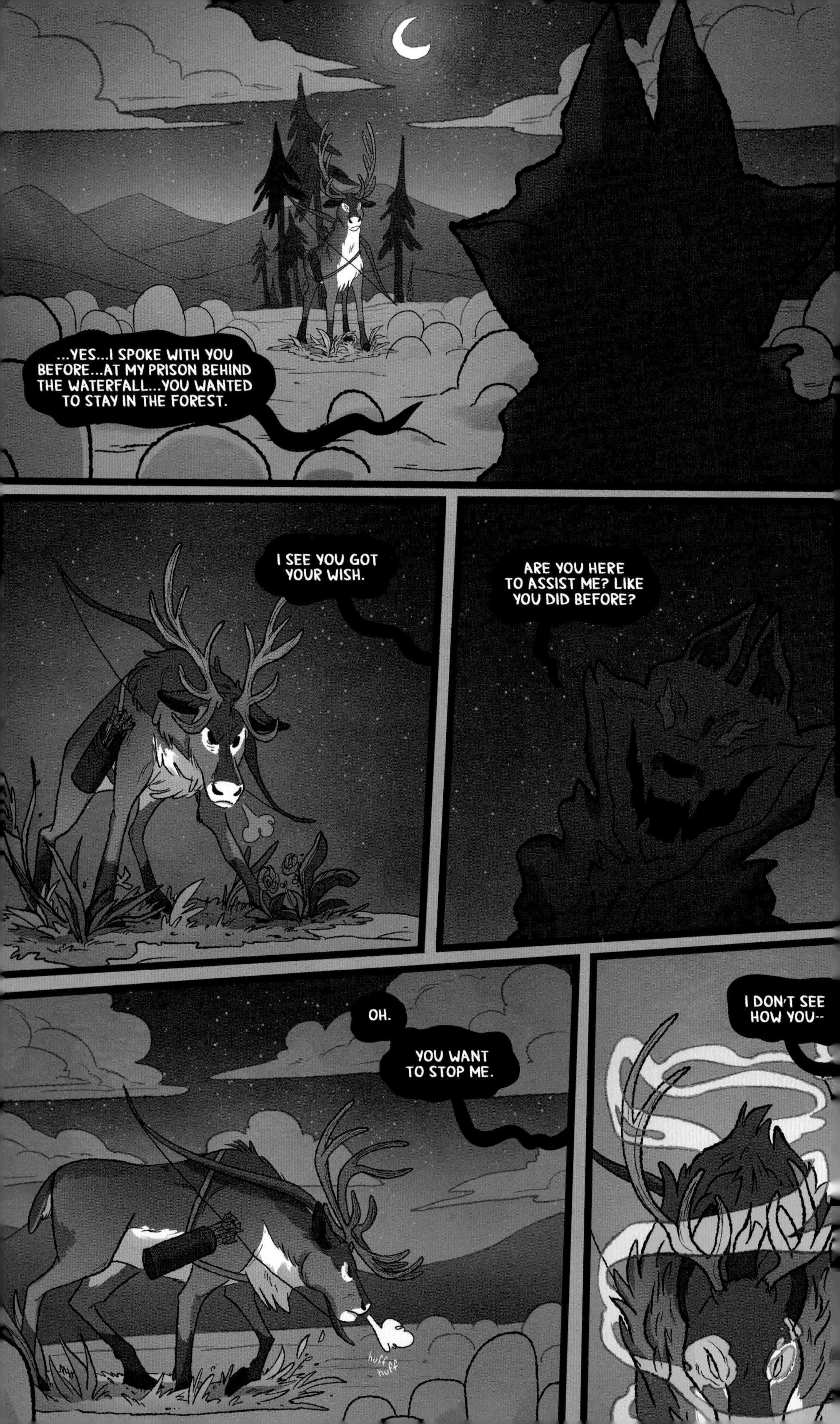
...YES...I SPOKE WITH YOU BEFORE...AT MY PRISON BEHIND THE WATERFALL...YOU WANTED TO STAY IN THE FOREST.
I SEE YOU GOT YOUR WISH.
ARE YOU HERE TO ASSIST ME? LIKE YOU DID BEFORE?
OH.
YOU WANT TO STOP ME.
huff huff
I DON'T SEE HOW YOU--

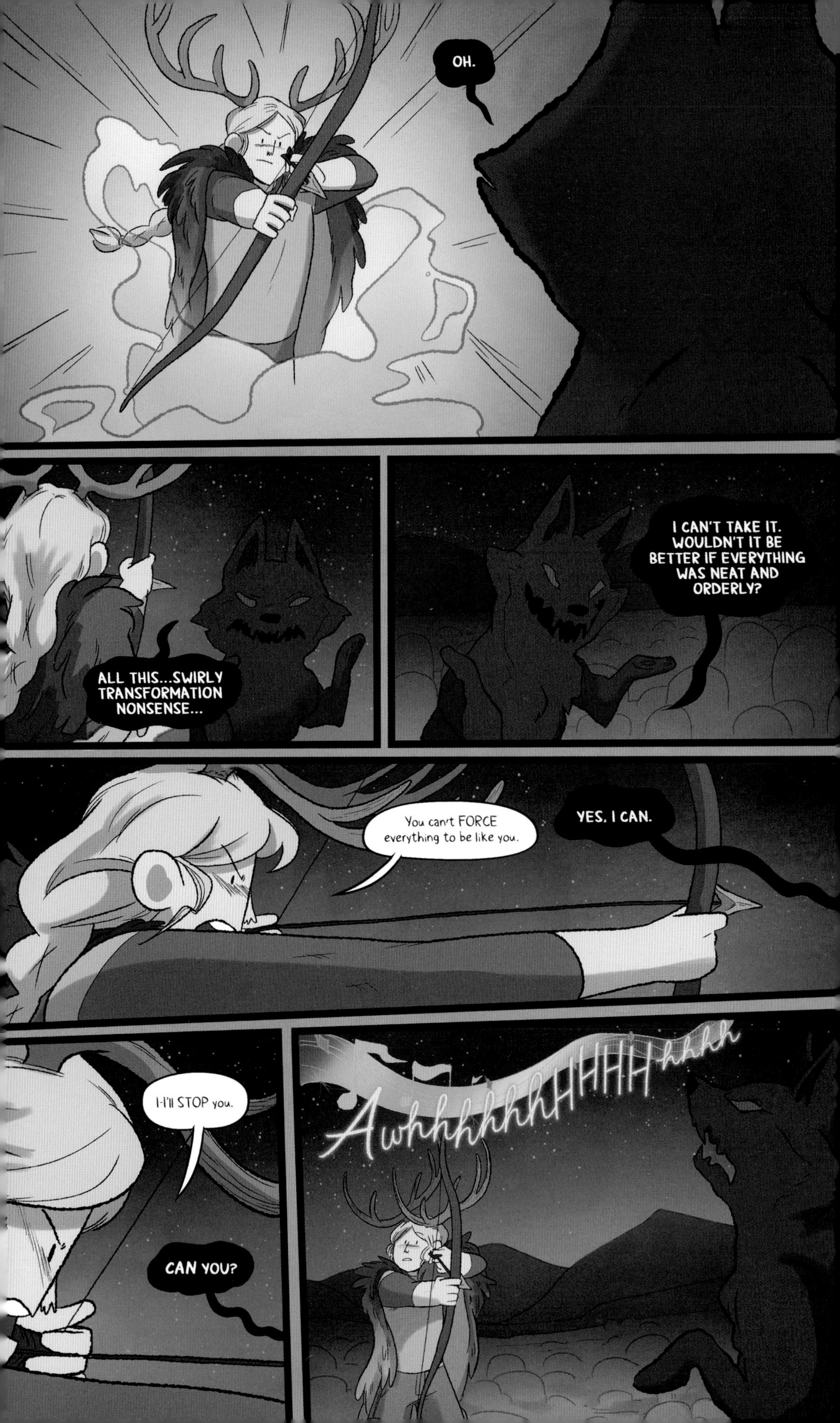
OH.
ALL THIS...SWIRLY TRANSFORMATION NONSENSE...
I CAN'T TAKE IT. WOULDN'T IT BE BETTER IF EVERYTHING WAS NEAT AND ORDERLY?
You can't FORCE everything to be like you.
YES, I CAN.
I-I'll STOP you.
CAN YOU?
AwhhhhhhHHHHHHhhhh

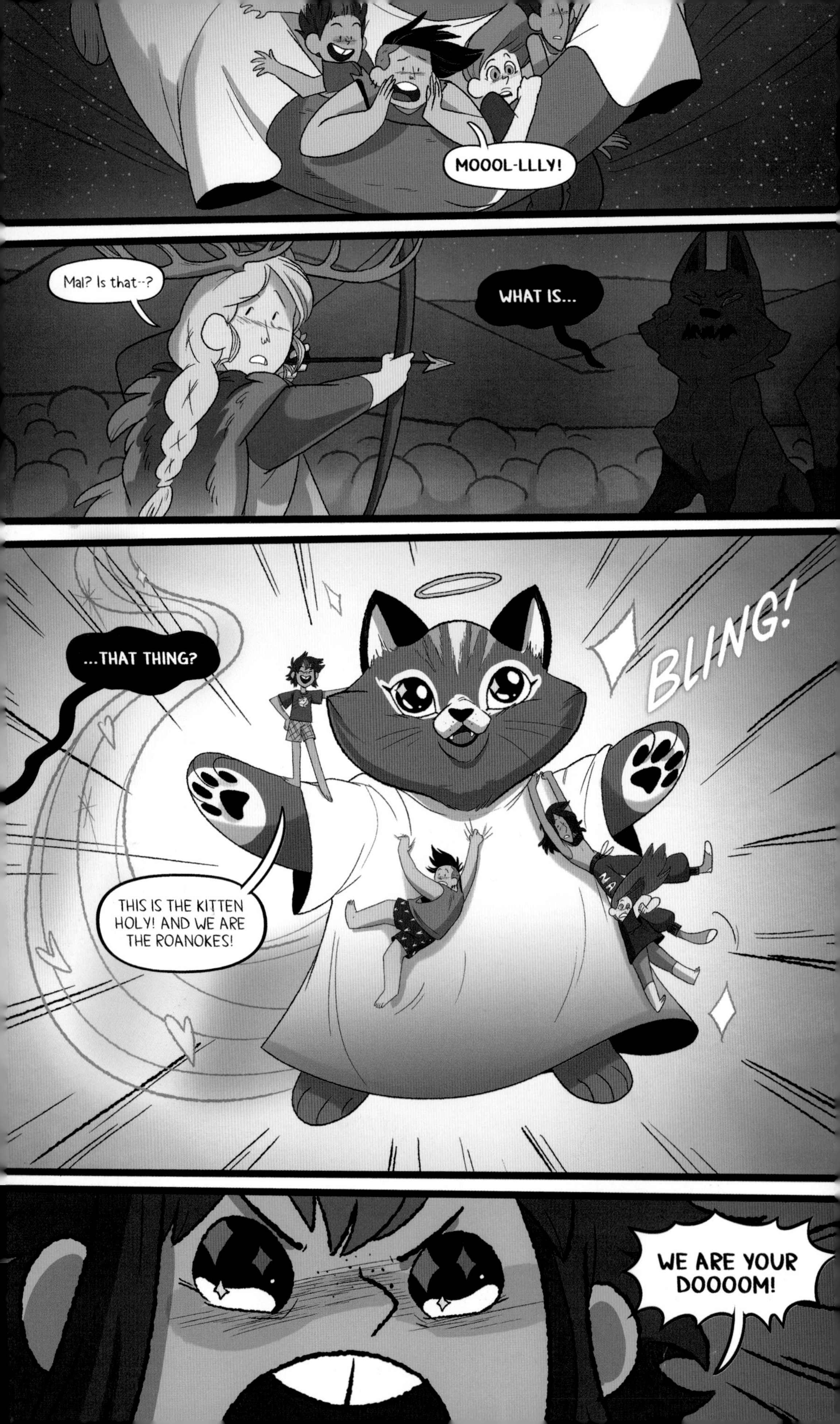
MOOOL-LLLY!
Mal? Is that--?
WHAT IS...
...THAT THING?
BLING!
THIS IS THE KITTEN HOLY! AND WE ARE THE ROANOKES!
WE ARE YOUR DOOOOM!

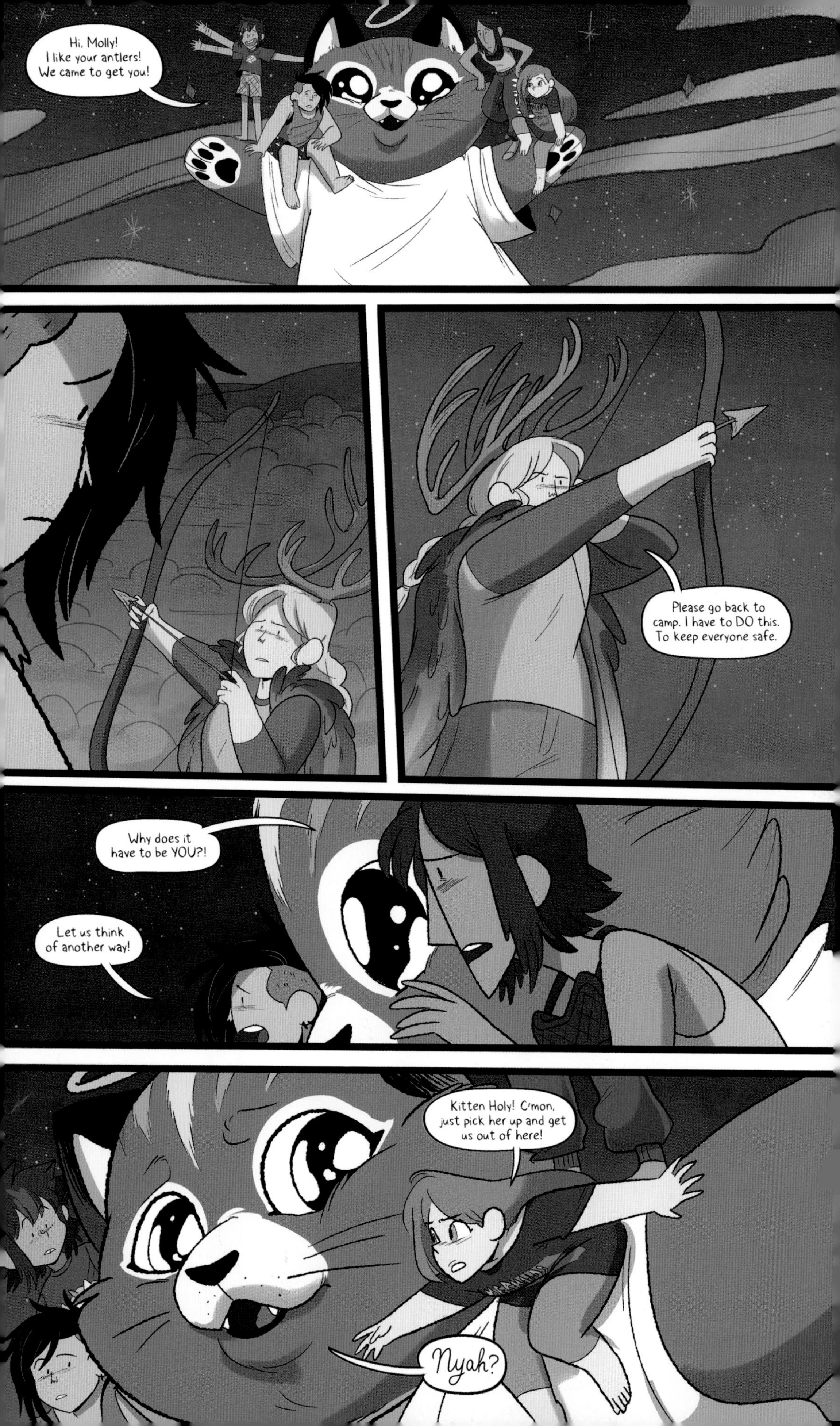
Hi, Molly! I like your antlers! We came to get you!
Please go back to camp. I have to DO this. To keep everyone safe.
Why does it have to be YOU?!
Let us think of another way!
Kitten Holy! C'mon, just pick her up and get us out of here!
Nyah?

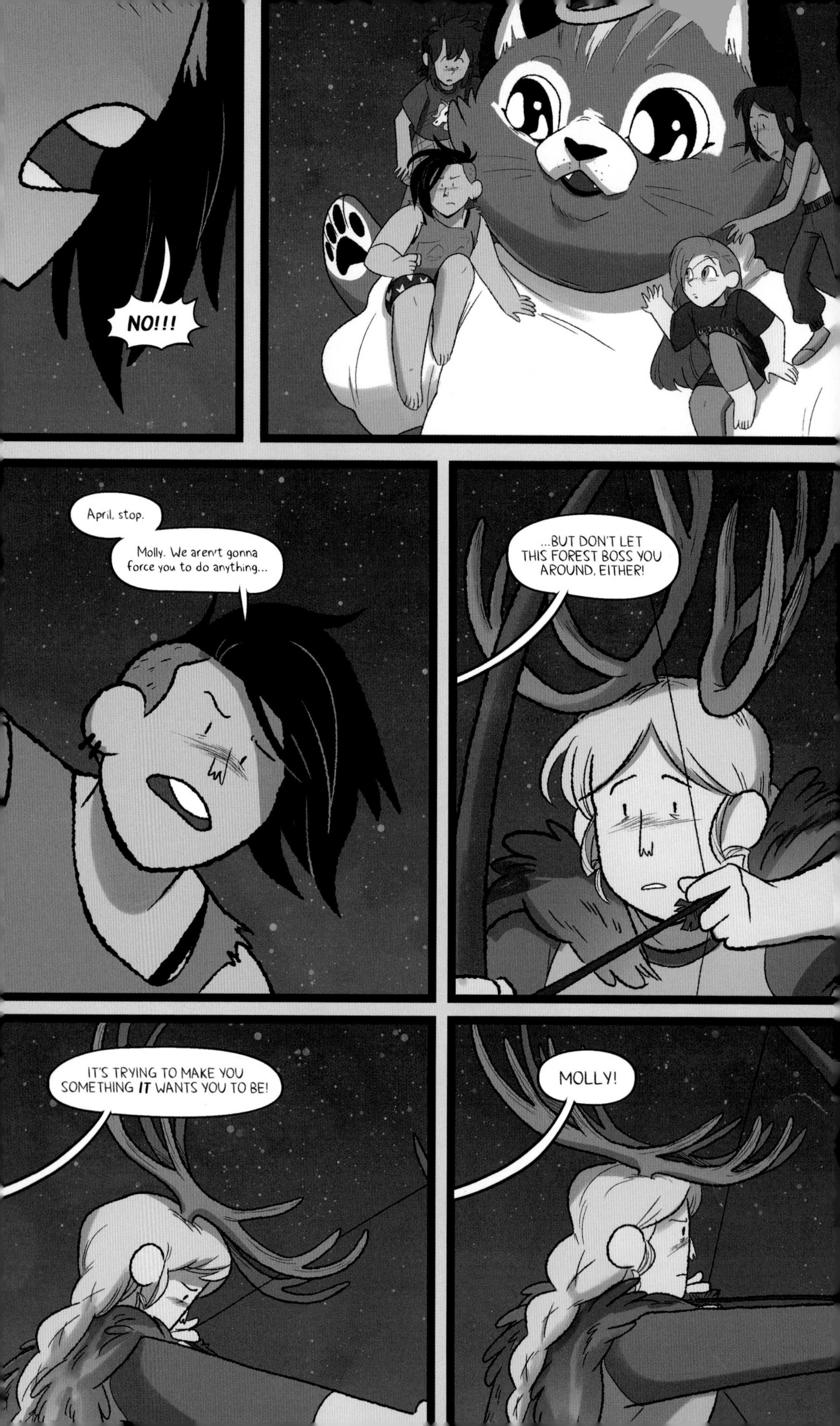
NO!!!
April, stop.
Molly. We aren't gonna force you to do anything...
...BUT DON'T LET THIS FOREST BOSS YOU AROUND, EITHER!
IT'S TRYING TO MAKE YOU SOMETHING IT WANTS YOU TO BE!
MOLLY!

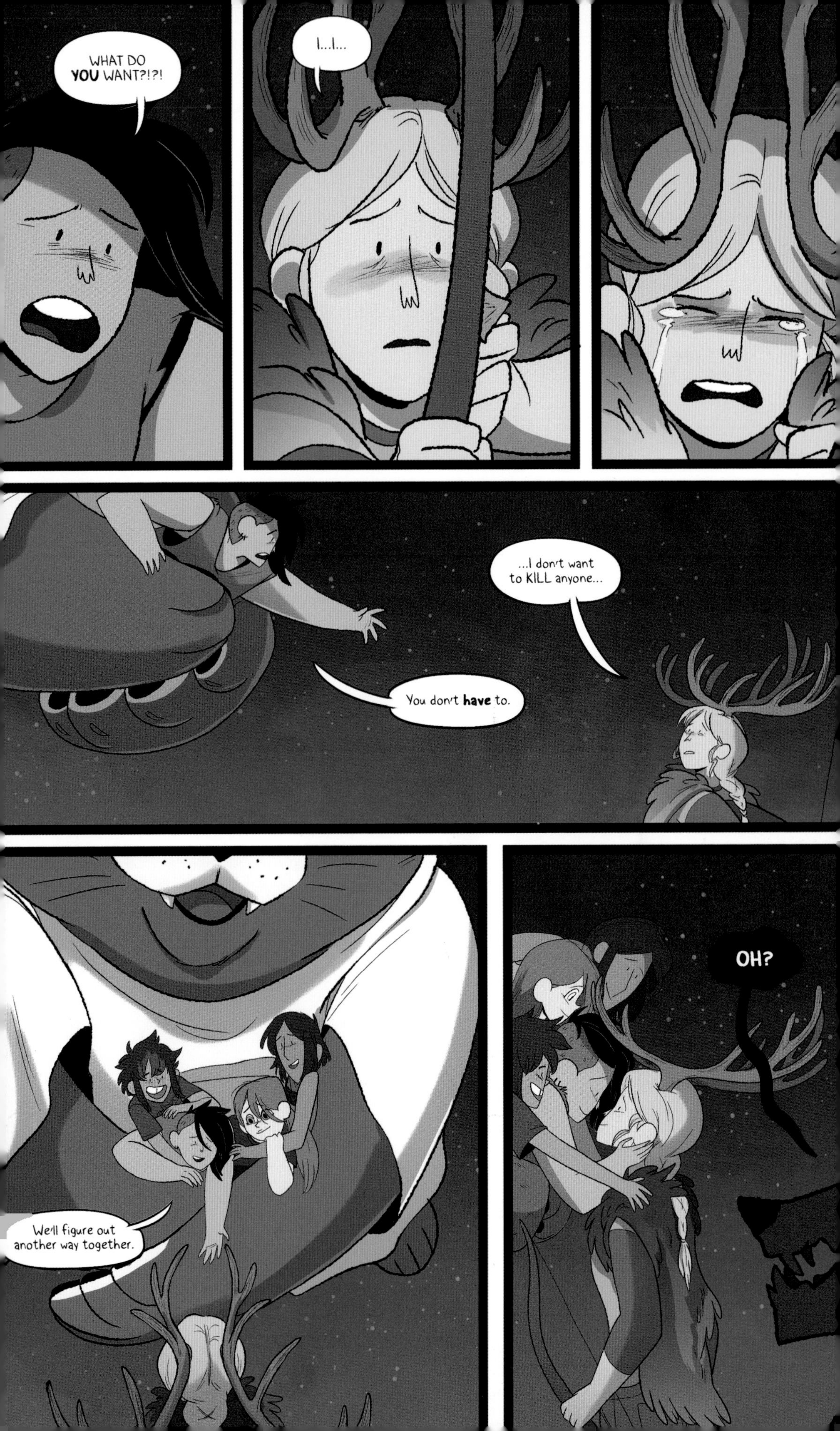
WHAT DO YOU WANT?!?!
I...I...
...I don't want to KILL anyone...
You don't have to.
We'll figure out another way together.
OH?

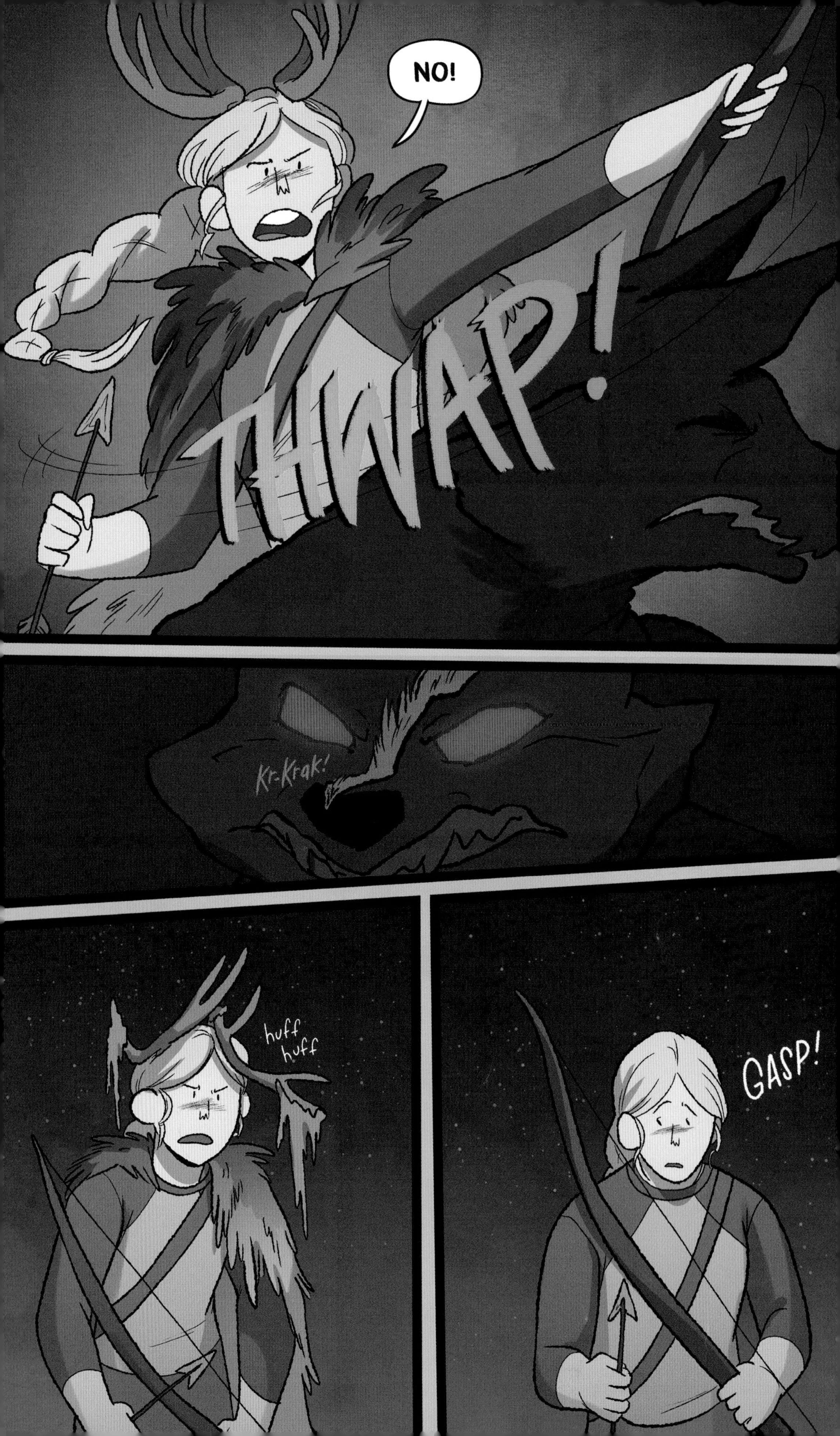
NO!
THWAP!
Kr-Krak!
huff
huff
GASP!

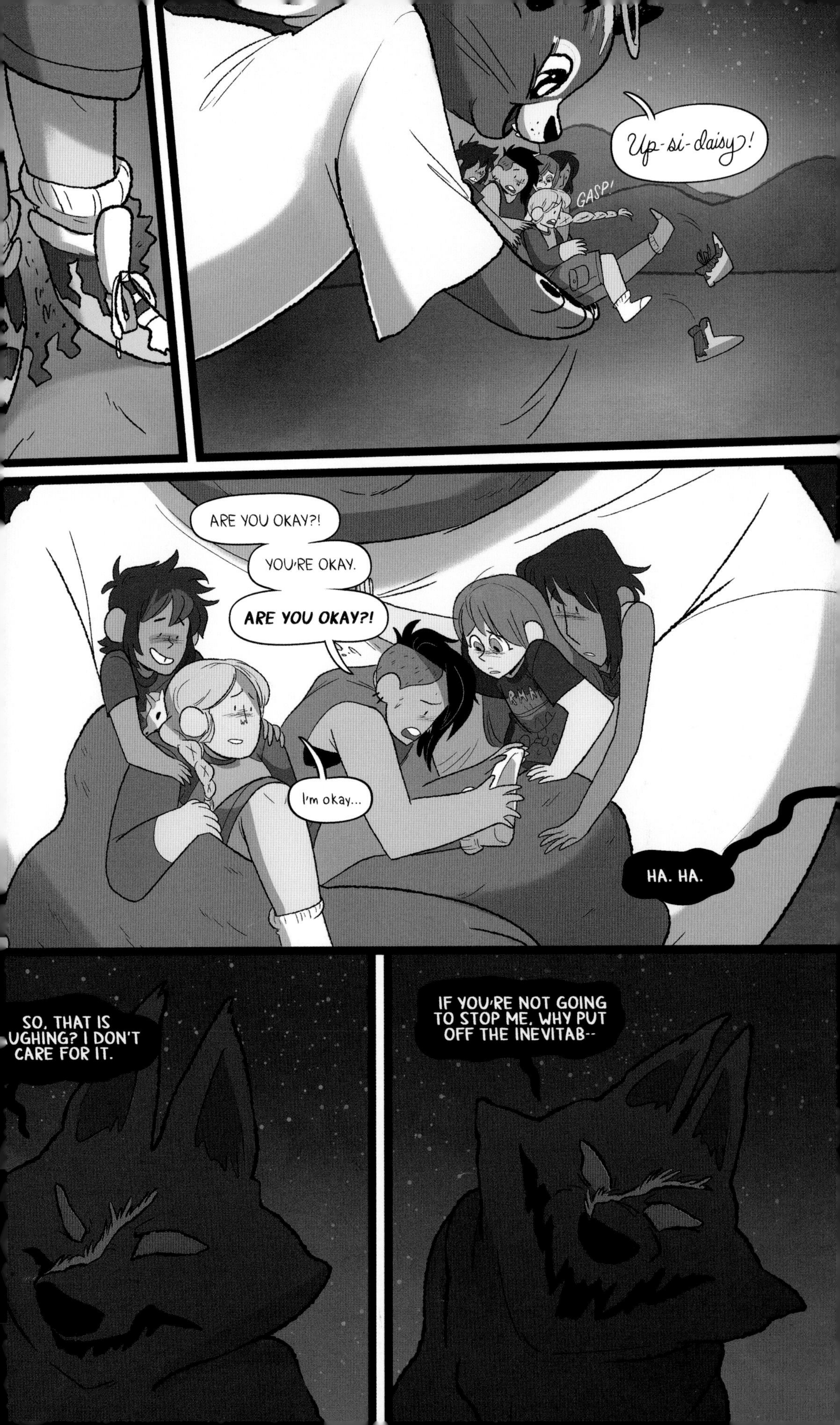
Up-si-daisy?!
GASP!
ARE YOU OKAY?!
YOU'RE OKAY.
ARE YOU OKAY?!
I'm okay...
HA. HA.
SO, THAT IS
UGHING? I DON'T
CARE FOR IT.
IF YOU'RE NOT GOING
TO STOP ME, WHY PUT
OFF THE INEVITAB--

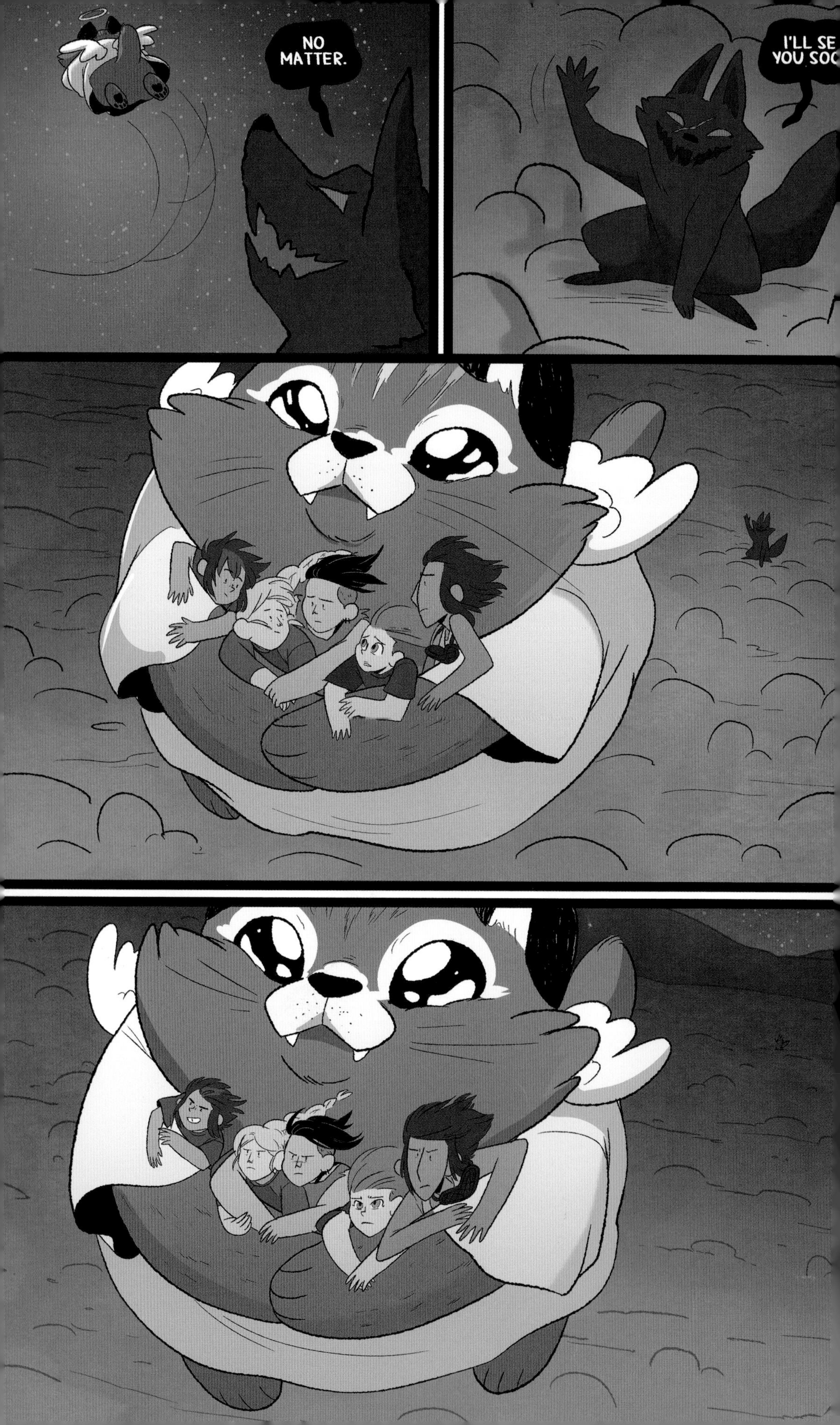
NO MATTER.
I'LL SE
YOU SOO

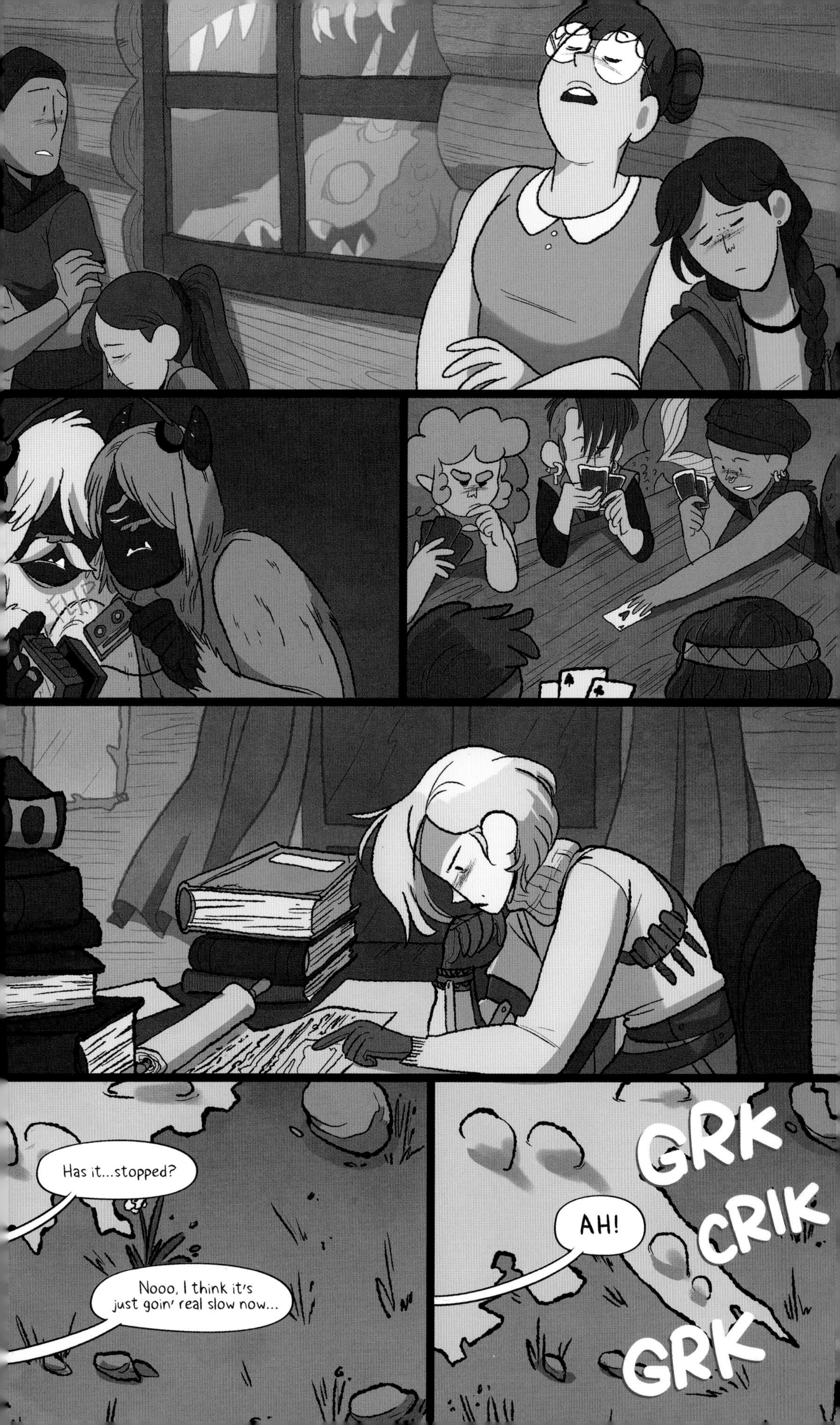
FLIP
Has it...stopped?
Nooo, I think it's just goin' real slow now...
AH!
GRK
CRIK
GRK

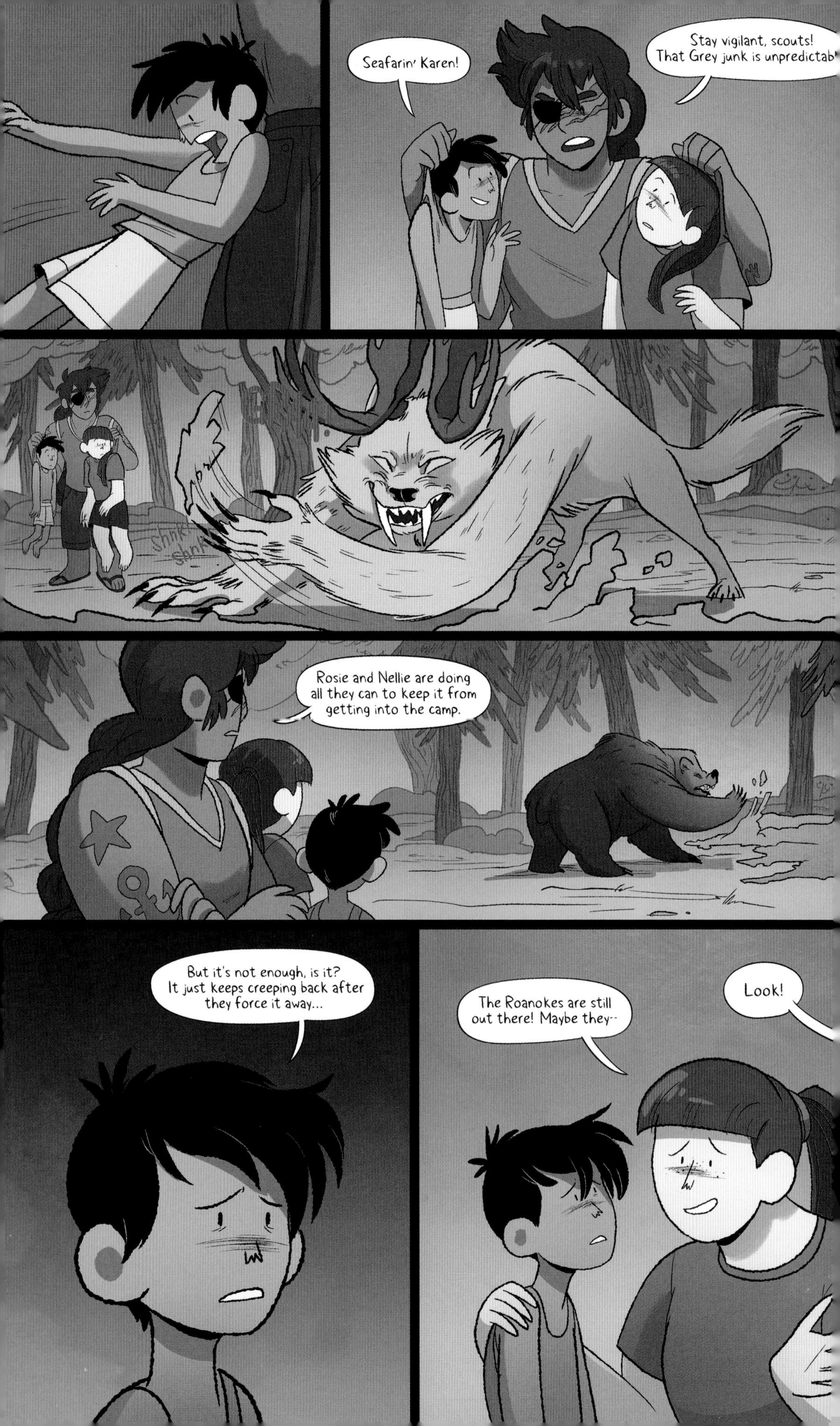
Seafarin' Karen!
Stay vigilant, scouts! That Grey junk is unpredictab
shnk! shnk!
Rosie and Nellie are doing all they can to keep it from getting into the camp.
But it's not enough, is it? It just keeps creeping back after they force it away...
The Roanokes are still out there! Maybe they--
Look!

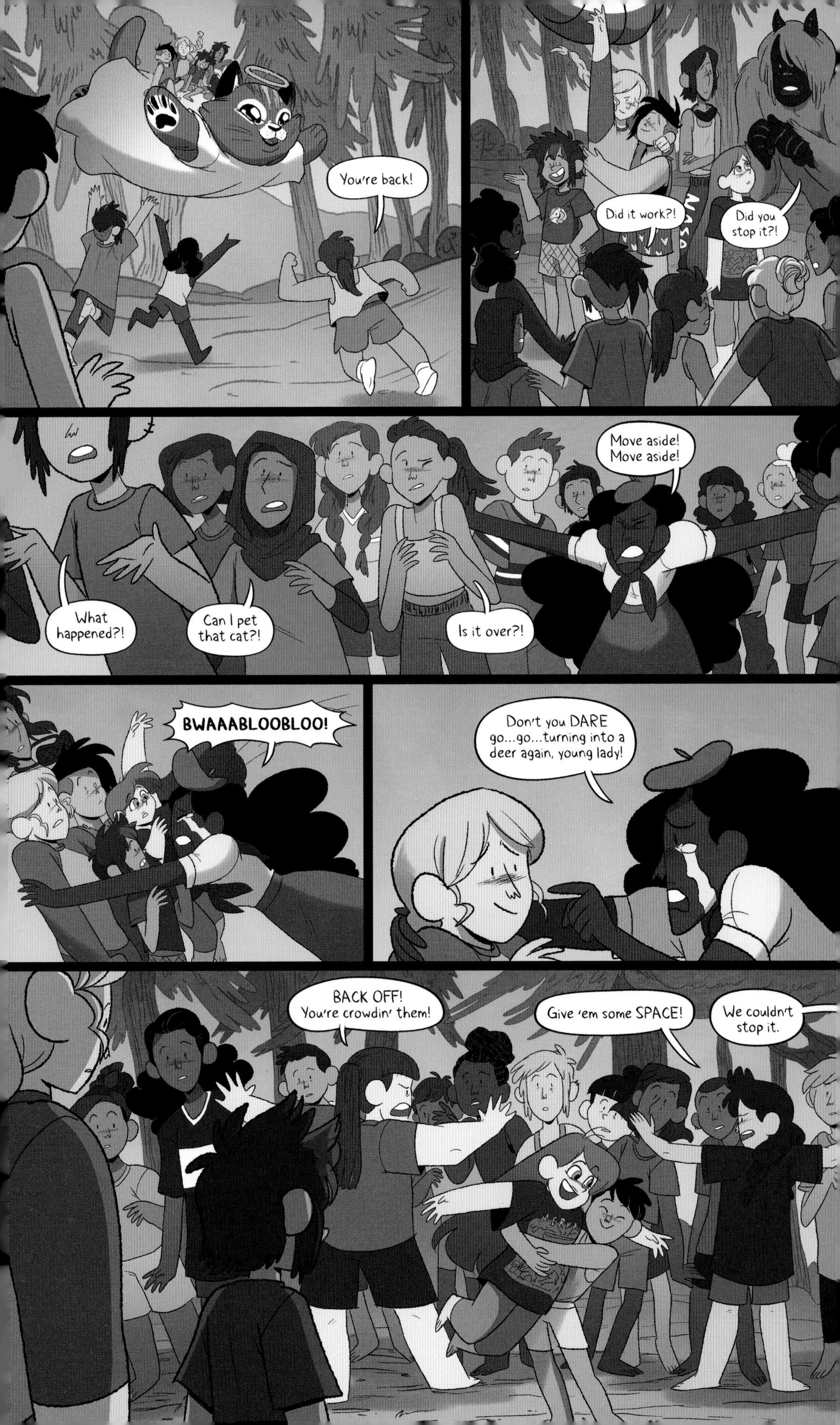

You're back!
Did it work?!
Did you stop it?!
What happened?!
Can I pet that cat?!
Is it over?!
Move aside! Move aside!
BWAAABLOOBLOO!
Don't you DARE go...go...turning into a deer again, young lady!
BACK OFF! You're crowdin' them!
Give 'em some SPACE!
We couldn't stop it.

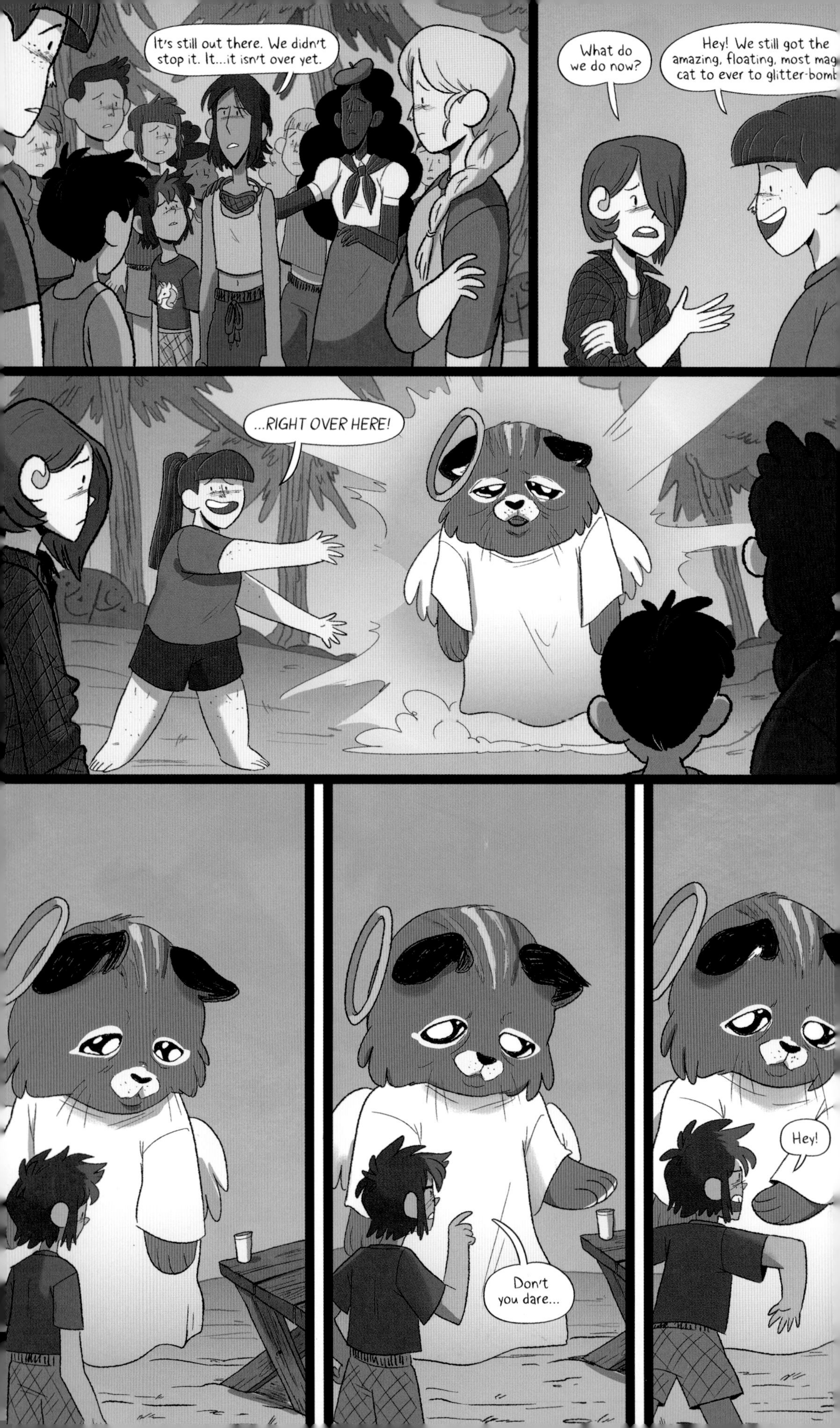
It's still out there. We didn't stop it. It...it isn't over yet.
What do we do now?
Hey! We still got the amazing, floating, most mag
cat to ever to glitter-bomb
...RIGHT OVER HERE!
Don't you dare...
Hey!

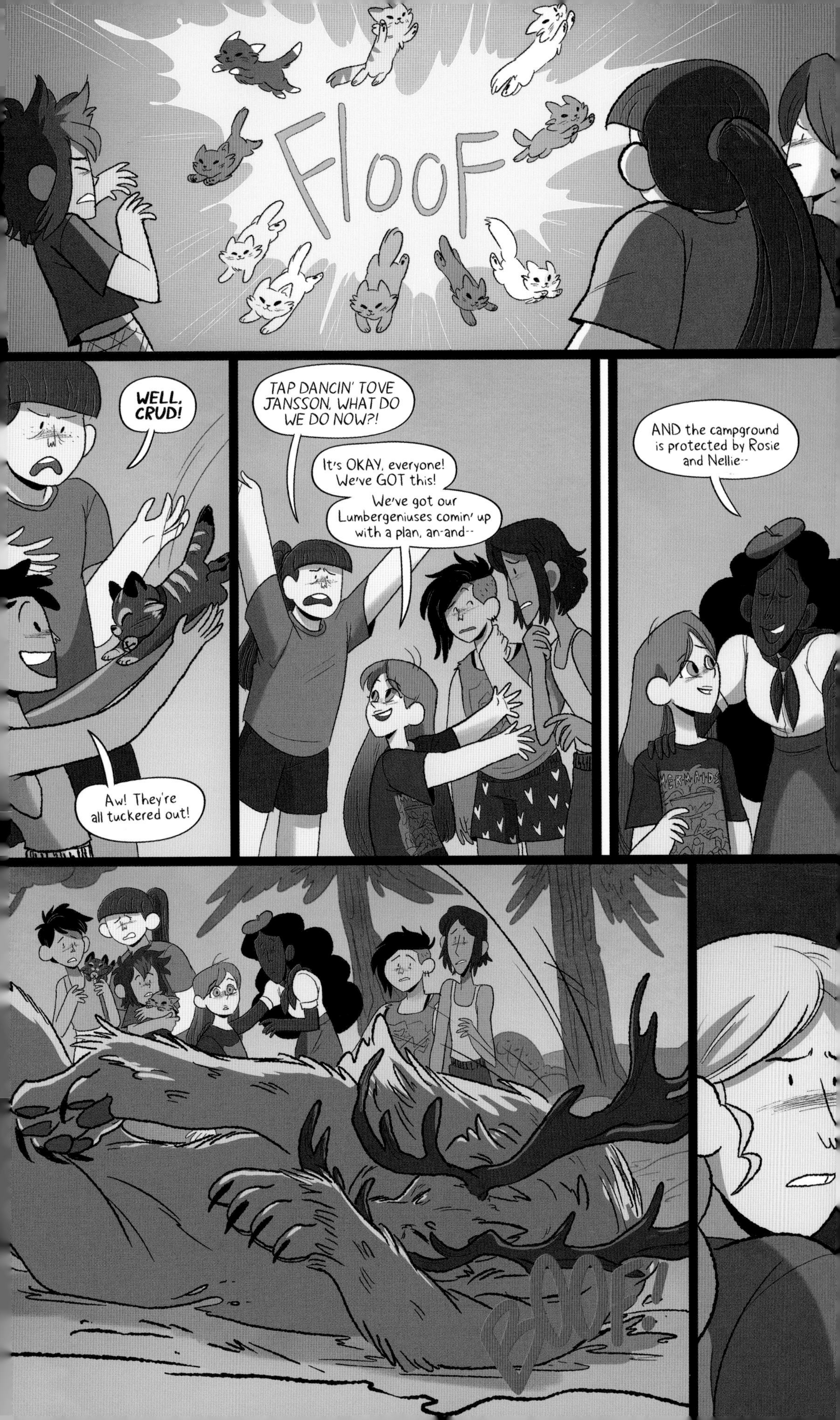
FLOOF
WELL, CRUD!
Aw! They're all tuckered out!
TAP DANCIN' TOVE JANSSON, WHAT DO WE DO NOW?!
It's OKAY, everyone! We've GOT this!
We've got our Lumbergeniuses comin' up with a plan, an-and--
AND the campground is protected by Rosie and Nellie--
FWOOF!

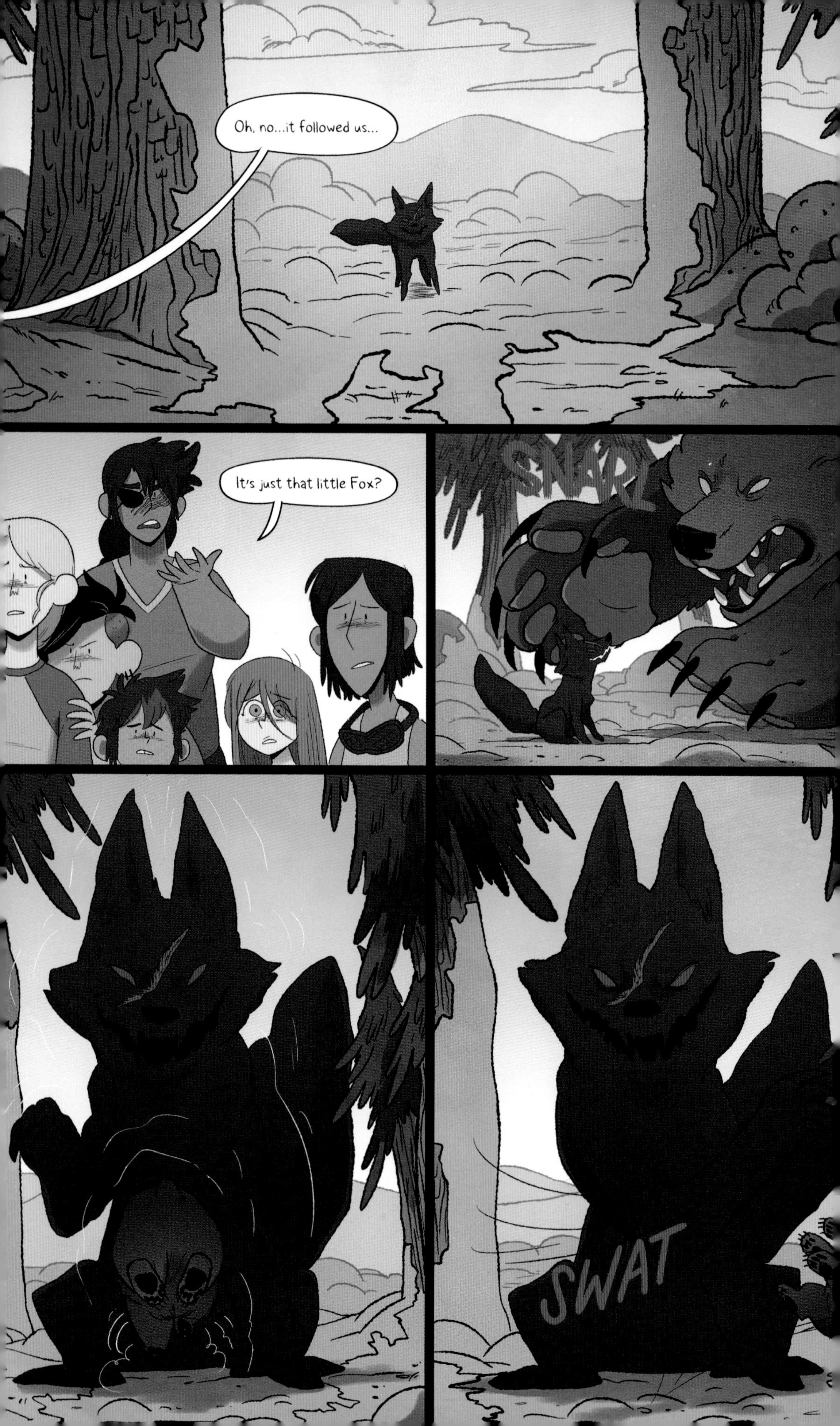
Oh, no...it followed us...
It's just that little Fox?
SNARL
SWAT

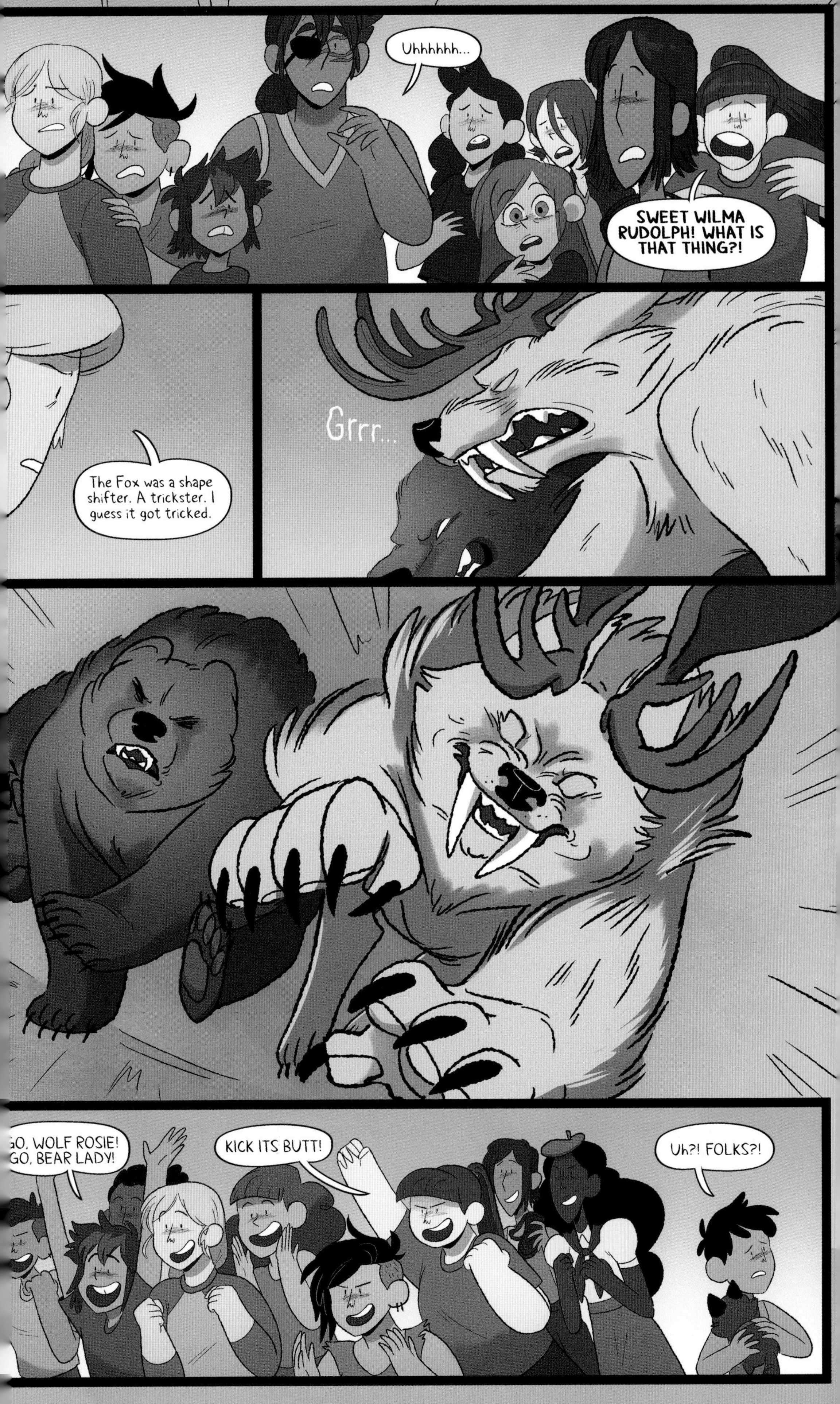
Uhhhhhh...
SWEET WILMA RUDOLPH! WHAT IS THAT THING?!
The Fox was a shape shifter. A trickster. I guess it got tricked.
Grrr...
GO, WOLF ROSIE! GO, BEAR LADY!
KICK ITS BUTT!
Uh?! FOLKS?!

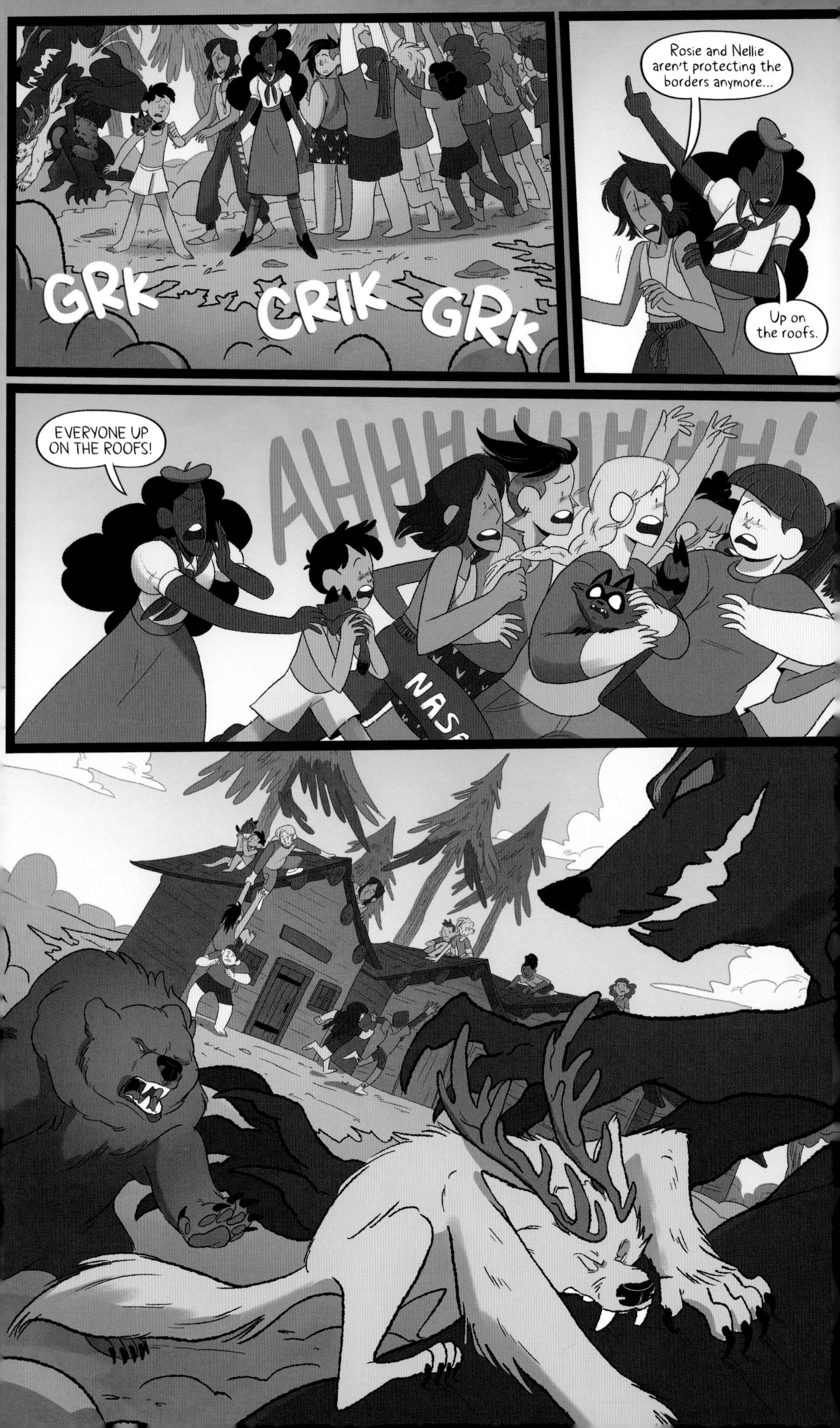
GRK
CRIK
GRK
Rosie and Nellie aren't protecting the borders anymore...
Up on the roofs.
EVERYONE UP ON THE ROOFS!
AHHHHHHHHH!
NASA

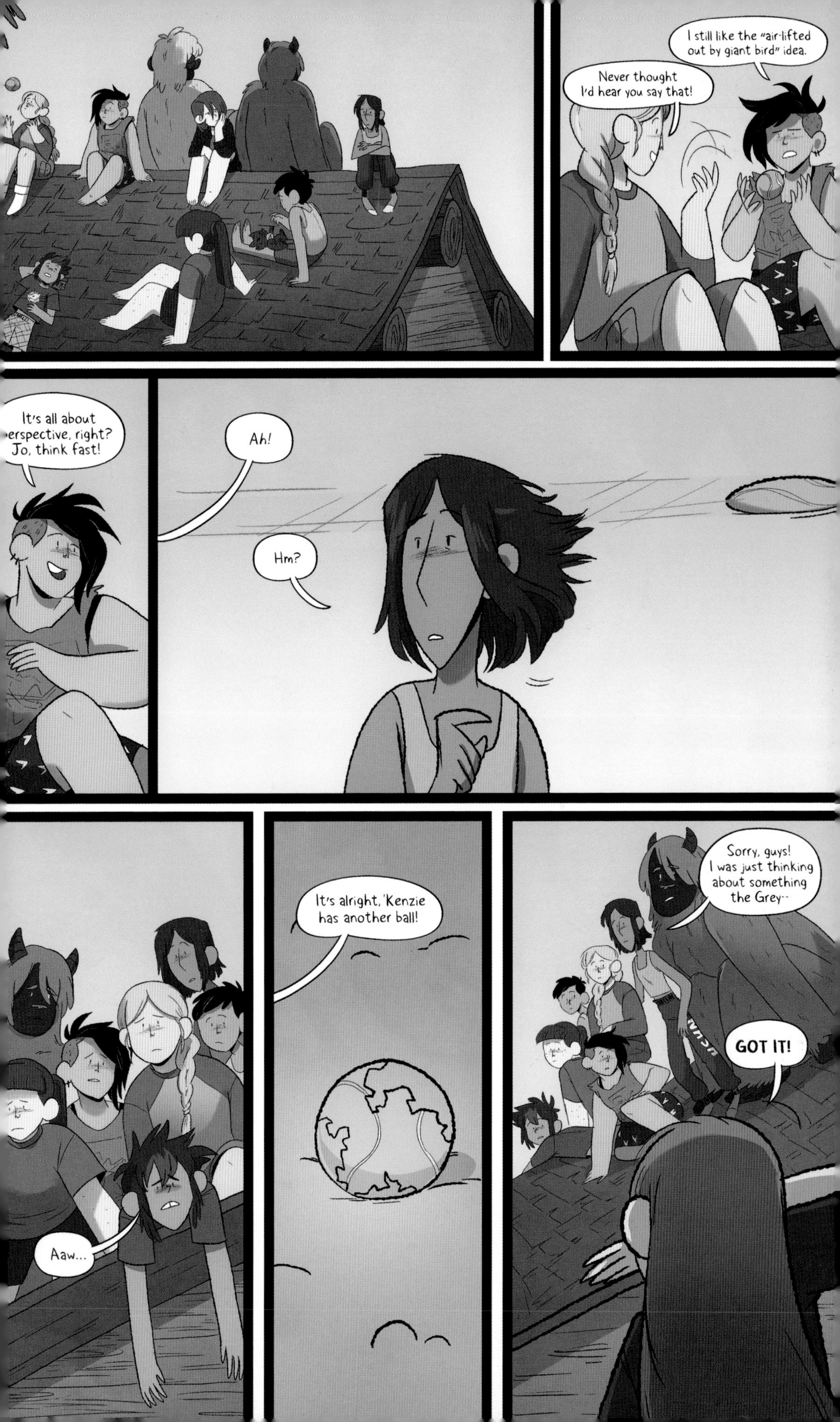
Never thought I'd hear you say that!
I still like the "air-lifted out by giant bird" idea.
It's all about erspective, right? Jo, think fast!
Ah!
Hm?
Aaw...
It's alright, 'Kenzie has another ball!
Sorry, guys! I was just thinking about something the Grey--
GOT IT!

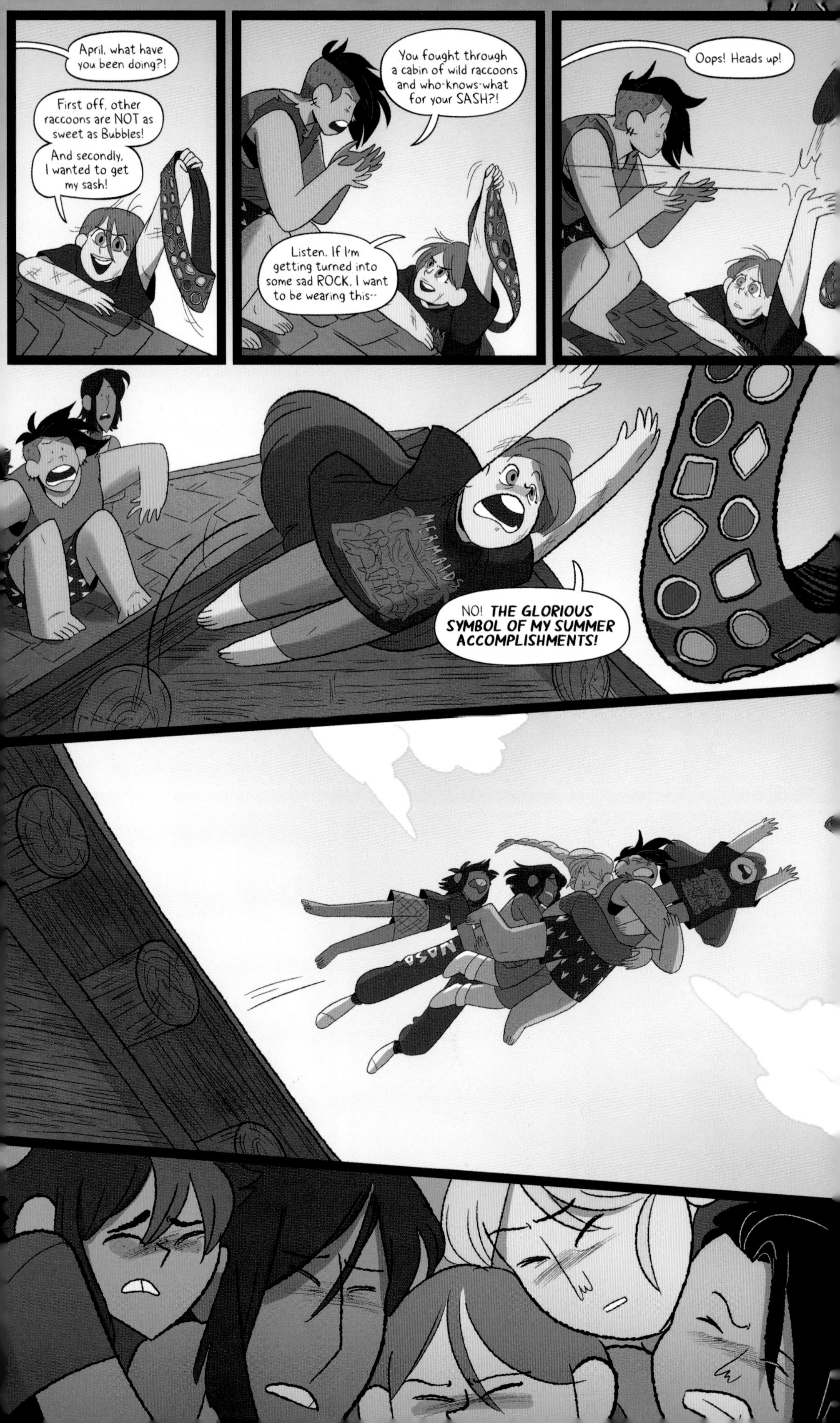
April, what have you been doing?!
First off, other raccoons are NOT as sweet as Bubbles!
And secondly, I wanted to get my sash!
You fought through a cabin of wild raccoons and who-knows-what for your SASH?!
Listen. If I'm getting turned into some sad ROCK, I want to be wearing this--
Oops! Heads up!
MERMAIDS
NO! THE GLORIOUS SYMBOL OF MY SUMMER ACCOMPLISHMENTS!

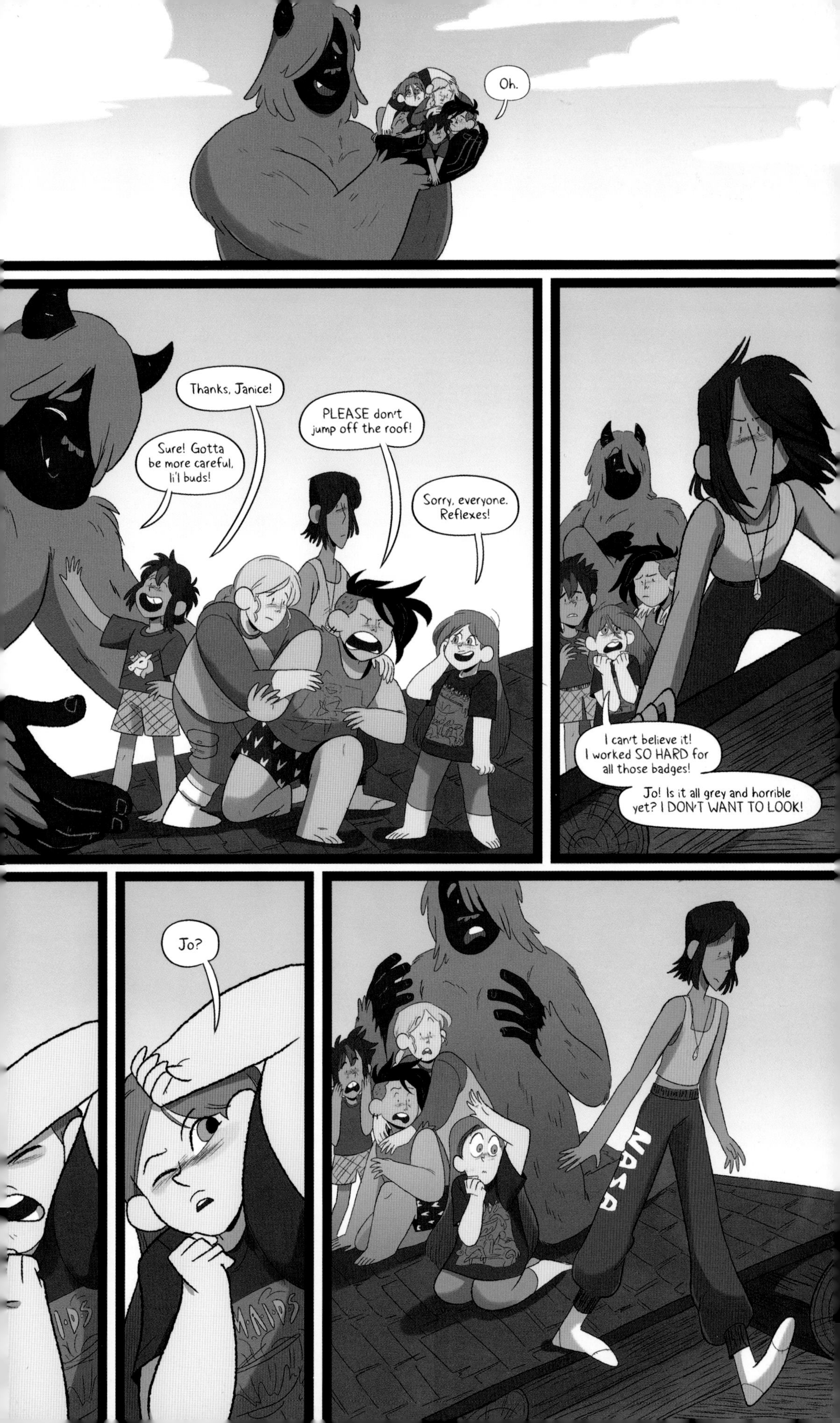
Oh.
Thanks, Janice!
Sure! Gotta be more careful, li'l buds!
PLEASE don't jump off the roof!
Sorry, everyone. Reflexes!
I can't believe it! I worked SO HARD for all those badges!
Jo! Is it all grey and horrible yet? I DON'T WANT TO LOOK!
Jo?
M·A·I·D·S
NASA

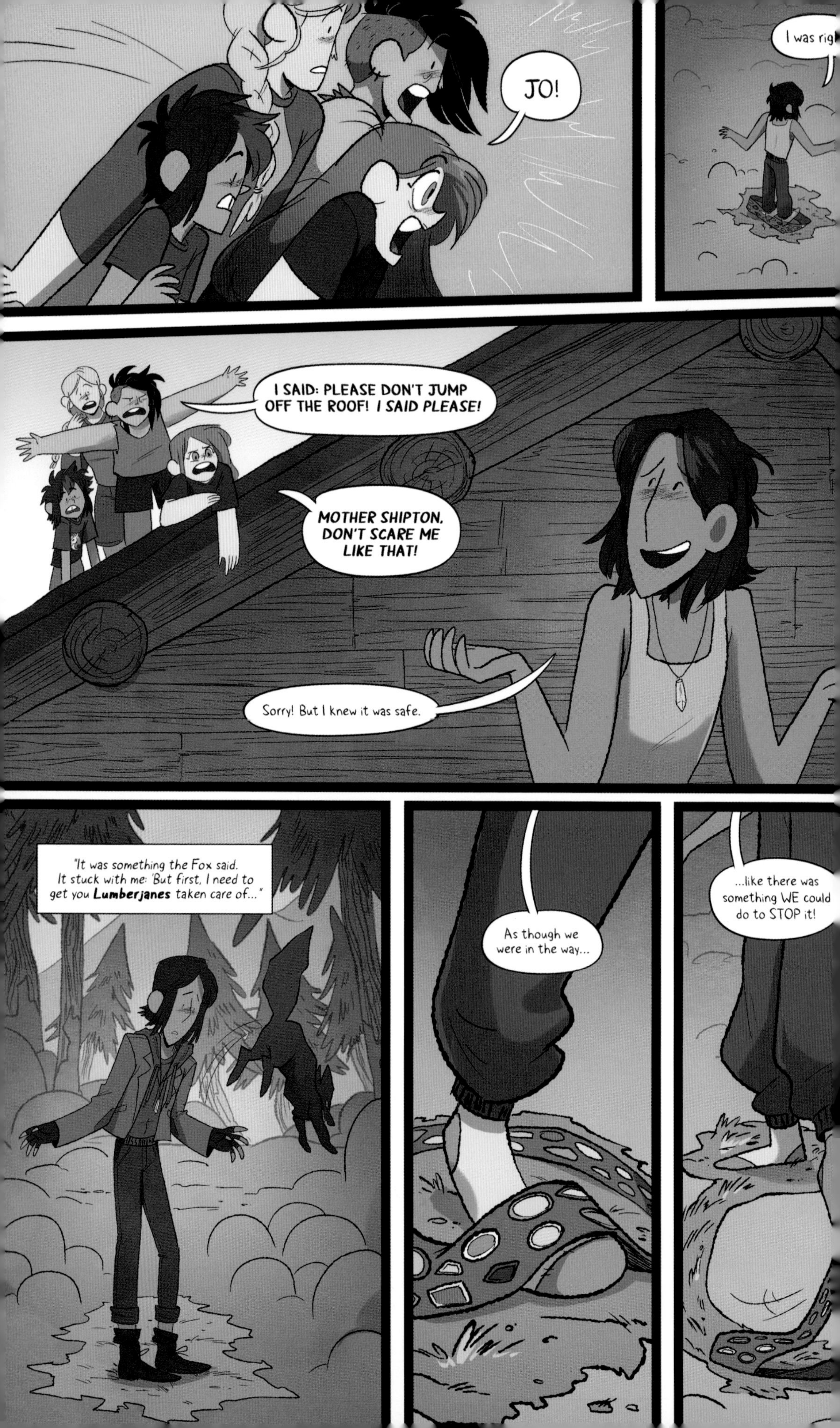
JO!
I was rig
I SAID: PLEASE DON'T JUMP OFF THE ROOF! I SAID PLEASE!
MOTHER SHIPTON, DON'T SCARE ME LIKE THAT!
Sorry! But I knew it was safe.
"It was something the Fox said. It stuck with me: 'But first, I need to get you **Lumberjanes** taken care of...'"
As though we were in the way...
...like there was something WE could do to STOP it!

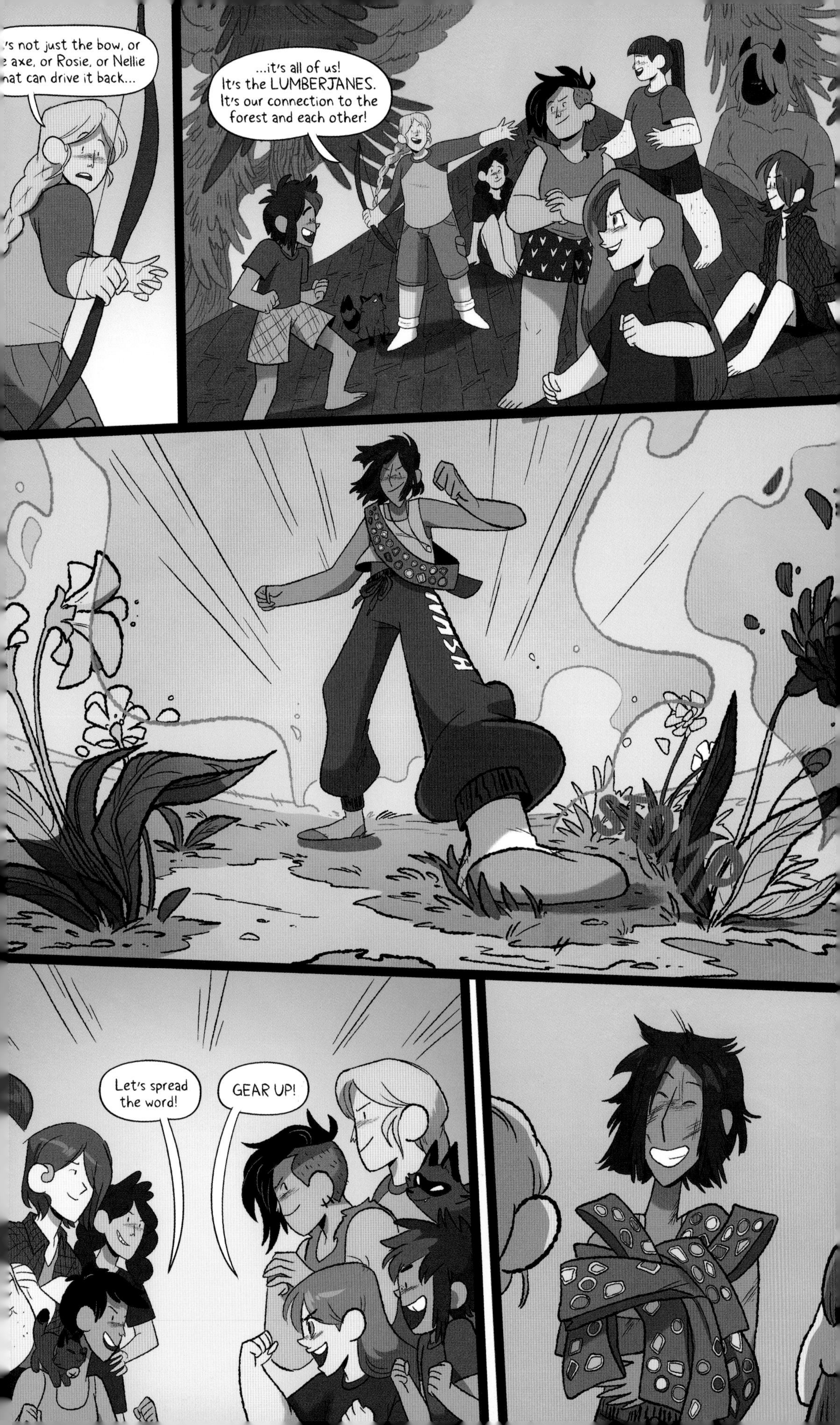

's not just the bow, or
e axe, or Rosie, or Nellie
hat can drive it back...
...it's all of us!
It's the LUMBERJANES.
It's our connection to the
forest and each other!
STOMP
Let's spread
the word!
GEAR UP!

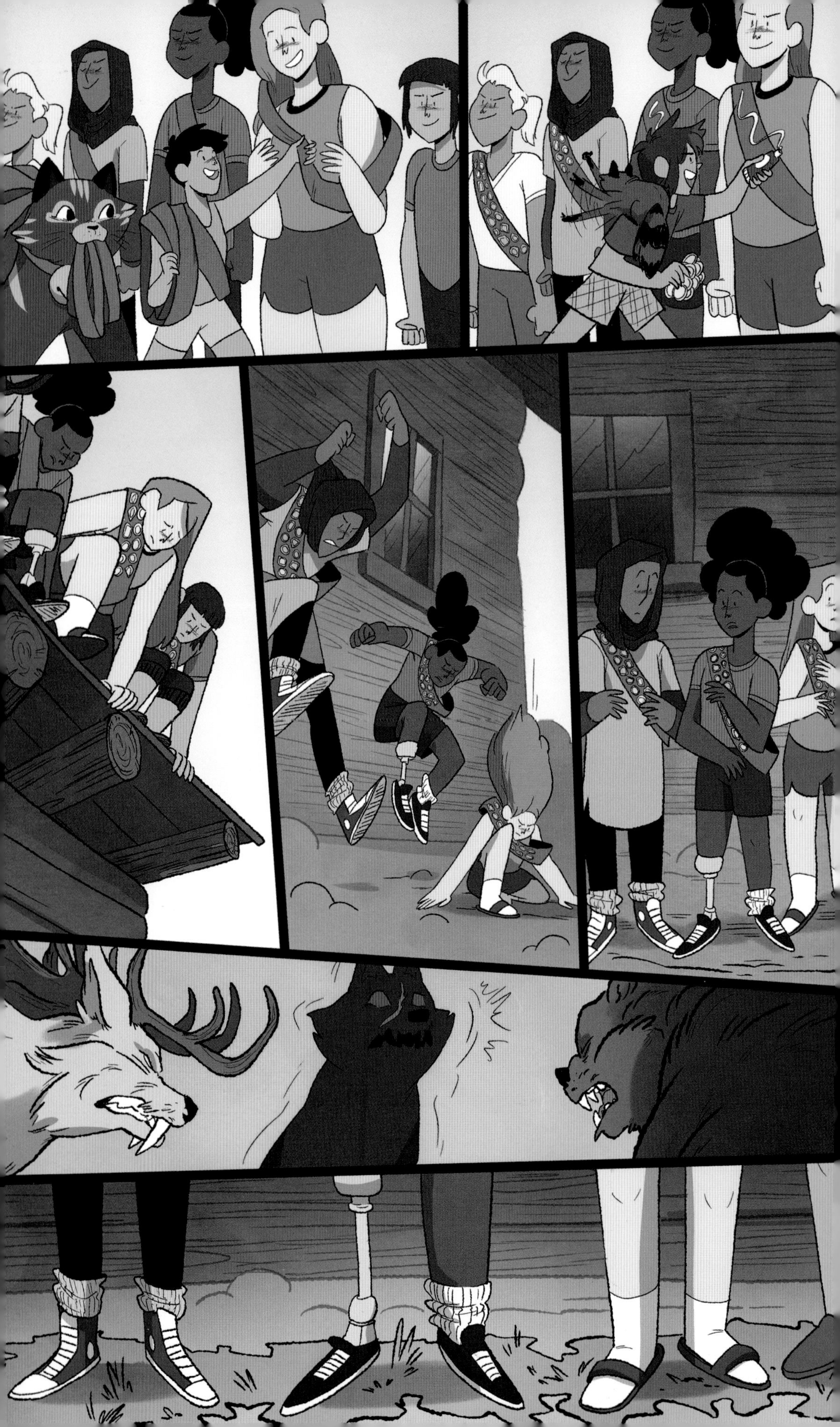

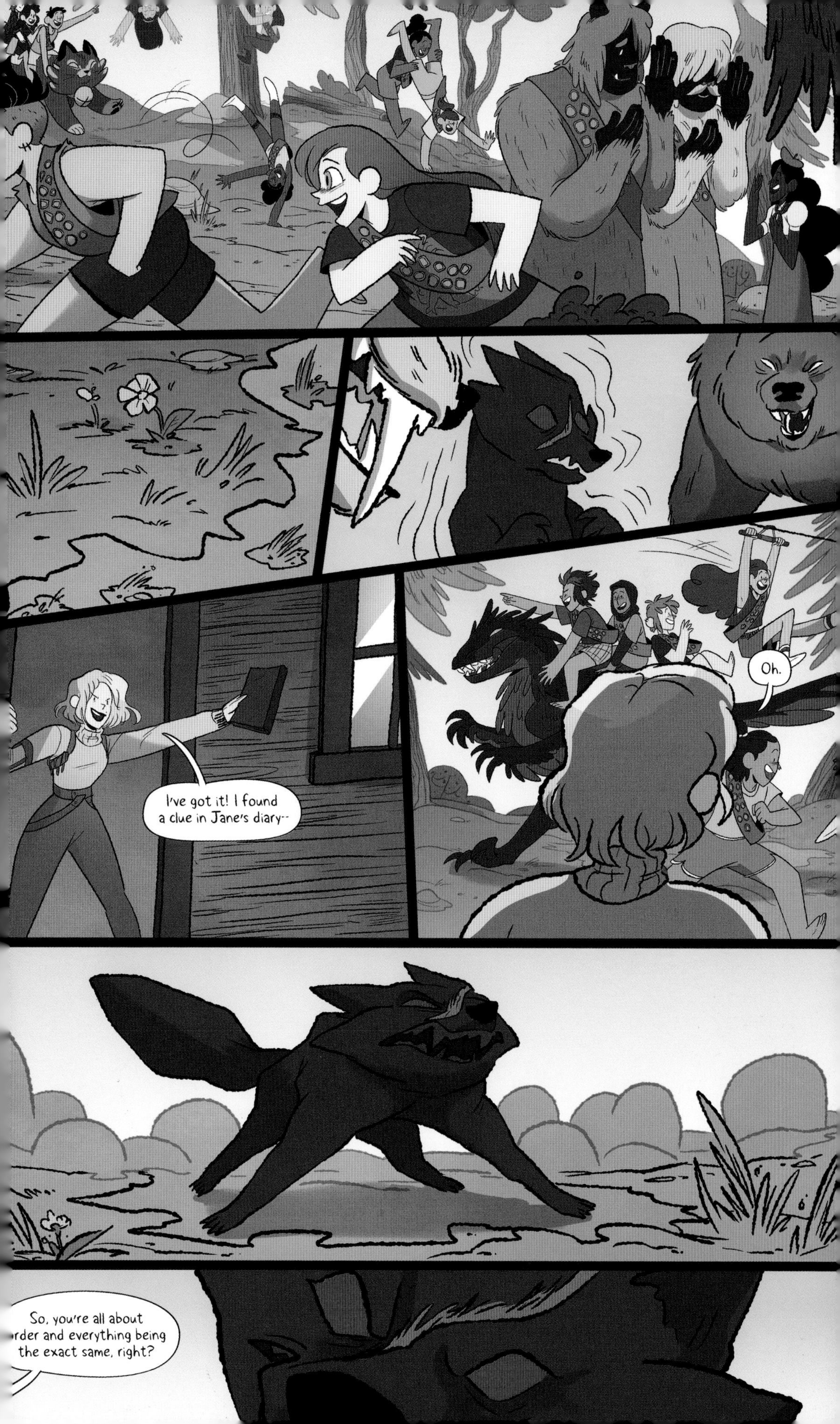
I've got it! I found a clue in Jane's diary--
Oh.
So, you're all about
rder and everything being
the exact same, right?

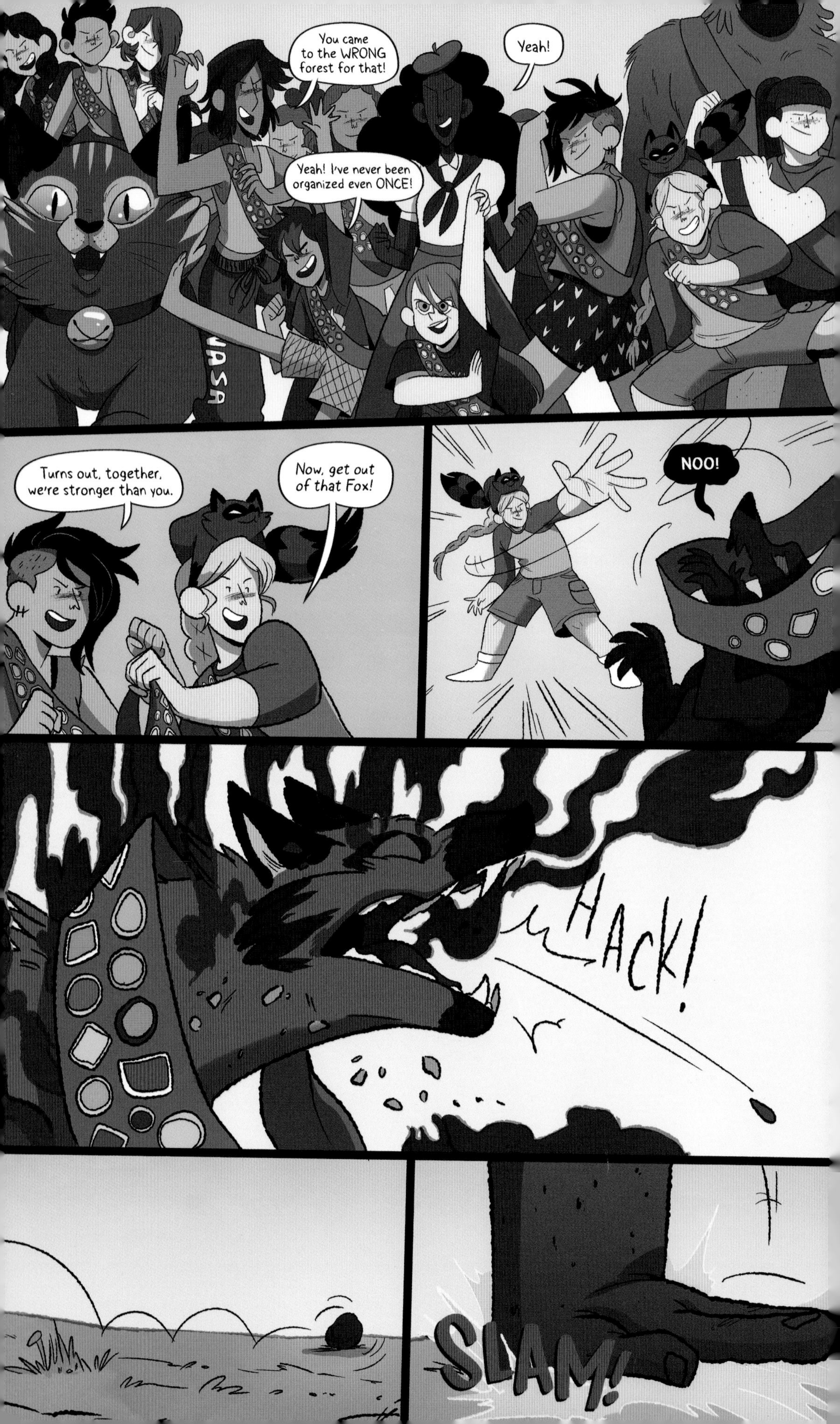
You came to the WRONG forest for that!
Yeah!
Yeah! I've never been organized even ONCE!
NASA
Turns out, together, we're stronger than you.
Now, get out of that Fox!
NOO!
HACK!
SLAM!

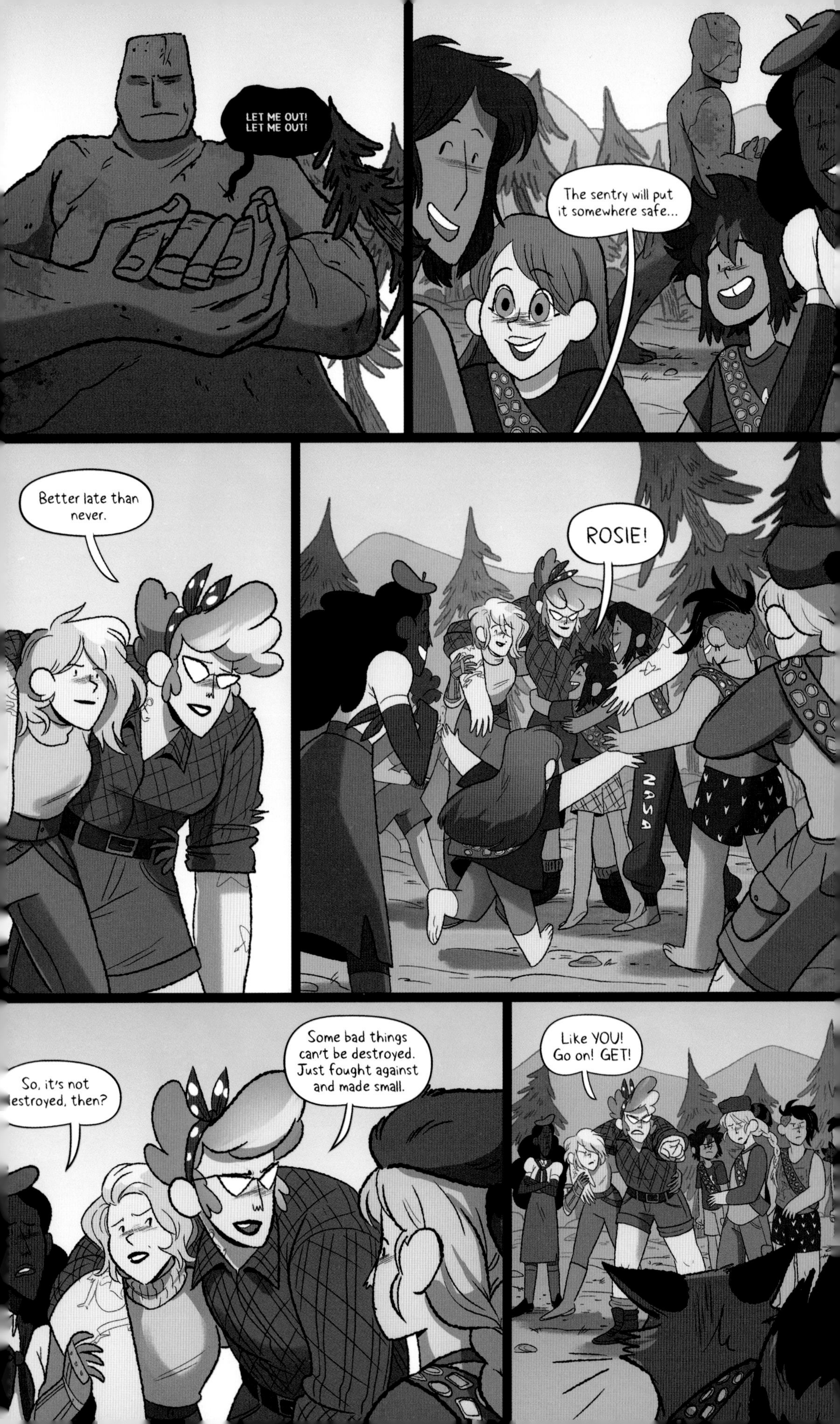
LET ME OUT! LET ME OUT!
The sentry will put it somewhere safe...
Better late than never.
ROSIE!
NASA
So, it's not destroyed, then?
Some bad things can't be destroyed. Just fought against and made small.
Like YOU! Go on! GET!

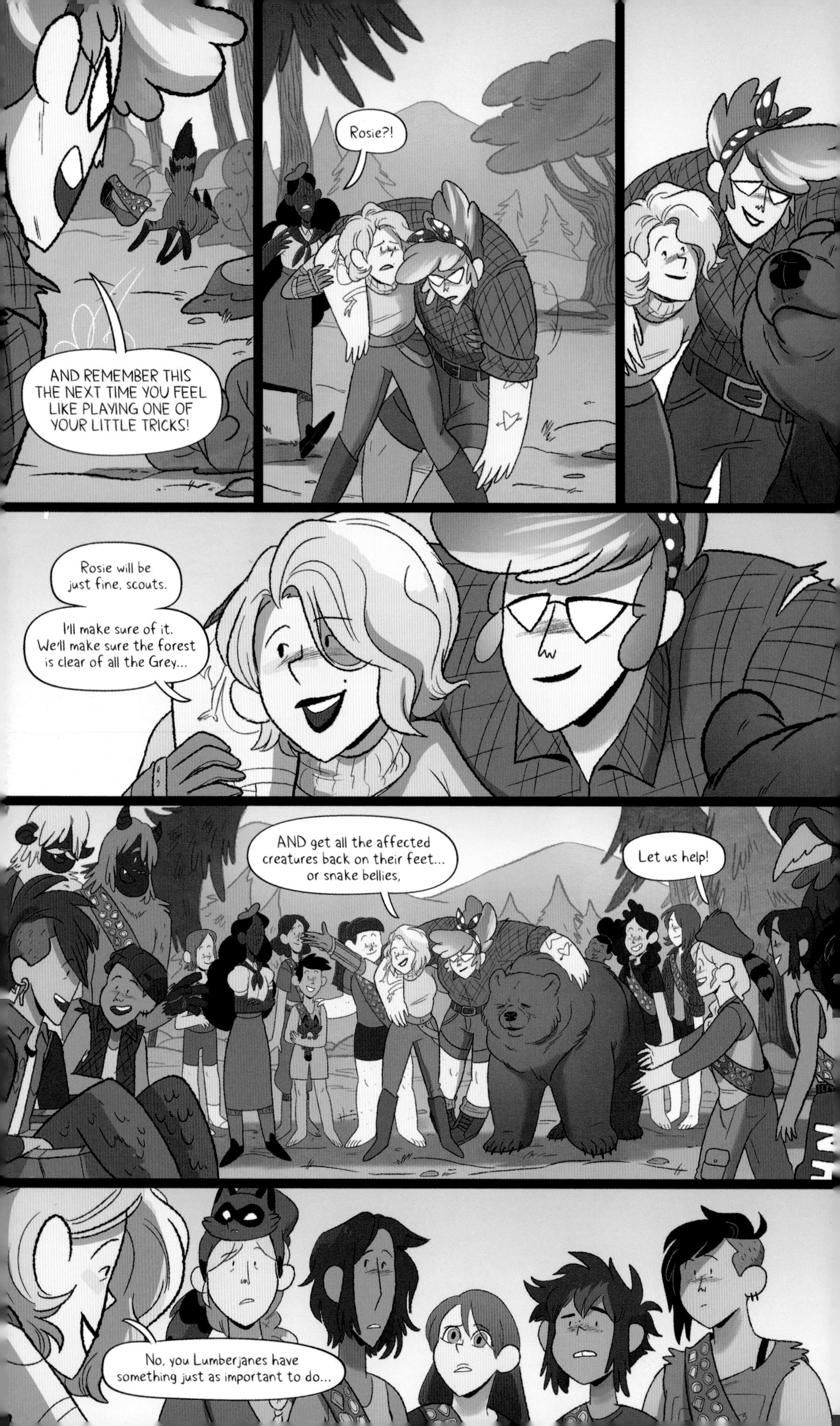
AND REMEMBER THIS THE NEXT TIME YOU FEEL LIKE PLAYING ONE OF YOUR LITTLE TRICKS!
Rosie?!
Rosie will be just fine, scouts.
I'll make sure of it. We'll make sure the forest is clear of all the Grey...
AND get all the affected creatures back on their feet... or snake bellies,
Let us help!
No, you Lumberjanes have something just as important to do...

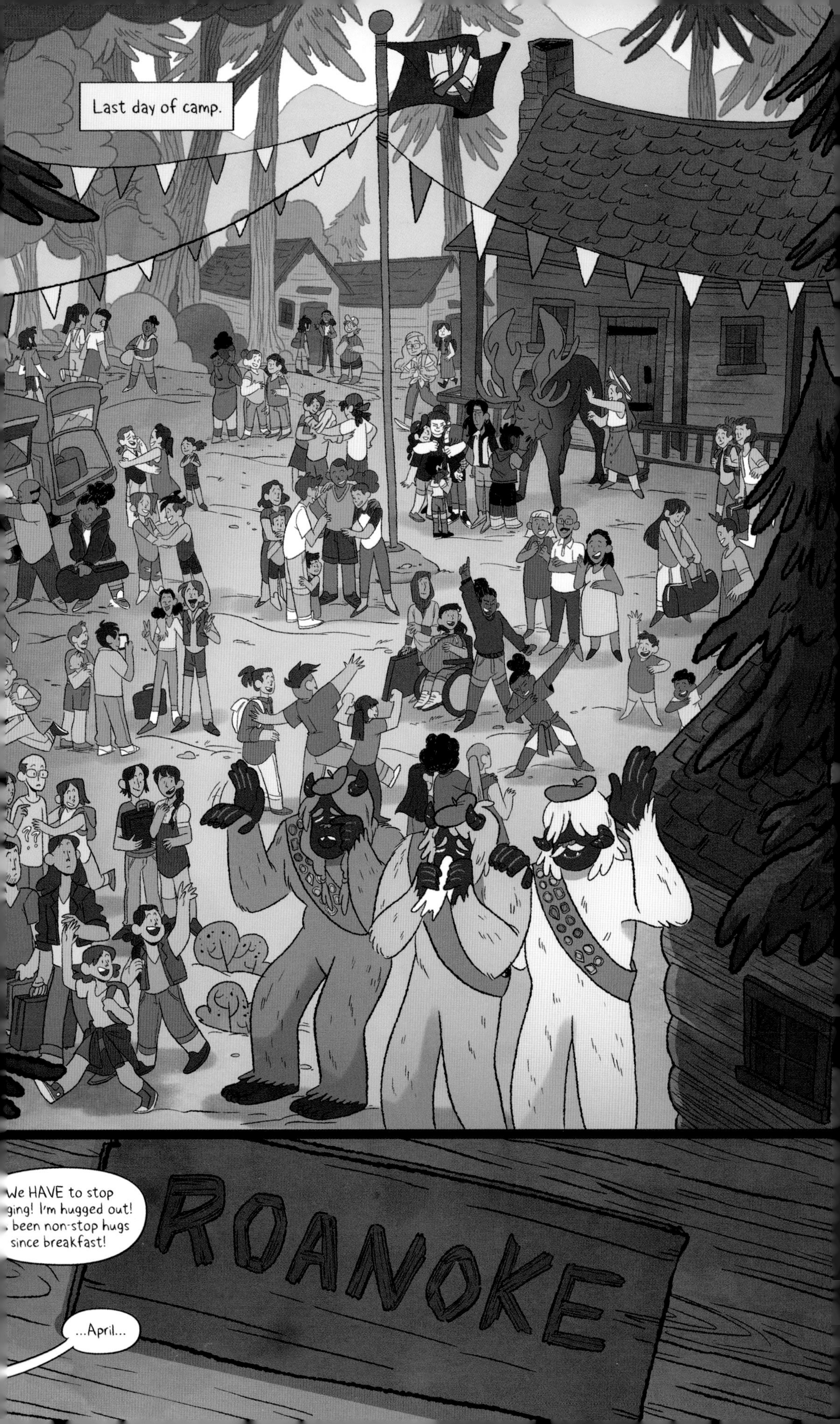
Last day of camp.
We HAVE to stop
ging! I'm hugged out!
been non-stop hugs
since breakfast!
...April...
ROANOKE

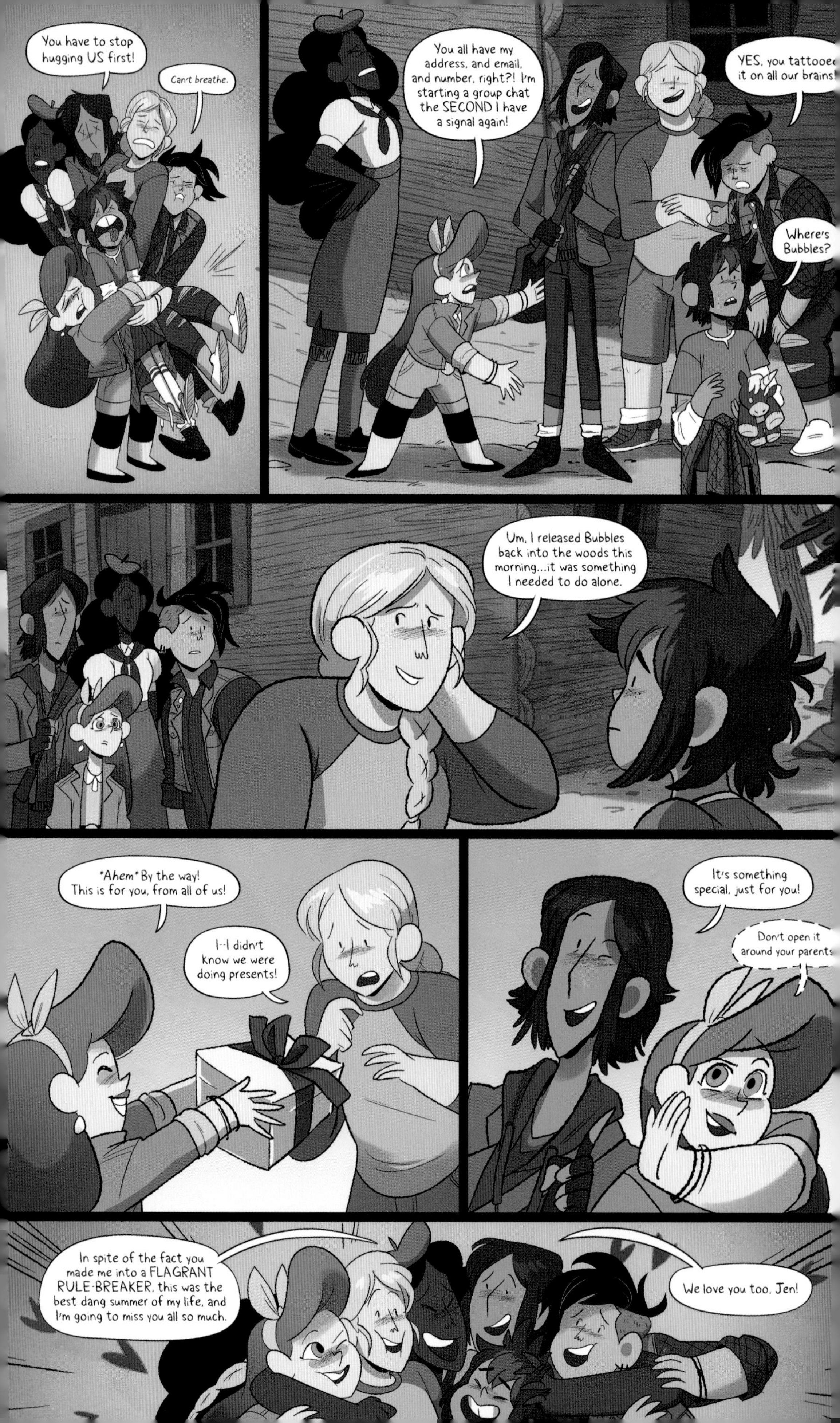
You have to stop hugging US first!
Can't breathe.
You all have my address, and email, and number, right?! I'm starting a group chat the SECOND I have a signal again!
YES, you tattooed it on all our brains!
Where's Bubbles?
Um, I released Bubbles back into the woods this morning...it was something I needed to do alone.
Ahem By the way! This is for you, from all of us!
I-I didn't know we were doing presents!
It's something special, just for you!
Don't open it around your parents
In spite of the fact you made me into a FLAGRANT RULE-BREAKER, this was the best dang summer of my life, and I'm going to miss you all so much.
We love you too, Jen!

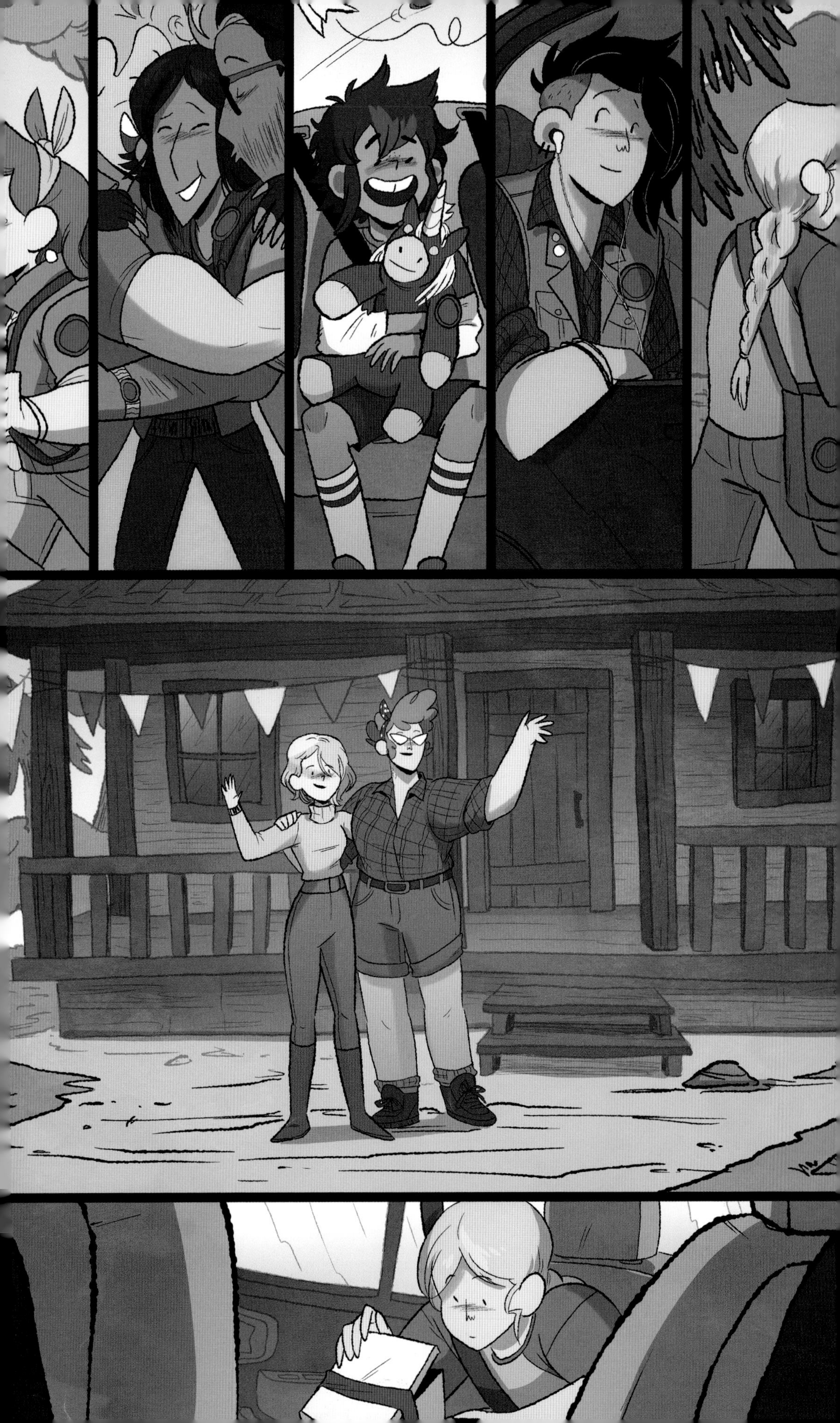

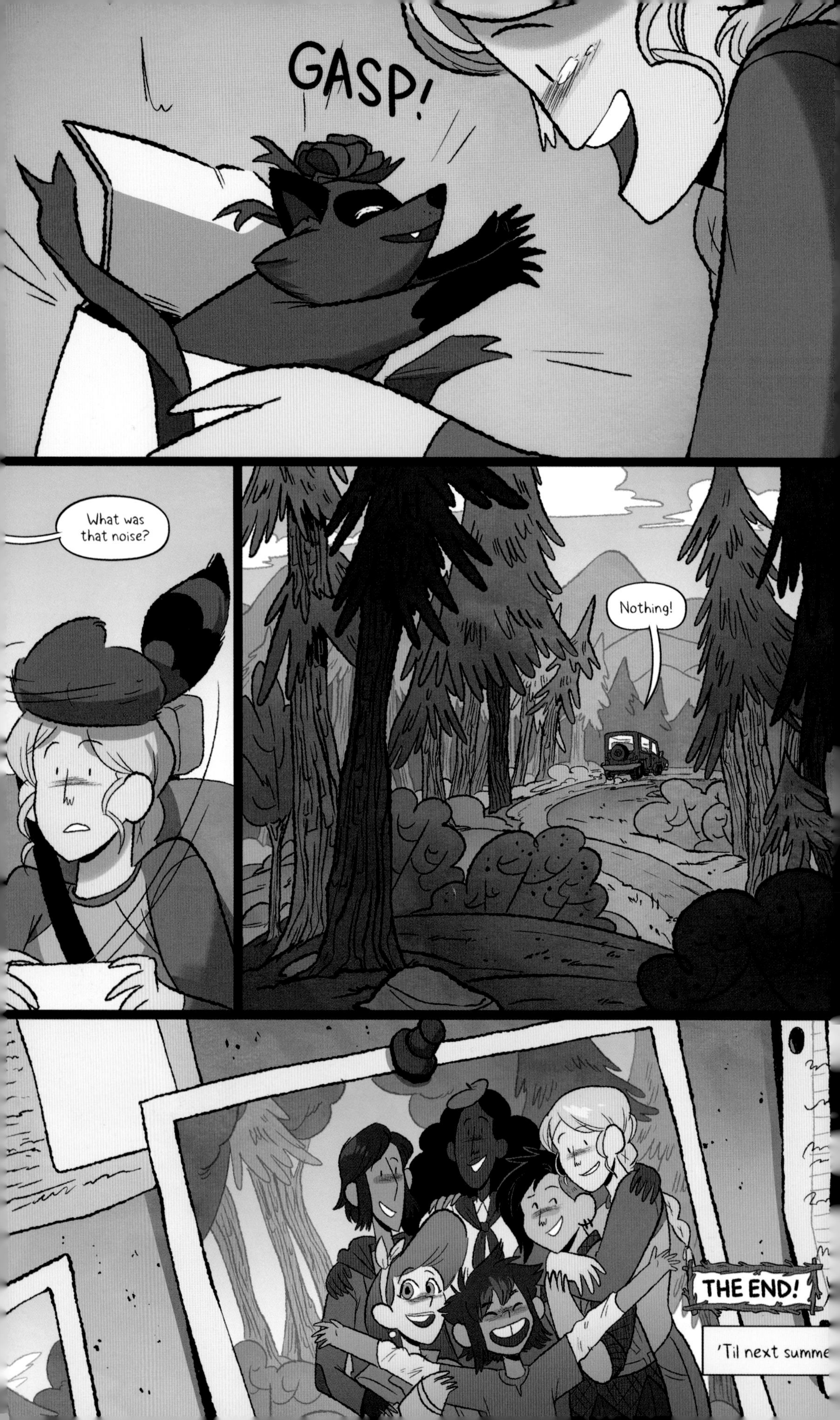
GASP!
What was that noise?
Nothing!
THE END!
'Til next summe

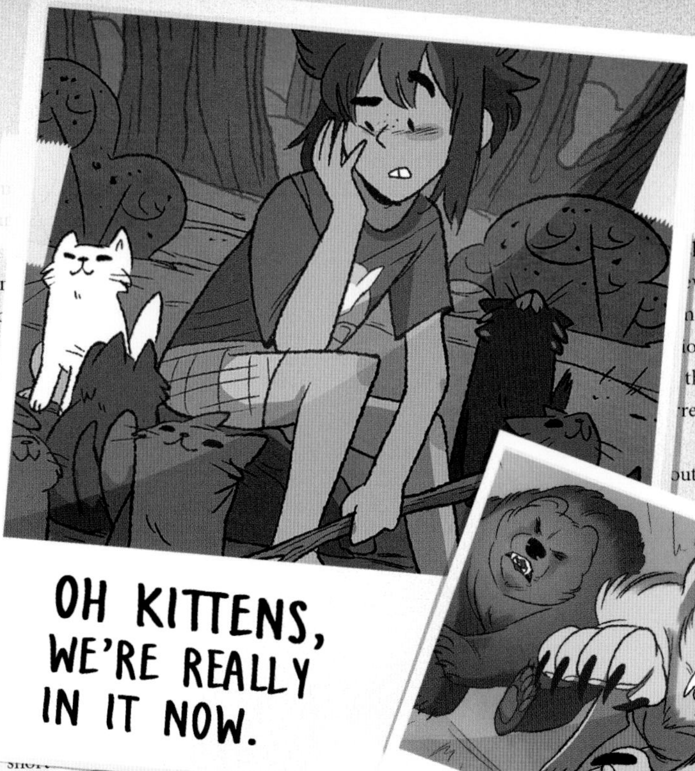
OH KITTENS,
WE'RE REALLY
IN IT NOW.

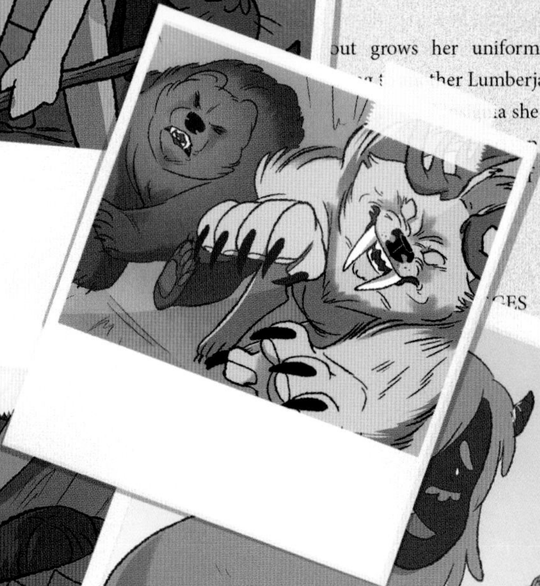

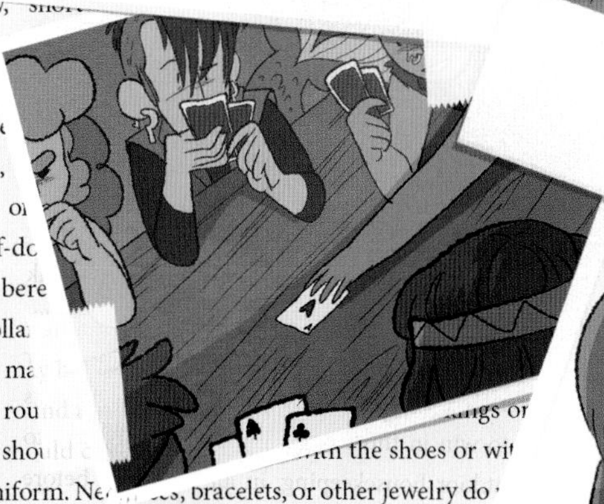

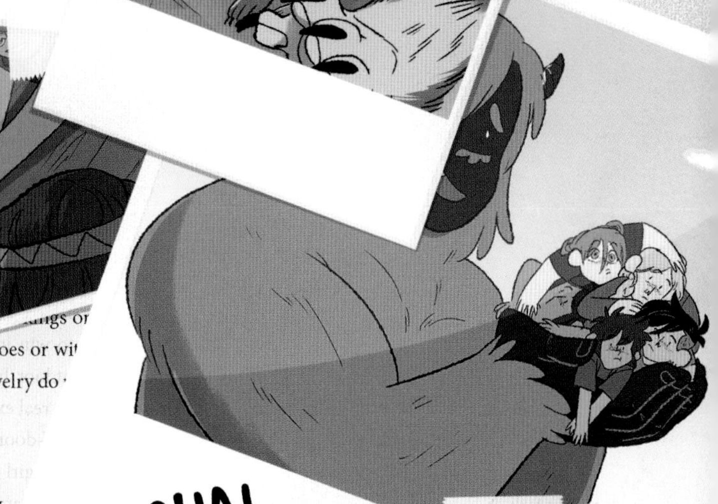
GOTCHA!

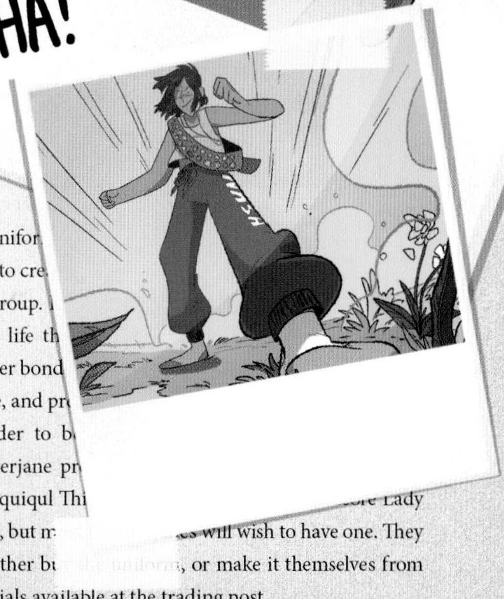

will co…

The u… It h… appearar… dress f… Further… Lumbe… to have… part in… Thiskw… Hardc… have … thems…

The … yellow, … emb… the w… choos… slacks, … made o… out-of-do… green bere… the colla… Shoes ma… heels, rou… …ings or socks shou… …ith the shoes or wi… the uniform. Ne… …es, bracelets, or other jewelry do … belong with a Lumberjane uniform.

HOW TO WEAR THE UNIFORM

To look well in a uniform demands first of … uniform be kept in good condition—clean … pressed. See that the skirt is the right length for your own height and build, that the belt is adjusted to your waist, that your shoes and stockings are in keeping with the uniform, that you watch your posture and carry yourself with dignity and grace. If the beret is removed indoors, be sure that your hair is neat and kept in place with an inconspicuous clip or ribbon. When you wear a Lumberjane uniform you are identified as a member of this organization and you should be doubly careful to conduct yourself in a way that will show everyone that courtesy and thoughtfulness are part of being a Lumberjane. People are likely to judge a whole nation by the selfishness of a few individuals, to criticize a whole family because of the misconduct of one member, and to feel unkindly toward an organization because of the

…E UNIFORM

…hould be worn at camp …vents when Lumberjanes …n may also be worn at other …ions. It should be worn as a … the uniform dress with …rrect shoes, and stocking or

…out grows her uniform or …ther Lumberjane. …a she has … her … her

…GES

The unifor… helps to cre… in a group. … active life th… another bond… future, and pr… in order to b… Lumberjane pr… Penniquiqul Thi… …ore Lady Types, but m… …s will wish to have one. They can either bu… uniform, or make it themselves from materials available at the trading post.

LUMBERJANES FIELD MANUAL

LUMBERJANES: FAREWELL TO SUMMER

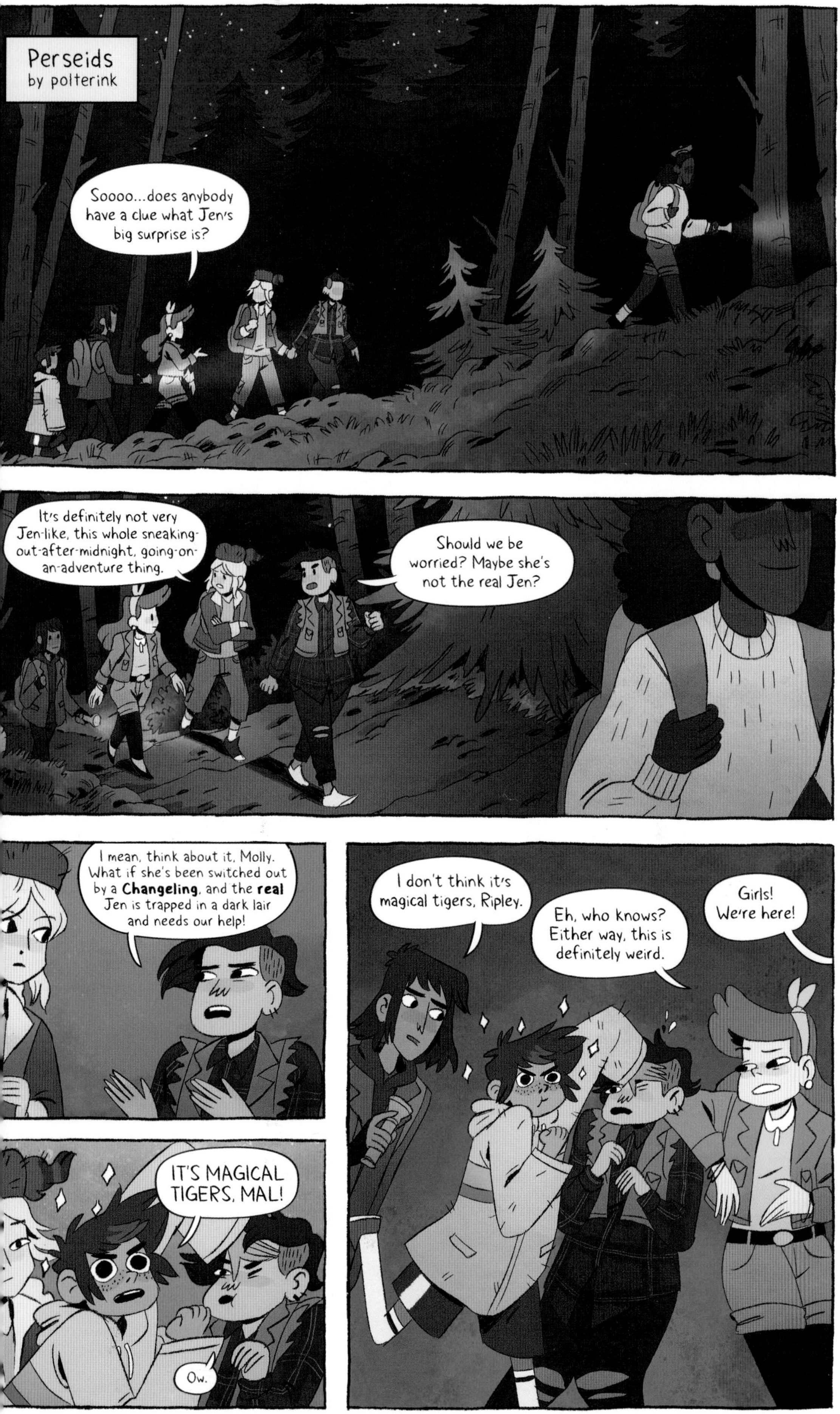

Perseids
by polterink
Soooo...does anybody have a clue what Jen's big surprise is?
It's definitely not very Jen-like, this whole sneaking-out-after-midnight, going-on-an-adventure thing.
Should we be worried? Maybe she's not the real Jen?
I mean, think about it, Molly. What if she's been switched out by a **Changeling**, and the **real** Jen is trapped in a dark lair and needs our help!
IT'S MAGICAL TIGERS, MAL!
Ow.
I don't think it's magical tigers, Ripley.
Eh, who knows? Either way, this is definitely weird.
Girls! We're here!

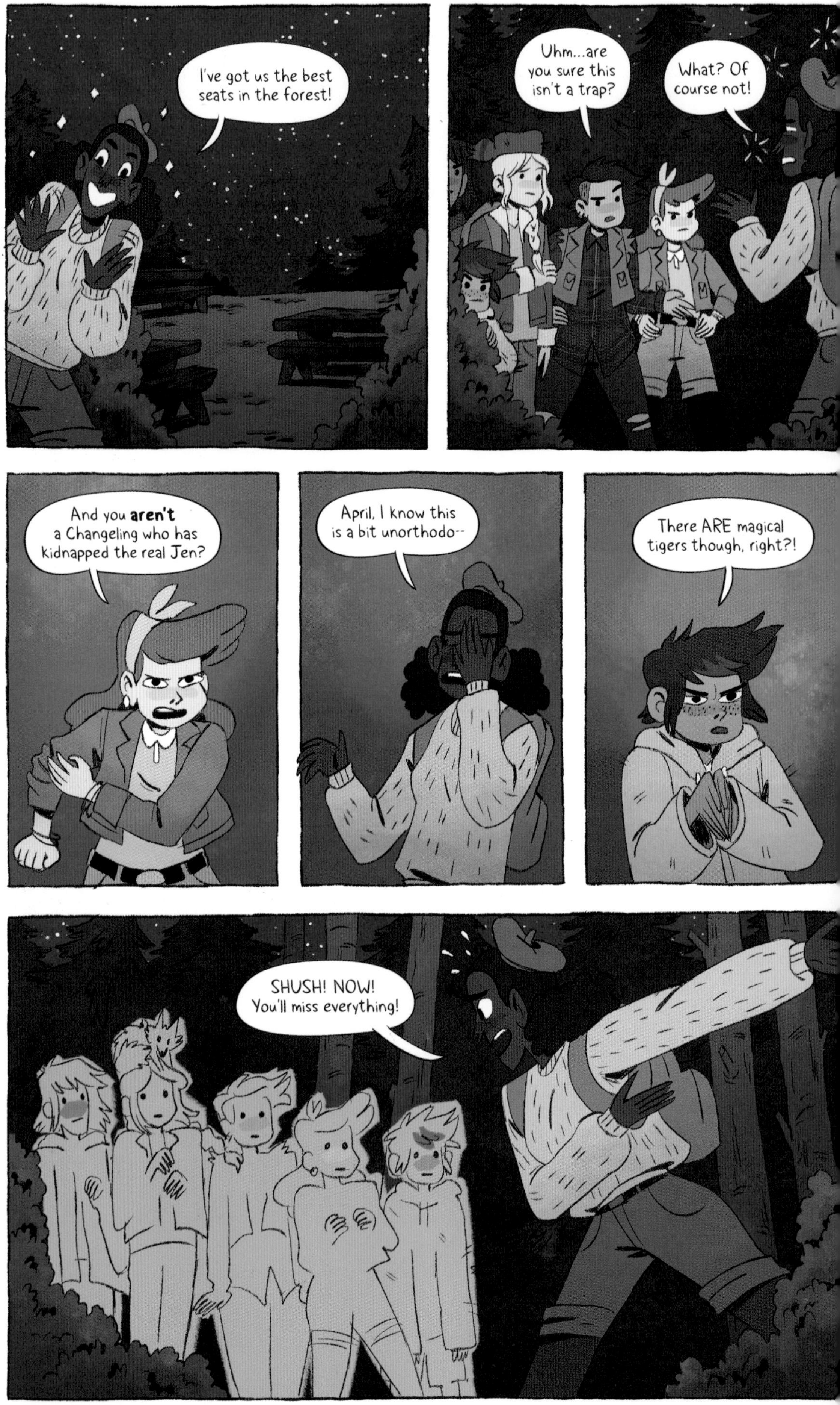
I've got us the best seats in the forest!
Uhm...are you sure this isn't a trap?
What? Of course not!
And you **aren't** a Changeling who has kidnapped the real Jen?
April, I know this is a bit unorthodo--
There ARE magical tigers though, right?!
SHUSH! NOW! You'll miss everything!

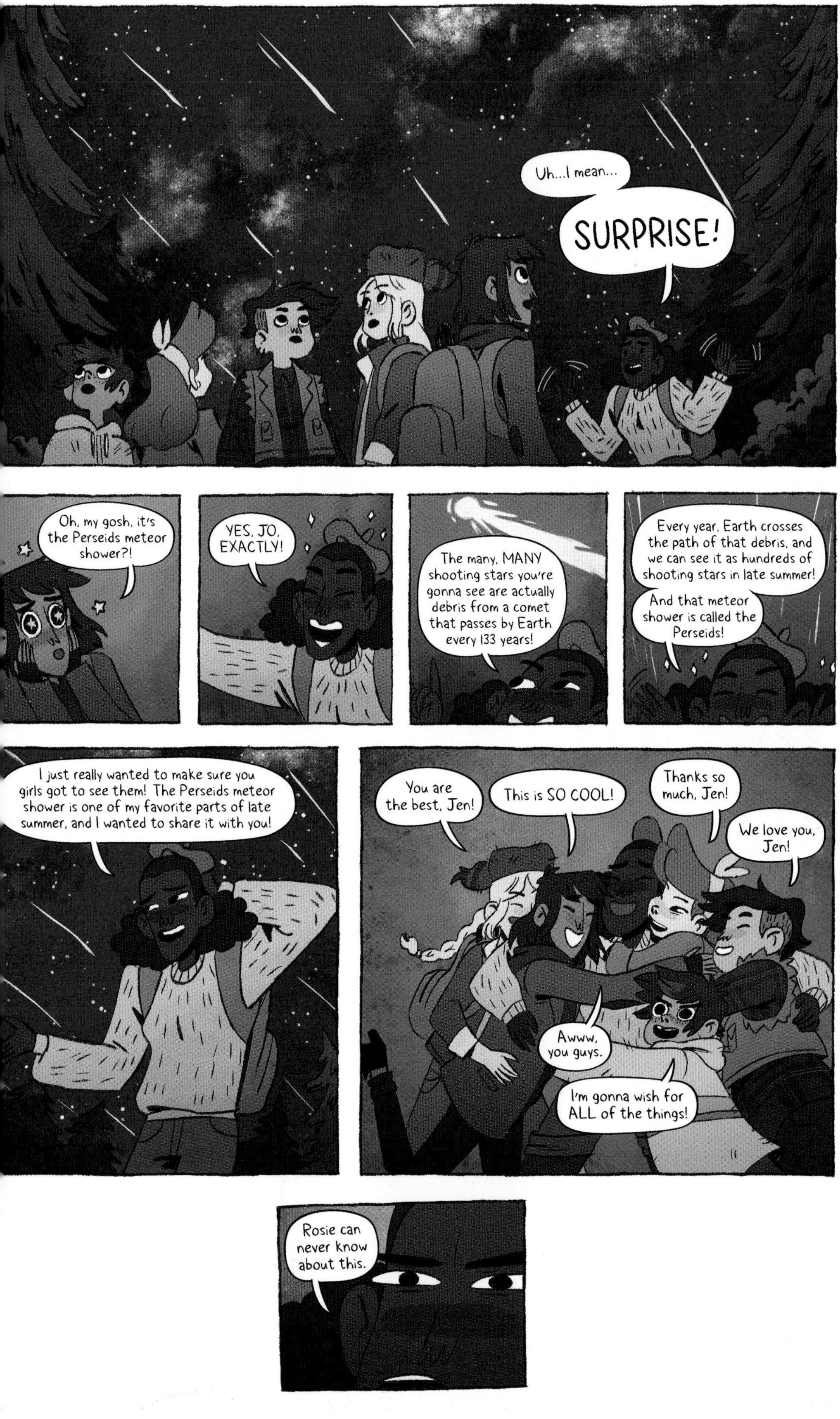

Uh...I mean...
SURPRISE!
Oh, my gosh, it's the Perseids meteor shower?!
YES, JO, EXACTLY!
The many, MANY shooting stars you're gonna see are actually debris from a comet that passes by Earth every 133 years!
Every year, Earth crosses the path of that debris, and we can see it as hundreds of shooting stars in late summer!
And that meteor shower is called the Perseids!
I just really wanted to make sure you girls got to see them! The Perseids meteor shower is one of my favorite parts of late summer, and I wanted to share it with you!
You are the best, Jen!
This is SO COOL!
Thanks so much, Jen!
We love you, Jen!
Awww, you guys.
I'm gonna wish for ALL of the things!
Rosie can never know about this.

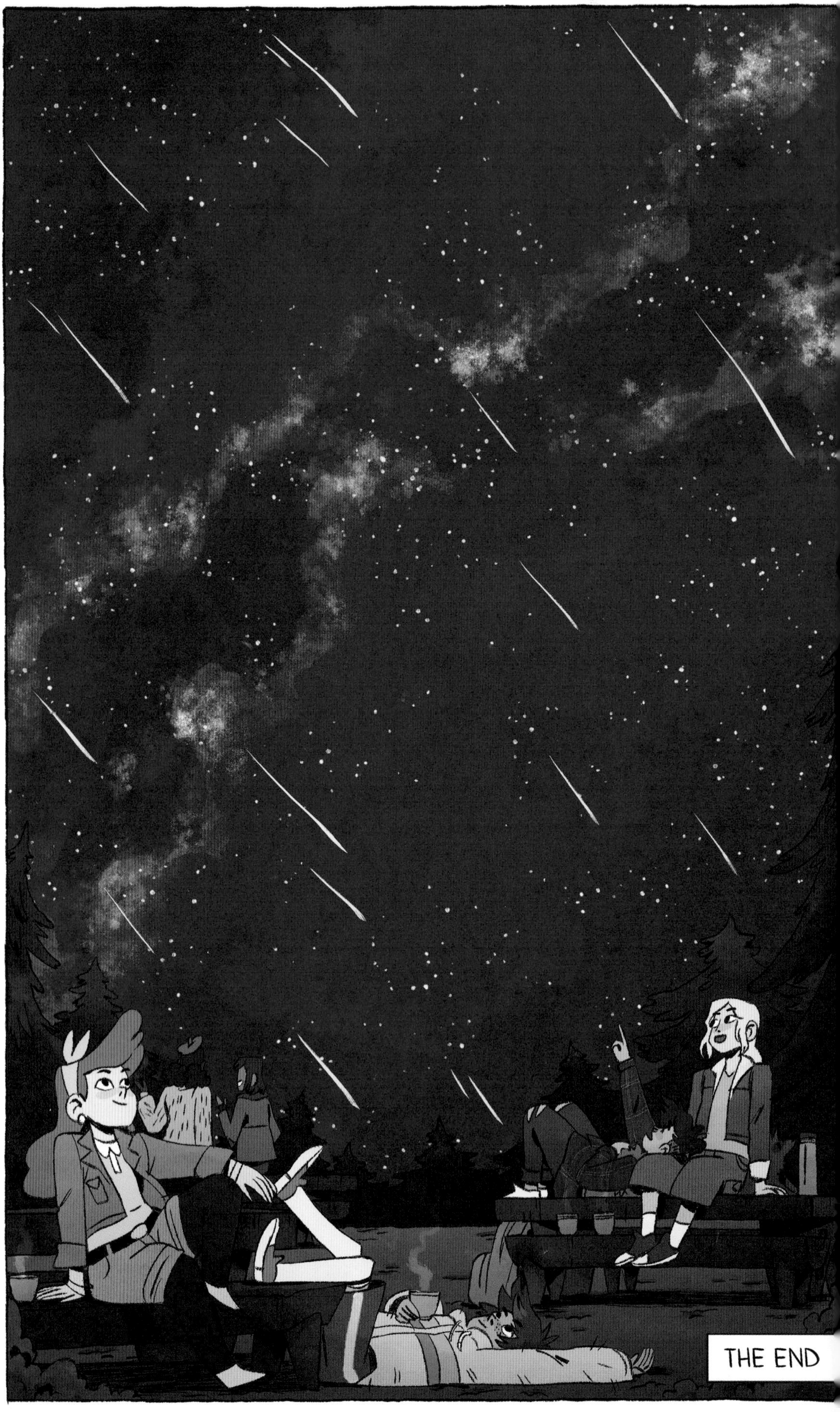
THE END

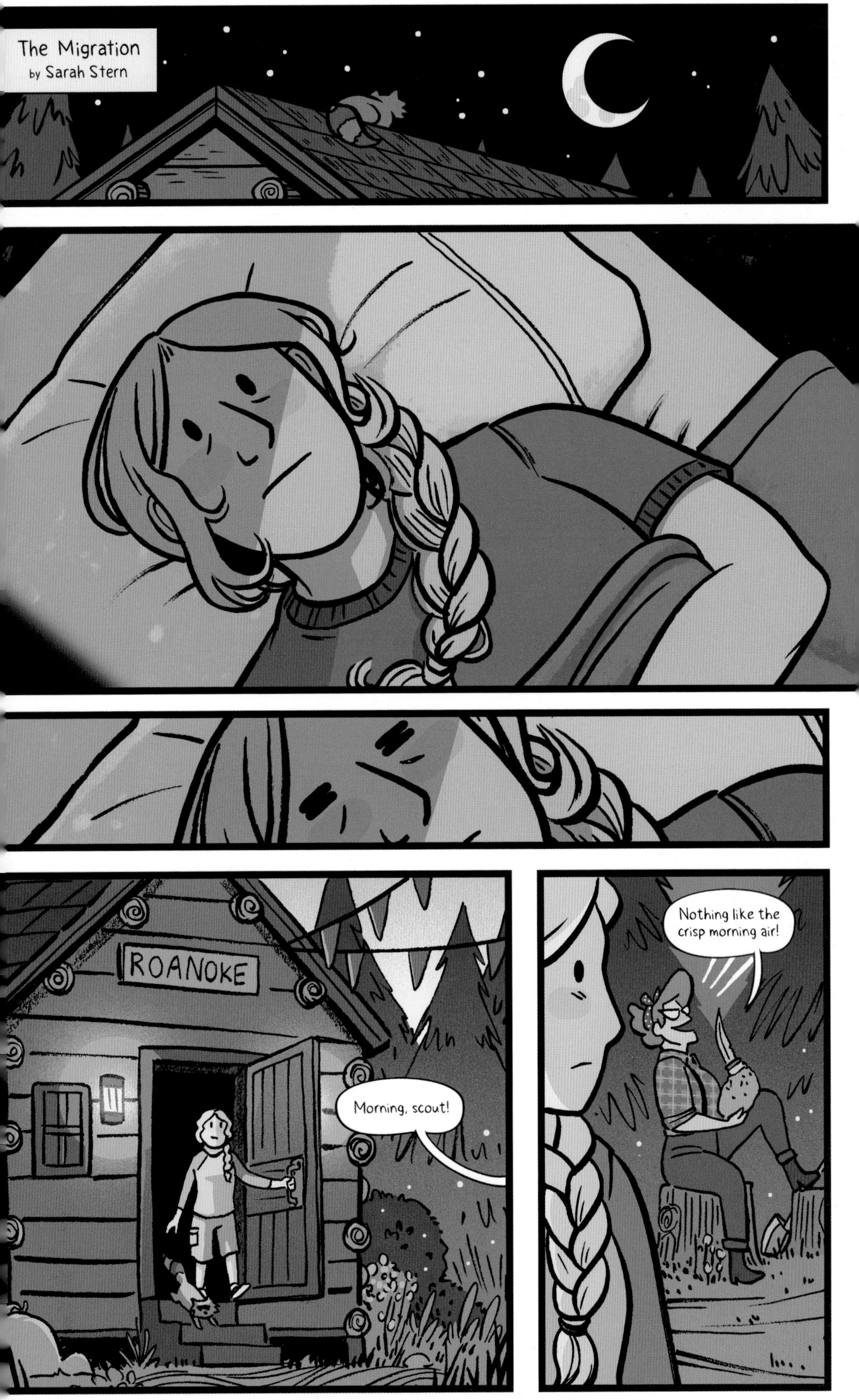
The Migration
by Sarah Stern
ROANOKE
Morning, scout!
Nothing like the crisp morning air!

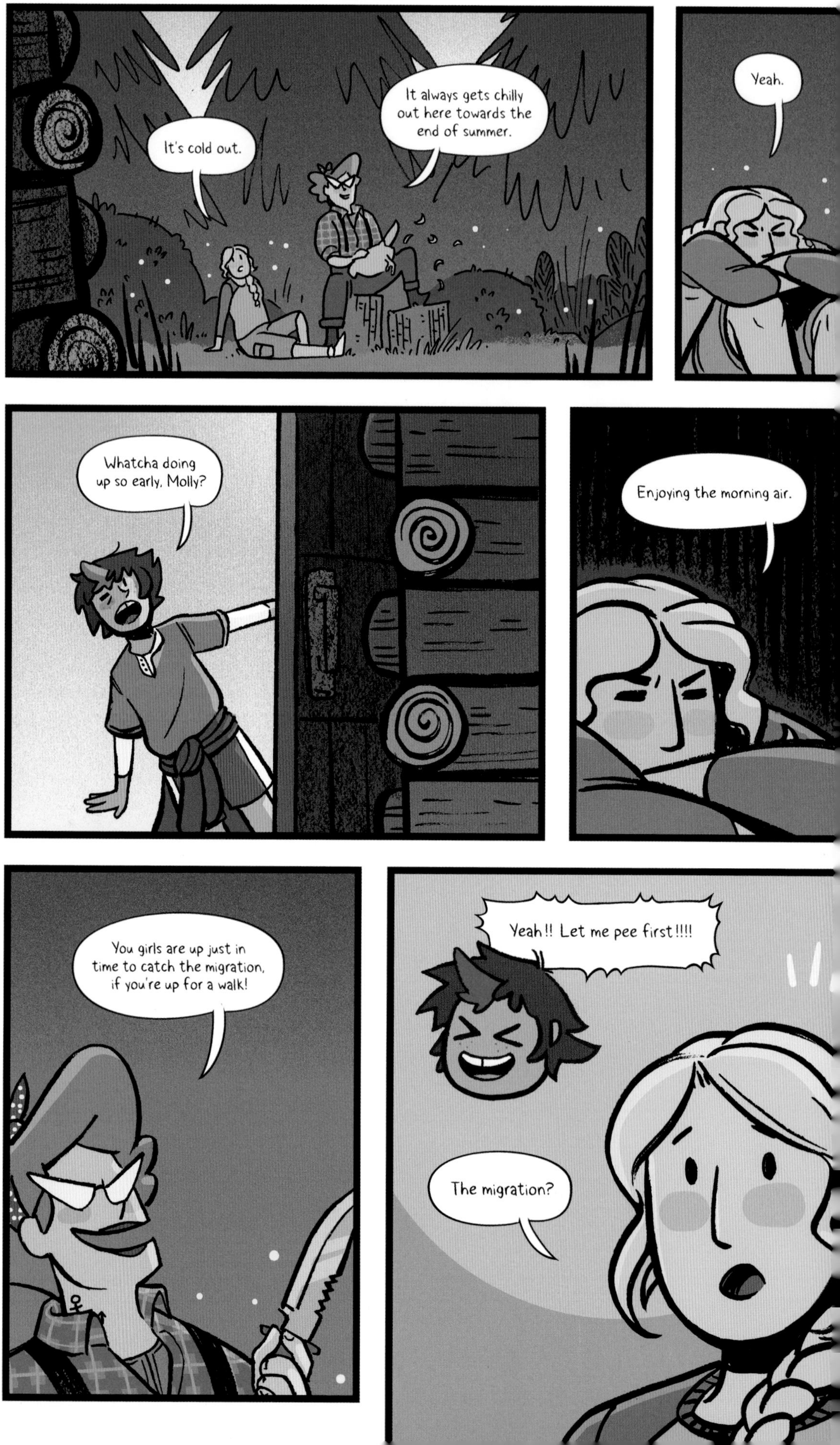
It's cold out.
It always gets chilly out here towards the end of summer.
Yeah.
Whatcha doing up so early, Molly?
Enjoying the morning air.
You girls are up just in time to catch the migration, if you're up for a walk!
Yeah!! Let me pee first!!!!
The migration?

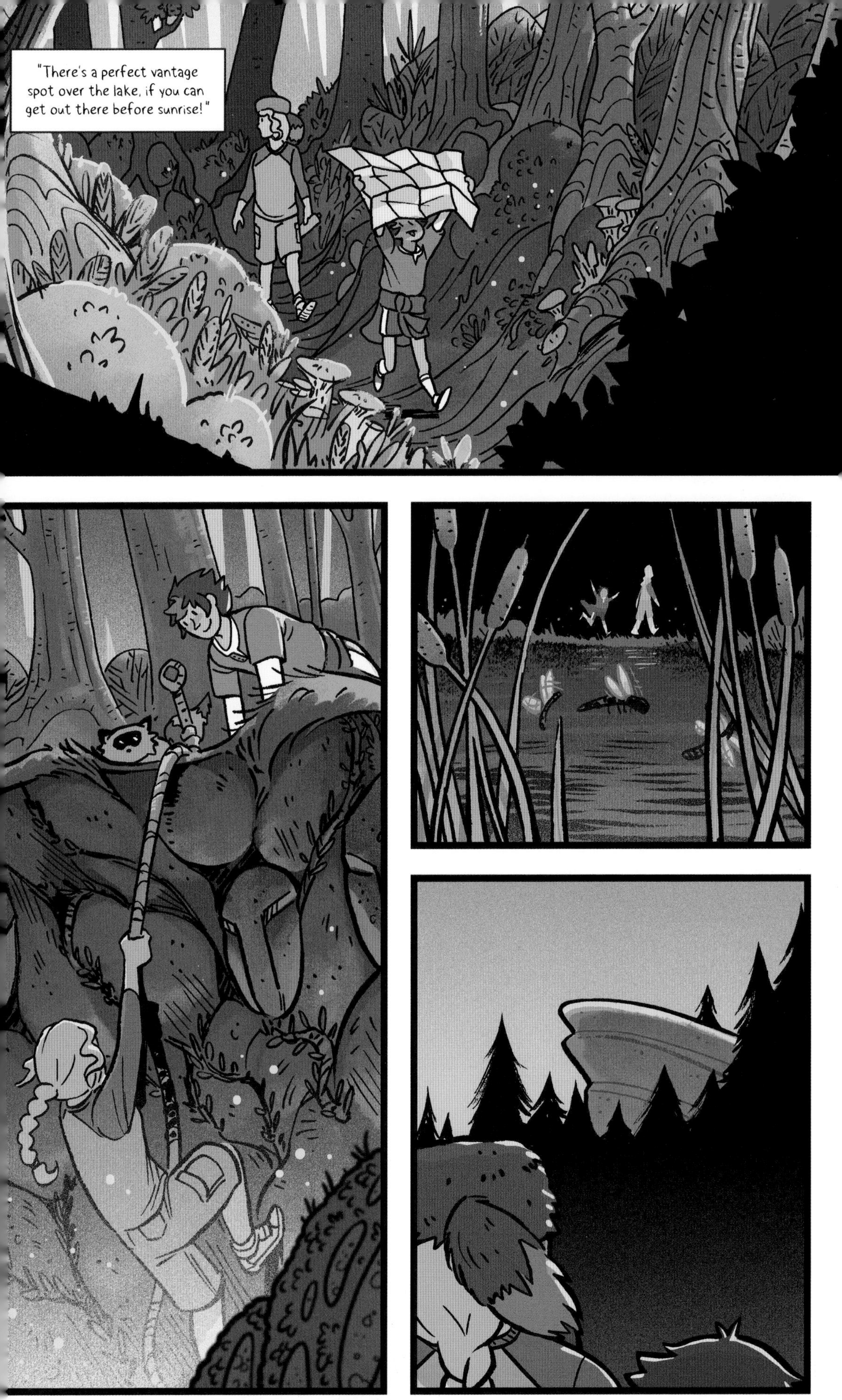
"There's a perfect vantage spot over the lake, if you can get out there before sunrise!"

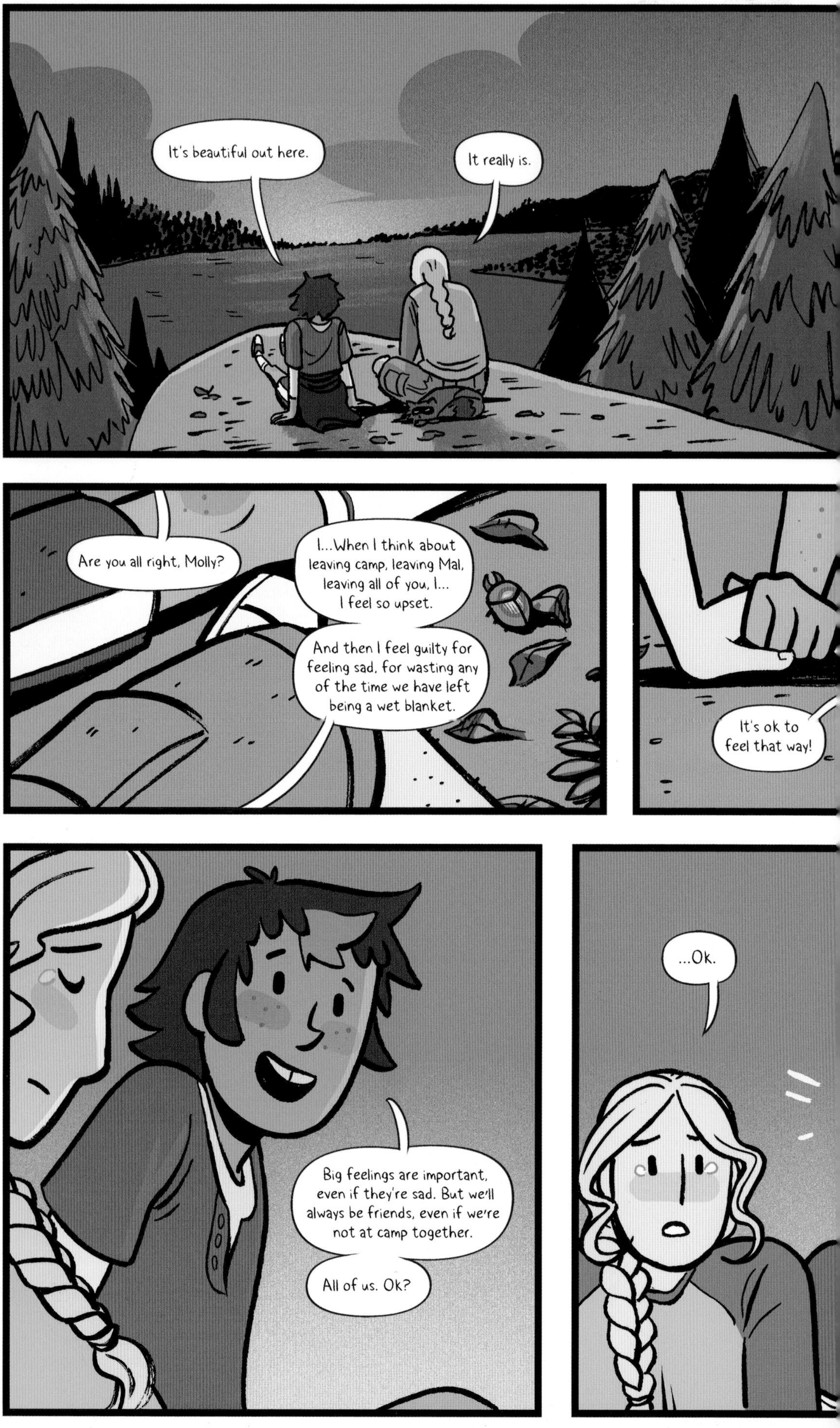
It's beautiful out here.
It really is.
Are you all right, Molly?
I... When I think about leaving camp, leaving Mal, leaving all of you, I... I feel so upset.
And then I feel guilty for feeling sad, for wasting any of the time we have left being a wet blanket.
It's ok to feel that way!
Big feelings are important, even if they're sad. But we'll always be friends, even if we're not at camp together.
All of us. Ok?
...Ok.

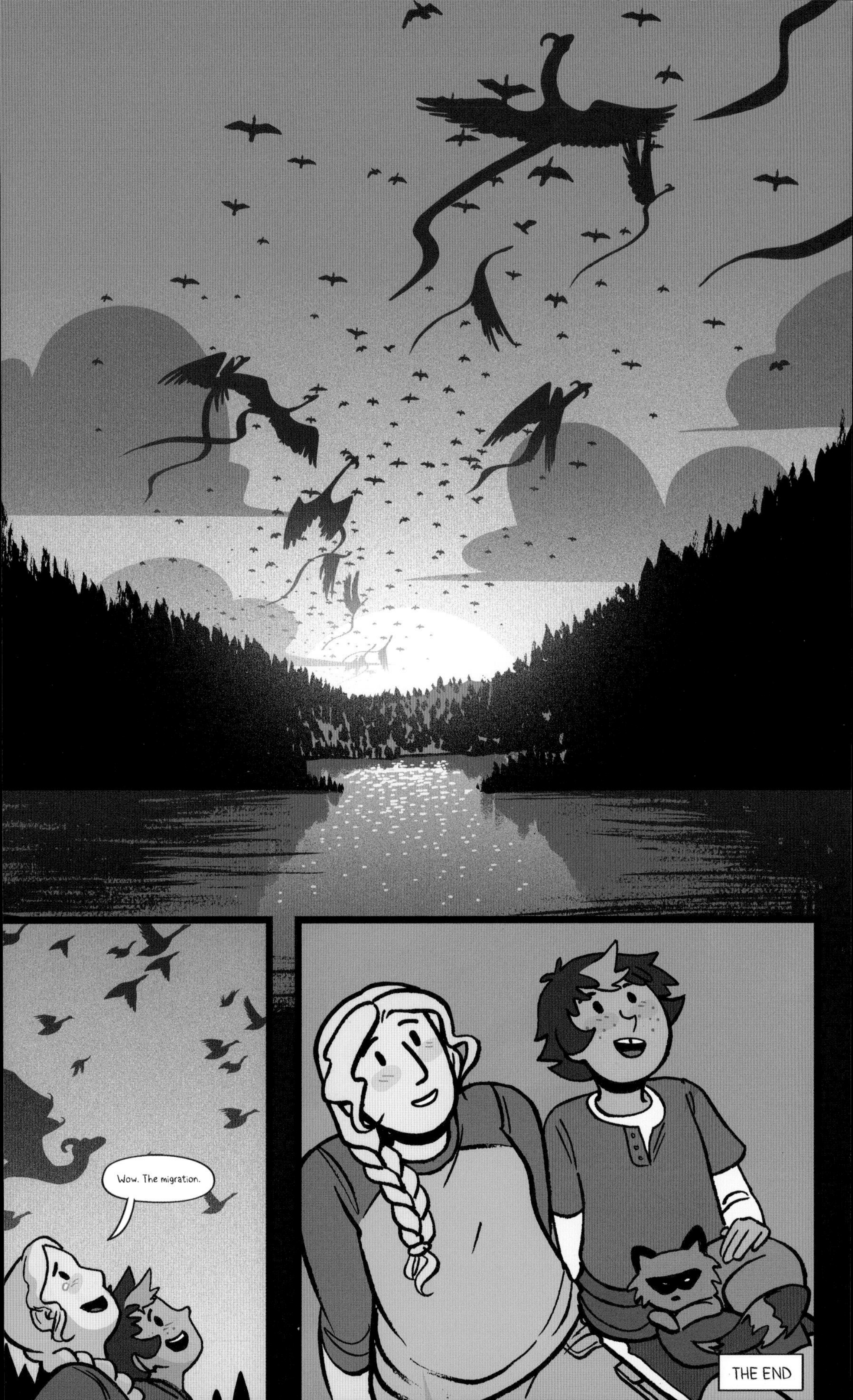
Wow. The migration.
THE END

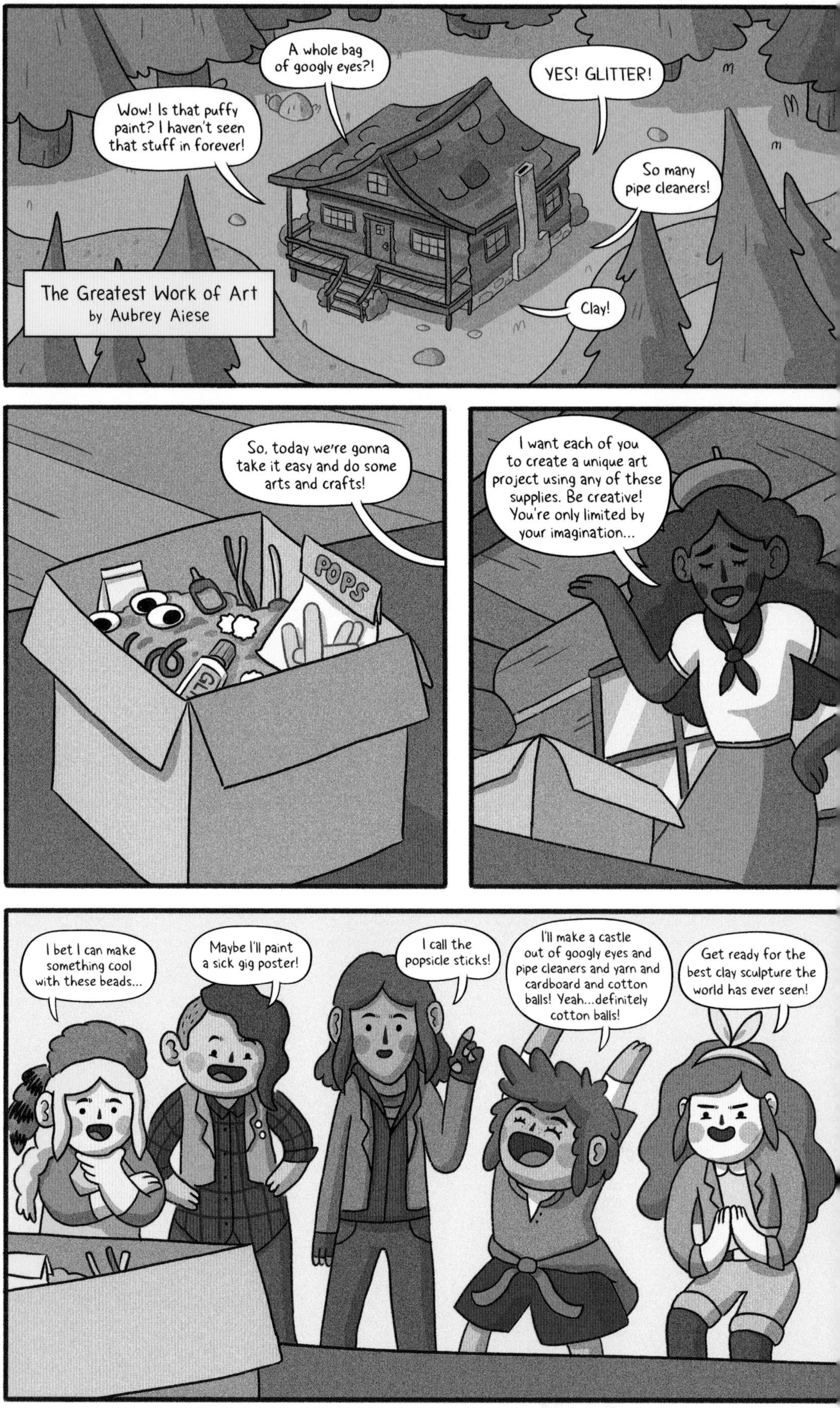

A whole bag of googly eyes?!
Wow! Is that puffy paint? I haven't seen that stuff in forever!
YES! GLITTER!
So many pipe cleaners!
The Greatest Work of Art
by Aubrey Aiese
Clay!
So, today we're gonna take it easy and do some arts and crafts!
POPS
GLUE
I want each of you to create a unique art project using any of these supplies. Be creative! You're only limited by your imagination...
I bet I can make something cool with these beads...
Maybe I'll paint a sick gig poster!
I call the popsicle sticks!
I'll make a castle out of googly eyes and pipe cleaners and yarn and cardboard and cotton balls! Yeah...definitely cotton balls!
Get ready for the best clay sculpture the world has ever seen!

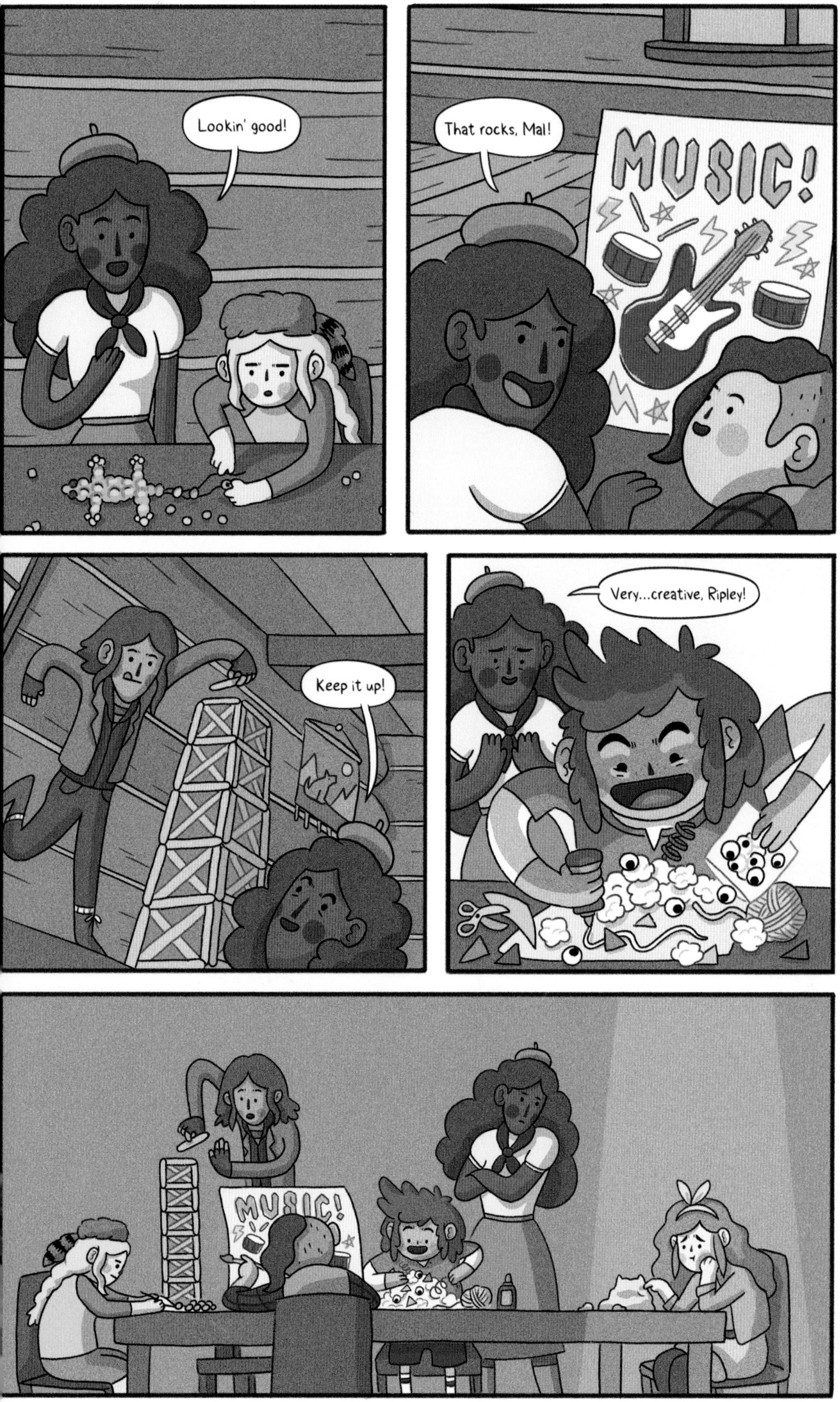
Lookin' good!
That rocks, Mal!
MUSIC!
Keep it up!
Very...creative, Ripley!
MUSIC!

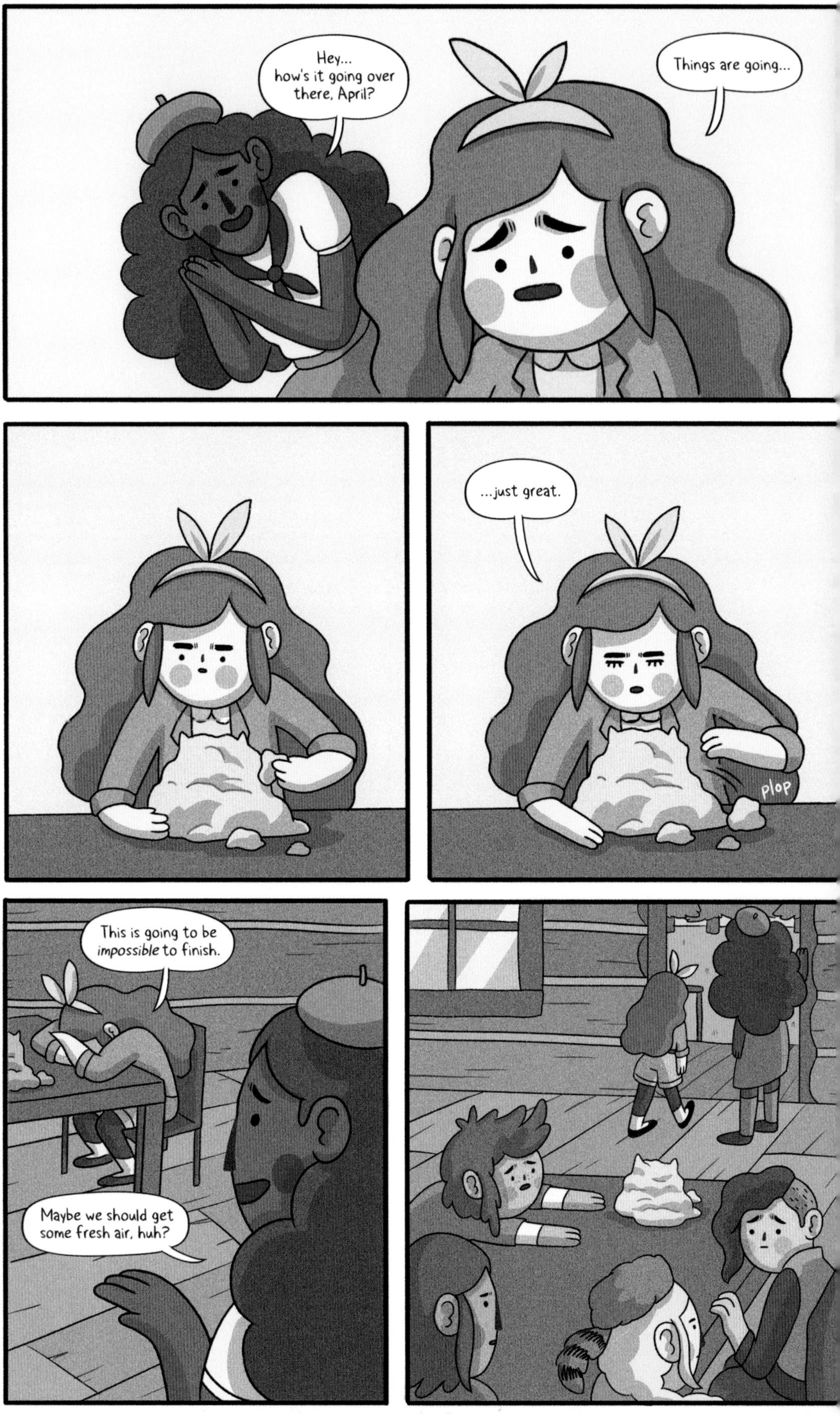
Hey... how's it going over there, April?
Things are going...
...just great.
plop
This is going to be *impossible* to finish.
Maybe we should get some fresh air, huh?

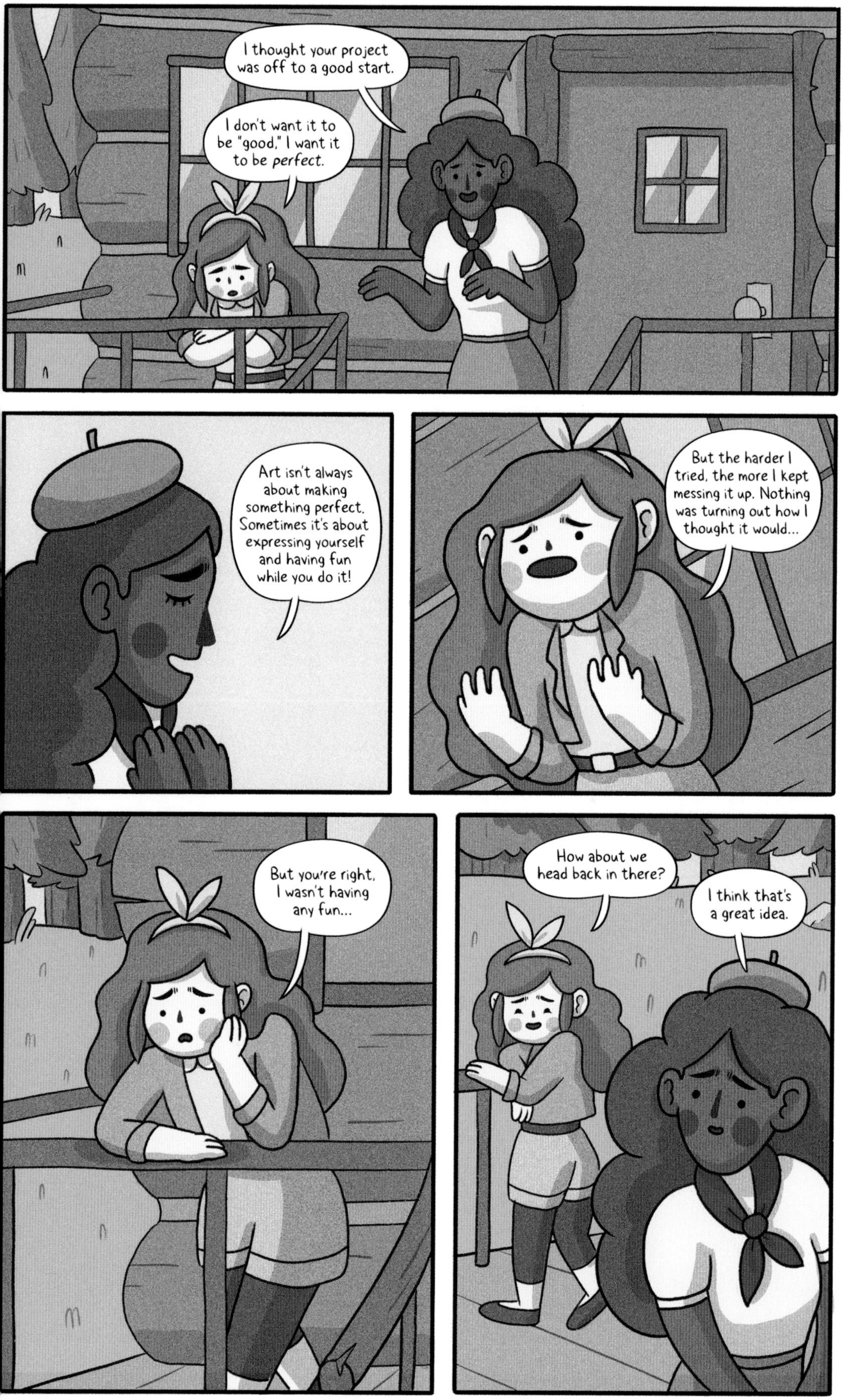

I thought your project was off to a good start.
I don't want it to be "good," I want it to be *perfect*.
Art isn't always about making something perfect. Sometimes it's about expressing yourself and having fun while you do it!
But the harder I tried, the more I kept messing it up. Nothing was turning out how I thought it would...
But you're right, I wasn't having any fun...
How about we head back in there?
I think that's a great idea.

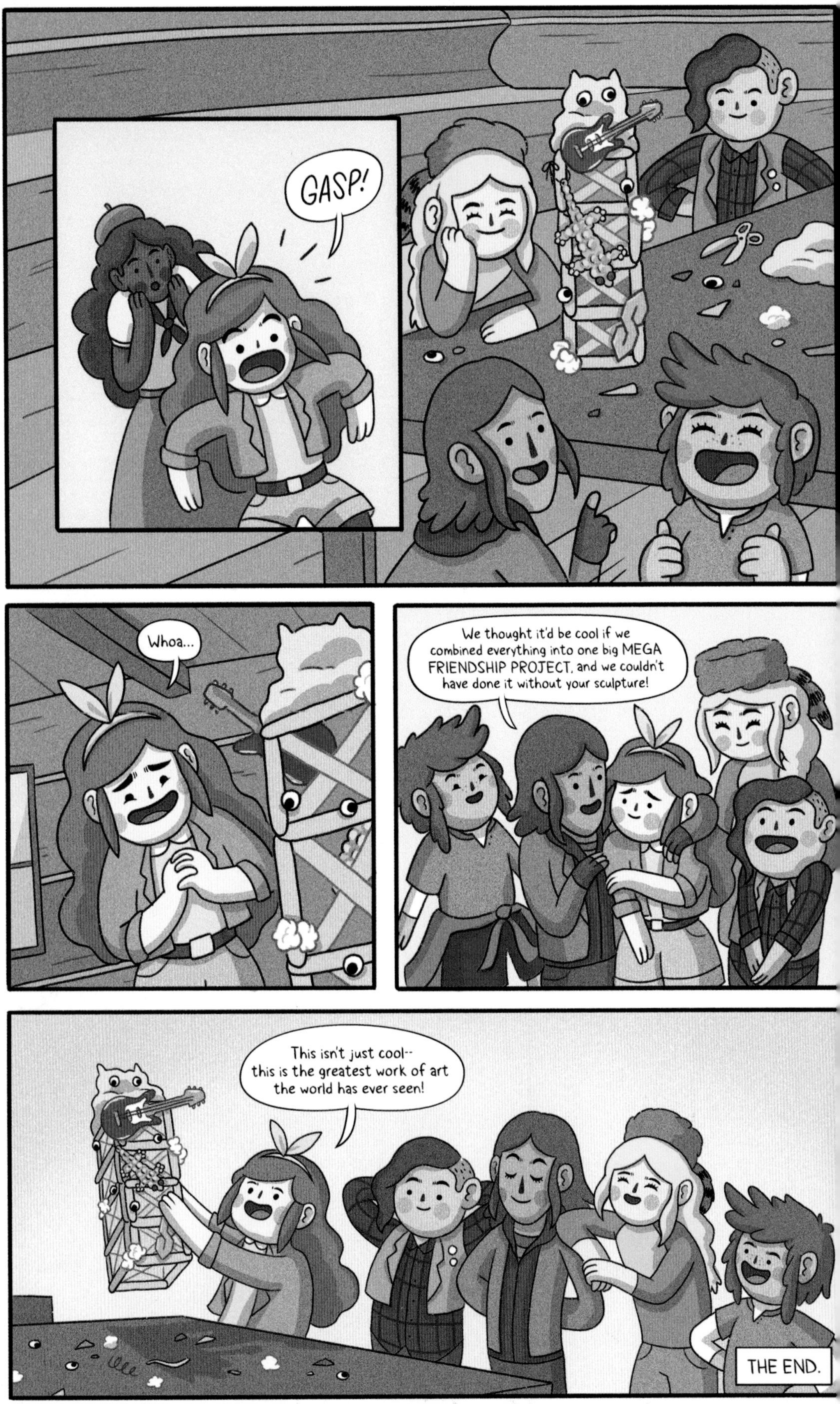
GASP!
Whoa...
We thought it'd be cool if we combined everything into one big MEGA FRIENDSHIP PROJECT, and we couldn't have done it without your sculpture!
This isn't just cool-- this is the greatest work of art the world has ever seen!
THE END.

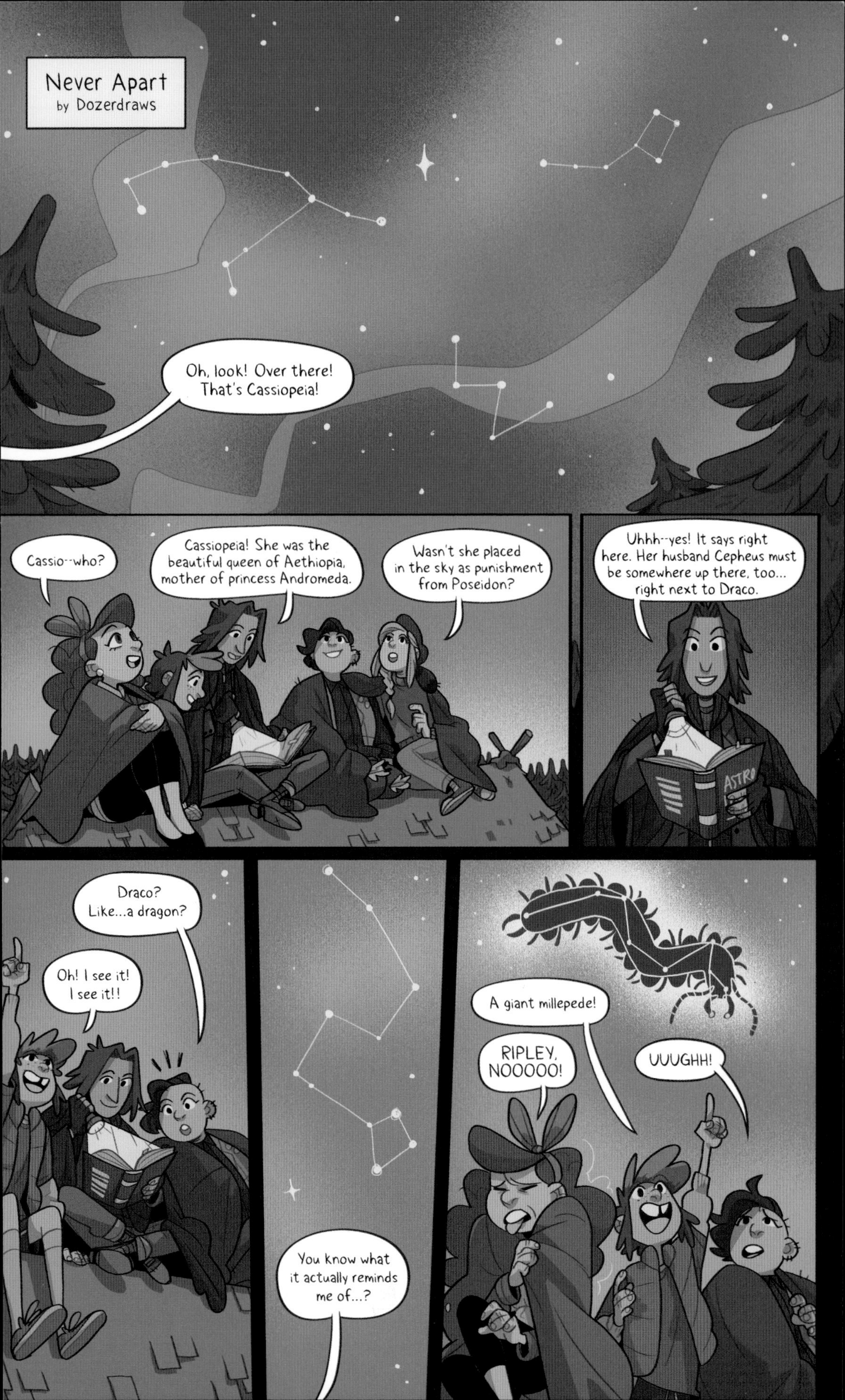
Never Apart
by Dozerdraws
Oh, look! Over there! That's Cassiopeia!
Cassio--who?
Cassiopeia! She was the beautiful queen of Aethiopia, mother of princess Andromeda.
Wasn't she placed in the sky as punishment from Poseidon?
Uhhh--yes! It says right here. Her husband Cepheus must be somewhere up there, too... right next to Draco.
ASTRO
Draco? Like...a dragon?
Oh! I see it! I see it!!
You know what it actually reminds me of...?
A giant millepede!
RIPLEY, NOOOOO!
UUUGHH!

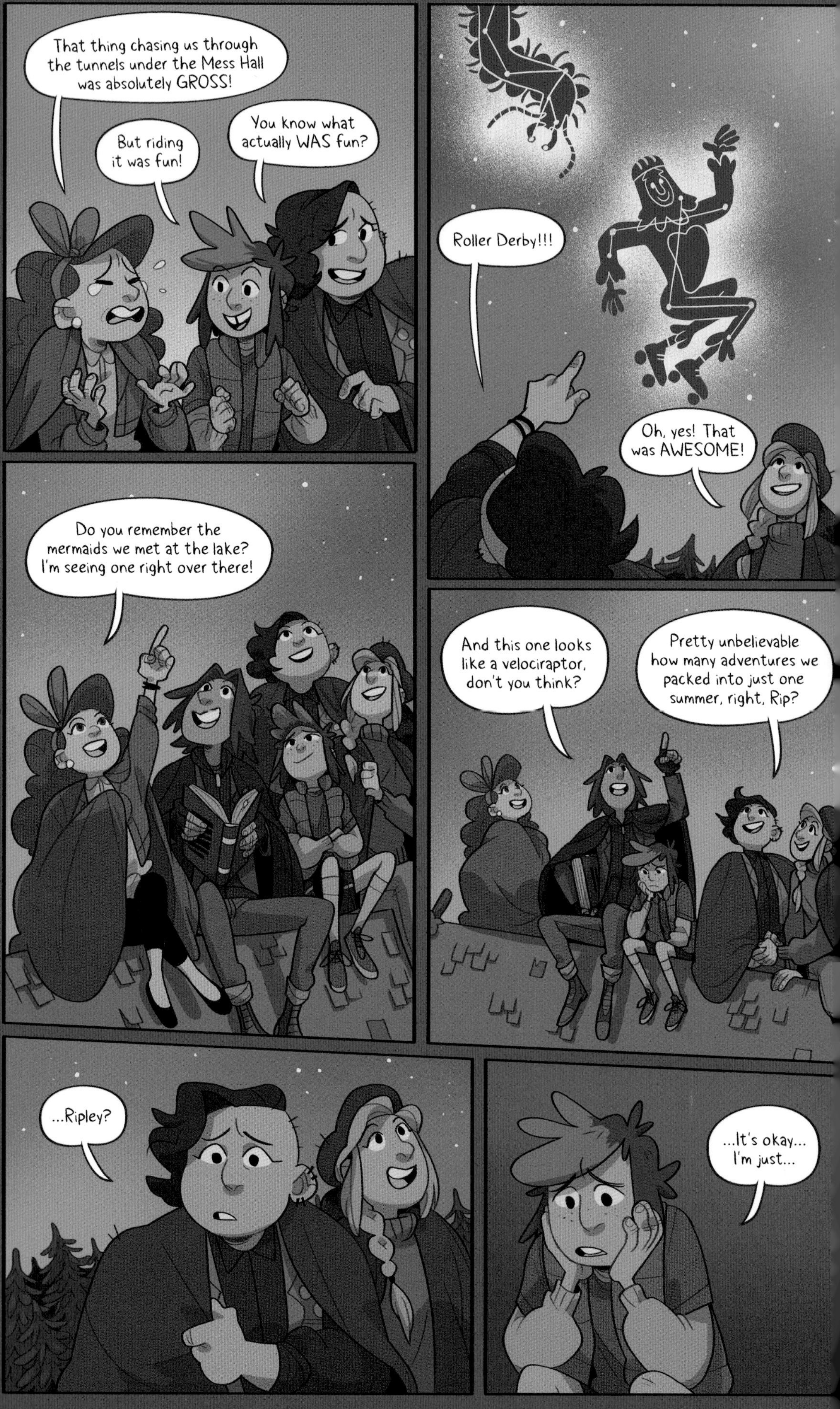
That thing chasing us through the tunnels under the Mess Hall was absolutely GROSS!
But riding it was fun!
You know what actually WAS fun?
Roller Derby!!!
Oh, yes! That was AWESOME!
Do you remember the mermaids we met at the lake? I'm seeing one right over there!
And this one looks like a velociraptor, don't you think?
Pretty unbelievable how many adventures we packed into just one summer, right, Rip?
...Ripley?
...It's okay... I'm just...

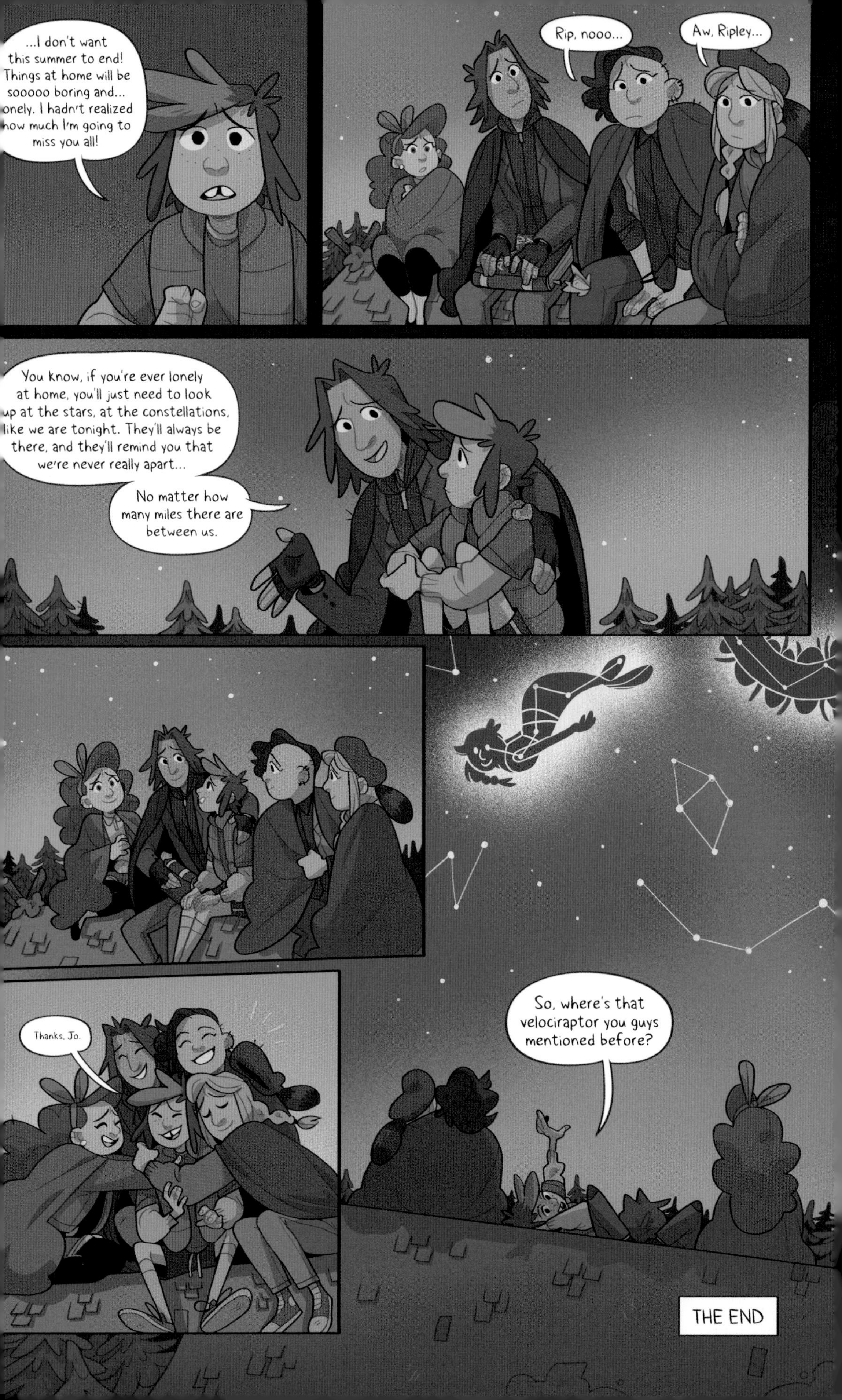
...I don't want this summer to end! Things at home will be sooooo boring and... lonely. I hadn't realized how much I'm going to miss you all!
Rip, nooo...
Aw, Ripley...
You know, if you're ever lonely at home, you'll just need to look up at the stars, at the constellations, like we are tonight. They'll always be there, and they'll remind you that we're never really apart...
No matter how many miles there are between us.
Thanks, Jo.
So, where's that velociraptor you guys mentioned before?
THE END

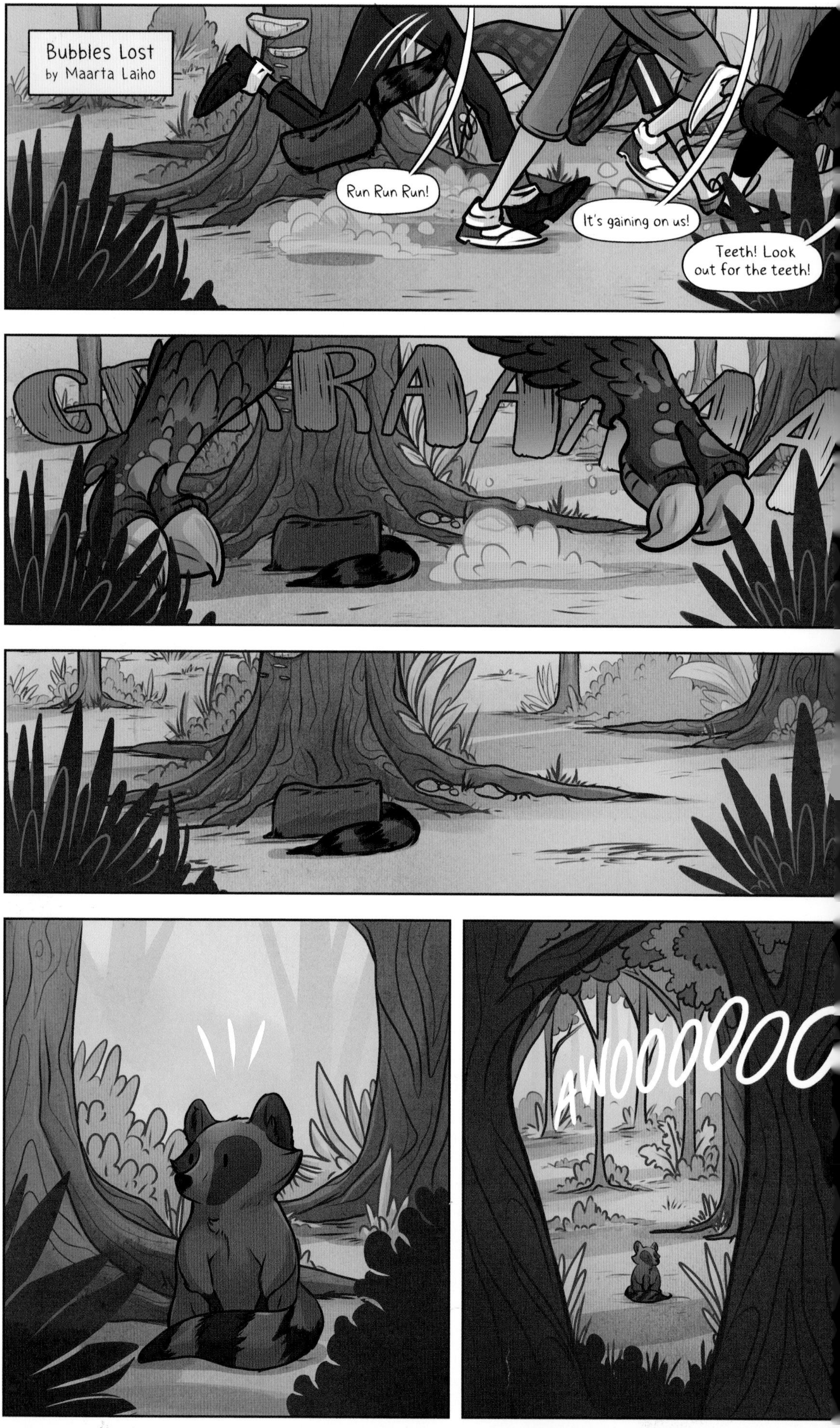

Bubbles Lost
by Maarta Laiho
Run Run Run!
It's gaining on us!
Teeth! Look out for the teeth!
GRRAAAA
AWOOOOOO

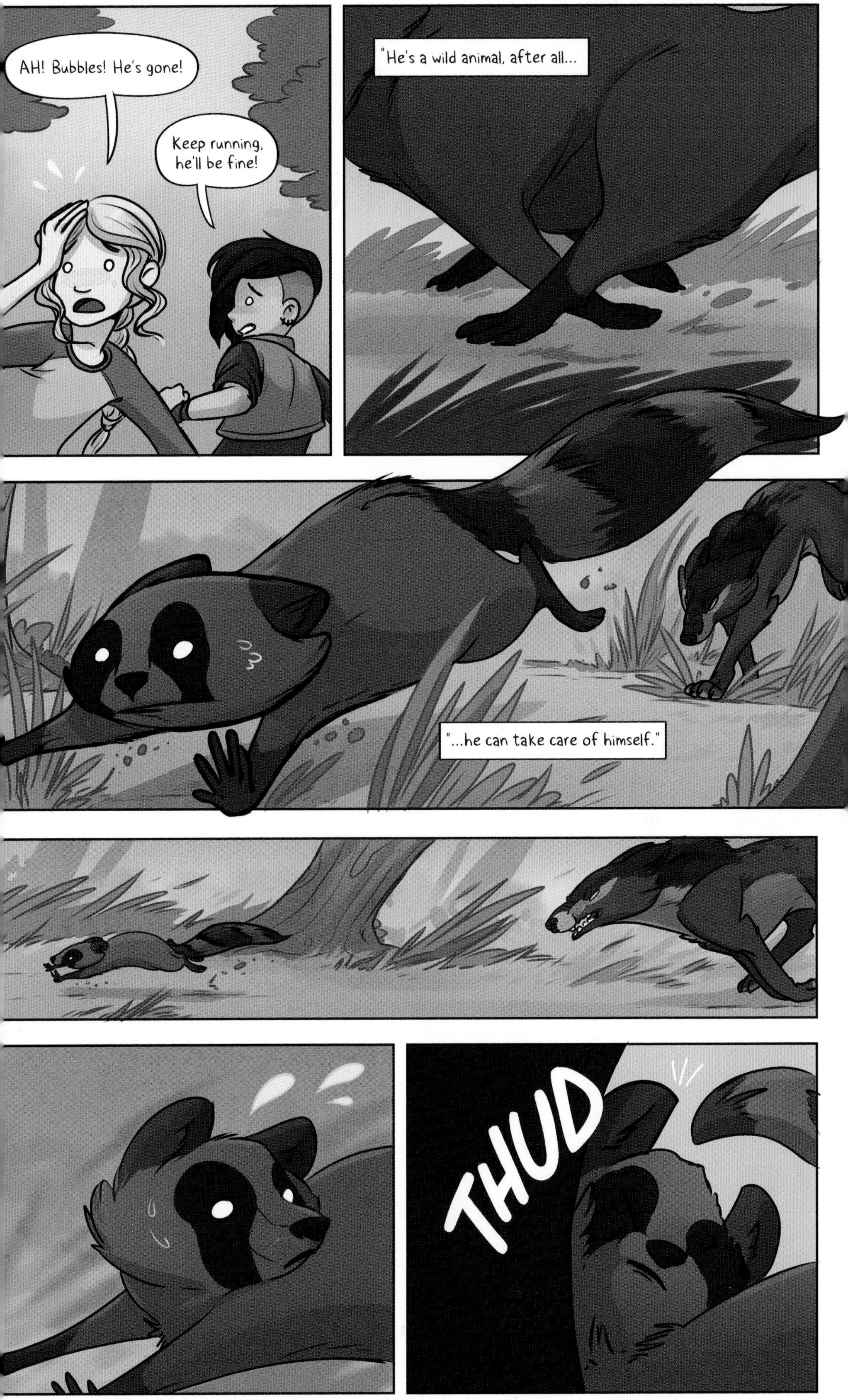
AH! Bubbles! He's gone!
Keep running, he'll be fine!
"He's a wild animal, after all...
"...he can take care of himself."
THUD

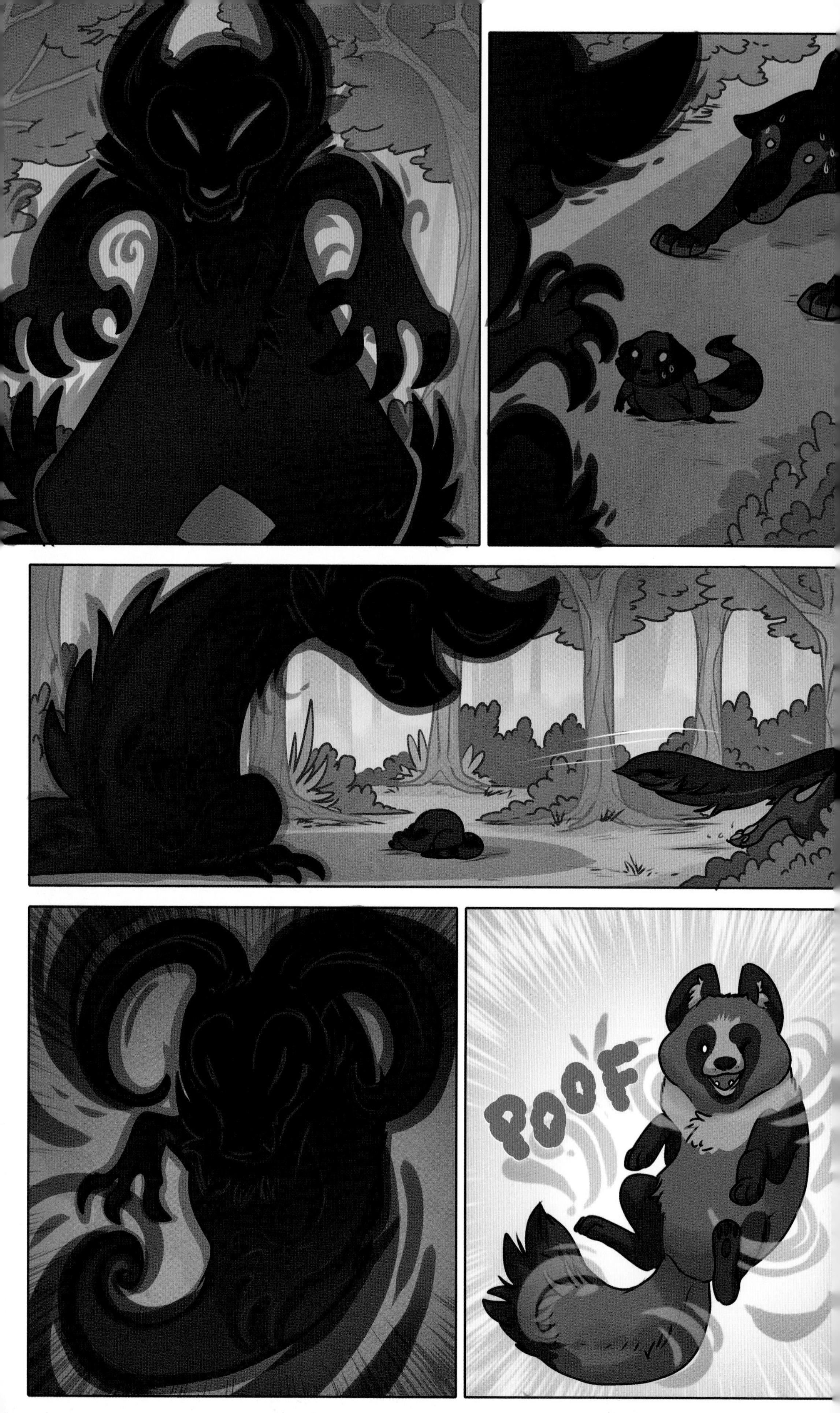
POOF

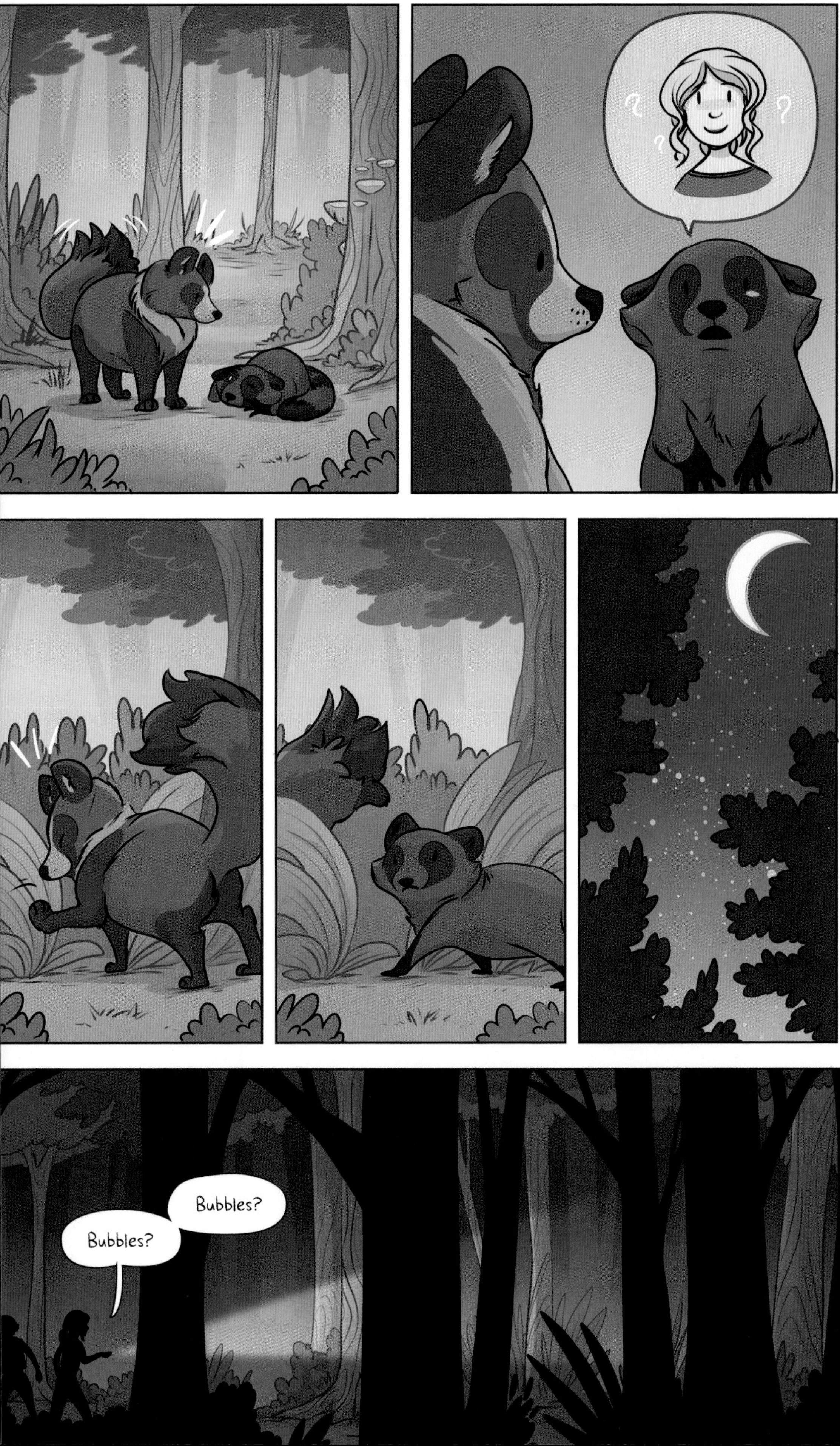
Bubbles?
Bubbles?

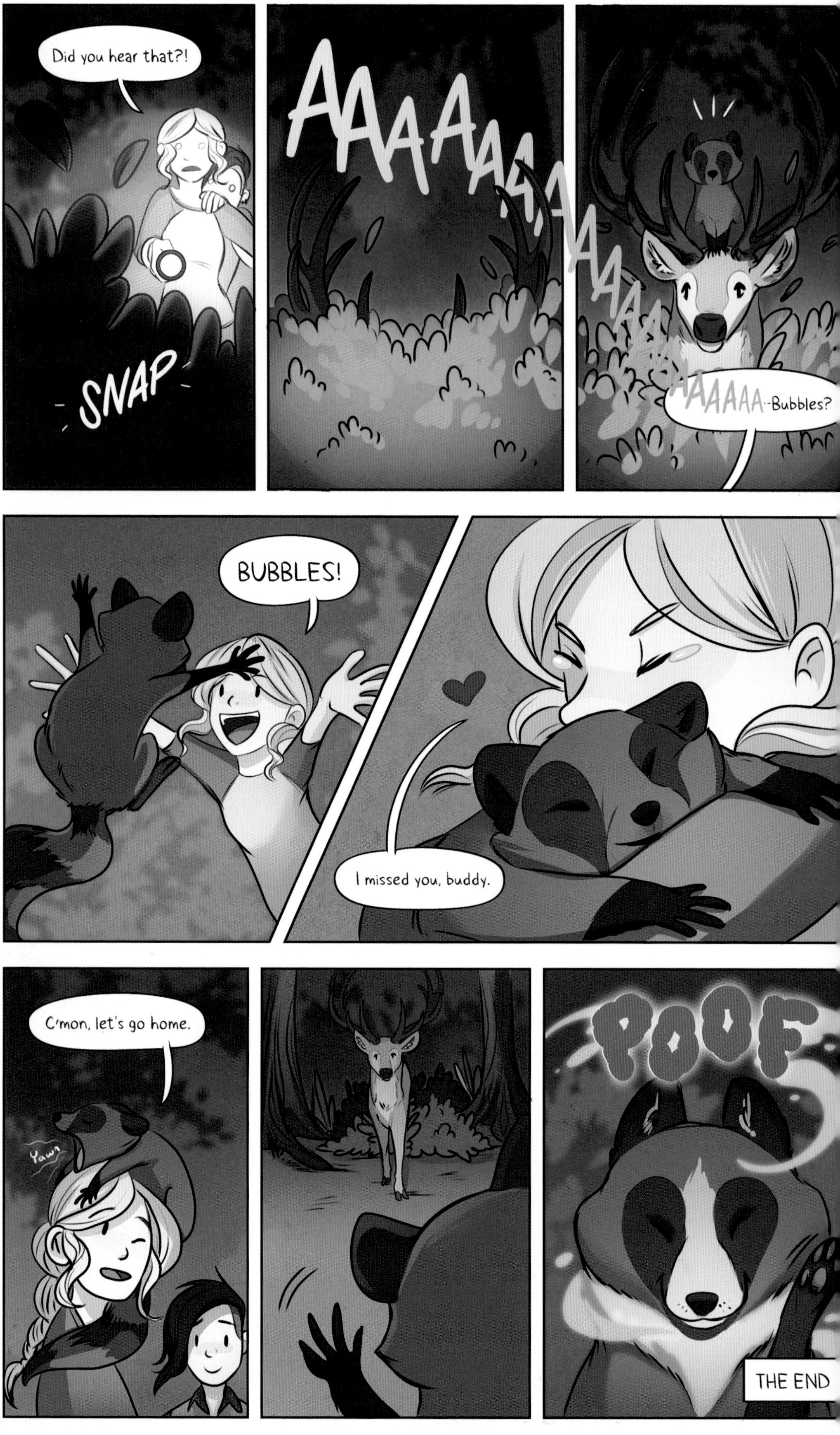

Did you hear that?!
SNAP
AAAAAAAAAAAAAAAAA
AAAAA--Bubbles?
BUBBLES!
I missed you, buddy.
C'mon, let's go home.
Yawn
POOF
THE END

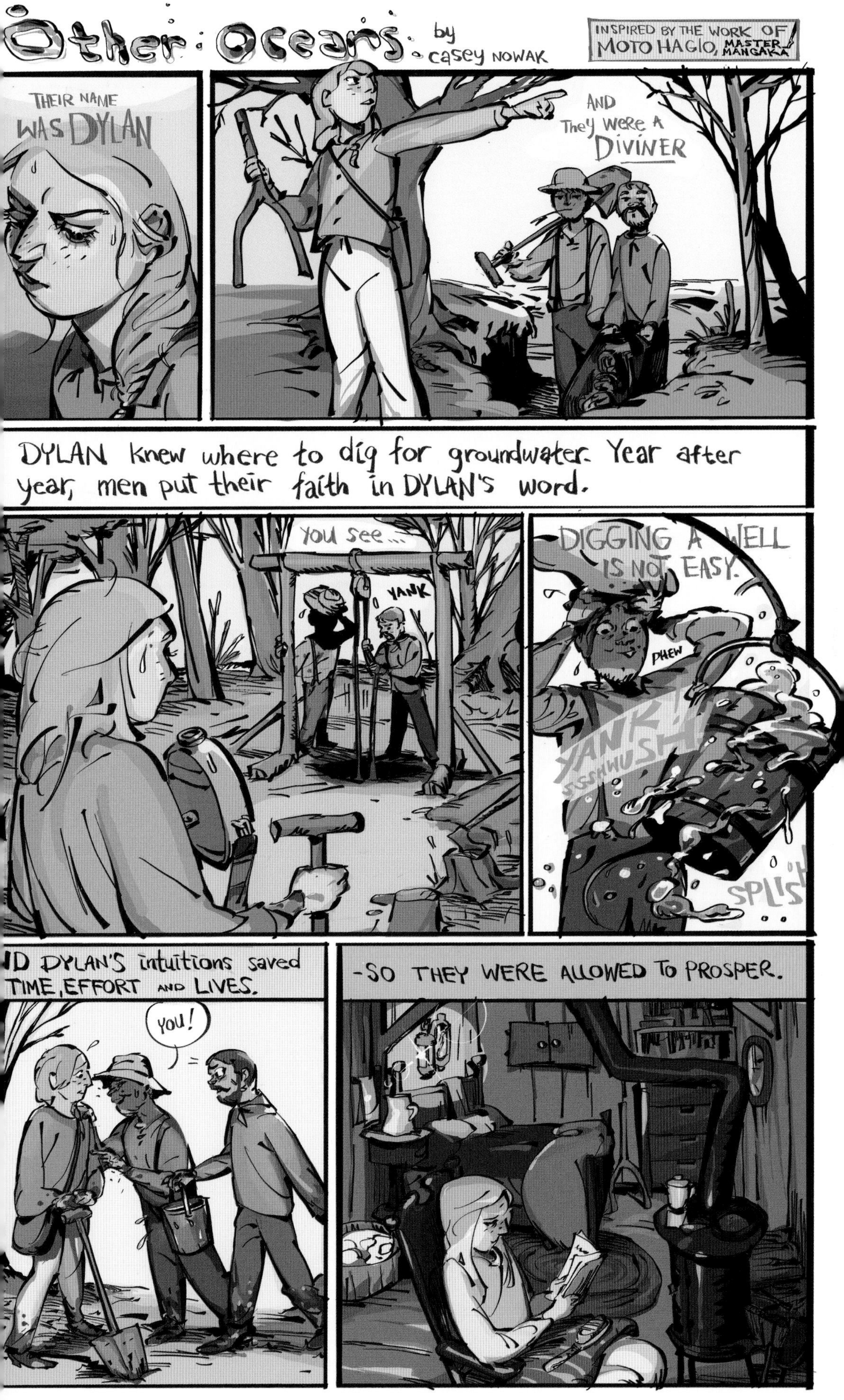
Other Oceans
by casey NOWAK
INSPIRED BY THE WORK OF MOTO HAGIO, MASTER MANGAKA!
THEIR NAME WAS DYLAN
AND They were A DIVINER
DYLAN knew where to dig for groundwater. Year after year, men put their faith in DYLAN'S word.
YOU See...
YANK
DIGGING A WELL IS NOT EASY.
PHEW
YANK!
SSSHWUSH!
SPLISH
ID DYLAN'S intuitions saved TIME, EFFORT AND LIVES.
YOU!
-SO THEY WERE ALLOWED TO PROSPER.

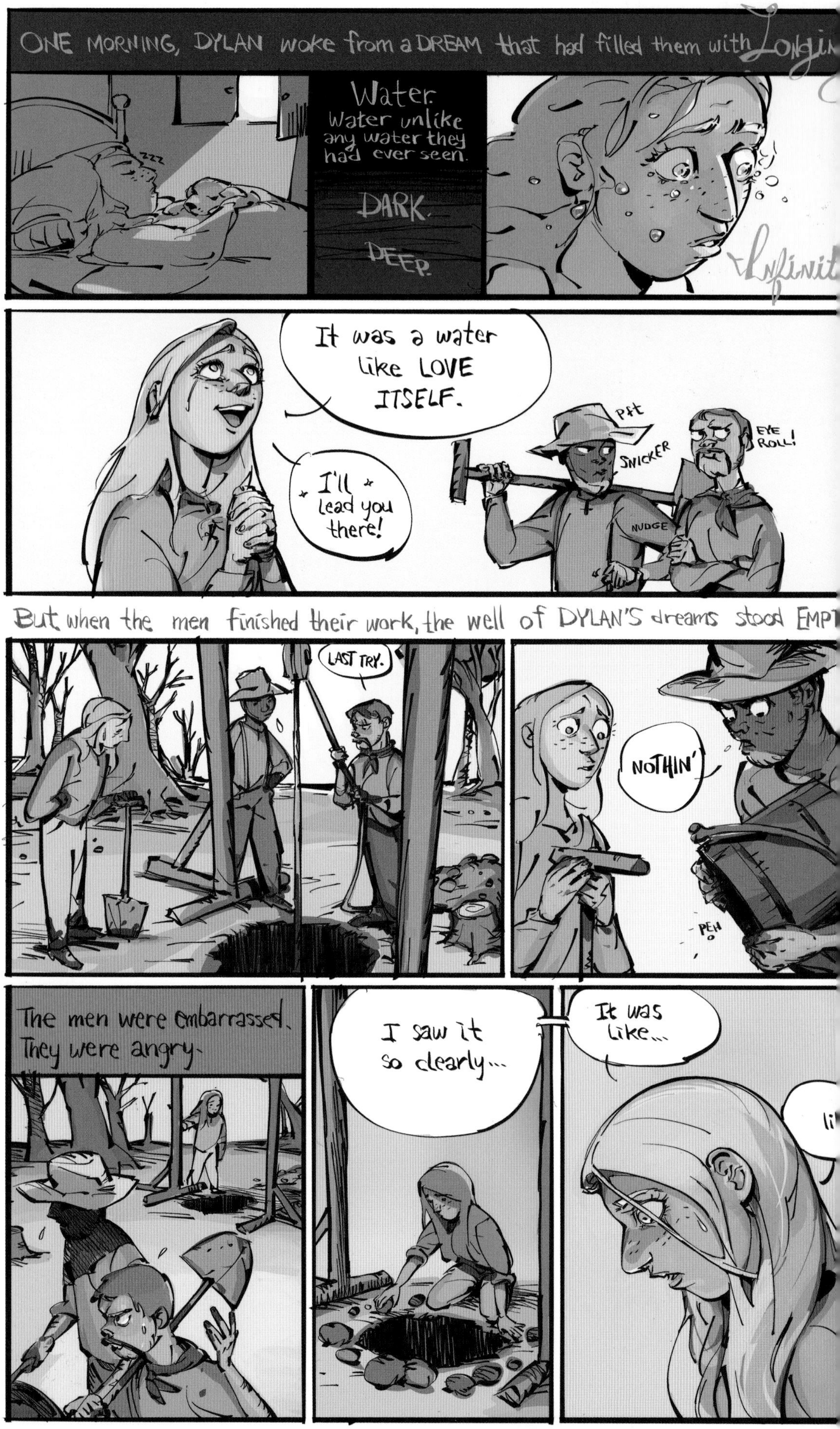
ONE MORNING, DYLAN woke from a DREAM that had filled them with Longin
Water.
Water unlike any water they had ever seen.
DARK.
DEEP.
Infinit
It was a water like LOVE ITSELF.
I'll lead you there!
Pft
SNICKER
EYE ROLL!
NUDGE
But when the men finished their work, the well of DYLAN'S dreams stood EMPT
LAST TRY.
NOTHIN'
PEH
The men were embarrassed. They were angry.
I saw it so clearly...
It was like...
li

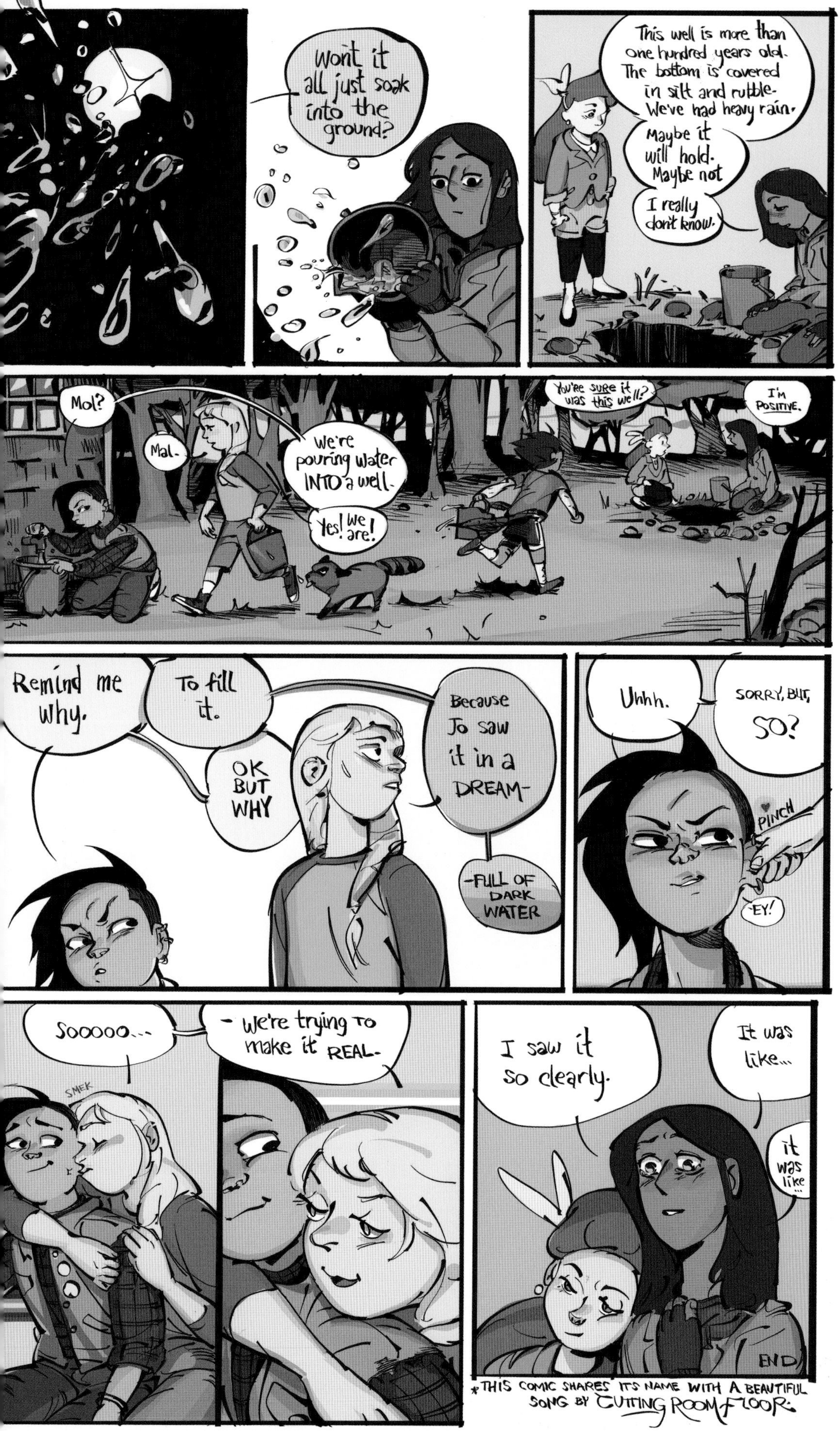
Won't it all just soak into the ground?
This well is more than one hundred years old. The bottom is covered in silt and rubble. We've had heavy rain.
Maybe it will hold. Maybe not
I really don't know.
Mol?
Mal.
We're pouring water INTO a well.
Yes! We are!
You're SURE it was this well?
I'M POSITIVE.
Remind me why.
To fill it.
OK BUT WHY
Because Jo saw it in a DREAM-
-FULL OF DARK WATER
Uhhh.
SORRY, BUT, SO?
PINCH
-EY!
Sooooo...
- We're trying to make it REAL.
SMEK
I saw it so clearly.
It was like...
it was like...
END
*THIS COMIC SHARES ITS NAME WITH A BEAUTIFUL SONG BY CUTTING ROOM FLOOR.

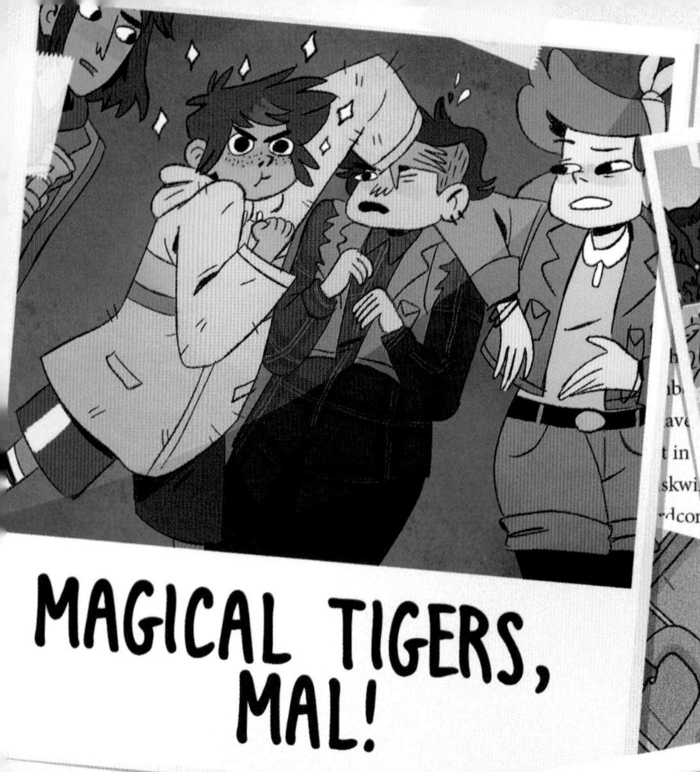
MAGICAL TIGERS, MAL!

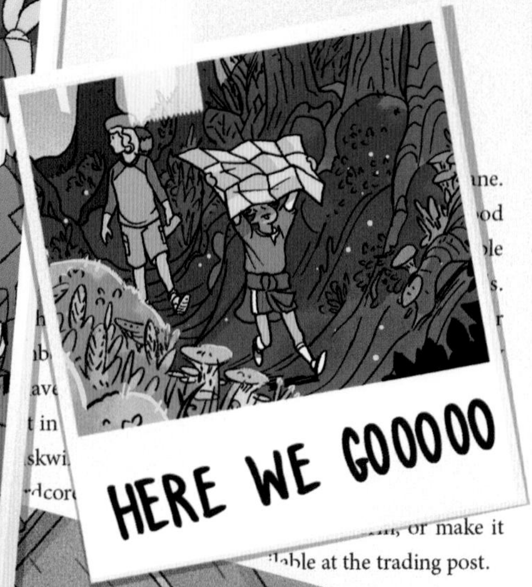
HERE WE GOOOOO

…m, or make it it
…ilable at the trading post.

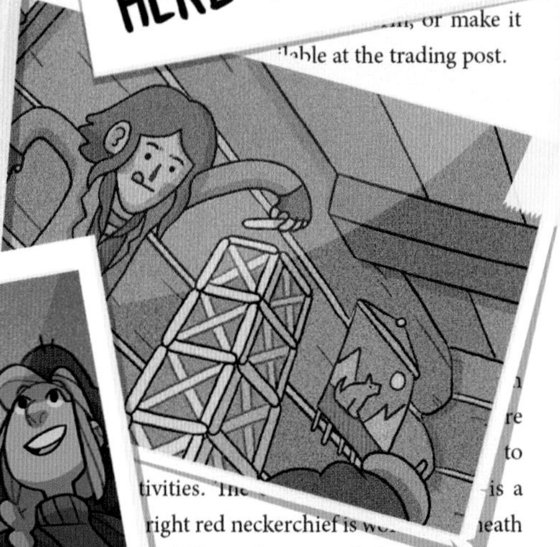

The Lumberjane uniform …
meeting…

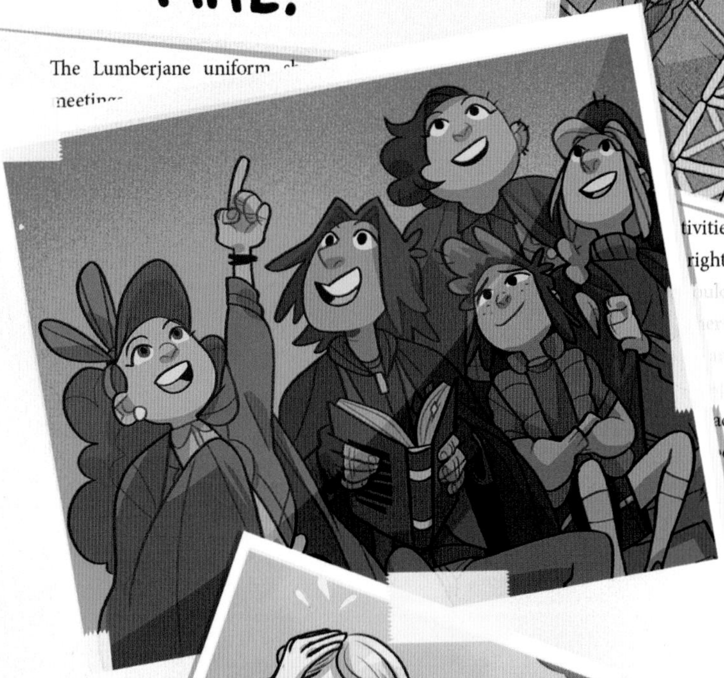

…tivities. The … is a
…right red neckerchief is wo… …neath
… be tied in a simple friendship knot.
…lack or brown and should have flat
… a straight inner line. Stockings or
…nd in color with the shoes or with
…aces, bracelets, or other jewelry do not
…erjane uniform.

…WEAR THE UNIFORM

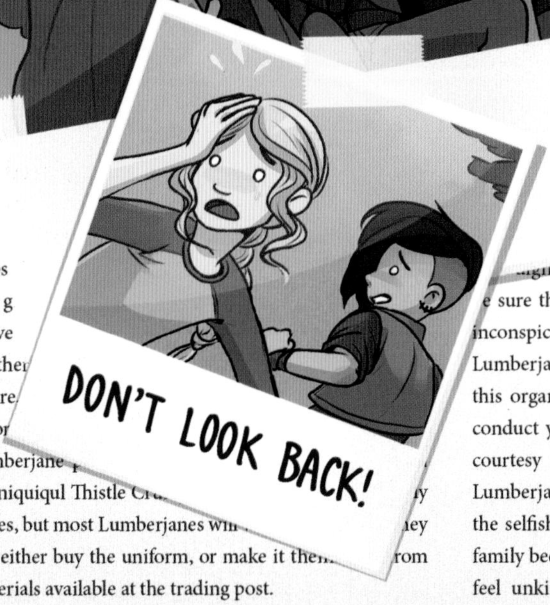
DON'T LOOK BACK!

The … helps … in a g… active … another… future… in or… Lumberjane p… Penniquiqul Thistle Cru… …y Types, but most Lumberjanes wi… …ey can either buy the uniform, or make it them… …rom materials available at the trading post.

…rm demands first of all that the …ood condition—clean and well …t is the right length for your own …e belt is adjusted to your waist, …kings are in keeping with the …our posture and carry yourself …ignity and grace. If the beret is removed indoors, …e sure that your hair is neat and kept in place with an inconspicuous clip or ribbon. When you wear a Lumberjane uniform you are identified as a member of this organization and you should be doubly careful to conduct yourself in a way that will show everyone that courtesy and thoughtfulness are part of being a Lumberjane. People are likely to judge a whole nation by the selfishness of a few individuals, to criticize a whole family because of the misconduct of one member, and to feel unkindly toward an organization because of the

COVER GALLERY

Lumberjanes "Out-of-Doors" Program Field

THE PERENNIAL PIN

"Year by year."

When you began your journey as a Lumberjane, you were just a little Seedling, and then, eventually, a Sapling scout. After a year or two of earning badges as a Sapling, you sprouted into a full Lumberjane scout, which is where we find you now. You've spent this past year learning, growing, and improving as a scout, as a friend, and as a citizen. In some cases, you may have attended a Lumberjanes summer camp, where you could focus as much or as little as you liked on earning badges and reaching your goals as a scout—on trying new things, learning, and working toward your next Spring, at which point you would become a Yearling Scout. It is on the occasion of your sprouting into a Yearling that the Perennial Pin is awarded, to commemorate your renewed commitment to Lumberjaning. Like the flowers that come back every year in our gardens, on the day of this Spring, you blossom anew, an older and wiser Lumberjane scout, refreshing your commitment to the words of our pledge, to the members of your Lumberjanes troop, and to the world around you. You promise to do your best. To be brave and strong, truthful and compassionate, interesting and interested. To treasure the world—natural, interpersonal, and intrapersonal. To question the things around you, and really listen to the answers. To help and protect those who need it, and to make the world better for friends and strangers alike. And as you Sprout to this new level of Lumberjane scout, we ask you to remember not just those words, but their meaning, and what they mean to you, as you head into your next year.

Issue Seventy-Five Cover
KAT LEYH

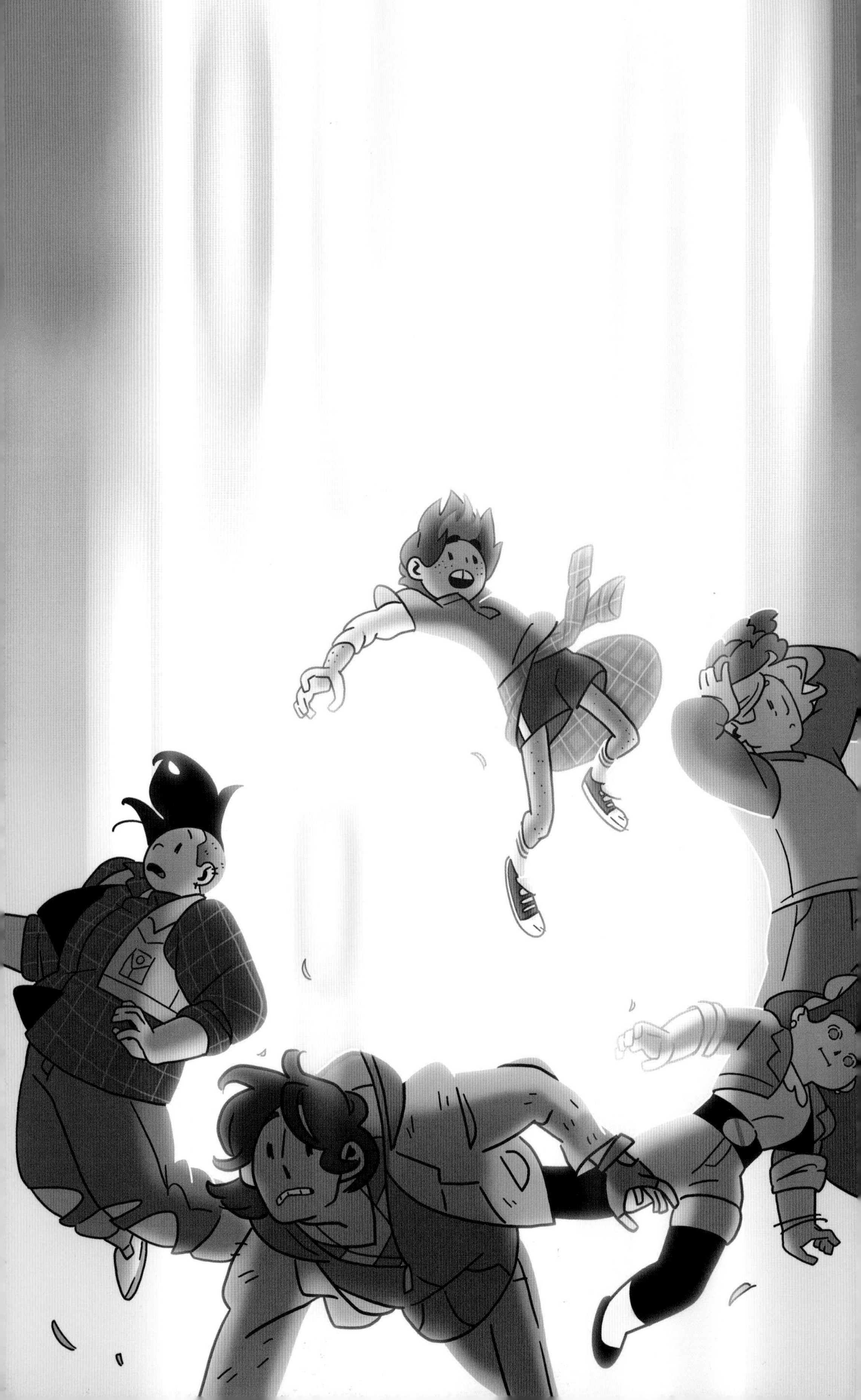

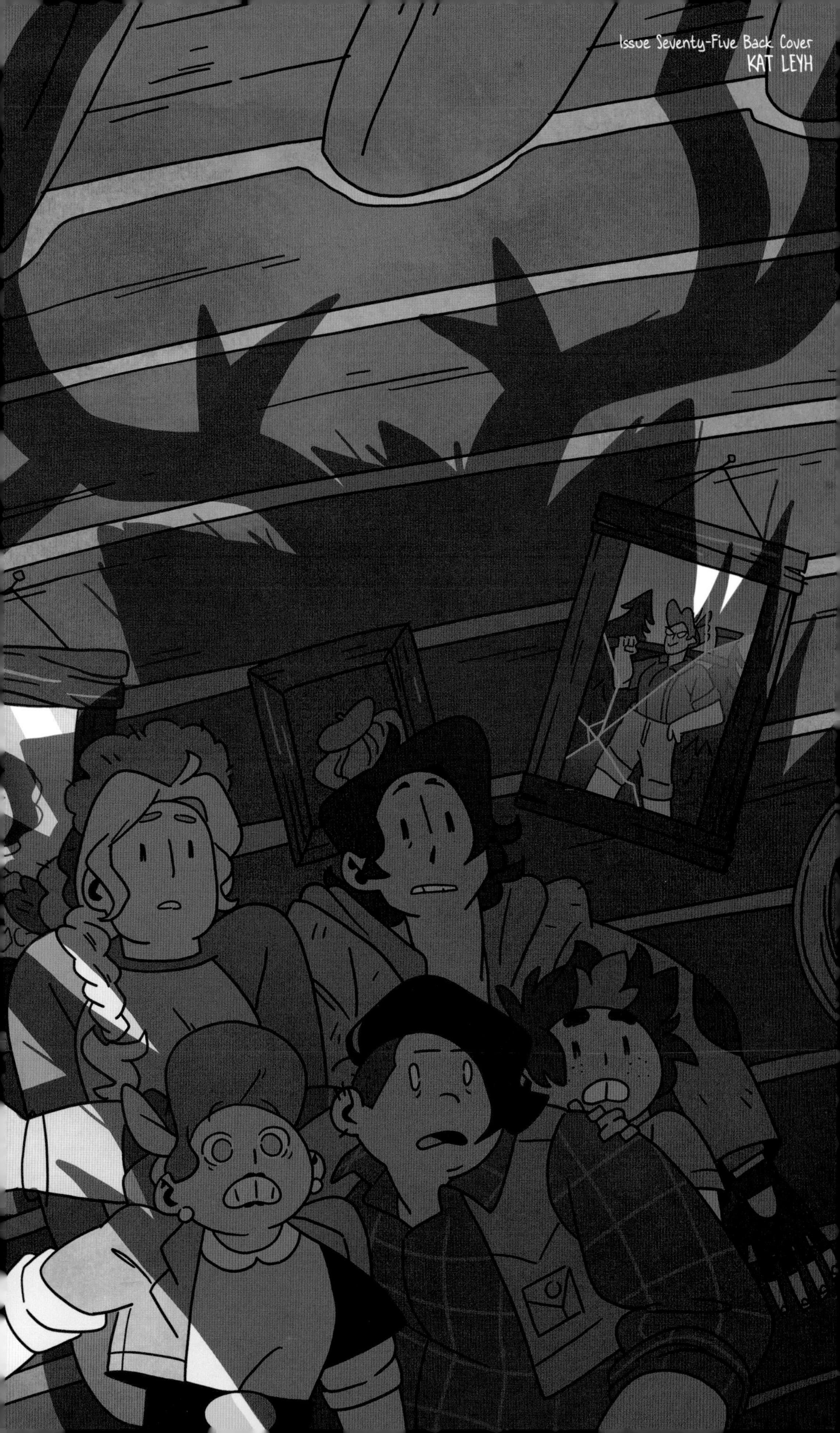

Issue Seventy-Five Back Cover
KAT LEYH

Issue Seventy-Five Variant Cover
HARRIET MOULTON

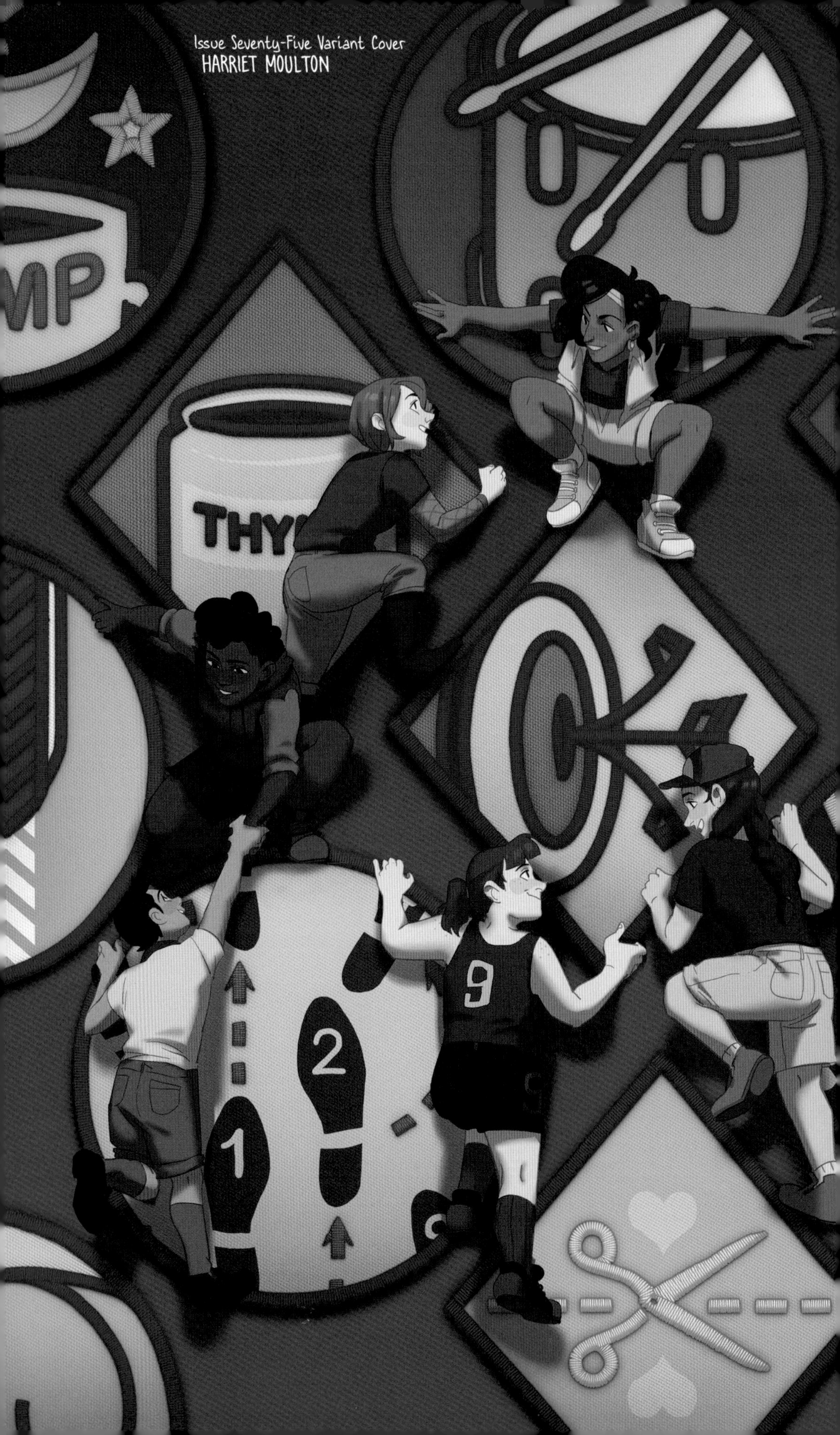
MP
THY
9
2
1

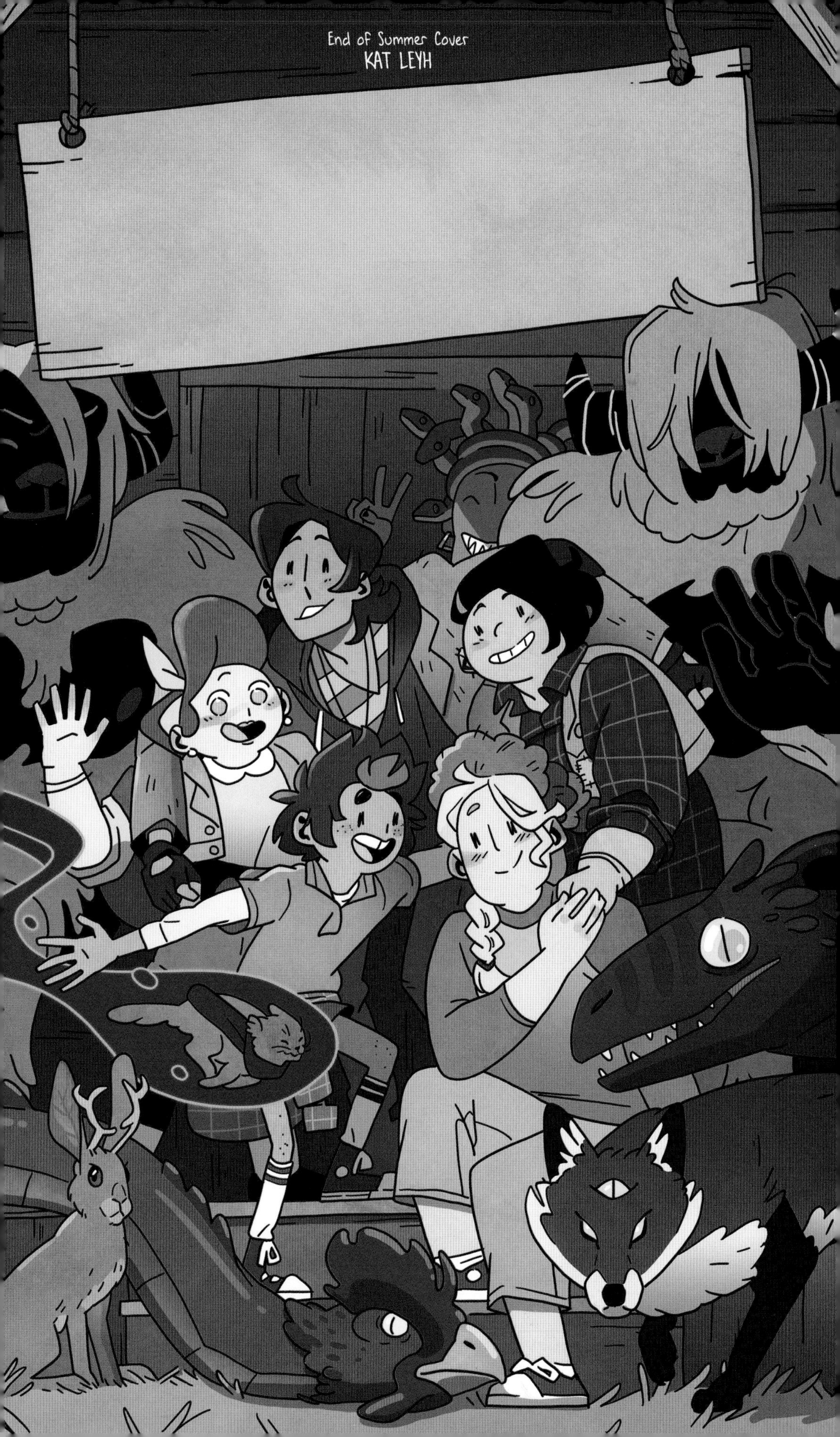

End of Summer Cover
KAT LEYH

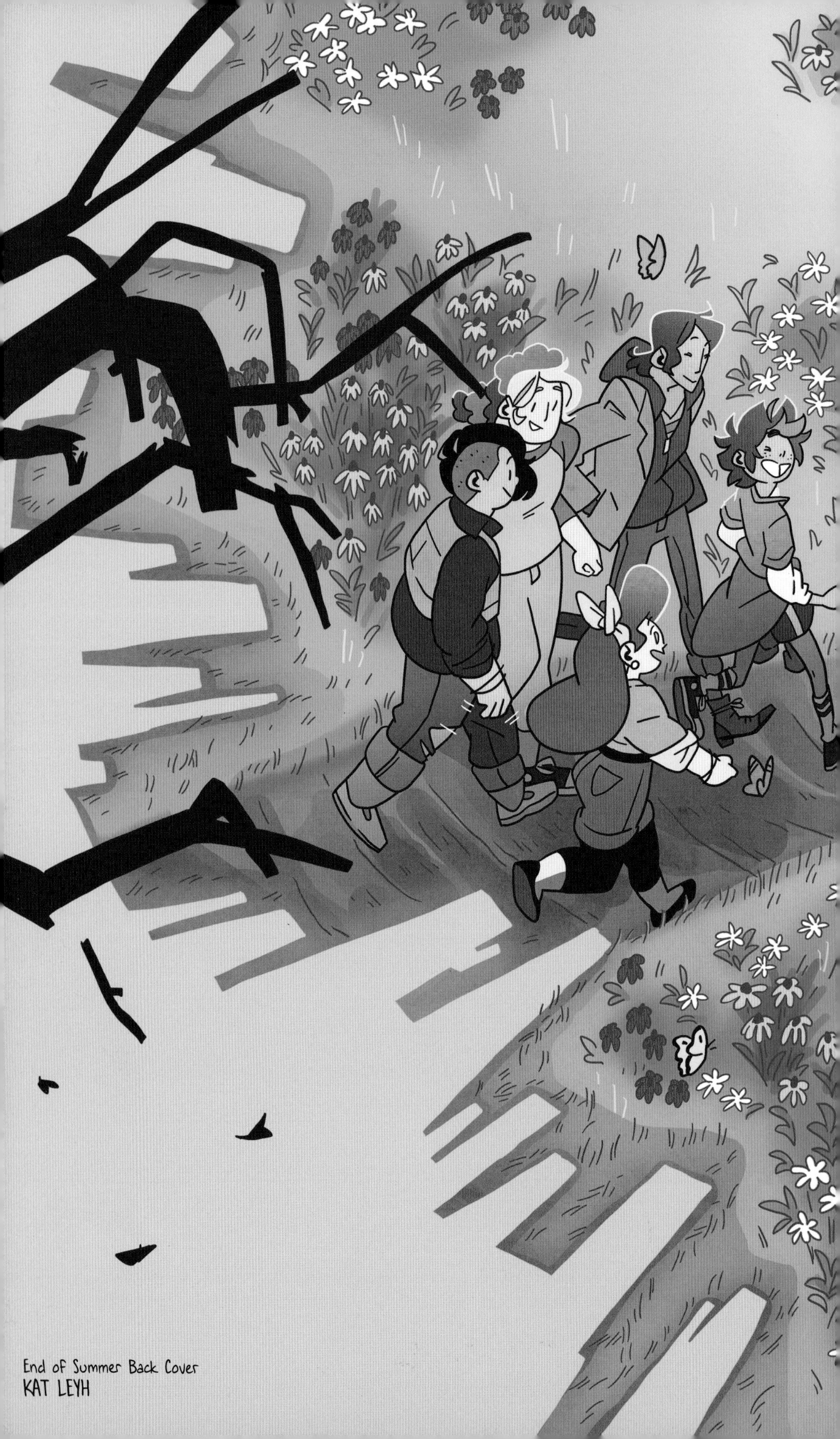

End of Summer Back Cover
KAT LEYH

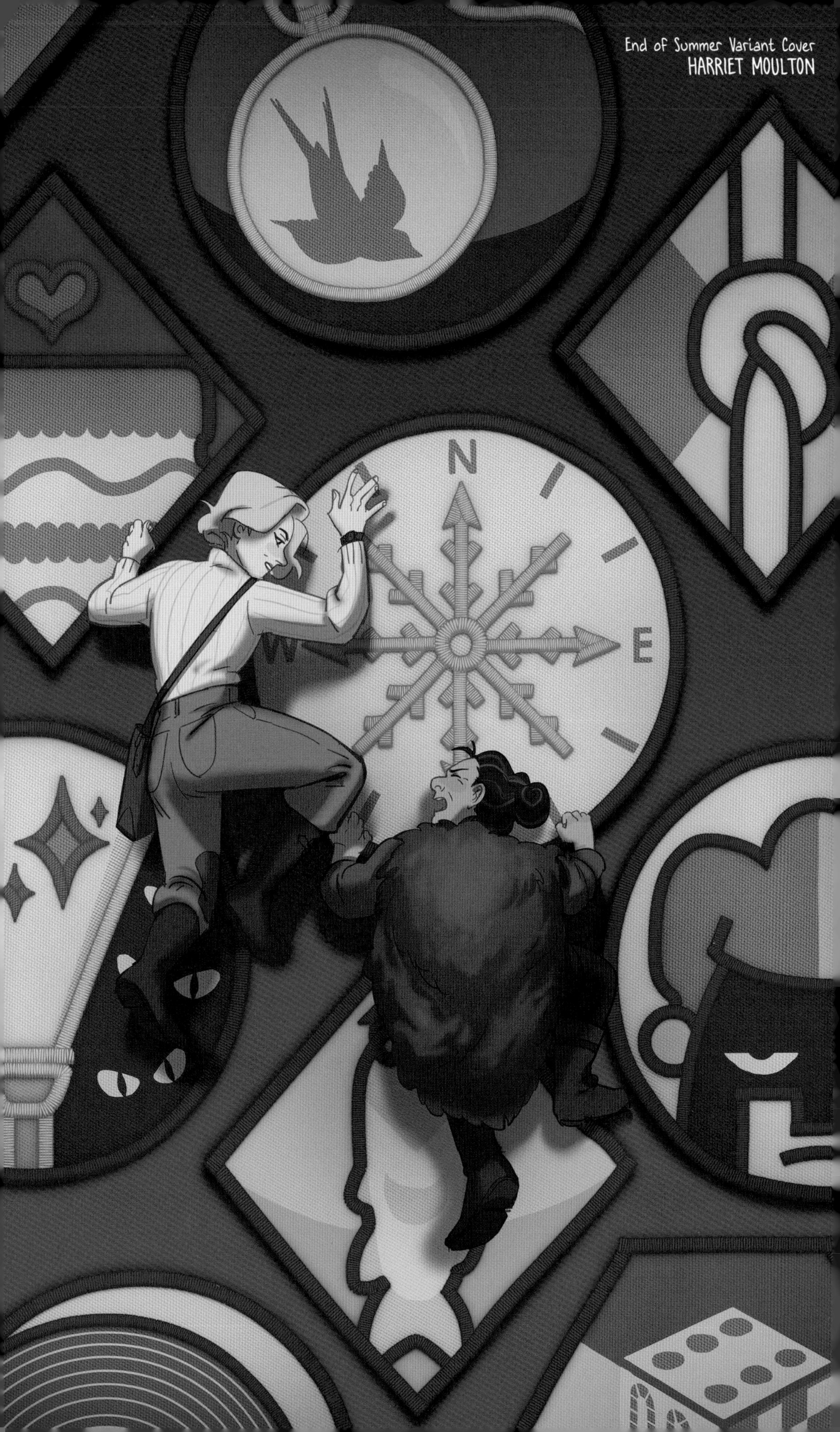
N
W
E

End of Summer Variant Cover
HARRIET MOULTON

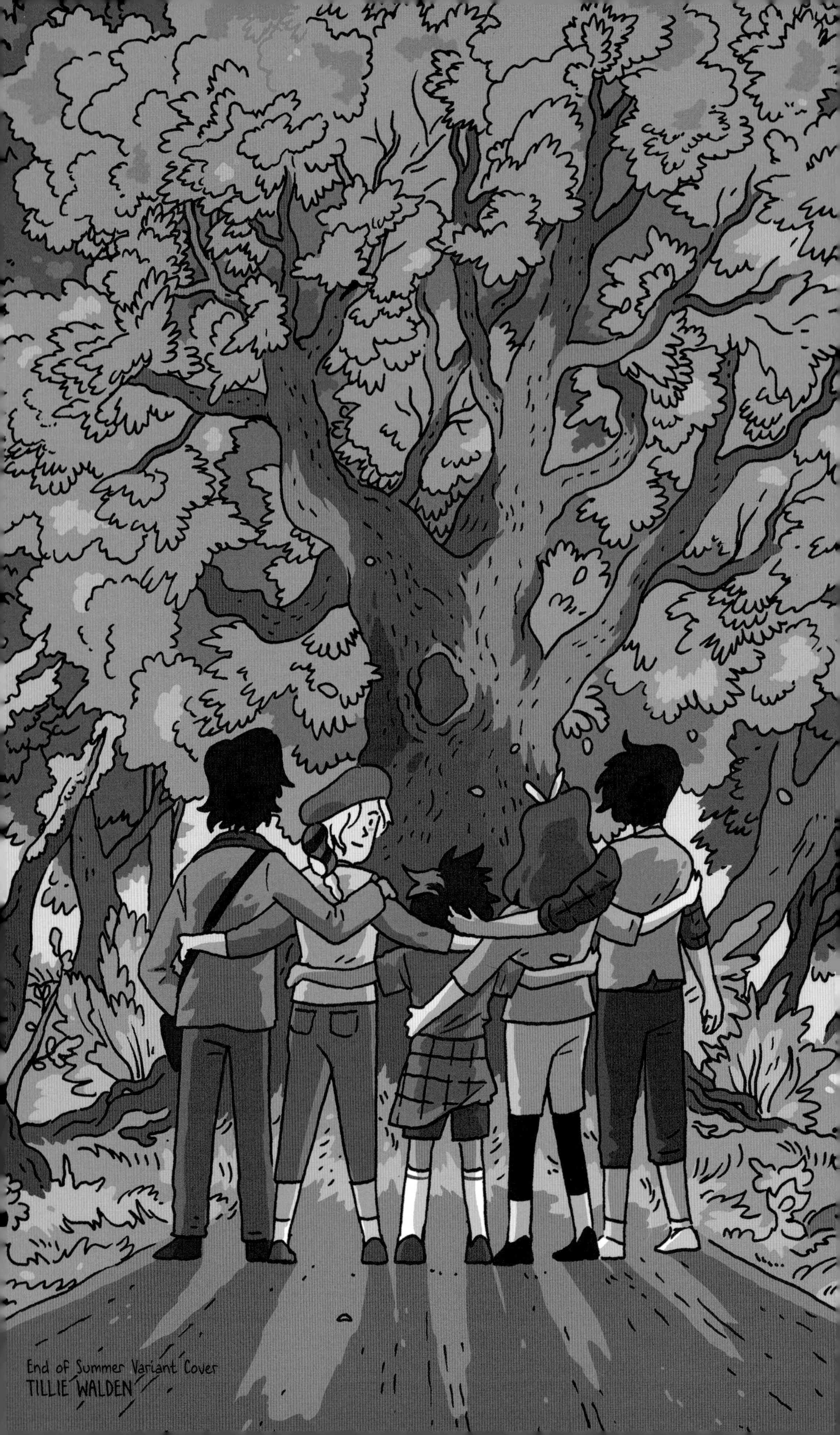

End of Summer Variant Cover
TILLIE WALDEN

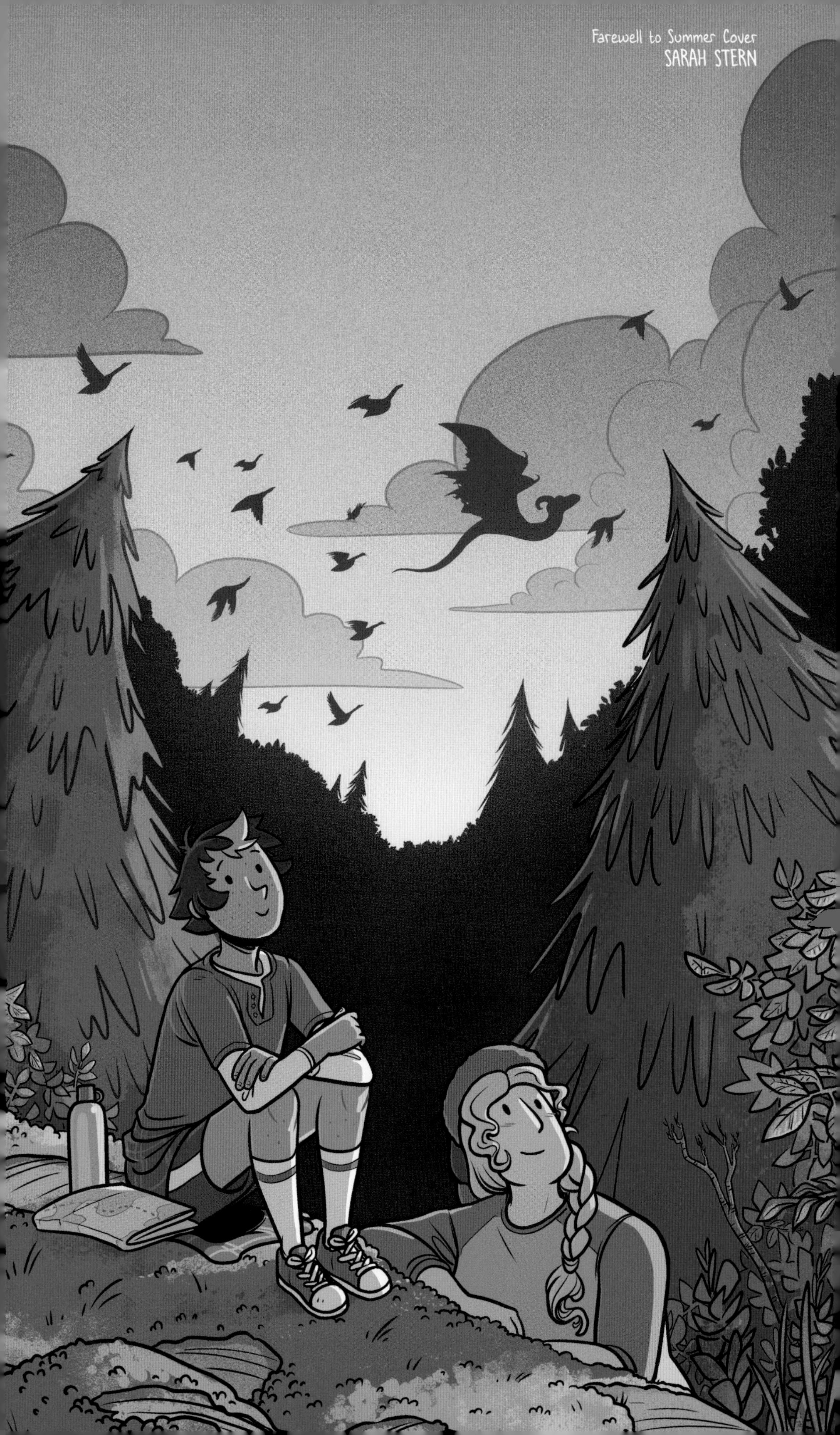

Farewell to Summer Cover
SARAH STERN

LUMBERJANES FIELD MANUAL

SKETCHBOOK

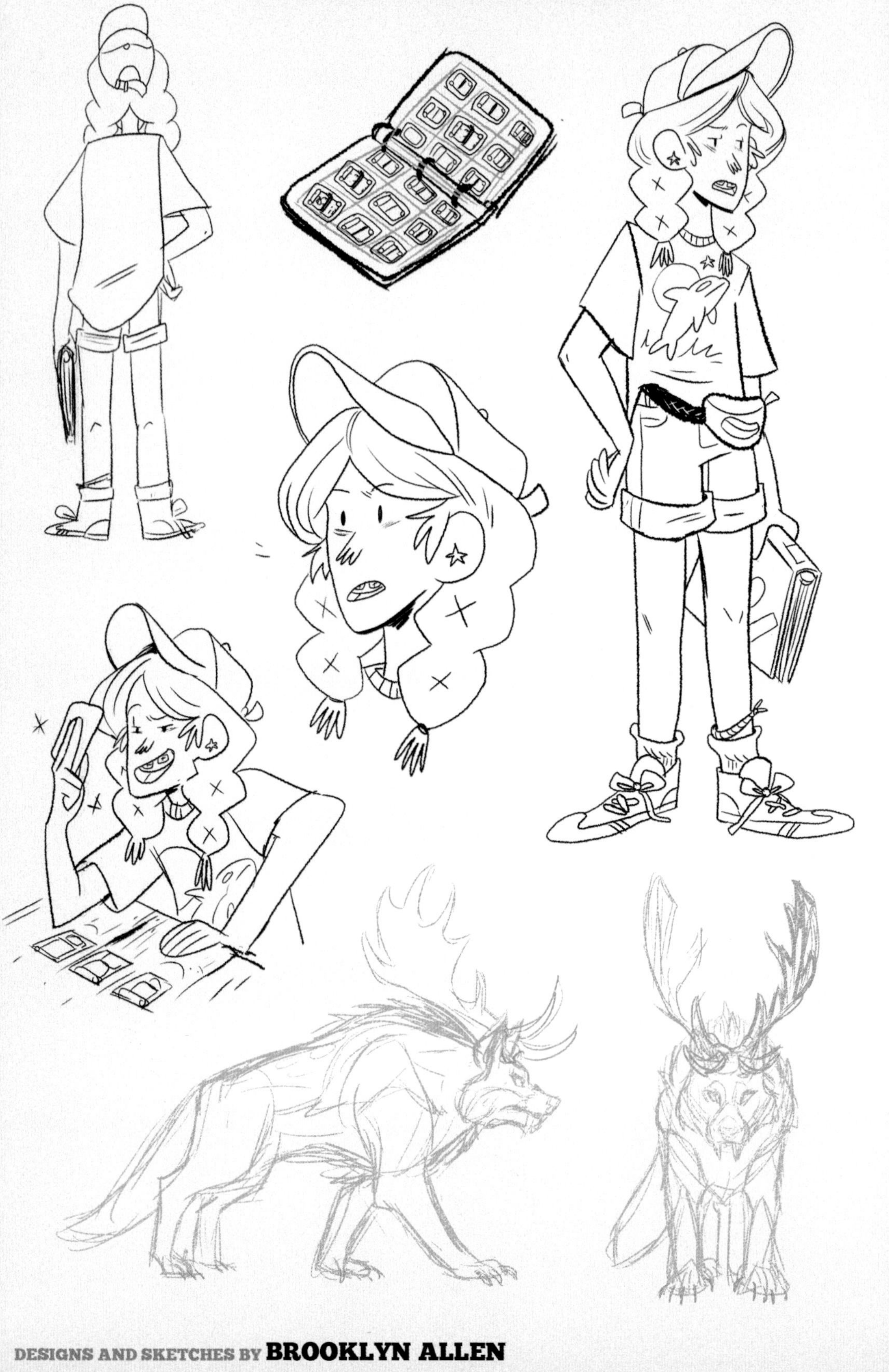

DESIGNS AND SKETCHES BY **BROOKLYN ALLEN**

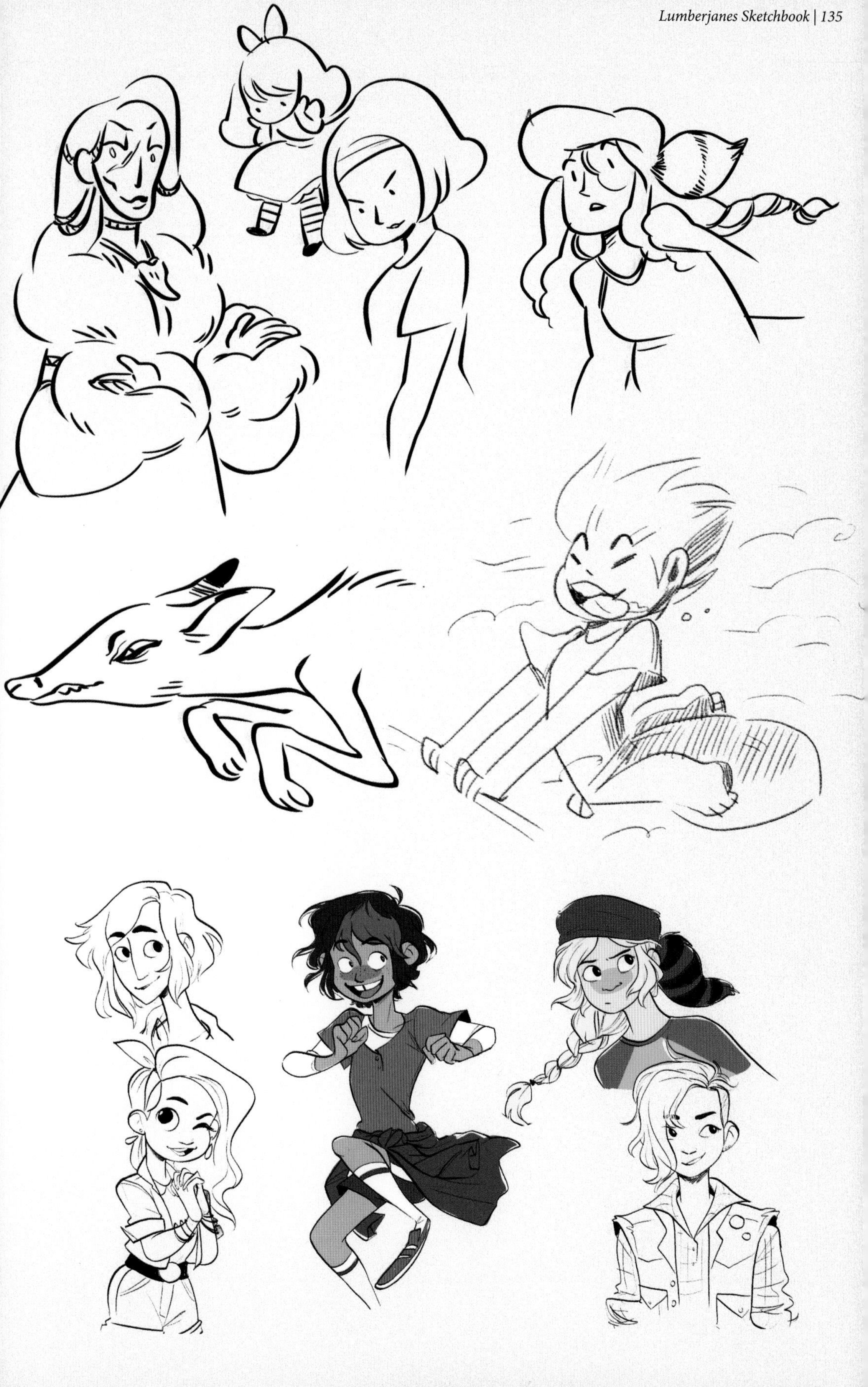

SKETCHES BY **KANESHA C. BRYANT & ALEXA BOSY**

Issue Seventy-Five, Page Nineteen

Panel 1: Wide shot. Rosie looks around.
ROSIE: Where's your counselor? Where's Jen?

Panel 2: The Roanokes look uncomfortable.
JO: We split up to try and get everyone to safety quicker…she's not back yet…

Panel 3: Ripley looks confident.
RIPLEY: It's okay though! She's Jen! She'll turn up right in the nick of time--
COUNSELOR: (off panel) ROSIE!

Panel 4: A counselor rushes up to Rosie. Other counselors and scouts are at her heels.
NAN: The other counselors and I have a perimeter check! The grey…*stuff* has us surrounded on all sides! We did a head count and have all the scouts, but--

Panel 5: A gathering is forming. Rosie looks grim. Questions are flying in from all sides.

    MOLLY: Rosie! Isn't there anything WE can do to help?!

    HES: Yeah! I don't like all this waitin' around!

    NAN: What should we do?

    APRIL: There must be a way to stop this!

    PUNCH: Hey, I was told there'd be cupcakes?

    SCOUT: Our cabin is full of giant bugs!

Panel 6: Close shot of Rosie's face. She has a determined, stressed expression. She's made a decision she's not happy with. The word bubbles are less important than Rosie's face, they can overlap and get cut off and stuff.

    OFF PANEL: How are we going to get home?

    OFF PANEL: Where's Jen?

    OFF PANEL: I tried to use the bathroom but there was a giant chicken in it!

    OFF PANEL: Rosie! What are you going to do!?

    OFF PANEL: What should we do?

Panel 7: Diane is sneakily sneaking away around the corner of a cabin while the frantic gathering mills in the background. Maybe have some blank words bubbles to indicate lots of chatter.

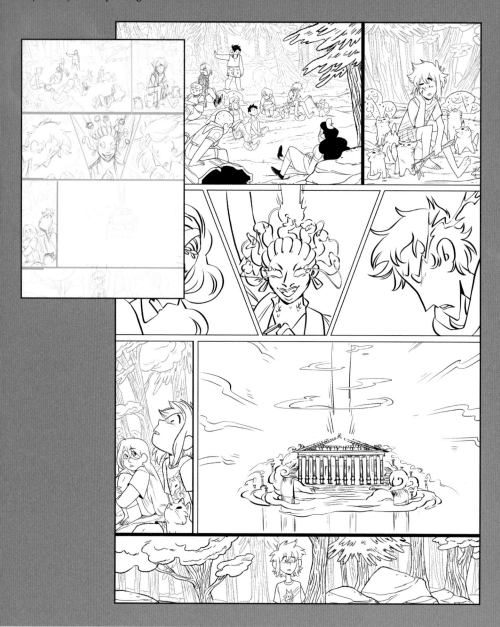

End of Summer, Page Seven

Panel 1: Cut back to camp. Group shot, various Roanokes, Zodiacs and Lads sit around downcast and grim. Amongst the campers, Ripley sits, dejectedly playing with some of the kittens.

> DIANE (caption): (from inside the cabin) "...just gonna have to TRUST them to finish it."

Panel 2: The various kittens around Ripley look up suddenly. Ripley notices them do this.

> SFX: Mrrp?

Panel 3: Quick splices of Apollo, Artemis and Ligo, glowing with energy and looking determined. This is it.

Panel 4: Cut to close shot of Ripley's surprised face. She's just noticed something as well but is not sure what.

    RIPLEY: Huh?

    APRIL: What is it?

Panel 5: Wide shot of Mount Olympus as a huge beam of energy bursts straight up, parting the clouds.

    SFX: *VWOOOM*

Panel 6: Contrastingly calm wide shot of Ripley.

    RIPLEY: Something feels--

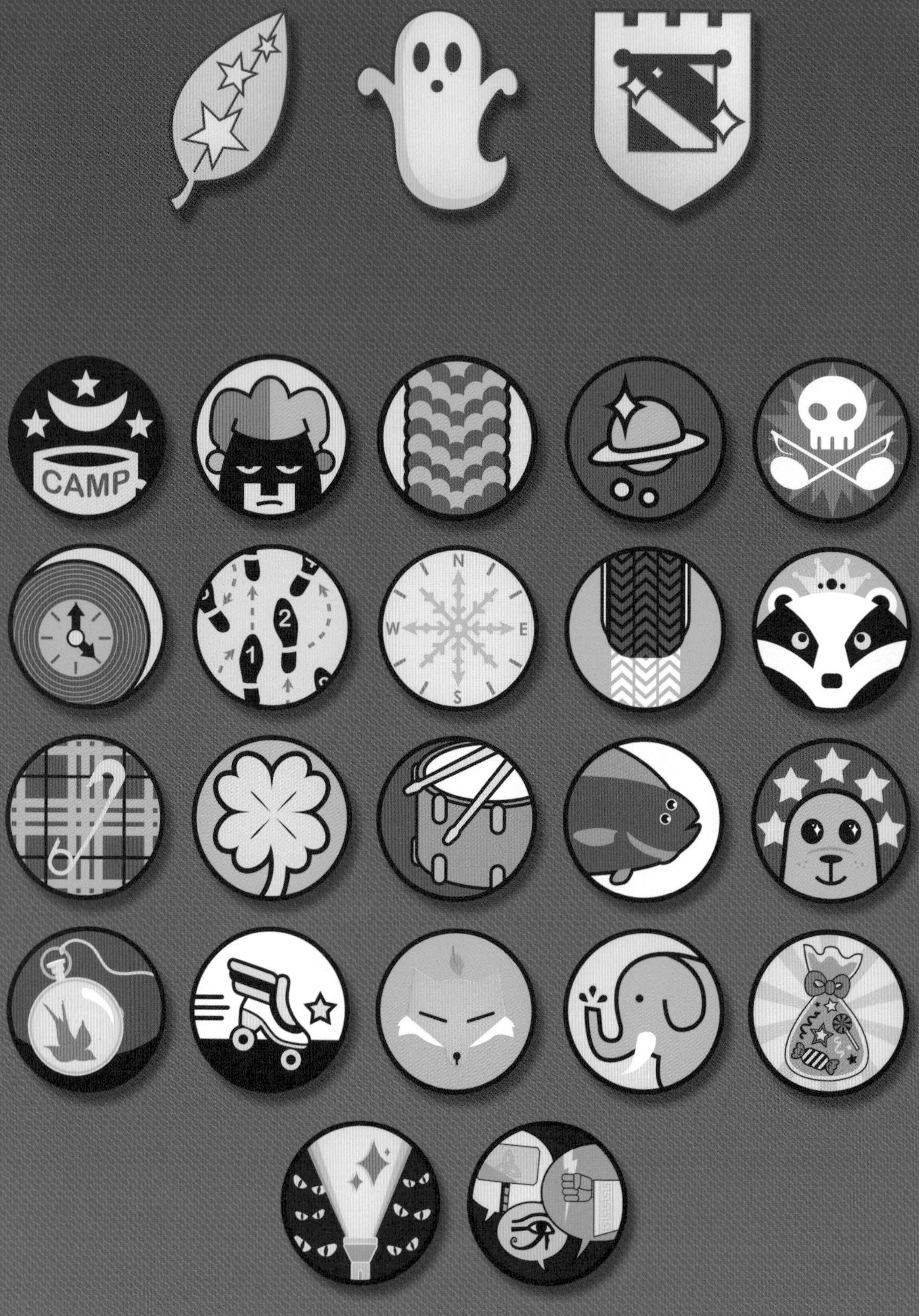
CAMP
N
W
E
S

BADGES DESIGNED BY **KATE LETH, SCOTT NEWMAN, KELSEY DIETERICH, BONES LEOPARD, MARIE KRUPINA, & GRACE PARK**

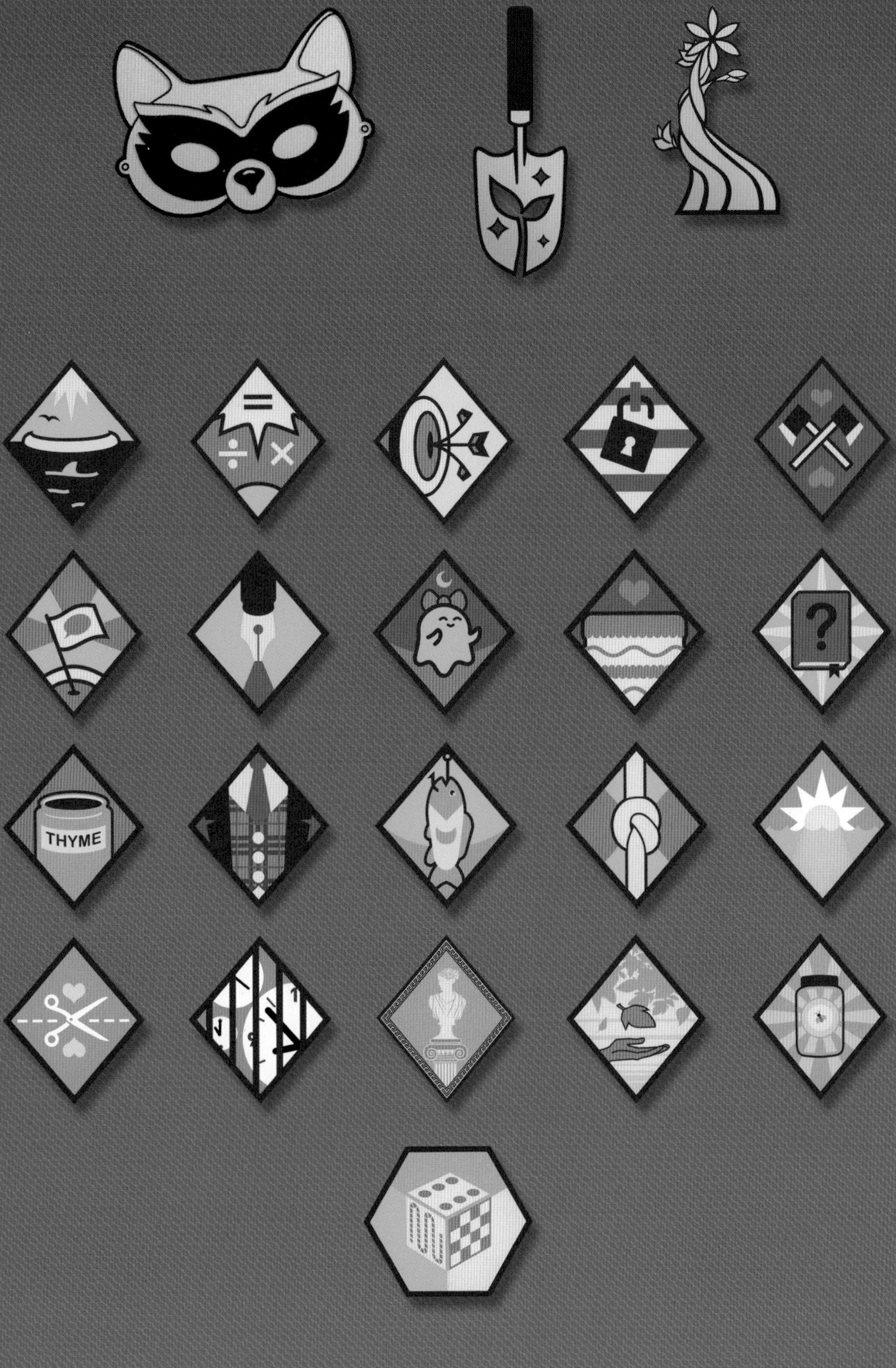
THYME

HELLO SCOUTS,

BY THUNDER, WE'VE COME TO THE END OF ANOTHER SUMMER! ENDINGS CAN BE HARD, ESPECIALLY IF YOU'RE AT THE CLOSE OF A JOURNEY THAT'S BEEN SPECIAL TO YOU.

YOU'RE NOT THE PERSON YOU WERE WHEN YOU STARTED, AND YOU'LL NEVER BE AGAIN. YOU'RE LIKE A TREE... YOU'VE GROWN. THERE ARE A FEW MORE RINGS INSIDE OF YOUR HEART.

YOU'VE MADE MISTAKES, AND YOU'VE LEARNED TO APOLOGIZE FOR THEM. YOU'VE LOVED, AND LOST THOSE YOU'VE LOVED. YOU'RE A STRONGER TRUNK TO LEAN ON.

THIS SUMMER IS OVER, AND YOU'RE MORE YOU BECAUSE YOU WERE A PART OF IT, AND I'M MORE ME BECAUSE YOU WERE HERE, AND FOR THAT, I THANK YOU.

I'LL MISS YOU, SCOUTS. COME BACK, ANYTIME. I'LL BE HERE WAITING FOR YOU.

LOVE,
ROSIE

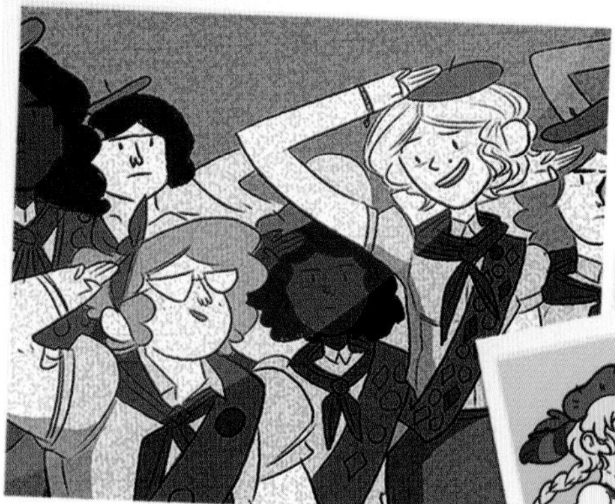

A CIRCLE IS ROUND
IT HAS NO END...

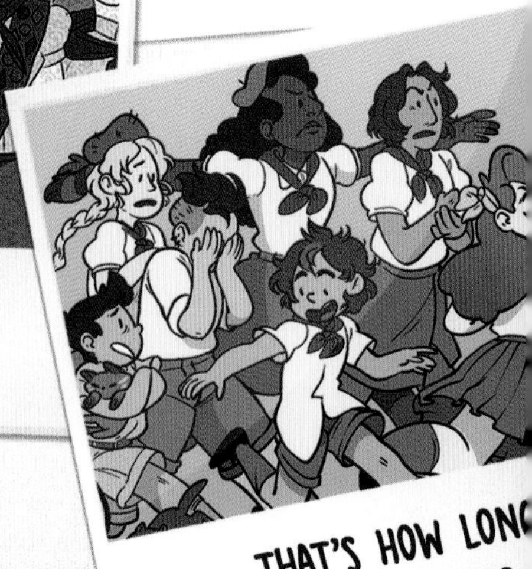

...THAT'S HOW LONG
WE'LL BE FRIENDS.

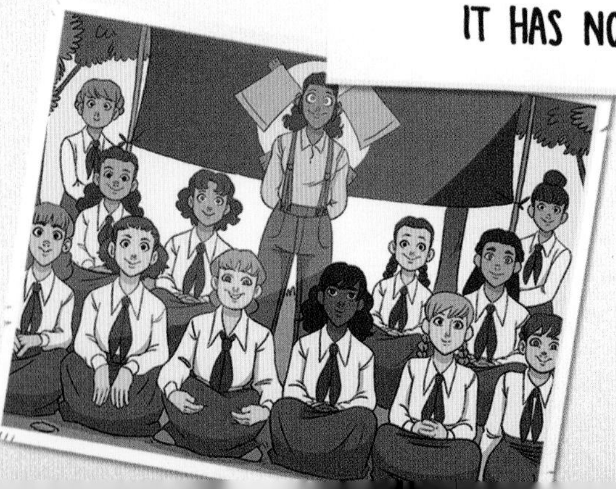

LJ

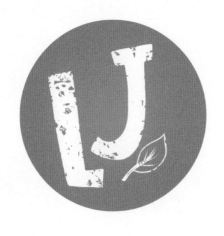

DISCOVER
ALL THE HITS

STEVENSON • ELLIS • WATTERS • ALLEN
LUMBERJANES
BEWARE THE KITTEN HOLY
NEW YORK TIMES BESTSELLING SERIES

Allison + Treiman + Cogar
GIANT DAYS
VOLUME ONE

From a writer of Disney's Moana
RIBON • FISH • PEER
SLAM!
VOLUME ONE

Hope Larson • Brittney Williams • Sarah Stern
GOLDIE VANCE
"Scoot over Nancy Drew..."
—Los Angeles Times
Volume One

JAMES TYNION IV • RIAN SYGH • WALTER BAIAMONTE
THE BACKSTAGERS

TYSON HESSE'S
DIESEL
IGNITION

BOOM! BOX

AVAILABLE AT YOUR LOCAL COMICS SHOP AND BOOKSTORE

To find a comics shop in your area, visit www.comicshoplocator.com

WWW.**BOOM-STUDIOS**.COM

Lumberjanes
Noelle Stevenson, Shannon Watters, Grace Ellis, Brooklyn Allen, and Others
Volume 1: Beware the Kitten Holy
ISBN: 978-1-60886-687-8 | $14.99 US
Volume 2: Friendship to the Max
ISBN: 978-1-60886-737-0 | $14.99 US
Volume 3: A Terrible Plan
ISBN: 978-1-60886-803-2 | $14.99 US
Volume 4: Out of Time
ISBN: 978-1-60886-860-5 | $14.99 US
Volume 5: Band Together
ISBN: 978-1-60886-919-0 | $14.99 US

Giant Days
John Allison, Lissa Treiman, Max Sarin
Volume 1
ISBN: 978-1-60886-789-9 | $9.99 US
Volume 2
ISBN: 978-1-60886-804-9 | $14.99 US
Volume 3
ISBN: 978-1-60886-851-3 | $14.99 US

Jonesy
Sam Humphries, Caitlin Rose Boyle
Volume 1
ISBN: 978-1-60886-883-4 | $9.99 US
Volume 2
ISBN: 978-1-60886-999-2 | $14.99 US

Slam!
Pamela Ribon, Veronica Fish, Brittany Peer
Volume 1
ISBN: 978-1-68415-004-5 | $14.99 US

Goldie Vance
Hope Larson, Brittney Williams
Volume 1
ISBN: 978-1-60886-898-8 | $9.99 US
Volume 2
ISBN: 978-1-60886-974-9 | $14.99 US

The Backstagers
James Tynion IV, Rian Sygh
Volume 1
ISBN: 978-1-60886-993-0 | $14.99 US

Tyson Hesse's Diesel: Ignition
Tyson Hesse
ISBN: 978-1-60886-907-7 | $14.99 US

Coady & The Creepies
Liz Prince, Amanda Kirk, Hannah Fisher
ISBN: 978-1-68415-029-8 | $14.99 US

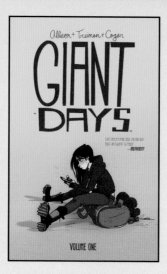